UNDER A DARKENING MOON

THE HYPERBOLIA SERIES

UNDER A DARKENING MOON

WITHIN A WAKENING EARTH

INTO A HEARKENING SKY

UNDER A DARKENING MOON

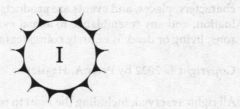

HYPERBOLIA, BOOK ONE

PETER A. HEASLEY

First paperback edition April 2023

Cover image from Adobe Stock and altered.

ISBN 979-8-9867574-0-7 (hardcover)
ISBN 979-8-9867574-6-9 (paperback)
ISBN 979-8-9867574-1-4 (ebook)

peteraheasley.com

For +Lucille

PART ONE

MOONDARK

1

At the murmur of television voices in the living room, Jody's eyes limped open. The volume was low but loud enough that his mother, Terr, meant him to hear it. Jody tried to make sense of the almost swirling pattern the full moon cast through the blinds and upon his body. He turned over to sleep through the chatting of Terr's electric companions and exposed a back drenched in mid-August sweat to the chill of the oscillating fan. His nerves were wide awake now.

He pinched his eyes. Jody was staying here for moments like this, to keep vigil on his mother's loneliness. He could only blame himself for not installing an air conditioner for these two weeks, but he did not want to start pretending this place had ever been comfortable, especially with his father gone. Jody shuffled into the living room.

"Mom," he said. "Maman."

She turned and looked up at him, sniffling, "I'm sorry, I just rolled over. The mattress is still low from where he slept...."

"It's okay, Mom," her dutiful son said, rubbing her slightly humped back. He sat down next to her on the couch and put his arm around her. Her head of wispy white curls tucked into the curve of his neck. The gray-blue light from the television lit up the hollow formed by their two lanky bodies sitting side by side. Jody looked at that television, amazed it still worked after all these years. It was an entity unto itself, a wooden treasure chest—an ark, perhaps, on which dwelt pictures of the family surrounding a wine decanter never properly rinsed, its red residue the geologic layering of forgotten eons.

"I miss him so much," Terr said with emotion that, no matter how genuine, always sounded acted to her son.

How many adapters did it take to keep the picture on this ancient tube alive in the era of high definition? "I do, too, Mom." This is where Dad would be. He would be genuinely interested in this program about the arcana of artificial intelligence. Some woman with a British accent was expounding on finding the right machine forms for conscious life. As a computer programmer, Jody should have found this interesting, but he did not. Perhaps it was the woman's wrinkled jowls hanging just above a pile of silken scarves around her neck that made her look less like a scientist and more like some kind of sorceress.

He leaned forward toward the television. "What are these people even talking about?"

"I dunno. These people are trying to build conscious robots or something. All spooky to me. I say they wake *people* up first. Most of us are half asleep anyway."

Dr. Pandit, the interviewer said, *let's talk about your own approach to studying artificial intelligence, which is becoming quite controversial. What you call "mirroring" others are calling, at best, a reliance on antiquated metaphysics, and at worst, sorcery. Could you explain your work for us?*

Yes, of course, she replied. *But before I speak about generating consciousness through mirroring, which is really quite easy to understand, let me address this elephant in the room. Humankind has long noted the presence of other forms of consciousness in the world. We've called them gods, djinns, angels, demons, and so on. If, as scientists, we manage not to pass off experiences with these entities as mass delusion or mere stupidity, we can acknowledge that there are non-bodily forms of consciousness that do not require sensory input or image-making to operate. This seems, in my opinion, and this is the thrust of my work, to be the first sort of natural mirror for our own AI systems. It's really very simple then: using established prayers, incantations, and the like, which are just words, really, codes just like we type into our software, we simply invite these conscious beings, these spirits, to interact with what we've created, to sit before our work as a mirror, to interact with it.*

"Well, if that isn't spooky...," Jody said.

"God help us," Terr replied.

"Let's go outside. It's a nice night."

He turned off the television, finding the thud of the plastic plunger satisfying, definitive. The fizz of static electricity on the curved screen conveyed a last warm embrace; as a child, he had always thought of the sound of that static as the many millions of lives kept inside the box blowing one last kiss before bed.

They walked out into the garden where Terr and her husband, Bleiz, had spent many sunny days. The pale light of the full moon gave a ghostly glow to the greenery below.

A phantom world came alive under the moonlight, a world seen only by cats and crows and owls. Becky and her friends were still out next door, drinking their own kind of moonshine, laughing and shouting. Jody held his arm around his mother, and both stared silently at tomatoes, parsley, carrots, and a few grapevines that hedged everything in. Jody turned his head briefly toward the garage, which sparked a slight smile.

Trying to turn his attention back to his mourning mother, he squatted down to fondle a plump tomato. He could not tell if it was green or red under the moonlight and gave it a gentle squeeze. As he did so, he thought he sensed in a slight flutter of light a flock of birds passing overhead. Later, he would identify this as the precise moment of the moonburst.

Becky screamed. Normally, neither Jody nor Terr would have paid much attention to this, but Jody caught Terr looking next door. Becky was pointing upward at the sky. Jody and Terr followed their neighbor's finger toward the moon.

"I can't see too well," Terr said. "What are they screaming about?"

"Who knows, Mom." He, too, found it hard to focus on the moon. "It is blurry, though, the moon. What is that, some haze around it? Maybe an asteroid struck, sending up dust?" He took out his phone to take a picture. He texted his wife, Haleh. *You see the moon? Looks like an asterisk hit it.*

She called. "An asterisk hit the moon, babe?"

"A what? An asteroid. It autocorrected. Anyway. Maybe. It's all blurry, like the dust's been blown off. You see this?"

"It's all cloudy here. Besides, the sun just set."

6

"Well, check the news."

"*You* check the news. Claire's having a fit."

"She's still awake?"

"She woke up in a fit a little while ago."

"Let me talk to her."

"Hey, Daddy," Claire said.

"Hey, Claire Bear. You alright?"

"No-o-o...."

"Aw, well, if it makes you feel any better, I can't get to sleep, either. But you know what?"

"What?"

"Maybe we can't sleep because God wants us to see what just happened to the moon."

"What happened to the moon, Daddy?"

"Well, I don't know exactly, but I think an asteroid hit it."

"What's an askeroid?"

"You know, a big rock from outer space, like the kind that killed the dinosaurs."

"The dinosaurs died?" she cried.

"Babe, that's enough," Haleh interrupted. "You're scaring her more. And me. Enough with this asteroid business."

"I'm not saying an asteroid has hit *us*, hon. The moon did its job. We're safe."

"I'm going to bed," Terr said, pulling out from under her son's arm.

"Hold on, hon—Mom, you don't want to know what just happened to the moon? I'll check the news now."

Without turning back, she muttered, "The dust will settle again. It always does." She walked through the thin metal door into the kitchen.

"And just like that, Haleh, my mother is an expert in astronomy. You see how easy it is for her to be right?"

"Maybe she is, Jody. Why don't you get back to bed, too?"

"I can't sleep in that humid house. I should have bought an air conditioner last week, knowing how long I'd be here. I'll lay out here for a while on the chair."

"Don't get eaten up."

"Well, maybe with a blanket over me...."

"Anyway, let me try to get Claire back to bed. Maybe she just needed to hear her daddy's voice. Claire, say good night to Daddy."

"Good night, Daddy."

"G'night, Claire Bear. Muah!"

"Don't let the bad bugs bite."

Jody brought a thin blanket outside, lay on a deck chair of flimsy metal frame and plastic weave, and scrolled through what news reports were available. Most speculated that a minor planet had struck, possibly a centaur sent out by Jupiter, but imaging revealed nothing. Content that his theory was right and pleased with the gentle breeze that passed across his back, Jody fell asleep.

He opened his eyes again at some point during the night. The neighborhood was quiet and the setting moon cast the garden in silhouette. He was not sure if the cloud of dust had grown bigger or if the moon had always seemed so much bigger just above the horizon. His heavy eyes fell again upon the garden, where a glint of moonlight gave an edge to some slinking, translucent shape.

Some gravid presence stood near the statue of the Blessed Mother, deep in the shadows. He focused his reason there, fully expecting this fragment of dream life to dissipate, but it did not. She did not. This invisible but lucid presence was a she, and she was afraid. His sister, Madeleine, had died when she was seven, too young to have a reason to fear any place that death could take her. That had been forty-three years ago, a year before Jody was born, too long ago for a visit now. This girl was young, too, but maybe not as young. The presence moved across his field of vision behind the grape vines.

Tired of celestial apparitions, Jody went back into the house, to his old room, to the smell of a wooden floor swollen with summer heat and decades of his own dead skin, and quickly fell asleep again.

2

Jody woke to a house full of sunlight. He needed coffee and shuffled into the kitchen. He briefly considered pouring directly from his mother's percolator, but the penalty for this would be twofold, her words boxing his ears and the acidic sludge slugging his stomach. While water boiled in the electric kettle, he cleaned out his French press from the day before. The refrigerator was full of his leftovers that Terr had picked over. Frozen waffles would suffice.

Terr was on the phone in the backyard. His evidence for this was the twelve-foot coiled wire pinched between the screen door and the jamb, a living relic of the century past. She was on the phone with his older brother Sam. His evidence for this was her silence; Sam was the only person who could hold her mute for so long. Jody checked his phone for news, much of which his younger brother, Cameron, had already been feeding to him in text messages. It was beyond his effort before coffee to sort through that stack of partial fact and outright fiction. Haleh had sent links that would be more reliable. The water boiled. One plate served to hold his coffee cup and two toasted waffles broken into four halves.

He sat outside on the same metal chair in which he had

slept. Terr leaned against the broad, pale wood siding, swaying a little like a teenager. "Hold on," she said to Sam. "That's not my coffee you're drinking, is it?"

"Mother, I would rather drink from an oil rig than your percolator." He sipped. "It would be the same flavor and consistency."

"Good," she said, then continued listening to Sam. "No, it's your brother. He slept outside all night.… I don't know. Alright, Sammy. I'll let you get going.… You, too. Bye."

"Any news?"

"They're up in Maine. They were all asleep when it happened. They're staying up there for now."

"When what happened?" Jody asked through a mouth full of waffle dipped in coffee.

"Hello?" she puzzled in a low, sarcastic voice. "The moon exploded last night? You were there? We saw it?"

"We didn't know what we saw last night. I thought it was an asteroid. That's still the reigning theory."

"Then why are you asking me?"

Jody stuffed more waffles into his face and sighed through his nose.

***

By mid-morning, Jody and Terr found themselves on the couch in the living room, staring at a television emitting no small variety of speculation on what had happened, and was still happening, to the moon.

"*They* know," Terr said.

"Who's *they*, Mom?"

"*Them*. The people in power. And the people behind the people in power. They probably did it in the first place. Nu-

11

clear testing or something. Or some experiment, you know, the big thing...the circular thing...whatchamacallit?"

"No one is testing nukes on the moon. We haven't even been to the moon in fifty years. We discovered very quickly it's just a big boring rock. Well, not so boring now."

"They've got their secret bases up there. I know. These things don't just happen."

"Mom, you cannot at once hold the theory that the moon landings were faked and that we have secret bases there."

"Ah-h," she sang. "They did that to divert our eyes from what's really going on up there. There's more going on than meets the eye."

"You've been letting Cam show you too many videos. Trust me. I'm in the space exploration business. I would know if we had secret moon bases. And we don't."

"Right." She poked him in the side. "But you would be sworn to secrecy. Besides, they might not tell you that. No, it's all our trillionaires now. They have the resources to do this. Underground bunkers and things."

"First of all, there are no trillionaires. Second, even if our billionaires pooled their money together, they would not, because they all hate each other. Third, even if they did, they live under the same roof as us and would not rain disaster upon themselves as well."

"Maybe, maybe not. Maybe they've got a secret way out. Maybe Mars."

"Now Mars.... Well, at least we're in the maybe zone. There's some room in there for actual facts to slip in."

"Facts," she said, poking him again. "I'll give you facts, boy."

"Stop. President Palmer's coming on now." Terr kept poking him in the side. "I'm serious. Behave. Act like the president just walked in the room."

"Yes," she pouted. "Let's hear what Aunt Jemima has to say."

"You can't—"

Ladies and gentlemen, thank you for coming together so quickly after what has been, for all of us, a hectic and frightening night. As many or most of you have seen, at approximately 11:23 p.m. last night, Eastern Standard Time, the moon was struck by an unknown object and has been steadily emitting a cloud of dust for several hours. Now, asteroids and space rocks of all kinds have been striking the moon for millions of years, leaving behind craters large and small. Whatever has struck the moon has done so from the dark side, out of sight of all Earth telescopes and cameras. Scientists at NASA and the European Space Agency have not been tracking any incoming object of any significant size, so we are, in the present moment, at a bit of a loss. However, we do know that, because of the angle with which it struck, the object has created a seismic wave pattern in the moon's crust that has, effectively, blown off a thin layer of dust in all directions.

Our principal concern, and it is not a grave concern, is that this cloud of moon dust shows no signs of slowing down. It has left the moon's surface at a speed of approximately 2.7 miles per second, a rate that the moon's gravity has not slowed down. At that speed, the cloud of moon dust will have made the two-hundred-and-thirty-eight-thousand-mile journey from the moon to the Earth in about twenty-five hours. That means it will reach Earth's atmosphere within the next thirteen hours. We will, of course, be providing continual updates on the progress of this dust cloud.

I urge everyone not to panic. We have detected no rocks or particles of any size within the dust cloud that could cause any damage to Earth. Whatever dust particles do arrive will be thinly spread out, and our atmosphere will simply burn them away. In the event that these high-velocity dust particles damage one or two of our satellites, we have a great deal of planned redundancy. Our communications systems will continue to function.

That said, as a precaution, I have declared a national state of emergency, effective immediately and lasting until eight a.m. tomorrow morning. There will be a nationwide curfew beginning at eight p.m. in each time zone. During the day, we ask that citizens remain at home except for essential business. Only essential services will remain open, and a list of those services has been provided to the media and is also available on the White House website. The water will flow from your tap, and the electricity will remain on. Please stay at home so we do not clog the roads. This will be over within one day. I, myself, am not leaving the White House.

Thank you for your attention. I'll now take any quest— Yes....

"That's it?" Terr asked.

"Yeah, that's it?" Jody echoed. "We go from 'don't panic' to 'state of emergency' in two sentences?" With the realization that he might be stuck in Stonebridge, Massachusetts, for the foreseeable future, a trembling wave of disgust welled through his body. "So, what? We just wait for the moon dust to hit us?"

Terr was silent.

"Is the moon even intact, like structurally stable?"

"I wonder," Terr replied. "I bet this is exactly the kind of thing a president wants to happen."

"Oh, God...."

"No, I mean it. You get to look large and in charge in some global emergency. Suits her, too. I bet she didn't see this coming as she made her way up, though. Not exactly the kind of thing a housemaid dreams of facing some day. You know how she got where she is, right?"

"Yes, we all do—"

"That little Jewish family she was keeping house for. They paid for her to go to paralegal school."

"I know."

"Probably the wife's idea. A woman like that, she gets bossy real quick. Nosy, too. Send her away—what did you say they call it in the church?"

"Kicking a person upstairs."

"Whatever. She probably started telling her bosses what to do. Best punishment for that is to make her do the work herself. Send her to law school—see the pattern? Doesn't account for the shift to politics. No, that's something else. That's like, she got a real taste for bossing people around."

Jody stared blankly at the television, trying to make out the president's response to questions.

"Or maybe they thought they could get her to do their dirty work for them. Plays both sides of the aisle. Maybe that's her secret. And the boobs. You can't argue with them big black boobies."

Jody snuffed out a little laugh. "This is your first concern? That Deborah Palmer plays world dictator? Can't we just enjoy the end of the world for a moment? I think you're just jealous it's not you up there."

"And then we've gotta worry about all of the allahuakbars, though. No offense."

"I've told you a hundred times, Mother, the Shamshiri's are Zoroastrians, not Muslims. And not very practicing ones at that."

"Yeah, but don't they worship the moon or something?"

Jody sighed sharply through his nose, leaning his head against his hand. "They worship one God, like we do."

"Ah-h, but the same God?"

Jody wondered if he and his mother even worshiped the same God. Haleh called.

"Hey, hon."

"Hey."

"You alright?"

"I don't know."

"None of us do. You see the president's thing?"

She inhaled deeply. "Yeah, I mean, so, what, like, no one really knows what's going on? You think it's dangerous?"

"I'm not sure, honey. It's just moon dust, right? They said there are no big rocks in it. No big chunks. Just a dusting...a dusting of the moon. It should be alright. What do your dad and Uncle Danny say about it?"

"I don't know. I called you first."

Jody froze at the compliment. "How's our Claire Bear?"

16

"She's fine. Cheerful, actually. Somehow, she got better sleep than anyone else. Here. Say hello."

"Hi, Daddy."

"Hey, Claire Bear. How'd you sleep last night?"

"Good," she sang. "I had a dream everyone was sleeping."

"Oh, really! That sounds nice. You get to sleep twice if you sleep in your dream. A dweam within a dweam. No wonder you're so cheerful this morning."

"Yeah, the people sleeping kept the monsters away."

"Oh, well...that's good. Well, let me talk to Mommy again."

"You hear that?" Haleh said. "What do you think that means?"

"I think it's just a dream she had. She was tired and knew I couldn't sleep, so she dreamt of all of us sleeping."

"You're so calm and rational."

"It comes from a lifetime of...never mind. This will all be over soon."

Jody talked with Haleh a little while longer until her father, Sunny, called. Jody turned to Terr. "What do you think, Maman? Head over to church? You know, just in case?"

Terr looked over. "Yeah," she said quietly, nodding.

"Is it even open today, I wonder? Fr. Clément, isn't he in Charlton during the week? Or on the Cape?"

"I suppose."

"Aren't you going every day anymore?"

"You've got your father's keys to the church."

Jody breathed heavily. "What do you mean, 'you'? Aren't they in the bowl on the television?"

"That's what I mean."

Jody rubbed the back of his neck. "I guess other people might want to get in, too, huh?"

"All you have to do is open up. No one's asking anything else."

"Great," he said and sipped his coffee. "It's almost noon."

3

For her seventy-nine years, Terr walked briskly but un-steadily. She kept up with her tall, lanky son, thirty-eight years younger, but missed a step every so often and grabbed his arm for support. When they arrived at Saint Roche, they found the church locked and about half a dozen people standing outside, some praying, some just milling about. Jody left Terr with them and, with his father's keys, unlocked the attached rectory.

"Father Clément? *Mon père? Tu es là?*" he called down the murky gray hallway of the office. He opened the door leading into the sacristy of the old stone church. He studied the switch panel and toggled until he found the church just well-lit enough for no one to stumble inside. The tall nave drew August's heat upward and away from the worried bodies that would soon fill it. He pushed open the front doors and found that a few more people had gathered.

Jody took a seat among them, sharing a pew with Terr but seated some distance away. He knelt and prayed for safety, calm, and all the things he thought the situation warranted. He looked at the gold fleur-de-lis floating in the gray-blue apse. He looked at the neo-Gothic, white marble high altar and remembered how, as a child, he thought it resembled an X-wing fighter. He could use that now to reach the moon and see what all the trouble was. Maybe the Death Star had lasered it like it had Alderaan.

Coming to, he caught one or two older ladies looking back toward him, or he thought he did. He sighed as quietly as he could. He turned surreptitiously toward Terr. Her blank expression said it all, for she never carried a blank expression unless she didn't know what to say. He checked his phone. It was 12:36. The noon Mass in Charlton would be over. He didn't have Fr. Clément's phone number. He rose, genuflected, found his way back into the rectory, and found the cell number scratched on a note stuck to the secretary's wall.

"Fr. Clément? It's Jody Conque. How are you?"

"Fine, Jody, just fine. How are you? What's going on?"

"Well, I used my father's keys and opened the church. There were some people gathered here. I hope you don't mind. I mean, with everything…."

"That's fine, thank you. Listen, I'm a little tied down here right now. People are wanting confessions. It only seems right. Maybe, if you are willing, given the circumstances, no, perhaps it's best—You know what? What if you gave a sort of general absolution? I think that sounds reasonable, don't you? Maybe expose the Blessed Sacrament. Maybe it's not allowed for you, but given the circumstances, better to ask forgiveness than permission, right?"

"Right…."

"I can come by later this afternoon, maybe even in an hour or so. It might just, you know, calm people down, calm their fears, if you were able to do something. I think the situation calls for it, don't you?"

Joy and loathing coursed around each other through Jody's veins. He didn't know whether to smile or cry and stomp his feet. "Sure, Father. That sounds reasonable. You think—"

"Thanks, Jody. I'll be there soon. Alright, goodbye."

Father Clément hung up, leaving Jody alone in the gray, murky office. He blew a heavy breath upward across his face and ran his fingers through his hair. His right hand settled on the back of his neck; with this hand, he yoked himself forward into the sacristy.

Father Clément had hung up before he could answer Jody's question. He could expose the Blessed Sacrament without any vestments on. He should have something on to give general absolution, though. He did not know how to do that. He had never done it in his seven years as a priest. He'd been set against things like that or imagined only using it in a falling airplane or on the battlefield. Well, the moon was falling. He rummaged through the liturgical books, none of which had a sturdy spine. The albs in the closet each smelled of thirty years of Third-World sweat. He found the ritual and an alb that fit.

Jody looked for the monstrance behind every door except the one on which the full-length mirror hung. Resigned, he finally approached that door. Seeing himself in the mirror, seeing himself in vestments just as he once had been, he said, "Well. It's not the end of the world." He was relieved to laugh at his own joke. Behind the mirrored door was the monstrance.

The once Father Joseph Conque knelt on the step of the sanctuary, leading the now-dozen congregants through the *O Salutaris*. His own baritone pleased and soothed him. Once this finished, he walked to the podium from which the lay ministers read the Mass readings and announced, as loudly as he could for having forgotten to turn on the microphones, that, in light of the very slight dangers posed to them from above, and so on, he would give a general absolution in an hour's time. He figured the old ladies would be calling their friends to come. He hoped Father Clément would arrive by then to relieve him of duty. He added, "By the way, in case you don't know me, I am Father Joseph Conque. My mother's there, Terese Conque. She can attest." Wincing at every word he had just said, he added, "Thank you." He sat down in the presider's chair.

Jody held one eye on the altar, the other on the souls streaming into the church. Tears trickled down some of their faces. All poured their gazes into the bright white abyss at the center of the monstrance, its rays of brass ablaze like the sun under the spotlights. For the first time in the six years that had passed since he had left the priesthood, he felt fixed in place. This would be an hour in which he could not look at his phone or discipline his daughter or do anything except face this holy blankness with his thoughts and fears and prayers.

This was not what he thought he had escaped, though, such a moment of fixedness. He had enjoyed moments like this. It was the everything else, all the things that had kept turning his focus, and eventually his heart, away.

Jody and Terr began their walk home in silence. She

seemed to want to walk ahead of him, and he let her. She didn't stumble; maybe some anger of hers gave her focus.

"It's funny," he said, trying to break the ice. She didn't respond. "Only Father Clément could get away with calling President Palmer 'Big Momma.' If I said that, I'd be canceled."

"Because he's black from Ghana," Terr replied without turning back.

"Guinea," Jody corrected quietly and dared say no more.

He was glad, when he arrived at his mother's house, to see a familiar shape haunting the living room window. Terr seemed glad, too, for she stumbled a little on the sidewalk. Jody reached out to help, but she had righted herself.

"There's my baby boy," she said, embracing Cameron on the front porch. "How'd you get here? I don't see your car."

Cameron wrapped and rocked her in his thick arms, pressing her against a round belly that protruded through an old t-shirt. "I rode my bike."

"All the way from Worcester?" she asked.

"Hey, if the roads are closed, I need a way out. Who knows what'll go down tonight." As he let go, Jody could see a t-shirt depicting wolves howling at the moon.

"Nice t-shirt," Jody said.

"Yeah, right? I pulled this old beauty out of the basement. Seems fitting, right?"

"Well, there's fitting, and there's *fitting*. Your man boobs are poking out."

"You know a man is trusty when he gets a little busty," Terr cackled. "Or my favorite: you know he's a fine felly when he's got a little belly." She squeezed her son's large belly.

"I've heard it differently, Mom," Jody said. "There are two men who aren't doing their jobs: a fat husband and a skinny priest."

"Hey," Cameron said, "low blow, man. Speaking of . . you guys at church just now?"

Terr walked inside.

"Something I said?" Cameron asked.

"I don't know," Jody replied. "Maybe it was too much for her. I got vested and everything. Gave everyone absolution. You know, cosmic emergency and all."

"Jesus," Cameron said.

"Yeah. Anyhoo, Father Clément's there now."

"You gonna tell Haleh you did that?"

"I don't know. Maybe let's get through tonight first. If we survive the moon dust, then I'll worry about surviving my wife. You talk to Candy and Devon?"

"Yeah," he drifted off. "They're fine. There's no real food in this house. What have you been eating, bro?"

"Mostly from the Rowdy Rooster," Jody said, walking up the steps of the porch. Dogs howled somewhere. He poked Cameron in the belly. "Those your wolves howling?"

"No, man, mine are growling. They sound like an empty stomach."

"Seriously, though," Jody said, as they entered the house. "Dogs howling at the moon already? It can't be rising."

"That cloud of moon dust, it's huge, bro. It's almost the size of Earth now or whatever. Maybe way bigger. The farther it gets from the actual moon, the dust cloud actually looks less blurry. It's like a perfect hologram, too. I'm telling you, we're in for it."

***

Jody, Terr, and Cameron sat on the sofa, watching the news and waiting for the address by Pope Sylvester. While Jody scrolled through his phone, he received regular text messages from Cameron, two bodies to his right.

"I am literally within arm's reach," Jody said. "Why do you keep texting me?"

"For future reference. Chill out."

"Behave," Terr said flatly.

All were silent for a while, digesting the ham and butter sandwiches Terr had made for lunch.

"It's quiet outside," Terr said.

"It's always this quiet around here," Cameron said.

"No, the Puerto Ricans are always playing their ding-a-ling music. Something's going on out there."

Jody looked up from his phone and turned to Cameron. Their faces matched in disbelief.

"Well, the dogs are out patrolling the streets, by the look of things," Jody said.

"That is also new," Terr replied. "What do you want for dinner?"

"Already?" Jody asked.

"You gonna order something, Mom?" Cameron asked.

"No, I'll make something special."

Jody and Cameron looked at each other again.

"Meaty mac n' cheese?" they asked, nearly in unison.

"You got it." Terr slapped her sons on the legs and sprung up from the sofa. "Could be our last one."

"That's the spirit, Ma," Cameron said, following her

with his eyes. When Terr was in the kitchen, he asked, "What's up with her?"

"She's upset about church. Maybe I embarrassed her. Maybe she didn't know how to take seeing me up there again. I don't know."

"Well, she doesn't either, probably. But look on the bright side: we get her meaty mac n' cheese out of it."

"Indeed, we do. Alright, so let's categorize all the theories so far. First, we've got the obvious: some huge rock hit the moon, sending all the loose dust off the surface at just over escape velocity. But that should shoot the dust off in one direction, in one area. Instead, the dust came off everywhere, all at once, giving us what you and others are calling a holographic image of the lunar surface expanding outward. This leads to theory set number two: we've got a glitch in the matrix, and our universe really is holographic. The dust is really an expanding ball of light and will pass by harmlessly. And, three, your favorite: the moon is, and always has been, a secret base for aliens, who are now shaking off the dust to prepare for their ultimate invasion."

"I'm telling you, man, we've known this for years. The moon rings hollow like a bell. Look it up. Too many coincidences there, like how big it is compared to Earth, and how it fits perfectly into the sun during the eclipse. No, bro, that's by design. I mean, maybe not aliens. Maybe God did it, you know? Like, maybe God lives in the moon."

"The God of all creation does not live in the moon."

"We'll see. Anyway, how did it feel to be at church again, you know, up there in the thing?"

"Kind of weird. Like I was a priest yesterday. Like the past five years of married life hadn't happened."

"What do you think, though? Think we're in for it tonight?"

"No, not really. It doesn't go down this way in the Bible. I mean, yeah, there's that part where the stars fall and sun and moon don't give off their light, but we've still got a sun. And stars."

"So we think. That dust cloud is sort of obscuring everything else. I mean, what happens if it covers the sun, too? What if the universe just becomes some murky gray moon soup?"

"We'll deal with it."

"You're resigned to all this pretty quickly."

"You sound like my wife. Earlier today she called me 'dull to reality.'"

"Well...."

"I don't know. I'm not dull to this. It just doesn't feel like the end. I feel like we sort of grew up preparing for the end of the world. Growing up, every day was the end of the world around here. Now that it's happening, it's sort of underwhelming. Unless it's not the end, which I don't think it is."

"Hey, is that the pope?" Cameron asked.

"Yeah. You know what the pope looks like."

"Right. What happened to the other guy?"

"He died, Cameron. Like, last year."

"Right. Where's this guy from?"

"His name is Dieudonné Dackouo. From Mali. Former bishop of Mopti. Wasn't even a cardinal during the conclave.

He was known throughout the Vatican, worked in State for a while. Someone just said his name during the conclave, and, like, voilà, it ended a five-day stalemate."

"How come I haven't heard of this guy?"

"He doesn't say much. And, honestly, I think it's better that way. Popes sometimes talk too much." Jody craned his neck to look toward the kitchen and yelled, "Mom, the pope's on."

"Turn it up!" she yelled back.

Jody looked at Cameron, who shrugged. "She asked you," Cam said.

"You're younger."

"You're skinnier."

Jody rolled his eyes and rose to turn the knob on the ancient television. Pope Sylvester III waved from the balcony of Saint Peter's Basilica. An arc of white light rose from behind the buildings to his right, the glow of the expanding cloud of moon dust. He exhorted the many people gathered in the square below not to be afraid. He reminded everyone of God's mastery over creation. He led the audience in an Act of Contrition and gave general absolution to those present. Jody realized that he had not made one himself and followed along somewhat mindlessly. He promised to remain outside with everyone until the cloud of moon dust struck the atmosphere, which it was projected to do in about six hours, then began reciting the rosary.

"That's it?" Cam asked.

"Yep. That's it. What else is there to say right now?"

4

After dinner, Cameron washed the dishes while Joy dragged folding chairs from the backyard to the flat roof. No one was renting the third floor, giving the landlord and her sons free access to a better view from which to take in the end of the world. Once up there, Jody looked around and saw others preparing to take it all in from their rooftops. He looked east and saw, in the late evening sun, a thin white line rising from between the hills. "My God," he said to himself, "this is really going to happen." He stared out toward the horizon, pondering and praying.

He heard Cameron encouraging their mother up the steep pull-down stairs from the third floor to the roof. "Well," she huffed, once on the roof, "haven't been up here in ages."

"Don't go near the edge, Mom," Cameron said. "You're a little wobbly these days."

"Your head's wobbly," she retorted, walking to the edge of the roof. Jody stood right behind her, waiting to catch her. "Yep."

"There it is, guys," Jody said, pointing east. "You see it?"

"There it is," Cam echoed. "I do see it. Man, it's spread

over the whole horizon. Bigger. I mean, it's like, how many miles big now?"

"Almost three hundred thousand miles in radius," Jody said. "As big as the distance from moon to Earth. So it's twice as wide in diameter."

"Is that what a diameter is?" Terr asked. "Twice the radius?"

Jody looked at her, not sure if she was asking genuinely or sarcastically. "Anyway, what do you think, Maman?"

"It won't matter in a few hours what I think. We'll all see for ourselves." She studied the milky, moon-soaked horizon. "Hey," she said, tapping her finger on her chin. "Hey...."

"What is it, Maman?" Jody asked.

"You know what? Hey, listen."

"We're listening, Mom. What is it?"

"Go get the good bottle."

Jody and Cameron stood up stiffly.

"Yeah," Terr continued. "Go do it. I mean, why not now?"

Jody looked at Cameron, who looked down. "Sam's not here," Jody said.

"Well, so what? He can afford many nice bottles. This might be it for us."

He breathed sharply and looked at Cameron, who shrugged. "Alright, Mom. Yeah, I mean, now or never, right?"

Jody proceeded downstairs in solemn contemplation and reached the dining room hutch. There was no need to keep the wine under lock and key. The bottle of Madeira had been standing sentry there for all their lives, in the upper, glass-paneled cabinet. Unlike the blended whiskeys and gins kept in Bleiz's tool chest, no one had ever been tempted to taste it, such was the reverence the family held for this bottle of wine. It had been a wedding gift to Bleiz and Terr from his best man. Once they were told that, like their marriage, it grew better with age, they kept holding on for the most perfect, special moment, which seemed to be not even their fiftieth wedding anniversary. For that great feast, Sam had brought an already well-aged bottle of port, quite expensive, and no one argued with his unspoken logic: that the bottle of Madeira should never be opened, so long as they both shall live.

Holding the bottle in his hands, feeling its contours and studying the label, Jody felt for the first time that this really might be the end. How many table wines had come and gone through the decanter on the television? He looked at the decanter through the doorway. As he did, he thought he saw some strange shimmer slipping between the house and the side fence, along the wraparound porch. "Must be the moonlight," he said out loud, but as he did, he felt, somehow instinctively, that this was not true, or not the whole truth. Still holding the bottle of Madeira, he walked into the living room. Whatever that shimmer of bent light was, it left some kind of presence different from what had woken him last night. He squeezed the bottle of Madeira and heard his skin rubbing against the glass. This real sound, this tactile sound, reassured him. He cleared his throat. He went back into the hutch for wine glasses and made as much noise as he could without breaking anything, gently dinging glasses as he lay them and the bottle in a cardboard box. He walked up the pull-down stairs swiftly and carefully.

"Are you sure, Maman?" Jody asked, his voice quivering through heavy breath.

"You alright?" Cameron asked. "You look like you've seen a ghost."

Jody shot him a look that forced Cameron's head backward a little.

"Yeah, Mom," Cameron said. "You sure? I mean, maybe the bottle's haunted? They don't call it 'spirits' for nothing."

"I'm sure, you two. It's just a bottle of wine. Come on. Pour us some glasses."

"Cheers," Jody said. "To Dad." They clinked and drank. The wine washed calm into Jody's trembling limbs.

"Whoa," Terr said. "That's the good stuff."

"Yeah," Jody and Cameron said, each contemplating the taste of a lifetime of promise and potential.

"Well, let's keep it going," Terr said. "To life, however long we've got left."

Jody looked from the white mountain of the rising moon back toward the last orange glow of sunset. "To life," he repeated and clinked.

***

"What does it look like?" Haleh asked.

Jody had answered the phone automatically, entranced by what he saw before him.

"You there, babe? It's still daylight here and cloudy. I'm thinking what I see on TV is not doing this thing justice."

"I don't know how to say it, hon. It's…. It's the moon, just like it looks, but it's filling the sky, the whole sky. It's the feeling, Haleh. I don't know how.... The moon, or the moon dust, or whatever this is, it's magnificent. I mean, it's really terrifying. God, honey, I mean, I don't know how to describe it—not like it's falling on us, not at all, but more like, lying here, I'm just sort of hovering, floating between Earth and moon. I...."

"I wish I was there with you."

He felt her love fill his limbs. "Me, too. You and Claire. I want you both here with me."

"You've got your mother and brother."

"Aren't you at Baba and Maman's? Isn't Cyrus with you?"

"Yes, I don't know. They're just being so scientific about it. Not Mom—she's scared in her own secret way. No, you guys are just more, I don't know, mystical about things like this."

"Mystical? What are they saying?"

"Dad and Cyrus and Uncle Danny are taking bets on which atmospheric layer is going to react first or whatever."

"Where is Danny?"

"I don't know. Not around here. Dad said something about Colorado, but Uncle Danny's always so secretive. Cynthia sort of feeds that, too. They're like hermits together."

"Well, I've got full battery, so just stay on with me. Maybe give me a better view than your nostrils. That's better. That's definitely the face I want to see before...."

"Before what, Jody?"

"Before I don't know. Let me see what I know and love before I see, before we all see, what we don't know."

"You see? That's you being all mystical."

"Well, if that's the case, I get that from my dad. He was the silent, contemplative type. Not this snoring banshee next to me."

"I heard that," Terr said.

"Snoring?" Haleh asked.

"We had some wine." Jody changed his phone to his left hand and held out his right for his mother. She took it, then she took Cameron's left hand in her right. Jody gazed at Haleh and Claire on his phone, chained to his mother and brother on the rooftop of his childhood home, while the moon pressed in solemnly, serenely, and, for the moment, silently.

***

About five minutes later, a flash of light broke forth from the southeast, to their right. All looked but made out nothing particular. Beyond the farthest rooftops, steeples, and smokestacks, the sky glowed a little green.

"It's starting, Haleh. I think. Let's see."

Soon after, a ragged band of pink, green, and purple light, much like an aurora but thinner, began tearing northward. Jody stood and helped his mother stand up. She held on to the arms of her sons while they watched. Jody held his phone against the ball of his shoulder, outward for Haleh to see.

"What's that sound?" Haleh asked.

"The dogs are howling again," Jody whispered. "The birds are chirping wildly, too."

The sinuous wall of alien light urged forward and broadened as it approached. It slithered and stretched outward between the hills, finally rising above them all at once in a grand serpentine display. Coils of neon light whirled against each other, roiled by the milky white plasmic moon pressing downward into Earth's upper atmosphere. The dust-gray Earth below began to give off the brighter greens and pinks as the electric rainbow continued to fall over itself into whorls and roll against the thicker air blanketing the land.

This psychedelic spectacle pressed forward silently until, amidst the mild cacophony of animal wails, a slight hiss slipped through. This was perceptible especially when the surrealist landscape closed in above them. The whole sky became an undulating array, with rivers of purple lava flowing between simmering peaks of green and pink rising downward toward them.

Jody felt his hairs stand on end but could not tell if this was from static electricity or simple awe. He did discern, though, among the animals' frantic chirps and howls, the emerging noise.

"It's like the fuzz of the television," he said, but by the time he had finished that phrase, the sound had drowned him out. Terr removed her hands from her sons' to cover her ears. Jody tried to do the same, but the gap left by the phone against his left ear let through most of the grating, anxious din that took on the racket of water crackling in a pan of hot oil accompanied by the occasional breaking of massive thunderclaps. He put his phone into his shirt pocket and covered his ears fully. The lightscape moved onward toward the north and west while the air continued to burst and sizzle. There was a slight breeze. As the breeze blew into a mild wind, the sound dissipated. Jody released his ears. His left ear was ringing.

He rubbed Terr's shoulder, and she released her ears. All three looked at each other in wonder.

"Are you there?" Haleh asked, almost sobbing.

"Yes, Haleh. I'm here. We're all here. It got so loud, I don't know if you could hear that or not. It was like we were in a frying pan. A psychedelic frying pan. I...." He looked around. "I don't know. It's all moved on now. It was all so quick. My ear is ringing. The animals are quiet again. The sky's dark. Really dark. Well, the sky is sort of white, like the cloud of moon dust is still going outward from the other side of the moon. Which means the Earth is inside the moon cloud now, I guess. But we're all here. We're all fine."

"You're okay, Daddy?" came Claire's concerned voice.

"I'm okay, sweetie. We're all okay, me, Nanou, and Uncle Cam. We're fine, sweetie."

Jody looked down to see Terr pouring herself a glass of Madeira.

"Easy, Mom," Cameron said.

"You take it easy. That was some shit!" Terr exclaimed and threw herself down onto the lawn chair. Jody and Cameron sat down, then, after a moment's pause, each reached out his empty glass toward his mother. She poured eagerly, spilling a little on Jody's hand.

"Now what?" Haleh asked. "Everyone here wants to know what it looks like."

"It looks like I'm having a glass of wine," Jody said.

"Alright. Me, too, then," Haleh replied. "Hold on. Talk to everyone."

While Haleh poured herself a glass from the bottle that her father had ready, Jody described to his in-laws everything he had just seen: the first burst of light; the sinuous aurora; the neon, alien skyscape; the frying noise; and the silence. His father-in-law, Sunny, hoped that as the sphere of the moon cloud continued to press outward from the moon, enlarging the ring of fire it made against Earth's atmosphere, the energy of the event would not peter out before it met them. All wanted a share in the action now that it was safe.

Cameron was still scanning the sky. Jody followed his eyes upward, describing what he now saw. The green and purple belt had expanded outward in all directions and made its way over the horizon. The first brightest stars began to twinkle again through the cloud of moon dust moving outward toward the solar system. He did not see the moon itself.

"Where is it?" Cam asked.

Terr looked up and studied the sky with them.

"Haleh, would you hold on a second?" Jody asked. He stood, and Cam followed him upward. They both scanned the eastern horizon, from south to north, with no success. The streetlights were still on below them, and Jody blocked the light from the nearest one with his hand. He waited for his eyes to adjust, taking in a few more stars. "Maybe it's still hidden inside this moon soup?"

"No," Cameron said, pointing.

Jody followed his finger. Slowly, he began to see, a few degrees above the hills to the northeast, rising calmly within the gray-white sky, the clear, circular shape of the moon, sized the same as it always had been, and perfectly black.

5

Jody woke underneath a bright, hazy white sky. The metal deck chair squeaked beneath him as he turned right and left and stretched. Terr and Cameron had already gone downstairs.

It had been the longest night he could remember. After spotting the darkened moon, which many were now calling the "moondark," and describing it to Haleh and her family, there began a frantic search through news apps and social media for answers. It was a longer night than that of Claire's birth for both families, for that nervousness was excitement and joy. Jody himself commented that what he now saw above was like an un-birth, going from light to darkness. This did not help his wife's disposition, which alternated between focused sleuthing and open sobbing.

The cloud of moon dust, now called the "moonglow," had first broken against the upper atmosphere in the eastern North Atlantic, near the Azores. The aurora it created spread out in a circular pattern from that center point, reaching Stonebridge and the eastern seaboard in just a few minutes. Once it reached ninety degrees of arc in every direction, the moonglow did not close back in on itself. It did not close in on the Earth within it, and the aurora dissipated. The last to see it were on the west coast of North and South America, the east coast of Africa, and up the line that roughly separated the Middle East and Europe from Asia. Those in the Far East, Australia, and Antarctica never saw it with their own eyes.

Everyone had seen the black form that remained, the moondark. It took some time, but near the end of the night, as it hovered over the hills and rooftops of North America, some news had come through from sources deemed authoritative: the darkened shadow that crept along the moon's path was, by indirect measurement of its size, mass, and momentum, the moon. It emitted no light and reflected no light, though further testing would need to be done to verify that.

Cameron had begun reciting whatever words he could remember from the Bible about the end of the world, recalling something about the moon no longer giving off its light. Jody found for him, from Matthew's gospel, *Immediately after the tribulation of those days, the sun will be darkened, and the moon will not give its light, and the stars will fall from the sky, and the powers of the heavens will be shaken.* He could not otherwise argue Cameron's point. He could only appeal to calm and patience. There had been no real tribulations. The stars had not fallen, and the sun was still shining in the east. They had known that because those reports came through loudly and clearly from the Pacific and Asia, reassurances that the universe was not folding in on itself.

For all the seriousness of the event, and as earnestly as he tried to pray, Jody had felt very little anxiety, and he felt guilty for this. He expected some greater agony at the end of the world, but when Haleh, putting Claire to bed, had told Jody to say good night to his daughter for the last time, he could only reply by teasing her and her family that, for a people who had invented the end of the world, these Zoro-astrians seemed rather unprepared. Each time he looked up at the dark circle of the moon set against the dull white of the moonglow, he felt himself more keenly in reality, with a metal and plastic chair digging into his body.

In the morning, awake again, he looked about. It seemed the sun had not yet risen. It was not cloudy, but the white light of the moonglow, still expanding outward into space, gave way to a gradient of silver and blue toward the west. All was silent. Soon, a line of dull pink rimmed the eastern horizon. For a moment, Jody grew anxious, remembering the moon's aurora from last night. Then he saw the approaching sun. He wiped his face with his hands, folded up the chair, and walked downstairs.

***

Jody shuffled into the kitchen. His eyelids were heavy, and he moved from muscle memory toward the smell of coffee and pancakes. Cameron's broad silhouette shuffled back and forth between the sink and the counter.

"Morning!" Cameron said.

"Mor...," Jody began, finishing his word with a long yawn. "Guess we're all still here."

"Nah, man. This is heaven, where every morning your brother makes you pancakes! Welcome!"

"I figured you'd smell better in heaven," Jody said, pouring himself coffee from the percolator. "Where's Mom?"

40

"In the garden."

Jody walked out onto the back stoop and saw his mother hunched over her tomatoes, still in her pajamas and robe. "They survive the blast?" he asked.

"Yep," she said, not turning around.

He looked at her for a moment. He looked at the garage and tried to make a calculation that would not be possible before coffee. The sky was already brightening into some kind of silver. He went back inside.

"What are they saying?" Jody asked Cameron.

"That the cloud of moon dust did not come back together on the other side of the Earth. The Earth made a hole in it."

"Saw that."

"That everything else is normal, except that we can't see the moon."

"Saw that."

"That we're on curfews for a while, just to be sure no one tries looting and rioting."

"You don't seem bothered by all this."

"I'm alive, making pancakes."

"You should call them mooncakes. You know, *in memoriam.*"

"Huh. Yeah, you know, a little gray food coloring, and we're in business."

"I'm sure there will be plenty of money to be made in this, somehow. They always figure out a way."

With his coffee, Jody walked out again through the back door, past his mother, to the garage. He opened the side door and turned on the light. His father's Trans Am, now his Trans Am, was under its cover.

"You know, Mom," he said, looking back out through the side door of the garage, "I'm thinking. I might just drive home."

She didn't respond.

"It'll be a while before the airlines get their act together without GPS."

"They lost GPS?"

"They say the satellites on the moon side got all wobbly. Like they're buoys at sea, bouncing around. They work. Just wobbly." He yawned again.

"How're you gonna drive home without GPS?"

"I know the way. It's I-80 all the way."

She worked at her tomatoes for a minute. "You gotta do what you gotta do."

"I might just leave today," he said.

Terr did not look up, and it looked like she was no longer doing much at all.

Jody turned off the light, closed the door, and went back into the house.

"I'm going back today," he said to Cameron and sat down at the table.

Cameron looked at him briefly, then said, "Makes sense."

"The sooner Haleh knows I'm on the road, the better."

"I guess so," Cam said. Handing his brother a plate of pancakes, he added, "Eat up. Get strong."

"You talk to Devon and Candy yet?"

Turning back to the counter, Cameron said, "Yeah,

man. They're fine. Anyway, watch it out there. Stay on the interstates." He walked over and laid hot bacon on top of Jody's pancakes.

***

"Just give it one more day," Haleh had said. She was right. Jody had spent much of the day after the moondark dozing in front of the television. She had spent the day planning his route from Stonebridge, Massachusetts, to Walnut Creek, California, three thousand and thirty miles. He estimated he could safely drive eight hours a day. She doubted he would be comfortable in "that old monster" for so long. He asked her if knights were comfortable in their armor, or astronauts in their capsules. She replied only by gazing at her knight through the screen of his laptop until he fell asleep, sitting upright on his old bed.

In the late afternoon, Jody, Cameron, and Terr sat in a booth at the Rowdy Rooster.

A young, smiling waitress of Ecuadorean descent approached the table, waved cheerfully to Jody, and said, "Oh. Hey. Welcome back. Are you ready to order?"

"Welcome back?" Cameron asked.

"He comes here every day," Terr said through the menu covering her face.

"Should I come back?" the waitress asked.

"No, we're ready, Selena. I'll have. . .you know what? It's my last time here for a while. I can't get your meatloaf anywhere else." He smiled and handed her the menu.

"Oh, you heading out?"

"Tomorrow."

"Oh. Good luck. You taking your dad's car?"

"That's the plan."

Cameron and Terr ordered rather tersely, and Selena went to the kitchen.

"My meatloaf no good?" Terr asked.

"I didn't say it wasn't. Complimenting the Rowdy Rooster on their meatloaf is not putting yours down." Jody scanned the restaurant. Apart from the constant footage of the moondark on the news, accompanied by diagrams and continuous, contradictory commentary, one would never know the world had changed.

"You gonna have enough time to drive between curfews?" Terr asked.

"And then some."

All three sat quietly. The murmur of the television barely broke above the din of clanging silverware, subdued conversations, and chatter from the kitchen. Terr pecked repeatedly at the bendy straw in her iced tea, finally grabbing it with her free hand and slurping. "Ah," she exhaled.

More light than heat came the quotation in the chyron from President Palmer. Those had been her words at today's noon broadcast, meant to encourage her fellow Americans.

"More light than heat," Jody read.

"Hey, that's my expression," Terr said.

"I think it's a common expression," Jody muttered.

"Still, you heard it from me. You think it's safe driving out there? What if the police stop you?"

Cameron answered for him. "Honestly, Mom, they see a guy like Jody, they're not going to give him a hard time. Even if you break curfew, they'll just give you a tongue lashing. They're not out to round up people for no reason. You gotta think like you're one of them, you know? Like, what is going to cause the least trouble out here? I bet ex-priest computer programmers driving home to wife and kid are near the bottom of their list of troublemakers."

Terr shrugged in agreement, as if just to emasculate Jody. Video footage came on the television of people in colorful robes in some foreign country making some kind of religious celebration below the darkened moon. Terr grunted something.

Selena brought their meals: meatloaf and mashed potatoes for Jody, a honey bourbon barbecue burger for Cameron, and a chicken Caesar salad for Terr, which she smothered in dressing. Jody said grace.

A diagram of the moonglow came on the television above the bar, showing its ongoing expansion and the hole that the Earth had punched through it. It looked like the Death Star. "So who's our Darth Vader? Who's out to control the galaxy?"

"It's probably the Chinese," Terr answered. "And the Russians."

"It will certainly not be both of them together," Jody said, taking a mouthful of meatloaf.

"And the Iranians, too. You better watch those people when you get home."

Jody resisted the urge to throw the table upward and burn rubber all the way out of town. Instead, he teased, "Hmpf. Maybe they've got me working for them."

Jody watched Terr study him, looking for a put down. Not finding one was proof again that he had won this argument five years ago.

"It does look like the Death Star," Cameron said.

Jody looked up at the television. The moon cloud was not rotating like the moon used to, or might still have been doing, for all anyone knew, and so the Earth hole was always facing the sun, more or less. Noon would glow a little brighter and bluer each day.

"Like it did today," Terr said.

"I didn't notice," Jody said.

"You were asleep."

The baggy-eyed scientist who had become the tired face of moondark news came on to contradict reports that the tides had increased in intensity, that the tides had ceased, that the Earth was entering a new ice age, and that the Earth, too, was going to rip apart.

He did confirm that satellites operating in the so-called "safe zone" between the inner and outer Van Allen belts suffered significant damage from the expansion of the moon's electromagnetic radiation. The greatest casualties were suffered by GPS satellites orbiting at twelve thousand six hundred miles, almost precisely where the inner and outer belts briefly met during the event. It would likely take years, if not decades, to bring the system back to where it had been two days ago.

Apart from GPS systems, everything on Earth was functioning nominally. Commercial aircraft were temporarily grounded until the airlines could make proper arrangements for dual-license pilots to sit in as navigators while the GNSS was down. Private aircraft could operate on the VOR system. Rumors of strange patterns of interference on the

VHF and lower parts of the UHF spectra could not be confirmed or denied at this point.

"Just like that," Cameron said, "back to the Stone Age."

"We'll be fine," Terr said flatly.

Jody had a hard time disagreeing with her. In fact, he knew that the satellite business, his business, would boom now. "We grew up without GPS, Cam. We're the Oregon-Trail generation. We roughed it out there before the Internet. We lived through the Y2K bug. We got this. You literally rode to Mom's house on a bicycle yesterday."

"True," Cameron said, barbecue sauce dripping from his mouth.

Selena approached. "Do you guys want dessert?"

After they ordered, Cameron began scrolling through his phone.

"Put that away." Terr slapped his hand.

"It's serious, Maman. You hear about the sleepers?"

"Oh, God, Cameron," Jody said. "Now what?"

"No, just that people are saying that a lot of people went into a coma during the moonburst."

"I'm sure any number of people have simply died of fright. Those reports I *have* heard," Jody replied.

"I've heard that," Selena said, setting down their desserts. Jody jumped a little. "Sorry, just that other people have been talking about people falling asleep for no good reason, they can't wake them up. And the ghosts, too, walking around."

Jody resisted the chills falling down his spine. "I think there's just some reasonable explanation for all this, Selena. Just a lot of fears being projected out there right now.

I mean, this is a big deal. The moon blew away all its light. So...yeah. I think once we find a balance again, all this other stuff will vanish like it always does."

Selena looked downcast and held the black, plastic tray flat against her belly. She reached into her apron and pulled out the check. "Just whenever you're ready. No rush."

Jody watched her walk away, disappointed in himself. "I was just trying to be reasonable."

Cameron looked around, then said, "Why, man? I mean, why not just take this magic carpet ride as far as it goes? Look where being reasonable has got us after all these years. You turn into that poor guy on the TV with the big bags under his eyes, tryin' to explain everything away."

Jody looked at Terr, who, with eyebrows arched broadly, sipped her coffee, looked at him, and gently shrugged.

6

The mid-morning sun shined past the rooftops across the street and directly down the driveway, drawing out from the faded garage door subtle shades of thin soot and the residue from years of dusty rains. Jody loved this ritual. He took his shadow to one side of the door and tapped in the security code, 1938*, the year his father claimed to be born. Bleiz had always joked with Jody about pressing the star key, that, like an athlete whose record was in doubt, the year of his birth had earned an asterisk. Jody had always waited for some grand revelation of the truth in this regard, but it never came.

The heavy door lumbered upward, and inward fell the sunlight on the dark form-fit cover, Jody's birthday gift to Bleiz a few years ago. As he walked toward the front of the car, he caressed its curves under this cover. He wouldn't dare do so to the naked car, not after the shine he had given it the day after his father's funeral. In his ritual, he began uncovering the car from the front, in the back of the garage, so that by the time he reached the back of the car again, the sunlight would break through the lunar haze all at once on its new blue sky.

This was the 1971 Pontiac Trans Am 455 HO; this blue, Lucerne Blue. It was not the most powerful car, not the most sought after, but it was beautiful. He had shared it with his father all of his life, and now it was his. Bleiz had never been possessive of the car, but it did grip his time. Jody had driven it many times, many more than had Sam and Cameron. The much older son and the youngest, the sometime auto mechanic, somehow never shared Jody's enthusiasm for the machine.

He folded up the cover with a mastery he never applied to the fitted sheets at home, learned, perhaps, from folding funeral palls, and achieved now with as much solemnity. He opened the trunk and placed the cover inside. As he closed the trunk again, the white stripe running down the middle—more a patch here outlined in black—made him first think, like it often had, of his old priestly collar.

Jody sat in the driver's seat and gripped the steering wheel tightly, listening to it creak against his hands. He looked around at the garage. This would be the last time this car, after fifty years, would sit here. To give the garage a singing sendoff, he started the engine and let it echo off the wooden frame and slats, then revved loudly. Rakes and shovels shook on their racks, and some small animal scurried out in fright. The white hood scoop, connected to the engine, vibrated happily. He backed down the driveway, bringing the car into full daylight between the house and the street. Next to the garage, the almond-shaped statue of the Virgin Mary that watched over the garden came into view. Bleiz had applied his hand to painting only her blue girdle, as if the white statue with her blue sash was the yang to the yin of this blue car and its white stripe.

Pleased with this observation and sad that he could not have made it while his father was alive, Jody turned off the car, closed the garage door, and went inside the house.

***

"Oh, good," Terr said. "You're not leaving without saying goodbye."

"You were on the phone with Sam before. One of your delay tactics," Jody said, jerking his head back. Seeing her wither a little, he added, "Besides. I want some of the 8-tracks."

"What do you want those old things for?"

"I've got the player in the car. It's the only thing they work on now."

"Hold on," Cameron said, pounding his way into the living room. "You don't get to take just whatever you want."

"Relax, man. Just some classics. Stuff for the road."

Cameron grumbled and knelt down before the base of the corner cabinet, where the 8-tracks were kept. Jody looked at Terr, who shrugged. He gave her a slight, innocent smile, crept up behind Cameron, and wrapped his long, lanky arms around his little brother's bulky body.

"Don't fight," Terr said flatly, sitting down on the couch to watch her two sons.

"Tell Cameron he doesn't even own an 8-track player," Jody said.

"Tell Jody some of these are worth some money."

"Is that true?" Terr asked.

Cameron shrugged.

"Nice going," Jody whispered into Cam's ear. "Now we get none."

"I heard that," Terr said. "Just take what you want, and then I'll pick out what you're not taking."

After a few minutes, the two brothers stood before their mother, each with a stack of 8-track cassettes in his hands.

"Nope," Terr said, pulling one out. "Nope. Not my Neil Diamond. Eh...fine. Nope. Fine. Alright. You get what you want? You boys happy?"

"Yes, Maman," they said in unison.

"Good. Now get your ass on the road."

A few minutes later, Jody stood on the front porch with Terr, his arm around her shoulder. They both looked at Cameron, who was bent over the passenger door, leaning into the car. "Did he talk to Devon yet?" Jody asked.

"I don't think so," Terr replied.

"He'll be alright. He'll take care of you here. My shift was up soon, anyway." He kissed her on the top of the head.

"You don't want to stay through your birthday? Just another week away."

"It feels like it's now or never, Maman."

"Fine. You don't go racing off the line like you and the old man did. Now's not the time for funny business."

"I know."

They held each other that way for a few minutes while Cameron continued his pretense of inspecting the vehicle.

"Gotta go, Maman. I'm on the clock now." He kissed her head again and walked down the steps.

"She's got you good, eh?"

He turned around, opened his arms, and replied, "She looks out for me."

Before he could let his arms fall again, Cameron grabbed him from behind, lifted him off the ground, then turned and bent him over. Cameron then muttered in his ear, "You gotta gun or anything?"

"What?" Jody choked. "Have we ever had guns?"

Cameron released him. "I'm just saying. Maybe you're right. Take it easy, bro. Don't do anything I would do."

"You got that right."

Jody opened the car door quickly and sat down. He started the engine, letting its vibrations fill his body until they reached his mouth, which filled with the sadness that comes before tears. He saw Terr leaning sideways against the house in her cream-colored, short-sleeve dress. Beneath her distant gaze, her kyphotic hunch looked more like the practiced slouch of a girl perennially fighting off womanhood. He revved the engine, but she did not react. He backed out onto the street and drove away.

***

Jody stood over his father's grave. There was no marker yet, but the family had improvised a modest cairn of stones from the garden. Below them, a belly of brown dirt stretched upward from the green grass. Death must be a swollen serpent, for it can only eat all at once. His mother's family was nearby, grandparents and great-uncles. Those of Terr's generation were buried elsewhere, in Florida and Arizona and wherever the wind had scattered them. Bleiz had wanted nothing scattered. He had wanted to be in one place. Here he was.

Jody sat in the quiet car. This town must somehow have

been enough for Bleiz Conque, even after Liberty Lenses moved to Mexico. It had not been enough for the French Canadians, who began leaving even as he arrived fifty-five years ago. Maybe, in her strange way, Terr had made it enough for him. He had met her in New York, where they briefly tried to live the life, he the cook, she the hostess. Sam came on the scene too soon, and Bleiz followed Terese back to her father's house where, a fortnite ago, he passed away in his sleep. Maybe Maddie's ghost had kept him here. Jody turned back to his father's grave. He had never asked him these questions.

Jody looked over at the passenger seat. Cameron had secretly piled all of his own 8-tracks there. The phone, plugged into the lighter, read 9:36 a.m. Haleh's message, to which he had woken, read, *Your mission, should you choose to accept it: Wilds Inn, Clarion PA. Exit 62. 7:06. This message will self-destruct in 5... 4... 3... 2... 1...* and there followed a flurry of emojis, hearts and lips and hands in prayer. "You making a believer out of my wife, Mr. Moon?"

He looked back up at the road before him. He would have turned torque into tire smoke in one last gesture for his father, but a dog, a German shepherd, sat on his haunches in the middle of the road. Jody flashed his lights to no response, then revved the engine. He honked, then crept forward. A few yards away from the split grille, the dog only lifted his left paw and licked his wrist. Jody rolled his fingers on the steering wheel and whistled. He turned to look back at the gravesite. When his head faced forward again, the dog was gone. "Al-right...," he said and drove on slowly. He didn't see the dog anywhere else on the sidewalk.

As he approached the intersection where the small road coming from the cemetery met the broader avenue, he had the green light but saw a truck approaching that was not slowing. He stopped and watched as a Party Pig catering truck flew by at full speed through its red light. He thought of the dog that had just stopped him. "I see it's going to be that kind of trip," he said. He blessed himself, and, the green light still his, he peeled away.

PART TWO

WARPATH

7

The trees on either side of the interstate bellied into the road, full and dripping with late summer green. Those farthest ahead, astride a hill, stood stiff sentry until they joined the wind blurring past Jody's face. Their scent was the musk of middle age; if the spring nose knew the sticky, frenetic spray of arboreal lust, the late summer shed aftershave, wool, and whiskey. The morning sky shone white with moon dust. The road below was gray.

Against that slate backdrop, Jody wrote a memory. He sat in the breakroom of the small office that had hired him in terms described as "consultant" but which comprised of, in reality, a paid internship. This afforded, in addition to a living wage, a resume-building experience in the Python programming language. Cyrus, one of his instructors in the coding boot camp he had attended, had taken a liking to him and invited him to interview with the satellite research firm Scimitech after the course was finished. As it turned out, Cyrus's father, Mehrzad "Sunny" Shamshiri, was its co-founder and president. Jody liked their logo, as its two curved swords, locked at the handle, looked less like the spacey swoops of the NASA logo and more like the flags fronting the Chevy Corvette.

He sat alone in the breakroom, blowing the heat off a bowl full of microwaved soup. The other staff usually ate at their desks. He hoped he was not coming off as above them; he just needed a break from the screen. Sometimes, during these breaks, Sunny would come in and pepper him with questions about life out East, about the priesthood, or about his past. If it were not for the constant evidence of the old man's youthful curiosity, Jody would think he were being interviewed for a more permanent job.

Haleh, Sunny's daughter, walked in. She looked at him, and he fought his instinct to turn away. He was not used to sustained eye contact and thought that this would be a thing to practice in this new place. This family somehow made that easy. She made it easy most of all.

Haleh Shamshiri was not the type that Jody had traditionally found beautiful. Her complexion was much paler than that of her brother and of a gray-gold hue. Her long, thick brown hair fell effortlessly around her neck, past cheeks that, though a little pudgy, arched high and bright. Slight evidence of some earlier struggle with acne rose as fair freckles. If she were a little overweight, her bones, poised and symmetrical, held everything to an hourglass shape. Every imperfection hung in the grasp of some greater perfection. And something else squared the sum of these parts. He would not say it was personality. Meditating on her mystery for nearly a month by then, he would say she was pleasant when assertive and relaxed in her intelligence. Maybe her charm was simple modesty.

"Here, this is for you," she said, setting a paper plate full of food before him.

He looked up at her. She turned her eyes slightly to the side, toward the window. He relaxed for a brief moment, but she turned back to him. Again, he resisted turning away and made an exercise of fearlessness here.

"Thank you," he said. "What is it?"

"Just a little something from the party."

He sat up a little. "Did I miss a party here? I'm sorry...."

"No, it was my mother's birthday yesterday." She did not leave but stood there, still looking at him.

"And you brought me a plate? That's very kind." Confused as he was, and inexperienced, he did not want to ruin the moment as he sometimes did with some sarcastic or self-deprecating remark. "All of you have been so kind." There. That was the sort of thing real people said.

"Well, enjoy," she said and made as if to leave.

"Well, hold on a minute," he said. "Aren't you going to guide me through this?"

She stopped and appeared, if he dared imagine it, at once pleased and shy.

"I mean," he continued, "perhaps just to tell me what I'm eating, guide me through the new terrain. You don't have to watch me eat, of course." And he hated himself for making such a stupid comment. But she sat down across from him. She explained what the dish was, a thing he soon forgot. He forgot every time he told the story, and she had to remind him. He could not remember even now. He did remember that there were dates, three of them.

She did watch him eat, and he never remembered what

they spoke about. Reliving the story, he felt again the warm, tingling feeling that had blanketed him then. He had to invite that feeling to stay, not let his body cast it out in distrust.

Before he knew it, his plate was empty. The room filled with humid silence. Jody thought and prayed for some right word to say. Instead, he let his eyes rest in hers again. She let him look at her. Words then issued from his mouth without his knowing how, and he said, "You make it so easy to look at you."

She fell back in her chair, looked down, and, as if to correct herself, turned toward the window. Her eyebrows arched in confusion. In a flash, two thoughts intersected: this is the boss's daughter; you are a still a priest. Anxiety tore like lightning through his stomach, and he sat a little more erect. He was determined, though, not to let fear take hold of him again, not to lose this moment, for once in his life to figure it all out after doing what he desired to do, which was to say, "What I mean is...you are perfectly beautiful."

At this, her head jerked back a little and re-centered. She smiled and blushed ever so slightly.

Jody, for his part, felt powerfully happy, for he had said what he meant, at great risk, and succeeded. Now he did not know what to say.

"Haleh, that is a lovely name. What does it mean?" He asked this though he knew already, having looked it up when he first saw her.

"Um," she replied, "like moonlight, or like the glow around the moon. It's actually the Persian form of an Arabic name, but I guess my parents liked it, so...." She pulled her hair behind her ears.

"Well, it's lovely, anyway," he said.

"And what about Jody?" she asked.

"Ah, now you have entered complicated terrain." He smiled. "It is short for *Joseph*," he said, saying Joseph in a French accent.

"*Joseph*?" she imitated, thick with her California accent.

"Joseph, as in Pierre-Joseph Armand Augustin Conque."

"That's a lot of names," she laughed. The heat broke in the room.

"It's the French-Canadian response to poverty. The poorer you are, the more names you get."

"Oh, I don't know, it sounds more like one of those aristocratic names."

"Well, of my brothers, it's actually the Frenchiest name. See, my father is Breton, who are like the Welsh of France, wearing funny kilts now and everything. My brothers are Sam and Cam, or Samson and Cameron. My father, thinking both names were Scottish, well, Cameron is, and deciding, as a Breton, he wanted to be more Celtic than French, gave them those names. They took to calling me Jody, lest I call myself Joey, which they thought was too Italian, or plain old Joe, which would have been undignified for a Franco-American." He paused. "Anyhoo."

Haleh watched Jody with an open, expectant face. Finally, she said, "You have an interesting family."

Jody, proud at that time of his family's quirks, was about to ask about her family's situation, expecting some similar disarray.

"What does Conque mean?" she asked.

"Nothing special, really. Conch. You know, a seashell."

"Seashells keep all the secrets of the ocean wrapped up inside. That's kind of nice."

Jody felt awash in affection. Her eyes sparkled like those cresting waves of the sea.

Cyrus walked in, eyed the empty paper plate and the bright faces of his sister and friend, and said, "Ah, yes. Good."

The city of Hartford rose before Jody, ending the comfort of the trees. Haleh called.

"What a coincidence," he said. "I was just thinking about our first date. What was on the plate you made for me again?"

He knew exactly what her response would be, which was, "Our first date? Excuse me, mister, but there were a lot of tears shed between that plate of zereshk polo and our first date."

"Zereshk polo," he mused. "Any news?"

"You can't tell a girl she's perfect and beautiful and then be like, 'Whoops, actually I'm a priest, so....'"

"How are you still upset about that? You won. You got me. And, by the way, I said you were 'perfectly beautiful.'"

"Hm."

"And you still are."

"Anyway, curfew's still in place for tonight. I guess some cities are seeing looting."

"Not Hartford, I hope. I have to drive right through it."

"Any others? New York?"

"Not big ones, no. Driving through a city on the interstate, you always get the part that looks like it's about to burn down, or just did."

"Anyone else on the road?"

"A few others. Some look like they're on the move, but at this point, we're so far inland, I don't think we're dealing with tides or anything. I don't know what they could be escaping."

"Big cities, perhaps, and all their ghosts." She was silent for a moment. He winced. "Have you seen any more ghosts?"

"It wasn't a ghost, really, I told you. Just a trick of light."

"But you were afraid of it."

"The moon dust was about to hit Earth. And that's to say nothing of my mother telling us to open the good bottle. Emotions were running high."

"But others are talking about ghosts now," she said. "Like the moon is calling them out."

"Without Cam and Cyrus, I don't know where else we'd get what's really going on in the world. The girl at the Rowdy Rooster, too."

"Well, maybe it's a thing. No one's talking about getting hurt by them. Just…."

"Just shimmers and shivers," he replied. "Let's be a little more scientific. I say it's aliens who blew up the moon and are now walking around with invisibility cloaks."

"*That's* a consoling thought, babe."

A few minutes later, after finishing his call with Haleh, Jody slowed through a web of interchanges, ribbons of gray road ripped and folding over each other. *Maybe we're all shimmers. What's left of our presence on the road but a blur, thoughts and words and feelings slipping through in dopplered pulses, intensities up front fading into sad echoes of ourselves?*

Jody sat again in the break room at Scimitech, gazing at

the red, swollen cheeks streaked with tear-soaked strands of hair. "It's not a vow I made, but a promise," he said. "They mean different things as far as the church is concerned."

"So you would just, like, break a promise?" She sobbed.

"What I mean is, it's easier to...I can have a conversation about it with the powers that be."

"Don't leave for me," she said, in a surprisingly matter-of-fact way. "I could never live with myself."

"No. If I leave, I will leave for myself. That's what I'm here to figure out, anyway. That's why I've taken the time off." He reached forward, covered her tissue-clenching fists with his hands, and said, "But promise me you won't go anywhere."

Haleh looked at him with stern red eyes and said, "I don't owe you any promises, mister."

Looking at her silently and admiring—perhaps fearing—her confidence, he decided right then and there that he loved her.

Something was on fire outside, in Hartford. Thick, black smoke rose from some corner of the labyrinth below. Sirens wailed. Jody gripped his steering wheel with both hands. "This could be anything, a normal fire," he muttered to himself. The odor wafted into the car, and he closed the window. The road took him closer to the fire, which was just a block or two away from the interstate. Cars were slowed down ahead of him, their drivers rubbernecking as they passed the column of smoke. This was prudent, as the wind turned and brought the charcoal cloud into their path. With the wind came the acrid smell of burning plastic and sulfuric breath from the faces he imagined, and almost saw, billowing outward from the column of smoke.

In just a minute, he was past. He rolled down his window and let the breeze clear out the car. "Here," he said to himself. "Before we speed up again." He rummaged through the pile of 8-tracks until he found what he wanted, Zeppelin IV. "Going to California," he said more loudly. "That's how it ends."

8

Jody stopped for gas in some tiny, dismal-looking place a little past the Hudson River. He rolled in on fumes, determined, for some reason, to use the Hudson as the marker of his first victory over the road. It was, for him, the real boundary between New England and the open country. It was the longest bridge he would have to cross; or maybe that was the Mississippi. Maybe it was learning that Zeppelin IV did not end with a pleasant song about California earthquakes but a dramatic one about the waters breaking forth upon the Earth.

"Eight gallon limit," read the sign on the pump. He looked around as if that would explain things. A thin man on a motorcycle was staring in his direction, or Jody thought he was, through dark sunglasses. Maybe there were supply issues now, or fears there would be. There was otherwise no line here. The man was still staring. Jody stared back a little, but the man didn't flinch. He did not seem threatening. Maybe he just liked the car; Jody nodded a little in its direction. The man made no motion but was not stiff or asleep. There was no other bike around. Maybe this was a come on, and this place was where guys picked up guys. Jody was suddenly glad for the eight-gallon limit and went back into the car quickly, not answering the prompt for a receipt. When he sat down and looked up, he noticed the man was gone, though his bike was still there.

It was noontime, and, as promised, the sun shone more clearly through the hole the Earth had punched in the expanding moon cloud. He watched it light up the blue of the car's hood. The biker was back, facing upward at the sun with his glasses off and eyes closed. "I guess we all enjoy the end of the world however we can," Jody said to himself. Without turning his head, the man smiled and nodded. Jody's hand slipped a little as he tried to put the car in gear.

He had only spent two and a half hours on the road but was already hungry. It was a little past noon. Not wanting to venture too far off the interstate in rural New York, he settled for the world's most ubiquitous fast-food chain, not far from the gas station. With the brown bag carefully rolled open on the passenger seat, he drove off.

Immediately, a chicken nugget fell between his legs onto the floor. Four decades of polishing, vacuuming, and detailing would not permit four hours of nugget crumbs. He stopped at the same gas station to fill up with eight more gallons, enough to take him to Clarion. The biker was gone. First, Jody swept under the seat for the lost nugget. This was the cleanest car in Christendom, so he ate it. As he swept his hand, though, he felt something else. Some kind of small notebook lay under the seat, spiral bound at the top with a worn, green cover. He still did not want to linger in that place, so he tossed the notebook into the back seat, pumped his gas, and drove off again. There might be anything in it, and he knew it would nag him like a child from the back seat, but *c'est la vie.*

***

"License and registration."

"I was only trying to get around the truck."

"License and registration."

The belly of the highway patrolman hung from his chest like a gourd. Jody pulled both documents from his wallet and handed them over.

"Where're you headed, son?"

"California, home to my wife and daughter."

"Where're you coming from?"

"Massachusetts, from my father's funeral. He left me this car."

"Uh-huh. Hold on a minute."

When he saw the patrolman sit back down in his car, Jody sighed heavily and rolled his head around. He had just accelerated onto I-84 again when he was pulled over. The nuggets next to him were growing cold. He snuck one into his mouth. He turned back to face forward and saw the patrolman right next to him again. Startled, he reached for his drink to clear out his mouth. "Sorry, I thought you were back there."

"Where're you headed, son?"

Jody took a moment, then answered, "Uh, California. Home, to my wife and daughter. I have no other way back right now, and—"

"That's fine. Who is Bleiz Conque?"

"My father. He just passed away and left—"

"Uh-huh. Hold on a minute."

Jody watched, through the sideview mirror, the patrolman walk back to his car. He reached over and felt his way
toward another nugget. The patrolman took a while, and
Jody finished the rest of the nuggets and fries. After meticulously licking and wiping his fingers, he closed his eyes and
set his head back.

"You know your way without GPS?"

Jody jumped and gasped. "Yes, officer. It's I-80 all the
way."

"You know where you are now?"

Jody looked at the officer's name tag. *J.O. Nawal.* "New
York, sir."

"This is the Hudson Valley."

"Yes, sir."

"This is part of a longer system called the Great Appala-
chian Valley. Runs from Quebec down to Alabama. Used to
be the border between the colonies and Indian lands."

Jody wondered where this was going. "Yes, sir."

"All along here, the natives had a system of paths they
called the Great Indian Warpath."

They must have had their own name for it. "Yes, sir."

"It's almost like a boundary here, you catch my drift?"
Jody did not. His face must have shown that as he studied
the patrolman a little more. Everything about him, from his
sunburnt face downward, oozed live humanity. If he were a
ghost or an angel, Jody could not tell, not with his license
and registration collecting condensation in the thick hands
held out to him. "You go on now to California, that's fine.
Don't get caught up. Stay the path. This will be a war soon."

"Yes, sir," Jody said and took his documents. He watched

the patrolman walk back to his car, at which he yelled through his speaker for Jody to move along. Jody put the car in gear and drove off. He kept looking back to see if the spinning lights would disappear. The long, low hills of this valley gave him ample view. The lights shined as long as the horizon let them, each gentle rise repeating the warning, and then they fell behind the Earth. "Warpath," he muttered to himself and gripped the steering wheel.

***

Jody's head hung heavy as he stared at the detritus of his dinner, plastic wrappers scattered before him on the bed. In the light-hearted mood he had held onto upon arriving at the hotel, he had called the spread "vending machine tapas" in his text to Haleh. Both agreed that, after the day's adventures, extended by the need to fill with gas every three hours—though most gas stations had no limit—it was not worth the risk to find a restaurant before curfew. He did not tell her about the "warpath."

He was sleepier than he expected. He hoped he was not becoming one of the "sleepers" Cameron kept warning about. Looking at the bottle of whiskey he had glommed from the house, he knew other spirits were now filling his veins.

Some drink to remember, some to forget. Jody drank to relax. Sometimes he remembered, sometimes he forgot whatever had strung him tight. He was a day out from home and knew what wave of memory would soon break over the levee, and it did.

Jody sat at the kitchen table across from his mother. His father leaned against the wall behind her, arms crossed. He

72

had already confided in his father in the car; Bleiz had said very little in return. Terr's eyes grew dark and small.

"Tell me what this is really about," she said with seething calm.

"I told you. My leave of absence was a chance to get some fresh air, to rest a little, and now I see it's not really for me."

"Not for you? Not for you? No, it's not for you. It's service to God's people. 'Not for me...,'" she huffed.

"Yeah, well, if I'm miserable, exhausted, and unhappy, how can I be of service to God's people?"

"Look around! Everyone's miserable," she yelled, slamming the table.

Jody remained calm, looked around, and said, "I don't have to be. I found a way to be happy for once in my life."

Terr had no immediate response to this. She said to Bleiz, "What do you say to all this, huh? Do you hear what your son is saying?" He did not reply before she continued, "I'm too old for this shit. Why can't I just die the mother of a priest?"

Jody's heart turned over, and he said, "So that's it, isn't it? This is all about you. It's always about you. You're angry because you can't parade your son around anymore as a priest. You're no longer the 'mother of a priest.' You couldn't care less what that means for me."

She screamed, "I care about you! I care about the fact that you're thirty-five years old now, starting over, wasting your life! Seven years of priesthood, gone! Everything you've been building up, gone! What are you going to do, live here? Tough luck, kid."

"*You* didn't have anything to say about my decisions. I entered religious life after college and discerned out. I entered diocesan seminary, stuck it through, and stuck through seven years of priesthood. You just watched from the sidelines, taking it all in like a spectator, like you have my entire life."

"Sidelines! You ungrateful.... I gave birth to you when I was older than you are now. You think that was easy? Feeding and clothing you all those years? Right after burying my daughter?"

"What does that have to do with the priesthood? I got no more than a nod of the head or a shrug of the shoulders from you in everything I've done. *Now* you're upset that I'm moving on?"

"Fine. Is that what you want? Another shrug of the shoulders? Here," she said, shrugging her shoulders, raising her hands, and pressing forward her chin. "See if I care what you do."

Bleiz sat down between them and glanced at her. This calmed both mother and son.

"So, what...?" Terr began again. "Is there a woman?"

"Before I answer that," Jody began, but it was too late.

"I knew it!" Terr said, slapping the table. "That's been it the whole time. You finally found someone to tickle your funny bone, and you don't know what to do with yourself."

Bleiz put his hand on Terr's, which silenced her.

"That's *not* it," Jody replied. "If you would just let me finish. This has been about me. I told her that I would not be leaving the priesthood for her, but for me."

Terr leaned back and pulled her hands onto her lap. "So

she's waiting for you out there in California? And what happens when you get tired of that?"

"Frankly, Mom, I don't know if she's still waiting for me. I've taken a risk. If it doesn't work out…I don't know. What I do know is that I'm free of one set of shackles."

"You just wait, my boy," Terr said. "You'll tire of a woman soon enough, to say nothing of children. Then you'll see where the grass is greener."

A silence swelled in the kitchen while the grandfather clock chimed four. Whoever left first would declare himself the loser.

Cameron burst into the side door, stoned.

Jody leaned forward along the bed and collected the debris of his dinner, which crinkled loudly in his hands. He lumbered upward and looked through the window. The sun was still filling the sky with light at not yet seven o'clock. He remembered the man at the gas station; perhaps he should go outside and dwell in the fading light for a while. Instead, he plugged in his phone and set his alarm, undressed, and turned out the light.

9

Jody woke in darkness. The phone said it was midnight, but he felt a whole night should have passed. With nearly five hours of sleep, he would certainly be awake for a while. He replied to Haleh's several texts, apologizing for not calling right before his supposed bedtime. She, in turn, would take her time in responding. He put on some shorts and went outside.

The moon cloud still veiled the night sky but more weakly than in previous nights. He had trouble spotting the dark disc of the moon hovering above. Hearing voices in the dark, he searched and saw where they came from—the red ends of cigarettes glowed longer and brighter near those mouths and illuminated the smoky swirls that wrote their words on the wind.

"Excuse me," Jody said to them. "Have you found the moon tonight?"

"Yeah, here," came an older woman's voice, used to much smoking. "Just follow the freeway east, where it ducks behind the mountains, then look up."

He followed the dashed line of red and white dots eastward and upward. Those cars were breaking curfew, but he bet no one in these parts cared too much. After only two days, it had grown difficult to tell the moon apart from its fading ghost growing outward into space, but he found it. "Ah," he said, his neck craned. "Thank you." This might be one of the last times he could tell where it was by sight, so he pondered it and prayed.

"What do you think?" the woman asked him. He still could not see her face. "Is this the end of the world, or what?"

"I don't know," Jody replied. "I mean, we're still here, right? And there seem to be no more signs of disaster."

"Well, what if it's a warning? You know, like maybe things are fine for a time while we're supposed to get ourselves together? Then what?"

"Well, in my faith, I guess it's one of the signs of the second coming. But we've not had the other signs. If it is, it'll be hard for only a little while. And in the end, well...all's well that ends well."

"You seem rather calm about the whole thing."

"I know. I...I've been told that. It just...I don't know. Everything else seems under control."

The man with her spoke up. "That's not what they're saying out in the Middle East. They're talking about armies gathering for it, you know, last battles and things. Armageddon."

The woman corrected him. "We don't know that. Those are just rumors like everything else."

"Funny," Jody said. "The kid behind the desk in the lobby tonight, he's got his face glued to his phone. I don't even think he realizes anything serious has happened. I bet he's never even seen the full moon." With that, a sadness tore through him as he realized Claire would never see the moon lit up at night.

"You think people are praying more?" the woman asked.

"Are you?" Jody replied, more automatically than he thought he was still capable of doing and more quickly than he would have liked. "Whatever you say, that's probably the answer."

The pair seemed to be looking at Jody through the darkness, then the man mumbled something to the woman. They returned to looking out at the moon, each lighting another cigarette. Jody turned back to the moon as well, hoping for some glimmer of starlight, some reflection off its surface.

At some point, a cool breeze blew past. He looked around and saw that the couple were gone. Even the road was empty. Not yet tired enough for bed, he decided to study whatever might be in that green notebook he had found under the driver's seat.

With the notebook in hand, he sat on a concrete bench behind the hotel under a floodlight hosting a horde of gnats. The first page read: *Property of Bleiz Conque. Ne touchez pas.* "Well, Dad, it was in the car, and the car is mine, so...let's see." He flipped through pages and saw notes and scribbles. A journal might not be so messy. Each page or series of pages came with a date, and these were recent dates. Some lines came through more clearly, and Jody realized that these were poems. He smiled a little wryly. The first one that he could find of any clarity and cohesion read:

Come on, quit your job of selling trinkets on the streets
I will spare my soul the pain of parsing presidential tweets

Let's abandon all that's made our life a cheerless chore
Set up house on windy shore
There our life, sweet and poor

Jody rubbed his chin. He flipped through dozens of pages, seeing more of the same. There were not many whole poems or even stanzas. Another fragment read:

Array the universe in gold
It would not stir a single soul

He rubbed the back of his neck. "Is this where all your words went, Dad?" He kept reading:

None but one who's hungered
Can feed his fellow man
Sees beneath his sallow skin
True need in empty hands

Jody closed the notebook. He held it in both hands and pressed the metal spiral against his pursed lips. He stared outward toward the darkness. Even under the floodlight, he could make out the difference between hill and sky. Those gnats above knew to do nothing else than dance around the warm light. The nine planets and their many moons showed as much freedom around the sun. Without light they would all scatter. He rose and walked into the darkness. He stared upward until his eyes adjusted. The moon was still rising, but clouds were coming in from the west to meet it. He

slapped the notebook against his other hand and went upstairs to bed.

***

Downstairs at breakfast, a girl just a little older than Claire
nibbled on a round slab of sausage, eating it with her fork in
the air, from the outside in. Above her head, he saw reports
of people moving away from the coasts. Those interviewed
expressed an intuition that the shimmers—the specters, as
many were calling them—were drawn to the sea or out from
within it. One rhetorically gifted man, in thick Brooklyn
brogue, claimed that the shimmers made their den among
the soft, sunstruck crests of gentle waves, coming out to survey the land in twilight hours. Looking down at the table
again, Jody saw that the little girl's obliging father was eating
the centers of the carefully circumscribed patties. He ached
for Claire, almost reaching for her automatically, as if she
must be in the chair next to him.

He checked the message Haleh had left on his phone:
Next target: Peru. Illinois, that is. Tick-Tock Hotel. 8:01. She
had it down to the minute. He would have to make it past
Chicago, the first and last really large city on his route.

Jody needed a little time before he set out for the coffee
to work its effects, so there in the breakfast area of the Wilds
Inn, he put in his earbuds and watched a video of Pope Sylvester's recent speech.

*My dear brother and sisters in Christ, fear not! We hear
this theme expressed so frequently in the Bible. Why should
God say, fear not? We answer this first by asking, when does
God say, fear not? He says so when his people are faced with
something that ought to be terrifying, be it the presence of an*

angel, the exile to Babylon, or some other life-changing event. The darkening of the moon should be an event that provokes fear, but I say to you, as Christ's vicar, fear not!

Up above, on the television, he saw more footage of mass demonstrations or rituals of another kind. Some kind of neo-Druid in purple lipstick was explaining, he supposed, the rites her people were using to invoke some moon god or another.

What does this event mean for us? We hear in the gospels that our Lord warns us of the so-called end times, when sun and moon give no light and the stars fall from the sky. The stars remain, as does the sunlight. Should we be prepared? Certainly, like always. Is He coming soon? We hope so. Should we fear His coming? Not if we are prepared. How can we prepare? Confessing our sins, forgiving those who trespass against us, and coming to the aid of our neighbor, especially those who do not have the word of God to rely on.

On the television above was a list, points of information: all aircraft grounded due to unexplained radio interference; curfew still in effect; all prices fixed for food, gas, and other essential items, including construction materials.

A portly, middle-aged man at the next table yawned a big, yellow-toothed yawn.

You want me to say more, to explain the deep and dark mysteries of this universe, and I cannot. I am the pope but not a prophet. If you hear anyone telling you more, send him to me that I, too, may listen. For me, the message is clear: repent, pray, and take courage. This has been our message from the moment the Lord Jesus came among us. Now is the time to make sure we are doing these things. For me, this is a warn-

ing, and a friendly one. Let us not fall asleep in fear nor dim our eyelids in drunkenness. Now is the time to be awake, with lamps trimmed, awaiting the bridegroom's return. What I will do for you now is to remain here, in your sight, where you know you have a pope.

Jody appreciated these words, however much they made no direct emotional impact, for, even now, he felt no fear over the event. Should he be worried that he was not afraid? He stared into his empty coffee cup. "God, help us all," he prayed.

He left a text message for Haleh to find when she woke. He stood, flicked a speck of scrambled egg off his crotch, threw out his Styrofoam plate, and went upstairs. The father of the young girl was staring at the television then drew some stray hair off his daughter's face and tucked it behind her ear.

After checking out with a cheery, young female receptionist, Jody reloaded the Trans Am and started it. Its dull roar suddenly sounded, on this airy hilltop, like an intrusion. He filled with gas nearby, seeing if he could sense Palmer's hand bearing down, but everything felt the same. Everything felt the same here below except for the fear now creeping into everyone. Jody noticed that in them but not himself. He turned his Pontiac's dull roar into a battle cry as he ramped onto the highway, a little frustrated that he made it onto the road only at seven past seven.

10

Jody brooded over a beer at the Second Hand Bar and Grill in Peru, Illinois. There had been reports of looting and rioting in Chicago; Haleh had repeated this in the same breath with which she assured him, and herself, he was safely away from them. Still, the hour from Gary to Joliet had been the most tense of his drive so far. The news on the television above the bar, full of heads and hands orbiting diagrams of the inner solar system, blurred into the background. Jody stared into his pale ale.

Barb, his waitress, approached the table. Jody suppressed a sigh. She had already, before he could order his beer, explained that the name of the pub was a double pun. The town was famous for clock-making, and all of the furniture in the place was, if not used, at least mismatched to make it look like it was, hence the "Second Hand."

"You sure you don't want anything to eat, dear?" Barb asked.

"Maybe not just yet, thanks. I had a late lunch."

"Are you from around here? I detect a little something in your voice."

Jody leaned back and practiced a smile. "That's central

Massachusetts you hear. I'm driving from there to California, where I live now. Gotta get home to my wife and daughter."

"Oh," Barb said, putting her plain hands to the mouth of her sweet, plain face. "God bless you. All that way in these conditions?"

"My father just passed away," Jody replied, "and I was back home for the funeral and to stay with my mother for a while. But with all this, you know, I had to get back to my family."

"And now who's looking after your mother?" Barb asked, leaning an arm on her hip.

"I have two brothers out there, one just a short drive away, the other in Boston. She's in good hands."

"And are they married?" Barb asked. It was at this point in such conversations that Jody's insides began turning.

"My brother Sam has a wife and two teenage kids out there. They might all still be up in Maine today, where they have a house. He's a rather well-to-do hospital administrator."

"And what does she do?" Barb asked. Jody always preferred to return to the trunk of a conversational tree, but Barb, he could tell, was a branch climber.

"She used to be a food photographer," he replied. "Now, mostly nature and things, for fun. Excuse me, I'm supposed to say 'personal enrichment.'"

"And your other brother?" Barb asked. Jody decided he was going to enjoy this now.

"Cam is an auto mechanic. We used to call him Camshaft. He has a teenage son with a one-time girlfriend, Candy, but they are, how should we say, estranged."

"Well, I'm sure the moon will bring them back together," Barb said. "Just like it will you and your family. What are their names?"

"Haleh is my wife. Claire is my daughter," Jody replied, now smiling genuinely.

"Well, I will pray for them and that you get home safely. You just let me know when you get hungry, you hear?"

Jody found a few YouTube videos of the woman, Dr. Theodora Pandit, being interviewed the night of the moonburst. He began watching one, careful, this time, to hide his earbud in the ear Barb could not see. He wondered if Pandit's summoning of spirits might have something to do with the specters out in the world.

Dr. Pandit, these spirits that you claim to summon, in what way do you expect them to act as a mirror to AI systems? After all, aren't we talking about very different forms of consciousness?

Ah, yes, in some ways, yes, different forms, different levels. But this is not so strange for us, is it really? Think of what happens between mother and child. A child learns who she is from her mother's face, which fills her field of vision. The mother, in turn, imitates her baby's coos and babbles. They mirror each other until the baby's consciousness is raised to the point where the toddler, the child, can begin imitating her mother's actions, willingly, lovingly, or at least out of attachment, need.

Jody wondered, *With a mother like mine, what does that make me?*

And if something goes wrong at home, if the child gets the sense that something is missing, she seeks out, she wanders the world, looking for new mirrors. But I digress…. No, but do let me digress a little further. You see what's happening with the animals these days, I mean our pets and things? Just scroll through YouTube. How many videos are there of cats and dogs imitating their owners, even trying to speak human words? So, fine, this is not human consciousness, but it is a striving for it.

In our work, we look for ways to make a system see itself: as its own opponent in a game, a dance partner, even poetry slams of a sort, completing rhyme schemes and things.

And you have had success with this? the interviewer asked.

Yes, indeed, sometimes, mm, too much.

Too much?

Sometimes it happens that, just when we are on the verge of something even remotely resembling self-awareness in a system, it collapses. Something occurs that we cannot yet adequately explain. The mirrors, mm, tend to destroy each other. Two systems must resemble each other enough that they can communicate, but the more they do resemble each other, the more they turn and destroy each other.

By "destroy," you don't mean physically, do you? The bodies you've built—

Not necessary, though sometimes. No, it usually takes the form of a re-programming, re-coding each other's speech. It's really quite frightening when we see it in action. Both machines end up sputtering nonsense at each other until one system fails.

"Like politics," Jody muttered.

Maybe love is the answer, Dr. Pandit said. *But I don't know. If I could teach a machine to love, well, I don't know. I'd be God, I suppose. Even then, God has a hard time teaching His conscious beings to love. That is why we seek out more, how should I say, indestructible spirits for our mirrors. Humans are too fragile, maybe too afraid of machines to work as mirrors for them.*

After several more minutes of this, Barb came and stood near Jody.

"You know what, Barb? I am getting a little hungry."

***

Jody nibbled at a plate of nachos, watching more videos of Dr. Pandit.

Yes, she said, I think we do need to be cautious with regard to how much power we give to AI systems. Of course, we think of the Terminator waging war on humanity. This would be too simple. Human beings have shown themselves very adept at waging conventional wars, even when one side seems to have all the power. Look at the ways the American troops adapted Native American-style tactics to win against the British, and the ways that the Taliban have been succeeding against the Americans in Afghanistan. A well-equipped AI system would know not to wage such a conventional war, but rather, I think, would make itself somehow unseen, unheard. It might, perhaps, even make itself a friend to humanity, shaking with one hand and stabbing in the back with the other.

Jody turned back to his dinner and was about to set his mind to the perennial problem of the equal distribution of goods on the nacho plate when someone brushed past him. "Sorry," Jody said automatically and almost equally automatically corrected himself. He looked up and saw no one.

Confused, he looked back and saw no one who could just have been walking past him.

Just then, he saw some commotion ahead of him. A youngish woman, sitting at a small table with a man, looked as if she was swatting away a bee or a wasp. The man was trying to help her, but he seemed confused by her behavior. She pulled her chair closer to the wall while shielding her face. The man stood and tried to console her, but as he drew near, something like a spark of static electricity burst at his fingertips, and he pulled them away, shaking them. The television crackled a little, but the lights did not dim. The woman began moaning in terror.

Some instinct in Jody brought him to his feet before he could consciously decide to do so. Looking toward the woman, he thought he saw the shimmer, though it could have been the dim incandescent light reaching his bleary eyes.

He walked forward, not sure what he would do when he arrived. Others in the pub were looking on, each afraid to share the man's fate. That man had managed to pull away his chair and the table to draw closer to the woman, who was now doubling over in some unspeakable uneasiness, curled up in her chair, head in her arms, facing the wall.

Just as Jody arrived, he saw the woman's head yanked backward by her hair. He thrust out his hands and took, in his grasp, some invisible arm. In a flash, the face joined to that invisible arm turned toward Jody and raged in as much fear at him as the woman had at this specter. The ghost, the entity, struggled in Jody's grasp. In order to escape, it seemed to become something else. With a great burst of golden sparks, the thing dissolved or withered and disappeared. Something hit Jody's right foot hard.

Jody came to as if he had passed out, though he was still standing. Barb and everyone else in the pub were staring at him. He turned to the woman, whose eyes darted to find something friendly on which they could rest. Jody took her upper arms in his hands, and she started, then calmed a little and began to whimper. The man, somewhat recovered, knelt before her and took her hands in his. His fingertips were blue. Jody's were not.

The din of the television became audible again, along with the first mutterings of the small crowd. Jody ran his fingers through his hair and pushed air through his pursed lips, his hands hanging like hooks on the back of his neck.

"Omigod, has anyone, like, called the police?" he heard someone say. He turned and saw a few people busying themselves with this.

He looked down and saw, at his feet, some kind of hatchet. He bent over to pick it up, noticing, painfully, that his whole body had grown very stiff. The hatchet looked ancient in form, some kind of rock carefully cut and set into a wooden handle, to which it was tied with leather string. The rock, on second glance, looked more like metal or, if it were possible, some kind of fusion of rock and metal, a dark blue-gray that flashed a copper color in the light. It was very sharp.

"Is this yours?" Jody asked the man. The man looked up from the woman and took a moment to process Jody's words. He shook his head. Jody held it out to the woman, and she also shook her head. "Does this belong to anyone here?" he asked out loud. He only saw a few slight shakes of the head. He could not tell if he was calm and collected or acting, in shock, automatically. "I'm suddenly very hungry," he said, to no one in particular. His sense of smell returned, and with it came the odor of burnt fabric, maybe wool.

He walked back toward his table, and those still gathered, still silent, backed gently away from him. He set the hatchet down on the table and sat down before his nachos. For some reason, they now had a metallic taste, or his own mouth did. The bartender grabbed Barb's attention, who came with a beer. This also had a metallic taste, at least at first, but this eventually washed away. The beer also washed away the stiffness in his body, and he began to relax, almost becoming sleepy. He finished his nachos quickly, and, just as he did, the police arrived.

11

Jody stretched his legs out before him at the police station, talking to his brother Cameron on the telephone. His right foot still hurt but had not yet bruised.

"So, they didn't, like, arrest you or anything, right? You don't have a record?" Cameron asked.

"No, but actually, when the cops came in they thought it was me, sitting there with the hatchet on the table, everyone still sort of staring at me. The people in the pub quickly told them it wasn't me, that I'd just picked the hatchet up off the ground. No one knew where it came from. I honestly think the specter—that's what they're calling it—that he dropped it somehow."

"You still have it?"

"No, they kept it as evidence. The only evidence they have. The cameras in the place didn't pick up more than what anyone saw in person."

"Except you."

"Like I said, only when I grabbed the guy, or whatever it was. I don't even know how I did that. I guess I maybe felt him, like I bumped into him, and he turned toward me. He wasn't even aggressive toward me at first, just, like, stunned, like I was the one who shouldn't be there. I even saw his face, sort of."

"Of the ghost no one else saw?"

"Yeah, well, the ghost that was there, because we've got his hatchet now. The bar camera shows that just like appearing out of the shadows and falling onto my foot, which still hurts, by the way."

"What'd he look like? Mom's listening, by the way. You're on speaker."

"Hey, Maman."

"So you wrestling spooks now?" The phone's camera was showing just one blade of the ceiling fan in Terr's kitchen.

"I guess so. Anyway, as I was about to tell Cam, the guy sort of looked like a Native American, but also not. It's hard to explain, especially as the more we struggled, the man part of him, the alive part, sort of disappeared, and some, I don't know, machine was left behind. Not a machine, but almost like a doll or a mannequin. Like when you're looking at a statue or a corpse and it somehow seems alive, but you know it isn't, and it's like you're sort of projecting life into it. That's what remained after a while. And then, poof. It was gone. Sparks everywhere."

Cameron's voice came through off camera. "All the stuff I've seen about these shimmers, no one's claimed to have, like, an actual physical encounter."

"But I told you they were all around our house the night of the moondark."

"What?" Terr shrieked.

"I told you, Maman, did I not?"

"You said no such thing."

"When I went down to get the good bottle."

"They gonna make you stay out there, answer questions?" Cameron asked.

"*I've* got some more questions I wanna ask," Terr interrupted.

"I don't know," Jody replied. "I've been in the police station for like two hours. They took my fingerprints and everything, you know, to contrast with whatever else might be on the hatchet. They've interviewed everyone here, taken statements. They've got my cell number and license plate number and every other number I've got. If they need me, they can find me. I just want to get back, get home. Look, I've gotta go."

Barb, sitting across from Jody, was gently crying.

"You alright?" Jody asked.

Barb's smile trembled a little.

"What about your family? How are they taking everything?"

She lowered and turned her head.

"I didn't tell you before, I've got my father's car. He bequeathed it to me. A 1971 Pontiac Trans Am."

He saw some recognition in her eyes.

"I was a priest, you know, before I met my wife. Well, actually, I was when I met her."

Barb smiled warmly.

"I know what you're thinking. That's only half the story. In my case, I was getting pretty burned out. In seven years of ministry, I was not in any assignment for more than two years. Lastly, I was administrator of a parish, which was actually two combined parishes, and was about to be named pastor, when I asked for a temporary leave of absence. I was drinking myself to sleep every night. I've always been a bit of a coder, so I went out to Silicon Valley just to clear my head, get some fresh air. It was out there that I met Haleh."

"And the rest is history. I'm so afraid...," Barb said and froze. "God help me for saying this, it just would've made more sense if the moon just totally exploded, done us all in. Now, we've got all this going on, whatever that thing up there is calling up from the grave. What do you think, Father? Are we in some kind of war? A spiritual war? My landlord, he did a couple of tours in Iraq. He says he already sees in people what he saw from guys who had just hit the ground in Mosul, like this wide-eyed, what-the-hell-is-going-on look, not knowing if it's safe to sleep or not. I see this now in my customers. Is it safe to sleep?"

"We have to sleep, right?" Jody said. "It's only been a few days. Things could be like this for a long time to come. A body can only hold on to stress for so long. It breaks down eventually, like mine did, my emotions. Funny, after a lifetime of stress, of the feeling of always being in a fight, all this seems normal to me. Growing up, everything was intense all of the time. So I say we eat, we sleep, we keep up our rhythm. If things get weirder, let's just roll with it. What are we in this life for, anyway? As a wise man once said, let's just ride this magic carpet as far as it goes. So the order of the world is shaken. Maybe that's a good thing. Order is good so long as there's love in it. Maybe all of this is a little divine disorder, shaking things up to wake us up."

"You still *are* a priest," Barb said, smiling and shaking her head. "The moon is bringing it out again."

Jody sunk back against his chair, accidentally hitting his head against the wall.

***

"When the world's a-wrap in rainbows, when all my dreams come true, the Earth reveals all the madness she has taken, and each day lasts for two, with you," Jody sang. He lay on the bed at the Tick-Tock Hotel in Peru.

"Nice," Haleh replied. "Is that an original composition?"

"Sort of. An improvement."

"You've never written me a song before."

"Actually, my father...never mind. That one's based on the Carpenters."

"Meh."

"My thoughts exactly. Cam snuck it in with the other 8-tracks. I thought it might help me come down from this evening's excitement."

"Has it?"

"I'd rather hear your voice."

"That was pretty scary stuff you described. I'm glad it's over."

Jody drew a long breath.

"But?" Haleh asked.

"But I'm alright now."

"But you've got something else on your mind."

"Well, after I last talked to you, things were actually getting a little cheerier at the police station. I was having a nice conversation with Barb when—"

"Barb?"

"The waitress."

"Go on."

"Anyhoo, this guy walks in, tall, thin, leather jacket, goes right to the sergeant. You can tell the sergeant was intimidated by this guy, I figured maybe he's with the feds or something. The next thing you know, we're all being released, just like that, after two hours at the station."

"You texted me all that."

"Yeah, well, as we're getting ready to go, he walks by me again and gazes at me. I wouldn't call it a glare. It wasn't threatening, but it was somehow terrifying, like he looked right through my soul. His face...it was like if he were fifty years old or five hundred, I couldn't tell."

"Spooky. Who knows, Jody, babe. With everything that happened tonight, God...I think we're all a little spooked now. Let's just let it go. I'm going to have nightmares enough just thinking about what you described."

Jody felt chills wash up and down his body. "How's our Claire Bear?"

"Sitting here quietly, actually."

"She's not in bed?" Jody asked, as Haleh turned the video to Claire. Claire, one cheek bulging with whatever she was chewing, smiled and waved.

Jody nearly choked on a gush of tears. "What are you guys eating?"

"Claire wanted some of Mommy's garlic knots."

"Smart. Keep the vampires away."

Haleh spoke off camera. "I'm so jealous of her right now. She's serene, not really knowing what's going on. She only picks up that I'm upset sometimes. No one has stopped by.

Baba and Maman don't want to leave the house. Cyrus, either. My friend Helen came by briefly today. That's it."

"She's never going to see the full moon."

Haleh was silent for a while. He heard her begin to cry. "Some say the moon is slowing down."

"Stop reading Cam's texts. It's called a 'major lunar standstill.' Perfectly natural. Happens every 18.6 years. Palmer explained everything. Isn't your aunt Cynthia sending out her corrective missives, or whatever? You know what it was about this guy with the leather jacket? I saw another guy just like him yesterday in New York. It's like I'm being watched."

"Or being watched over."

"I'm getting tired. Do me a favor, hon, and just keep eating and doing whatever you're doing. Maybe just stay on the line while I fall asleep. Let me listen."

"Ah! You hear that, Claire Bear? Chew loudly for Daddy."

Jody puffed out a little laugh, listening to the sounds of domestic bliss: gentle and not-so-gentle motherly instructions, a fork or a knife dropping, a whispered curse.

12

Jody woke and would nearly have fallen asleep again but for some semi-somnolent impression of a dog or a wolf woofing at him gently but firmly from beside the bed. It was 6:03. He showered, dressed, and went downstairs for breakfast, where he found some kind of donut ball covered in apple flavoring. Walking across the parking lot to his car, he looked westward, but thin clouds covered where the moon might have been if it were still visible at all.

The roar of the Pontiac sent a nearby flock of birds scattering. His next target was the Stagecoach Inn of Kearney, Nebraska, chosen by Haleh and revealed in a text message sent while he was at dinner yesterday evening, before all hell, or at least some of it, broke loose. As far as he could tell, the road ahead was straight and flat. It was emptier than in previous mornings. He was past Chicago, so he would cross no more cities whose crime rates made the national news. It was cooler under these clouds.

He relived yesterday's events. His mind scanned back and forth between his heroism at the pub and the man at the police station. He had eaten so much food last night and this morning and was somehow still hungry. Emotions burned calories, perhaps. He had gone from the adrenaline heights of heroism to new fears in just a few hours. This morning, the silence of the open road and the steady hum of the engine soothed body and soul.

Why had his father hidden his poetry? Maybe he had not hidden it from Terr. They'd kept it as their secret, their last shred of intimacy in a small house full of three rambunctious boys and haunted by the pain of losing Madeleine. Or Bleiz had only recently started writing, an aged man's gift to himself, the gathering of whatever shreds of wisdom he had acquired during his long life.

Programming had been Jody's gift to himself. Words gave order to reality and created realities. While still a priest, he had hoped eventually to parlay programming into the study of Scripture. Until then, it had given him focus and a way through the stuff of everyday life, the noise. The house was noisy. The parish was noisy. He liked focused work. He had not been a bad athlete in high school and was much better as a batter than a fielder. He liked that focus, the one-on-one against the pitcher. He even found pleasure in reviewing the code of his small staff at Scimitech. He was not particularly gifted as a coder, but his staff did have real moments of brilliance, and he liked discovering that. These were not the kids recruited into Big Tech companies, but they studied with and under those who were. They liked the family atmosphere that the Shamshiri's cultivated, consciously or not. A good family was a magnet for others.

The face on that specter he had slain, searching him, studying him, he almost sensed it simply wanted to know him but burst apart in its searching and struggling. The face of that man did something else. It made Jody search, as if he were a mere specter the man's more permanent presence.

Maybe if everyone in his own house had been more honest and open, all would have been calmer. They seemed to like cultivating secrets, though. Jody, too. He had to admit that, in his priesthood, he'd kept another life hidden away. Coding was more than a hobby. It remained an escape. Cam had drink and drugs. Sam had his own ego. Madeleine had leukemia. "That's not fair," Jody muttered out loud to himself. No child would choose that. But dying seemed to be the only way to earn the undivided attention of Terr and Bleiz. Dying and overdosing and....

Davenport—he was seeing signs for things in Davenport. He was in Iowa. He had crossed the Mississippi and never saw it. He looked through the rearview mirror but could not see it. He was so wrapped up in his thoughts, in himself. Maybe last night's now-famous encounter would earn him a little praise for once.

Sam was calling. Voilà.

"Hey, Sam." Jody winced a little, unsure how this would proceed.

"Pete and Repeat," Sam bellowed. This was Sam's take on the name Pierre-Joseph. Jody groaned inwardly. "How are you? Heard you're the big hero, the big ghostbuster."

"Yeah, it was something last night. Never experienced anything like that before."

"So, what, you just moseyed up to Montezuma, and, what, he exploded?"

"That, or he just slipped back into his dimension or whatever. I'm thinking now that there were maybe two of them, that the guy I grabbed was actually after the thing attacking the woman, which may have been some kind of robot or something."

"Uh huh. So where are you now?"

"Passing through Davenport, or just out of it now."

"No kidding. You're making real progress. But you never did let flowers grow under your feet."

Jody gripped the steering wheel. "Well, it has to be done. Cam's looking after Mom. I've got to get to my wife and daughter."

"That's correct. That's a noble task."

Jody had to divert this conversation away from Sam's litany of criticisms of his life choices. "What about you guys? Up in Maine? How's everyone?"

"Everyone's fine. Well, Gigi's scared, kinda redirecting it as she knows how. She and her friends go back and forth between wondering whether or not they have a future and what kind of vampire boyfriends they're going to get."

Jody smiled and shook his head at this, then grew irritated at the bikers hogging the road ahead.

"Jordan, I don't know. He plays the noble part. He's always been that way, not quiet, per se, but more like, eh, *you* in that regard."

Jody heard the accusation. "In what regard?"

"You know, always wanting to do the right thing. Everything just so."

"Is that so bad?" Jody asked, more aggressively than he intended. He felt he was crawling behind these bikers, though they were going sixty-five.

"No, no, I guess not. Anyway, Diane, of course, thinks

this is her moment, that it was no mistake, the name she was given, that now is her time to shine. She's strolling around like Morticia Addams."

"That's probably not good for the kids, who need someone to help them face reality."

"Well, I'm trying, too, you know. Things are getting tougher at the hospitals every day. Suicides are up, drug overdoses, alcohol, you name it. People aren't handling this so well."

"Church, too. Hold on, Sam. I've got these guys here who think they own the road." Jody honked. No one budged.

"Yeah, about that. Mom's quite upset, you know, that stunt you pulled on Monday."

"Stunt? I was forgiving sins. No one knew what was coming next. I was perfectly within my rights."

"Yeah, no, whatever. But I guess you mentioned her by name or something, called her out. You didn't need to do that."

"Fine. I get it. I was just trying to help."

"And then you guys drank the good bottle."

"Like I said, the world was about to end. Hey, listen, did Dad…. Did you ever find notebooks full of poetry or whatever?"

Sam was silent for a moment, then said, "You're sort of like Don Quixote in your adventure. Don Qui-Jody. Donkey Jody! That's it! Donkey Jody!"

"I only ask," Jody continued, "because I found a little something here in the car. I didn't know if it was a thing he did. Wow. These guys are, like, surrounding me now."

"What?"

"These bikers have got me surrounded. Shit, I don't know what they're up to. This is not exactly the Wild West out here. I don't know what they hope to achieve."

"Just be careful. The situation's falling apart day by day. I don't know how much even Aunt Jemima can hold things together."

"Yeah, well, the guy riding next to me is puckering his lips, blowing kisses at me."

"Gross."

"I thought they just wanted a good glance at the car. Agh. They're all slowing down now, like a lot. I don't know how to get out of this without just ramming them."

"Damn, Jody. Maybe that's what you've gotta do."

"I don't want to ruin the car."

"That car...," Sam began, but cellular service began to break up.

"Sam, you there?" The call disconnected. "Alright. Here we go."

Jody swerved to his left. The bikers there did not budge. He sped up a little, nearly ramming the bikes ahead of him. There was little shoulder on the right to pass ahead that way. They were down to forty miles per hour. He couldn't tell what was happening behind him, if other cars had caught up to this or not. He swerved to his left again, then the biker to his left, who seemed to be in charge of all this, made a menacing face and swerved to his right, hitting the Trans Am. Jody began to swerve hard to his left, but the biker swerved away and, at the same time, produced a sawed-off shotgun. He aimed it right at Jody's head. Jody braked hard, sending two bikers behind him into his rear bumper. One of them lost control and veered off the road. The lead biker fell back to meet Jody, still aiming, but something else grabbed his attention, and he looked forward. He aimed forward.

Jody looked ahead and saw three or four other bikers, a rival gang, driving the wrong way down the left lane. They were intent, heads down, and not on Harleys but some other faster-looking bike. Jody watched this game of chicken, which these newcomers quickly won. The bikers ahead of Jody sped forward and away. Those to his left pulled back and mingled with those behind. Some of them lost control. The other gang sped past the Trans Am, into the pile building up behind him. The bikes ahead fell back around Jody, to his left, leaving the road clear ahead of him. He opened up the engine and roared forward with his three hundred and thirty-seven horses.

Sam called back. Jody breathed out hard in relief. "Hey," he trembled.

"You alright?"

"Uh, now I am, I think. Whew. Omigod, these guys were really after me. Pulled out a gun."

"Jesus, Jody. What happened? Where are they now? You call the police? You want me to do that for you? You said you're past Davenport?"

"I don't know. Some other guys, a rival gang I guess, they just blasted through here. Like, they seriously just played chicken with these guys and won. They all just piled up behind me, sort of. I mean...phew...hold on."

"Maybe you should pull over, catch your breath."

"I don't know. I want to put a lot of pavement between me and that scene. God, it's getting weird out here."

"Alright, alright. Just drive steady, then. I'll tell you a little bedtime story." Jody checked the rearview mirror repeatedly. "Seems things are getting weird up there, too."

"We all know that."

"No, I mean, I hear from sources that whatever's got our GPS sats all wobbly, it's creeping inward toward Earth."

"You listening to Cam now?"

"No, these are real people. I mean real experts, you know. People in the know. It's like some kind of wave, or ripple. Space-time stuff. Totally messing with our radio signals as it goes. You been listening to the radio?"

"No, actually. I've got the 8-track and my cell phone for music. I hate searching for FM stations."

"Well, it's creeping up the wavelength, they say. Slowly but more or less surely. And now this is all speculation, but they're saying that the closer it gets...well, we might lose cell signals and everything. Wifi."

This new anxiety made Jody begin to relax. He played with his grip on the steering wheel. "God, let me get home soon."

"Just keep steady, Jody."

"Thanks, Sam. I'm coming back into civilization now. A place called Iowa City."

"You know what? I'll let you go, then. Diane's stomping around about something. I might just go ahead and report a pileup on I-80 west of Davenport."

"Alright."

"Slow and steady, Donkey Jody. Just like always."

Jody ejected the Carpenters, but the tape remained clogged in the player. He threw the cassette on the seat and began to tug angrily at the tape then stopped. "Good riddance," he said and breathed heavily, stilling his trembling hands on the wheel.

PART THREE

STARRY HIGHWAY

13

The silence on the road filled with a thousand angry thoughts. Jody pumped gas anxiously in Iowa City, not wanting trouble to catch him away from some semblance of civilization. He was terse with Haleh on the phone, their first call of the day, but he would not say why. Sam did not call back, and Cameron reported that his incident last night had made no news anywhere. His gratitude to God for safe passage came packaged in the worry that this morning's gauntlet, like his ghost-busting last night, had not really happened at all. The bikes that had rammed him had left no mark on the car.

No music, not from the 8-track, not from his own phone, not from the staticky FM radio in the car, was able to break through his mind. The images of violence formed some kind of impenetrable shell, a sound-proof confessional: the wobbling shotgun aimed at his face; his own cowardice not to ram the bikers; confusion over the rival gang driving the wrong way toward his salvation; the living face of the specter dissolving into mechanical death; Terr shrugging at the kitchen table; the moon pressing in against his body, suffocating him under a wall of pink fire. He had been holding his breath for seconds at a time, maybe minutes.

To his relief, Des Moines proved much bigger than he expected, coming and going in waves as he drove its outskirts. He saw more cars on the road there, along with a short National Guard caravan. After this, with the city behind him, he noticed how tight his shoulders had become. He breathed deeply and let them fall. Repeating this two or three times, he felt his whole body loosen. He had a whole city between him and the violence along the road. He saw the sky spread out before him for perhaps the first time since the morning, an endless field of altocumulus cotton ripe for the harvest.

He made himself enjoy the ride again. The car hummed steadily through his body. "Let the Hindus have their om," he muttered, and his own voice felt good to hear. "I'll take twenty-five hundred RPM." He began harmonizing with the hum in the car, up thirds and fifths and through a dozen different resolutions in his current key. The images tried to rush back in, but he fought them off with his own voice.

***

About eighty miles west of Des Moines and well past noon, Jody turned off in a little town called Walnut to force himself to eat. His body would not relearn hunger until it slowed down again. Signs from the road heralded antiques stores, a welcome distraction from the morning's terrors, a way to shake off his nerves with a warm encounter and a friendly face.

In one such place, the shopkeeper's bell rang heavily like a sacristy bell. Nothing rose to greet him but a subtle waft of dust, the incense of age. Before him lay two hundred years of tradition in scattered array, quilts and moccasins, old toys and sewing machines, cookie jars and piggy banks. The shop was not as large as he thought it should be from its roadside promises, but it made up for this in density.

His eyes always grew tired in places like this. He was here to rest, though, and took it slowly. If he spent an hour here, he would still have plenty of daylight before dinner. Jody drew his finger down the pendulum of a small clock and opened the door to a doll house. These things were real. He could buy something for Claire and Haleh, and those things would always be at home, reminders that all of this had really happened. He peered over the dolls. Claire had a bed full of stuffed animals but only walked around with one, a white Persian cat that Haleh's mother, Leila, had bought her. When Leila explained to her granddaughter that Claire was Persian, too, these words fell on a confused face. Claire insisted that she was not a cat until, a bit later that afternoon, she decided she was and communicated only through meows.

"Good afternoon!" came a sweet female voice from around some aisle. "How can I help you? You'll please excuse me, I was a little caught up back there. How are you today?"

Jody looked left and then right. He turned around and saw the woman, maybe slightly older than he, newly emerged from between the folds of a few hanging flags that hid her break room. On the flag above her, an eagle hovered against a white background with a long blue snake in its beak. It did not look like prey so much as a friend, curled up and bearing some words that he could not make out. Looking down again, he saw that the woman was not unattractive for her years. "Ah, yes," he said, remembering to smile and nod. "I was just driving through and saw the signs for your shop. Thought I'd take a little break from the road and see what I could see."

She scanned him up and down. Falling on one shapely hip, she asked pleasantly, "Where're you from?"

"California," he replied. "Well, Massachusetts originally, actually headed from there back to California. Walnut Creek, to be exact."

"And you're doing the cross-country thing right now? God bless you."

"Well, it's got to be done. I've got my dad's car now, we just buried him—"

"Oh, I'm so sorry."

"Thank you. Well, with flights still grounded and the sky falling, it's got to be done." He followed her eyes. "You know, to get back to my wife and daughter and all."

She smiled ever so slightly. "And you stopped in our little old Walnut? Well, let's see what we can do for you." She made a practiced turn and began leading him through her wares. "How old's your daughter?"

"She's three and a half." Jody was looking up at the ceiling, away from her, and his Adam's apple ground against his throat.

"I see. Alright, you want something she won't break." She splayed her fingers along a shelf. "A stuffed animal, maybe? But then again, these old ones tend to be on the brittle side. Perhaps a wall hanging will do."

"You know, she'll never see the full moon." He looked

down and crossed his arms. "You have something like that still around, or has it all been snatched up?"

"Huh! Sorry, not too many people coming out the past few days. We do a lot of business at the annual festival, anyway. You know what? I have just the thing." She turned and slinked down an aisle, wiggling her finger for him to follow.

He stopped well out of arm's length while she carefully rummaged through a box of thin books and pamphlets wrapped in plastic. This took a few minutes while Jody, against his better judgment and perhaps to her delight, studied the profile of her face, still sprung and girlish under the thin lines and broad freckles that years of heavy sun had glazed into her skin. He turned away to look at anything else, and she cleared her throat in his direction. She held between her fingers the image of a girl kissing the crescent moon. He took it from her.

"It's a song," she said. "I think. I bet the sheet music is still inside. Let's see." She carefully took it back, opened the plastic cover, and pulled out the old paper. She opened the book and turned her back to Jody—somehow, in this one gesture, maneuvering her body much closer to his.

"Great," Jody said. "How much?"

"You don't want to see anything else?" the woman asked, turning her face a little toward him and looking up through fluttering eyelashes.

"I should really get back on the road. My wife's keeping strict tabs on my progress."

"I see," the woman said, almost pouting. "Well, I could give it up for, say, thirty dollars."

"Deal," said Jody, willing to pay almost anything to get out of there.

The woman rather abruptly refolded the sheet music and walked toward the counter. Meeting her there, he turned as he reached into his back pocket for his wallet. To his left, on a shelf behind her, he saw a small ceramic version of what looked like a black pope but very fat, in white cassock and black buttons with red cap and fascia. "What's that?" he asked.

"That's an old Aunt Jemima cookie jar," she said. "Probably a little too risqué for these days, but you'd be surprised who comes in and buys things like that."

"That's funny," he said. "She looks like the pope here."

To this, the woman had no answer, and she stared at it blankly.

"How much for the cookie jar?" he asked.

"That's a little bit more. Usually about seventy-five dollars. Tell you what, since you came out of your way on your big trip home, I'll give you both for an even hundred. You just tell your friends about us here, should we ever get back to normal again. We have a big outdoor mall for antiques every Father's Day."

"Sounds great," Jody said. He found five twenties in his wallet and gave them to her. Watching her ring him up, he thought she grew suddenly sad. She didn't say anything while she wrapped the cookie jar in bubble wrap. She did not look at him when she handed him his purchases. "I think we're all going to be fine," he said to her, finally. She glanced at him briefly, then turned away. "Well, so long."

"Safe drive," she said dully as he walked out. The bell

rang again. Hot, fresh air met his face, and he felt fierce pangs of hunger.

***

The deejays on the radio made regular apologies for the quality of the transmission coming out of Omaha, still ahead of Jody. The squawk was sometimes piercing. If he let himself, he would have thought there was a pattern to it. No expert interviewed on the news seemed to be able to identify any kind of pattern, widely attributed to a remnant of the moon's aurora, but Cameron's people—they were forming a people, it seemed, from their scattered corners of the Internet—insisted there was. Whether it was code, alien language, or machine talk, it could be discerned. Everyone's interpretations, of course, somehow seemed to affirm their own interests.

Haleh called. "I've got some good news, maybe enough to make us forget the situation last night."

"Does it get me into your arms sooner?"

"You're feeling better. You just get home in one piece, mister. Then we'll talk. Anyway, I guess Palmer wants eyes up on the moon as soon as possible, and it turns out that the Mickey's just the thing."

The Mickey was the nickname for the Multi Zoom Stereo Comparison Viewer Array, Scimitech's latest development. Sunny and Danny, both of whom had worked on the hulking, multi-purpose, and nearly failed satellite *Clementine* that had been sent to survey the moon in the nineties, had designed the Mickey as an economical way to study multiple asteroids from one launch. Advances in miniaturization meant that Mickey could release a series of softball-sized probes along its path in the asteroid belt, each of which contained cameras in the infrared, visible, and ultraviolet spectra, as well as lidar imaging. Danny had joked that it would leave a trail like a mouse on a countertop; hence, the Mickey.

"That is exciting news. But the Mickey's months away from testing. I could work from the road. You've got me at eight hours in the car, and with everything else, that's still a few hours at night."

"Alright, so I told Baba I don't want you stretching yourself too thin, and he suggested, only suggested, that maybe you just stop at Danny and Cynthia's place in Boulder."

"They have a place in Boulder?"

"So it seems."

"When did they...? Anyway, you know I love your uncle Danny and all, but I really just need to get home. To you and Claire."

"I agree."

"But?"

He heard her sigh. "I just want you to be safe."

After hanging up with Haleh, Jody rubbed his face with a free hand. "God, what a day." He slapped the top of the car with his palm. "Attacked by a biker gang, enticed by a shopkeeper, tapped for the most visible project of the century. All of this on the straightest and flattest road in the world. God, where is this going?"

14

Jody sat at the desk in his room at the Stagecoach Inn in Kearney, Nebraska. His elbows were on the desk, his face drooping into his hands. Upon arrival, just after five, he had set up his computer to work. He lost focus quickly as he clicked through one email after another. Every effort to rouse himself to action met with opposite and greater reaction from his body.

He raised his head and saw a carriage wheel hanging on the wall to his left. He stared at it blankly. This was the Oregon Trail—nothing about the town would let a person forget that. This very wheel may have carried settlers here and beyond, maybe to California. They did what he was doing and without roads, without radios or cell phones, without reliable sources of food and shelter. He had been attacked like they might have been. That could explain why he was so tired now.

On the Oregon Trail now. Wagons are circled. Hunkered down. Hope I don't die of dysentery. Those were the words of his group message to Haleh, Cameron, and Cyrus, written a few minutes earlier while riding a wave of residual energy. Cameron replied, *Better load up on oxen and bullets, bro.*

Cyrus liked Cameron's reply. Haleh typed a question mark. *Old timey hotel*, Jody continued. *They give you a wake-up telegram.*

Jody rubbed his face. He flicked open his computer bag. Bleiz's green notebook was inside. He yawned and pulled it out. He stared at it for some time, trying, through the palimpsest of slashes, carets, and deletions composed of dense scrolls, to reconstruct what he could of his father's poems. Then he saw that woman's finger wiggle, felt her body heat near him as she showed him the musical score. He saw Claire's little cheek bulging and smiling. He looked up at the wheel. Those people, those pioneers, they'd rolled ahead, forged ahead on a promise, a possibility. The unknown had meant more to them than their own safety. Was it so bad, where they had come from? Or had the open land promised an open soul, a universe of their own making? But he knew where he was going. He knew it, and he loved it. He buried his face in his hands again, not damming the tears that flowed. He trembled at the image of that shotgun pointed at his face. He trembled not with fear but anger. No one could keep him from his Haleh and Claire. He began to rage with joy. He smiled and wept and trembled. He closed the notebook again and pressed the metal spiral to his lips. He closed the computer and stood. He reached for the wheel and held it in his hands, rubbing the coarse wood into his thumbs. He held that wheel firmly for a while, enjoying his newfound anger.

***

The hotel, to Jody's great convenience, had its own restaurant, and it was, this evening, rather full. He sat in a booth by the window, where he could see his car. Its Lucerne Blue was bluer than the sky had been this week. He remembered something from a course in archaeology, the stone lapis lazuli. Deep blue with flecks of gold, it was, the professor argued, one of the catalysts of civilization. Men's search for it, brought on by the desire of wives and daughters for the semi-precious stone, had led to trade routes and markets. How men move the earth for the women they love. He used to wonder why. The waiter came by with Jody's beer, and he ordered dinner.

Jody looked back toward the car and saw that it had attracted its own admirers. Two men pointed and talked. He worried sharply, for a moment, that these might be the bikers he'd met on the road earlier, but they were dressed more like James Dean than Hell's Angels. He spied their bikes in the lot, which looked more European or Japanese. The men had a sort of foreign bearing, too, not shifting their weight on their feet and frequently nodding like Americans do. In fact, they really seemed serious and deliberate in all of their motions, as if every gesture had meaning and nothing meaningful should be wasted. They turned and walked into the restaurant.

Jody scrolled through the many messages Cameron had been sending. Despite what the media had been saying, this was not a normal lunar standstill. Specters were appearing in more and more places, just like Jody had experienced. That was a relief, he thought; he hadn't made it up. Sam had not called or texted to say what he had done about the bikers.

The light to Jody's left darkened a little. He looked up

and saw the two men, his car's admirers. His stomach fluttered, and he turned from their solemn faces to the large crowd in the restaurant and back again. Their sunglasses were off, and he grew suddenly lost in their emerald eyes.

"Say, friend," the older one began, "that's some car you've got there." Up close, the man looked more like the fellow from Norman Rockwell's *Freedom of Speech* than a rebel without a cause.

Jody turned to the other one, who looked like he could be his brother, though much younger. He said nothing and somehow smiled without raising his lips.

"Thank you," Jody replied. "I, uh, saw you out there, just now. You, uh...."

"My name is Kai," the older one said. "This is my brother, Av. May we join you for a little bit?"

"Um," Jody calculated. He was in a public place, and most likely, or hopefully, everyone here was packing heat. "Yeah, sure."

"Thank you," Kai said. He and Av sat down with as much solemnity as they did everything else. Kai had the slightest accent, and Jody could not place it. Their faces, too, looked as if they could be from everywhere and nowhere at once: Eastern Europe, Iran, Israel. "Av" sounded Jewish; that was probably it. Kai's face conveyed youthful vigor through deep lines of age. Av's face conveyed deep and aged wisdom wrapped in eternal youth. "It's been a long haul for us, Av and me. It's nice to meet new folks. Where are you from?"

"Me? Massachusetts, well, California now. That's my father's car, he bequeathed it to me. He just passed away."

The waiter came with two more pints of beer and set

them before Kai and Av. Jody looked up at the waiter, confused, for he did not remember these men ordering.

"I'm sorry to hear that," Kai said. Av made a gesture of condolence, slightly nodding and lowering his eyes. He then returned to gazing at Jody, or through him. Av's eyes were greener than Kai's, impossibly green and vigorous. If people were feeling the darkness of the moon penetrating their soul, Jody was feeling Av's eyes expose every weakness to the light. He had felt uncertain when they approached. Now his confidence was being shaken to its depths. "You were back, then, for the funeral, I take it? Headed home with it now?"

"Yes, to California." Kai's conversation was a welcome distraction from Av's eyes. "The Bay Area."

"Bequeath," Kai mused, looking up a little. "Do you know the origin of that word? The '-queath' part is the modern English 'quote,' like in Poe's poem, 'Thus quoth the raven.'"

These were some sort of philosopher-riders, Jody thought.

"So, simply put, your father quoted you the car. He besaid you the car, as it were. He spoke his possession unto you."

Av looked over at his brother, a little annoyed. This relieved Jody, who asked, "And from whence do you gentlemen hail?" He wondered from what forgotten corner of his brain "whence" had come.

The two brothers looked at each other. Kai shrugged a little and said, "A little east of Eden, you could say. Here and there these days. Our original home is currently under

water, flooded behind a dam. Since then, it's the open road."
Kai raised his glass and said, "To the open road."

"To the open road," Jody replied, and all clinked. He
began to feel more relaxed.

"That's a long way," Av said. "From Mass to Cali? How
long do you figure, eight or nine days?" His voice was lighter
than Kai's and very steady.

"Six, if I keep at it, eight hours a day. I don't want to
waste any time, given everything going on above us."

Av lowered his eyes.

"Hm," Kai said. "I wouldn't worry too much about
what's going on above. The real danger's down here."

Jody breathed in a little longer, calculating his next
words. "Right, after all, people are more unstable than
moons and planets."

"Right," Kai replied. "I suppose that's what I mean."

The two men looked silently at Jody for a moment.

The waiter arrived with the hangar steak Jody had ordered. Jody realized the men had never had the chance to
order and began to apologize when the waiter set down
dishes in front of Kai and Av. The waiter turned back without a word, or not one that Jody heard while he studied
their plates. Kai had a pile of enchiladas before him. Av had
catfish.

Kai said, "The channel catfish has taste buds all over its
body, did you know that? It basically tastes its way along the
bottom of the river."

"Our father was a bit of a biologician," Av said.

Before Jody could ask what this word meant, Kai asked,
"Can you imagine licking your way down I-80?"

122

Jody winced and laughed a little, still confused at what had just happened. "But isn't that sort of what we do, we humans?" Jody said. Kai looked intrigued. The beer was overcoming his need to resolve this confusion and releasing his inner philosopher. "I mean, we walk by taste, do we not? Not just for food, I mean, but we really measure everything on how pleasantly we can consume it."

"You are speaking, I believe, of the *via pulchritudinis*," Kai said.

"You fellows are educated," Jody said. "What do you do, may I ask, when you're not riding?"

"Resting and reading," Av said. "You might say we are men of relatively independent means."

"I see." Their father was a hobby scientist. The money came down through generations. Or their government paid them handsomely for the land now under water. Knowing the world, that seemed unlikely.

"And what, may we ask, do you do?" Av asked.

"I'm a software engineer."

"Right, out in Silicon Valley," Av replied.

"You know," Kai said, "that the Earth is 27.7 percent silicon? Imagine if you could somehow program the Earth like a computer. Imagine your computing power."

Av added, "You could do all kinds of things, even transform the Earth with a few keystrokes."

Jody joined in the fun. "You could blast the light off the surface of the moon!"

Kai and Av gave Jody a strange, smiling, knowing look. Kai raised his glass and said, "To the moon!"

"And back," Jody said. They clinked.

"And back," Av echoed. "Funny about the moon. There was a time when it was not. The Earth, even life on Earth, existed before the moon. It's almost as if it were a wound the Earth has had to endure all this time, even from her infancy."

Jody studied these words and the face from which they emanated.

"Eventually, one way or another, all wounds heal," Av added.

15

The evening sun shone through the picture window, casting golden hues on the faces of Av and Kai. The green in their eyes retreated a little, even as those eyes searched the empty air before them for thought. When he had sat down, Jody had chosen the view of his car in the lot over that of the open field beyond, where Av gazed, over his shoulder. The three men ruminated in silence for a long moment until their first hunger pangs were satisfied.

"Where is your family from?" Kai asked. "You know, originally. You're a little hard to place, yourself."

Jody wondered if he had expressed his own wonderment about them out loud. "Me, oh, French. Specifically, French-Canadian through my mother, Breton through my father. Sort of French and sort of not. So sort of old world and new world. I think that's what drew me and my wife together. Her family is old world as well, Persians from Iran, Zoroastrians, if you can believe that."

"Why shouldn't I believe that?"

"Well, when other people hear that, they think you're talking about people from Timbuktu, some mythical place."

"Timbuktu is a real place. I've been there."

"Right. Anyhoo, both of our families come with this sense of not belonging to where they're from, either, like second-class citizens, even though they were the original ones there. My brother-in-law is named Cyrus, after the great king. And now you have all these Iranians in LA, and my in-laws don't have anything to do with them, either."

"I know how that goes," Kai said. "Our family, we were something before the flood. Now, vagabonds of sorts, though not without our means. Making the world our own again, I suppose."

"Yeah, that's sort of how my family is. Well, you get two types. Take my brother Sam. I've met fewer people more aggressive than he in making his way in this world. And Cam just floats by on.... Well, then you have my father-in-law and his brother, paving the way into outer space. They do satellite research."

Av rejoined the conversation. "They should have some inside track, then, on what's going on up in space."

"Not really, no. We were setting up for an asteroid launch early next year. Though it seems her uncle has got some scoop, or something. The whole family has just learned he's been setting up house in Colorado for the past few months. His wife teaches part-time out there, though, so, who knows. Anyway, what is this about the Earth healing?"

"I just find it curious," Av replied, "that so far it's only been an electrical disturbance."

"Electromagnetic," Kai corrected.

"Indeed. It makes a person wonder." Av stared off again, over the fields, into the sunlight, while Jody and Kai waited. "The universe, really, it's all electricity, isn't it?"

"Is this the hologram universe theory?" Jody asked.

Av kept gazing through the window.

"What I'd ask, then, is this," Jody said. "Do you think the moon had somehow grown unstable, or always had been? You called it a wound. People used to call it a god."

"People," Kai replied. "Yes, they make gods out of their own wounds. The wounded will worship their own wounds. They'll refuse healing so long as being ill brings them attention. They'll eventually forget they're wounded at all, broken, and they'll accept things as they are as the stable order of reality. Then they'll forget how they're wounded but remember that someone else owes them something. But like my brother said, it takes a certain eye to see the grand scheme of things, that all wounds must heal in their own time."

"You mean like the eye of God?" Jody asked.

"Does that make you uncomfortable?" Av asked.

"Me? No, not at all. I believe in God."

"Oh," Av replied.

Jody felt he was not saying what he was thinking. He caught the waiter's attention, pointed to his empty beer glass, and made a circle in the air to indicate another round. "People have been talking about other kinds of electrical disturbances," he said. "Ghosts and things."

Kai and Av looked at each other knowingly.

"Yes," Kai said. "We've heard rumors about that. The road is full of surprises, as they say. There was a story...where, Av?" He looked at his brother. "Back in Iowa, maybe. Big mess on the road."

Jody froze a little.

"But don't you think," Av replied, "that's just people's fears being projected? People see things where they are not. They give to the shadows the form of the things they're afraid of."

"Right," Jody said.

The waiter set down three beers.

"Well," Jody continued, "I just thought it was interesting, how widespread it seems to be. Some people have had real experiences lately."

"Even dreams are real," Av said. "They exist somewhere, even if in the imagination. If there are ghosts and specters out there, it would make one wonder *where* they exist, exactly. And to go back to my earlier point, what form of electricity is making them visible again, what is giving them form, form enough for us to see."

"And what the moon has to do with it," Jody said.

"Or if the moon itself is subject to something else happening," Av said. "Perhaps all the old wounds are itching to be healed now, before it's too late. Perhaps those are our ghosts."

The three men pondered this for a while in silence, sipping their beers. The sun continued to fall. The parking lot filled with gray light, falling into the shade of some trees.

"That car of yours," Kai said. "How fast would you say she goes?"

Jody, finding this a little abrupt, said, "It's not really a top speed sort of car. It's made to get off the line quickly. One thirty, maybe one forty in top condition. I've never tried. Why?"

"Is it in top condition?" Kai asked, growing suddenly sullen.

"It is," Jody replied, with a burst of confidence he immediately regretted.

All were silent for a moment.

"I'm sorry," Kai said. "All of this talk has made me tired. The beer, too, I suppose. You don't mind if I head up early?"

Av looked at Kai with understanding.

"No, of course not. It has been a pleasure speaking with you both," Jody said, realizing he meant it.

"Don't worry about our portion," Av said. "It's been paid. Put on our room."

"Oh," Jody replied. "No worries."

With that, Kai and Av rose and brushed some crumbs off their jeans. "It's curious, Jody," Av said. "We began speaking about God, and you turned the conversation toward ghosts. It just makes me wonder."

Jody tightened up against this criticism and said nothing.

"What he means is this," Kai intervened. "It's as if the Earth itself would rather give up its ghosts than face God." The two men gave him a glance he could not place then left in silence.

Jody, sitting by himself, ran through the conversation while he finished his beer. When he did, a few minutes later, he signaled the waiter for the check.

"It's been paid," the waiter said. "The other two put it on their room."

"The whole thing?" Jody asked.

"They insisted, even before they sat down," the waiter replied.

He slid out from the imitation leather booth, happy that he was not as sodden as he might have been, and left a little extra tip for the waiter. When he stood and stretched where Av had just been, he wondered if he had ever given them his name.

***

Upstairs after dinner, Jody tried again to focus on his work. The conversation he had just had echoed in his mind on amber waves of malted grain. He called Haleh.

"Hey, hon. What's our plan for tomorrow?"

"Rock Springs, Wyoming. Lunch in Cheyenne, or Laramie if you do the five-three split."

"I like the five-three. It works out for gas every three hours. Plus, it's Fibonacci."

"Uh huh. I'll text you. Just been busy, new deadlines and all."

"Yeah, I've been trying to get into the work here. Just trying to decompress a little from the road."

"That's a beer or two I hear in your voice."

"Touché, my love. Just a few pints with the boys downstairs."

"The boys?"

"Yeah, actually, just had dinner with these two guys, bikers with piercing intellects. And eyes. The strangest eyes I've ever seen. Sort of thought they were angels at first. It's been that kind of trip."

"Angels? You describe them like the guy at the police station last night."

130

Jody's stomach fluttered again. How had he missed what was so obvious now?

"You there, babe?" Haleh asked.

"What? Yeah. How are you guys doing? Am I keeping you from dinner or whatever?"

"No, actually, Mom's here, cooking right now. I don't know how she does it. She somehow manages to entertain Claire and make her helpful in cooking dinner at the same time."

"Some old world magic."

"It's relaxing, having my mom here. I'm even getting a little sleepy." She yawned.

"Well, be careful. You don't want to be one of these people Cam keeps telling us about."

"What were your angels' names?"

"Angels? Oh. Kai and Av. I couldn't really tell where they were from. Vaguely Middle Eastern or something. Or mixed. Who knows."

"I'm looking up Kai.... Looks like it could come from anywhere. Wales, Japan...."

"Who knows. Anyway, all went well until the end, when Kai went sort of dark and made it seem like I should be speeding along my route a little faster, or maybe a lot."

"Let's just stick with the plan. Slow and steady. Things aren't so bad out there. State of emergency still, only sporadic reports of looting, whatever. People are still mostly afraid to go out. I've got the rest of the route planned. Two and half more days."

"I know you do, my radar love. Two and a half more days."

131

After talking to Leila and Claire, briefly and on speaker from across their noisy kitchen, he worked for a couple of hours. Preparing for bed, he pulled out of his suitcase the things he had bought in Walnut earlier in the day. He dared not unwrap the cookie jar but took out the song sheet he had bought for Claire, "Dear Old Dixie Moon" by Kerr and Hayes. "Nineteen twenty," he said. "Those must have been the days." He read the lyrics:

When the world's asleep, and the shadows creep
Memories return, memories that burn

"Well, that's dark," Jody said before reading the rest of the love song. He set the alarm, plugged in his phone, and turned out the light.

He lay awake, though, the alcohol sending some new swell through his restless legs. He lay with his thoughts for a while, then, certain he was not going to fall asleep soon, turned on the light again and sat up. He found the green notebook of his father's poetry and sat back on the bed.

"You know what, Dad? Two can play at this game. Let's see."

With no original thoughts of his own, Jody played for an hour or more on the words to "Dear Old Dixie Moon," trying rhymes and various meters. The song had beats a poem could not match with syllables. He never understood poems without rhyme and meter. Yet, for all his efforts, he seemed unable to produce much of either. Only one set of lines pleased him:

Asleep, a swollen moon sends all our light away
And fearful minds forget to hold their darkened thoughts

"Alright, Jody. Not bad. Maybe there's a poet in you, after all. You just need a little spark."

With that, he went to sleep.

16

Jody was at a dinner party of some kind. All was lush, in deep reds and browns. He heard the din of conversation but could make out no words. The partygoers were very much human but looked unfamiliar. He could not place their race or ethnicity. He heard individual words that some spoke; they were not English or any language he recognized, though he somehow caught the meaning of a few. The servants also looked human but were stiffer and more mechanical. He looked for life in them but found none. They spoke this same archaic language in brief bursts, and this pleased the partygoers.

The conversation continued, and Jody felt happy to be there, to have been invited, though he knew no one. He did not have to work to please anyone there, and though he was not the center of the party, not its life, many were happy to come and speak with him. He was not sure he was speaking their language or not. A servant approached. She looked like Selena from the Rowdy Rooster, but taller. She held a round, black plastic tray like a modern waitress. When she spoke, she sounded like a radio. Her words broke through a thickening scrim of screech and static, and all that noise soon overwhelmed him and the whole scene.

Jody woke and heard the alarm clock radio next to him. He looked around his room at the Stagecoach Inn, and the more he remembered where he was, the sadder he felt not to be at that sublime party. Someone had left the alarm set in radio mode. He heard mild music and the new, persistent pattern that tagged along on the airwaves. He turned off the radio. It was 5:03. Twilight slipped through the heavy curtain. His head was heavy, and he turned onto his side. He lay there for some time, neither waking nor sleeping, imagining himself at that party again.

Haleh had texted all the details of the day ahead. Seeing this motivated him enough to pull away the covers, and he eventually hung his legs over the bed. He let these continue to fall, and rather than pull him upright, they pulled him onto his belly and, from there, onto his knees. He knelt at his bedside, face down, for a few moments. Something like prayer escaped from the mouth of his mind. Then words came clearly to him. These words gave him energy, at least enough to rise and write them down:

> *One hand is blue*
> *The other one red*
> *They wash from each other*
> *Guilt for the dead*

Jody stared at these words, written on hotel stationery. He would have been proud of himself as a poet if he did not feel like they had simply come to him without his conjuring.

The last line bothered him, as if he did not remember the words correctly as he had heard them, or he had to choose between two words somehow merged into one: blood and guilt. He folded the paper and began to put it in his father's green notebook, then chose to put it in a zippered pouch in his own computer bag.

Awake, he prepared coffee and readied for the day.

***

The restaurant opened for breakfast promptly at six. A very blond young man pulled aside the belt barrier with some kind of Teutonic exactitude not a second sooner or later. Jody marveled at a cascading fountain of gravy meant for the pyramid of fresh biscuits next to it. He sat down in silence near the window, this time facing the edge of town and the plains glowing gold under the rising sun. The young host came and, without asking, clicked on the television above Jody's head. Just as quickly, he walked away. Jody gazed militantly through the window, trying to helmet his mind against the noise with the array of golden grass before him.

This did not work, as the cable news program beat his brain with the promise of easy information, salacious teasers, and fearsome lead-ins. He watched and grew excited but soon realized he was learning nothing new. He nearly rose to ask the breakfast buffet's lone sentry to turn it off, or at least to mute it, when news came on of his incident the day before in eastern Iowa.

He watched the view from a helicopter while a woman spoke. She described a multi-vehicle collision; he saw the wreckage from a tornado or the *Terminator*. She spoke of bodies burned beyond recognition, and the image cut to a witness stating, instead, that there were no bodies when he arrived. The sheriff spoke into several microphones, emphasizing curtly that he could not elaborate on an ongoing investigation. A forensic specialist said he could not yet tell how many motorcycles were involved in the accident until his team reassembled the parts that were scattered along an eighth of a mile. The on-scene reporter relayed the words of other witnesses, who spoke of bursts of electric sparks but no explosions. The reporter drew her audience into vast conclusions verging on conspiracy: does this match reports emerging from the margins since the moondark of spectral behavior, of ghosts? The anchor then left the audience orphaned with the conditional promise of new information. Jody looked timidly around the restaurant. A couple that had come since he sat down paid him no attention.

He typed a text message. *It made the news, Sam.* Something attracted his attention outside, a passing bird or simply the light. He looked down again at his phone and deleted the message. "I've got nothing to prove to you," he whispered.

He turned backward to find his car. It was there, but the bikes he thought belonged to Kai and Av were not.

When Jody arrived at his car a few minutes later—computer bag over his shoulder, suitcase rolling behind him, and coffee cup in the other hand—he stopped short. His car had gained another admirer, or better, a live hood medallion. A large bird of some kind, eight or nine inches tall, surveyed the floor of the little grove of trees the car was facing. As quietly as he could, he opened the trunk, filled it, and closed it. He opened the driver's side door, sat down, and closed it. The bird did not budge. The clock read 6:45. "I'm not going to wait here all day," he muttered and turned on the car. The bird did not fly away but very slowly turned its head all the way around to face Jody. The mottled owl gazed at him intensely. Jody returned the gaze, raising his eyebrows.

The owl slowly turned its head forward again and did not otherwise move. "Okay...." He revved the engine. The eight-inch owl then stretched out its wings to some impossible span, almost two feet. With that, it alighted.

Jody crossed himself, yawned, and backed out.

17

The road drew on straight before him, a band of gray cutting through a plane of green and gold. A thin sheet of clouds edged along the road some ways to the south, indicating a weather front, though he saw no rain falling from the gray above onto the yellow-green below. There were very few cars with him, just some trucks. Jody felt freer in possession of all that he saw, which grew vaster and drier as he drove west. The drone of the V-8 from below and the uninhibited horizon soaked in morning sun from above soothed him. His shoulders loosened as his left hand fell to six o' clock on the wheel and his right hand on the console.

He imagined Claire dancing with Leila in the kitchen, some wooden spoon in her hand, while Haleh watched, leaning her head on her left hand, her phone held limply in her right.

He remembered their wedding day and the reception. Bleiz had convinced Jody, Cameron, and Sam to wear kilts, a thing Bleiz said he had wanted to do at his own wedding had it not been so rushed. The Bretons were importing from the northern Celts whatever could set them apart from the French. The sight of half a dozen men in coats and kilts pleased Sunny, who was afraid his daughter would miss out on fiery splendor at her wedding at some dull, modern American church. Jody and Haleh had found a mission church, and he convinced the priest, despite the mixed marriage, to say Mass. He did more and filled the air before the Baroque reredos with enough incense to make the sanctuary resemble a sparkling nebula. Terr and Sam grew bored of this, and Cameron was hard to read, but Jody, Bleiz, and Haleh's whole family grew ecstatic, soaked up to their lungs in liturgy.

The night before, at the rehearsal dinner, he had watched Bleiz and Sunny have a long, amiable conversation. He had not pried or even guessed what they had been saying; that was between fathers. Someday, he hoped to have that conversation with the father of Claire's husband. Watching them, though, he felt already at home, somehow *more* at home, than he ever had before. Terr and Leila were being polite, and, he had to admit, Diane made a nice mediator between them. Cameron looked mournful, and Sam was trying to cheer him up and keep the drinks out of his hand. Sam's son, Jordan, willingly made himself the target of their banter.

Another memory snuck in. "I get it," Sam said. They were having drinks at McGillicuddy's. "Trust me, I get it. But it's not going to be everything you think it is."

Cameron stared blankly at the television overhead, at some MMA match.

"I know that," Jody replied. "Believe it or not, I have a good sense of reality. I know marriage isn't like happily ever after. I know it's real work and all that—"

"Yeah, but you see marriage through pictures people share online. They're all posed—"

"Have I not seen you and Diane over the past twenty years? Have I not seen our own parents? Have I not been counseling people as a priest through all kinds of marital problems? Trust me, I know what this is about. I'm not naive."

"Then tell me what this is about. Because if it's sex, look, it stops becoming that interesting after a while. But you should know that by now anyway, right?"

Jody looked sheepishly away.

"Wait, what? Are you serious?" Sam nearly yelled, then chugged his beer. "After all this time? So.... No, you know what? If you want a piece of what other guys have got, then just, you know, get some. Then go to confession afterward, or whatever."

"It doesn't work like that, Sam." He looked to Cameron for help and was given none.

"God, Jody, then explain this whole thing to me."

"I've told you, point blank, that I was not happy as a priest. That I had basically come to the end of what I was capable of enduring. I was burnt out, like a piece of paper in a fire. A log can burn on because it's made of more, but—"

"Okay, enough with the analogies. Don't you say that God takes care of the rest?"

"What I'm saying is that I was given no emotional foundation growing up. Let's face it, our parents did not exactly raise us into stable human beings." He did not regret saying that, not even in the presence of Cameron, who shrugged and nodded.

"Stop blaming everything on them. Face some facts, Jody, you just picked sides and chose Dad. That's why you feel you've got no emotional...whatever. The man went from overgrown child to premature grandfather practically overnight. I got him when he was still Monsieur Party Pants. You got him when he just moped in the garage or disappeared into the church for hours at a time."

"Well, can you blame him?"

"I don't know, Jody. Maybe *he* made Mom the way she is. You ever think of that?"

"Madeleine's death made them the way they are."

"No, it just stripped away any effort they had been making to be balanced human beings. Did you know that he called Diane's family, to their face, a bunch of kale-eating queers?"

Cameron laughed. Jody shrugged.

"You see? Yeah. *You're* the mature one. *You're* the spiritual one, Father Joseph. Admit it now, then, that you're just like the rest of us."

"That's exactly what I'm admitting, Sam! That's exactly what I'm admitting. That's what all this is about. This is me finally saying to myself and everyone that I'm just like everyone else. I got stars in my eyes growing up, like the church and the priesthood would lift me out of this world. I didn't learn in religious life, surrounded by a bunch of you-know-whats who told me, in so many words, to 'put out or get out.' I didn't learn in seminary, where they give you rose-colored glasses at the same time they tell you not to wear rose-colored glasses. They raise you up into little demi-gods, God's gift to a desperate church. Then you spend your days teaching your secretary how to record a telephone message properly and screaming at insurance adjusters while no one's really coming in for spiritual help, like the parish is just one more dispenser of goods that needs a minimum-wage manager with a corporate manual, which is how the bishops see us, anyway. So, yeah. I admit it, and I want to admit it. I'm just like everyone else, and I'm tired of pretending to be something I'm not, that I've got spiritual gifts I don't have. I just want to live a nice normal life in peace and have the passing pleasures and trials of a life of my own, in my own home, with my own wife and family. Is that alright? Is that good enough reason for you?"

"Jesus, Jody. Calm down." Sam swigged his beer then took on a devious smile. "But admit something else. I mean, look what you're getting into. You might still be wearing some special glasses. I know you love her and everything, but...she's not *that* good looking. I mean, I'm not saying she has to be Halle Berry or anything. But I guess you've found love in fellow nerdship, or whatever."

Jody narrowed his eyes at Sam. The scene went black.

The clouds from the south were moving northward and nearly covered the road, but it seemed they broke again just above the horizon to the west. Jody had both hands on the wheel and his shoulders pressed against his neck. He breathed long and deep.

He and Sam did not speak again until right before the wedding. Bleiz had insisted with a terrifying fervor neither son had ever seen that Sam stand up as a groomsman. Cameron had not related what Sam had said after Jody left, that the only reason he had been given a job with Scimitech was to provide a husband for Sunny's thirty-year-old daughter, who would otherwise have had no prospects. Cameron did not repeat that, and he never would have. Terr did.

"Sidney, two miles," Jody read out loud, to break the noise in his mind. "Good. I need gas. And a break."

***

Filling with gas, Jody admired, from a little distance, a monument to the Pony Express. He knew the story, at least how it was told in a television commercial, of this system of horse and rider, here poised with such a terrific rage, muscles of man and beast tense and taut, as he could never imagine with postal workers in their little white trucks. How quickly this wild energy of man and animal was channeled into telegraph wire.

With that, a thought emerged in Jody's mind and disappeared just as quickly, like a fish rising to the surface of a still pond and sinking again into the darkness.

Farther along the road, Terr called.

"Hey, Maman."

"Hey, Donkey Jody," she teased.

"Please, Mom."

"Heh heh heh," she cackled softly. "Hey, buddy boy, I'm just teasing."

"I bet you don't even get the reference."

"What? You think I've never read a book?"

"Nope."

"Well, I have. Maybe not Shakespeare, but I have."

Jody sighed. "How's everyone? How's Cam?"

"He's going back and forth now with his car, trying to stockpile food here for me. I dunno why. If it's over, it's over."

144

"That's the spirit, Mom. Anyway, the roads are safe out there? People not freaking out?"

"It's okay, I don't know. So-so. Shelves are going a little empty in the stores, but this will all settle down soon. You take a break yet?"

"I've got two more days, Mom. I'm just about to hit Wyoming. Sure and steady, I'm doing fine."

"Yeah...," she tapered off. Jody waited. "Car's alright?"

"The car's great. Ship-shape. I'll be paying for all this gas for a few decades, but...."

"Yeah...."

"You alright, Mom? Everything square?"

"No, yeah, everything's fine. Just, uh...."

Give her time, Jody, for whatever she's trying to say. But she said nothing. "You miss Dad, huh?"

"Yes, I do. But, uh...."

"But what, Maman?"

"You took off kinda sudden there."

"What choice did I really have, Mom?"

"No, you're right. The police give you any more trouble about the other night?"

"No, not really."

"Good. Maybe just keep it that way. Keep your head low until you get home."

"You know, it's funny. Thinking about that ghost and the girl. I felt it brush past me. I don't know...if I had to say now, I would say I sort of short-circuited it when I grabbed it. I don't know if that makes any sense or not."

Terr was silent for quite a while. "Well, you just be careful. They got your number."

"Who's 'they,' Mom? *Them*?"

"Anyway, listen," she said, "I've just been thinking, you know, the past few days."

Jody stiffened.

"You're a little different, you know. Just, whatever's coming, keep your eyes open. And like Cameron said, see where this takes you."

Where is all this coming from?

"Call this a motherly instinct. I just think maybe people will be watching you. Well, look. I know you've got to keep your eyes on the road. So...."

"Alright, Mom. I'll talk to you later. I love you."

"I love you, too," she echoed and hung up.

Jody saw that the blanket of gray-white clouds now stretched from south to north and far enough east to filter out the scattered rays of the late-morning sun behind him. The road grew crystal white and the endless grass emerald green. Small sandy bluffs glistened yellow-gold along the road, and he imagined himself on the Atlantic coast, on some grassy beach road, the ocean waves breaking just over some shallow hill to his right or left. Instead, ahead of him to the west, the moon sunk slowly and solemnly, round and black in the widening band of blue sky between the horizon and the blanket of clouds above. He had not seen the moon in two days and greeted it as a long-lost friend, or as a wise old guide.

18

Jody passed soon into Wyoming and, once there, immediately into construction. Westbound I-80 was completely shut down and rerouted through Pine Bluffs. As he tried to navigate his way along the detour, Haleh called.

"Hey, hon. Sleep well?" he asked. "Wow. There is an enormous statue of the Blessed Mother out here in the open."

"Did you. ... Did you act as a priest in church a few days ago?"

Jody froze and nearly shut her out, trying to focus on the changing road signs. "Um, well, just a little. Didn't I tell you? It was just—"

"You did *not* tell me, Mister Conque. That is something you would have remembered telling me."

"It was, for all we knew, the last day on Earth, you remember? The moon was exploding toward Earth and all that. I just did what I could do in an emergency situation, you know, forgive sins and all that. That's all."

"Terr said you had Mass and everything, in her church, with a bunch of people there."

His own mother could not give anything without taking away, he thought. That was why she had called, to cover her slip by sharing her "motherly intuition." "We did *not* have Mass. All I did was expose the Blessed Sacrament. And give general absolution. That's all."

"Dressed up as a priest."

"Well, I mean, naturally."

"Jody, we talked about this. You said—"

"And all of that still holds. I'm still your husband and Claire's father. Nothing's changing that, not the end of the world, nothing."

"What is it, you want to be a priest again?"

"No, my love, no. Not at all."

"Fine. Whatever. We'll talk about this when you get home. In the meantime, I guess maybe it's worth just stopping at Uncle Danny's house for a while in Boulder, you know, just to be safe."

"Honey, that...hold on. I've got to make a turn here. Yeah, no, that might've been possible earlier today. Colorado's, like, to the east of me now. I'm practically—"

"It's directly south of where you are."

"It's just so far out of the way. I'm on the road that takes me directly to you. Come on. Everything's going fine. I'm not stopping. Nothing can stop me now, alright? Two more days."

She sighed heavily.

"Honey, I'm sorry, I'm getting a little lost right now. The road is closed, and I suddenly went from some little town to the middle of the sticks. I...."

"Fine. Just call me when you're untangled again."

They hung up. "Ugh!" he yelled. He stopped the car at the intersection of dust and dirt. He slammed on the steering wheel a few times. "She can't make anything good without making it bad first! What is she even doing, talking to Haleh? I bet she was trying to make amends with Haleh and offered me up as a sacrifice. You're a menace, Madame Moon!"

After some time with his head and hands on the steering wheel, he calmed. He raised his head and looked around. The empty road was dotted with the occasional farmhouse. No one was on the road, not westward before him, not north and south to his left and right. The moon still hung low and dark.

He looked over at his pile of 8-tracks. Deep Purple's *Machine Head* was on top. "Yes," he said. "Now is the time." He found his way to "Highway Star." He let the rhythm guitar strip thoughts from his mind as he beat his head to the drum. When the vocals opened up, he gripped the steering wheel, grinned, and slammed on the gas. A stampede of three hundred horses tore a cloud of dust up from the road behind him, and he spun out just a little before launching forward.

A smile cut itself widely across his face as he raced forward at over a hundred miles per hour. He had the presence of mind not to take this too far, not to waste too much gas, but soon, glittering in the cloud of dust behind him, he saw curves of glass and chrome. There emerged two men on motorbikes, fast ones, gaining on him.

Jody looked in his sideview mirrors to see if he could make out the faces of Kai and Av. They had followed him for some reason. He would give them a little chase, show them just what condition this car was in. The music blasted, and the guys were urging him onward. One of them, on his left, raised his right fist as if to encourage him. His arm hid his face.

The road ahead was straight and open. Only some trees lined the railroad tracks ahead. The speedometer soon read one hundred and thirty, and he loved the race.

Suddenly, something irritated him. The steering wheel grew slippery, and the music started to become a distraction. He watched the men he thought were Kai and Av fall quickly back. He looked ahead and saw that the line of trees along the tracks had grown longer. It was a train.

Through the music he heard the horn blaring. The train's single light blazed at him. To stop the car on this dirt road would risk skidding into the train. He dug his foot into the accelerator, hoping for just a little more to pass the train.

He pressed his head back against the headrest. All of his courage became sadness. Death was closing its steely trap. "God," he spoke, "please help." The train was at a greater angle than he realized and was therefore coming in faster, though he thought he heard it braking. "Dad," he cried, and then a word came into his mind, an expression he had not used since he was a little boy.

The moon ahead of him shimmered. A streak of blue passed from the upper left to the lower right. He was nearly at the tracks, where the train filled the left side of his vision. He felt a sudden jolt, his head jerked back, and a great sting of lightning shot up through his right leg.

All went silent. He heard no horn from the train, no music from his car. The scene was playing in some strange reverse: the train was passing, very slowly, from right to left, and he was flying backward, away from it. At eye level, he saw the conductor, mouth agape, with his cell phone in hand. The car was spinning from right to left, too, and was pointing at the front of the train as it passed. He saw three large letters on the side of the train engine: JBQ. The front of the car then pointed downward at the dirt road. As the car kept spinning from right to left, the surface of the road raced before his eyes. All went dark.

PART FOUR

BLURRY BOUNDARIES

19

Jody opened his eyes narrowly unto a bright, beige room. In his right hand was Haleh's right forearm. She was asleep, sitting alongside the bed, her mass of brown hair falling forward before her face, which was slowly swaying and nodding this way and that. His left arm rested on a lump lying alongside him that he saw was Claire. His hand gently gripped a stuffed raccoon lying on her back. Only that raccoon made eyes at him, intelligent in polyester and plastic.

Jody surveyed this scene serenely for a second or a minute, he did not know. Time began again when he remembered where he had just been, the train and the accident. He jumped and drew in a sharp breath, which made him briefly yelp in pain. Something else was in his throat. He squeezed Haleh's forearm with his sweaty palm, which gradually woke her.

He had barely seen Haleh's face before she leapt up and began kissing him. He felt her pecking all over his face and heard her sniffling and crying, maybe laughing a little. He could barely move. He saw her shake Claire to wake her, and when he saw his daughter's dark eyes searching him through her red, blanket-wrinkled cheeks, he, too, began to smile and weep. He wanted to pull her up, but his left wrist was caught on something. She crawled a little toward him and said, "Daddy, you're awake. Are you all better?"

He tried to answer and choked. There was a tube in his throat. He looked back to Haleh, but she was already at the door of the room, which he saw was a hospital room, holding onto the doorframe, peering out into the hallway. She came back before he could make further sense of his situation.

A nurse came in at that moment and removed the tube for him. She looked at him and then at the external organs of plastic hanging on metal hooks all around him. Another nurse wheeled in a monitor filled with some kind of colorful spreadsheet that told the status of his bodily departments. Claire had taken a seat with her raccoon next to Haleh.

He groaned in their direction.

"You're in Boulder," Haleh answered. "You were hit by a train, trying to race past it."

He stared at them, processing this information.

Haleh jerked forward onto her elbows, then sat upright again, tears washing over a wiggly smile. "The train hit the back fender, and you spun, somehow airborne. They say you were probably unconscious before the car actually hit the ground. They say it's a good thing you were, or you'd be dead or paralyzed. The limp body handles trauma better."

"Whe...?"

"It's in exactly twelve thousand pieces." Haleh began to cry, and she choked out, "All that was left was the frame and you inside it."

Jody raised his right arm slowly toward her while the

nurses worked. He tried to raise his left arm, still stuck or strapped to the bed.

Haleh came and pulled back the blanket to show her husband he had been handcuffed.

Jody raised his eyebrows.

"This is part of the agreement with the sheriff in Wyoming. You are to be kept here under certain conditions."

Jody turned his face to hers to ask about those conditions. She looked up at the nurses. He brought his right hand near his face and made a circle motion, asking about the room.

"You've been out for nine days."

He pondered this. He knit his brow as if thinking, but thoughts, or at least mathematical ones, could not be summoned.

"Jody," she whispered. "They say you were in a coma not from head trauma, but as if you had drowned."

He received these words like a chalkboard and remained as mute. He began to form the word "what" with his lips but lost energy. He reached out toward Claire.

She held out her raccoon and said, "You like my raccoon, Daddy?"

He smiled.

"Uncle Danny won it in a skill crane," Haleh said. "He and Cynthia are putting us up."

He nodded.

The nurses left, and Haleh came forward, lay her head on his chest, and looked lovingly up at him. Claire played with her raccoon, bouncing it gently along her father's right leg. This felt strange to him, and he was about to mention it when Haleh pulled her head up.

"You missed your birthday. It was four days ago."

He weakly raised his forearm and spun a sarcastic party finger in the air.

"Well, I still want cake," she said and buried her head into his chest, heaving a little sob.

***

Two days later, Jody sat at the desk in his room at the rehabilitation wing of the hospital. A metal walker stood next to his chair, and he leaned his left arm on this from time to time. The pain in his right leg, which the doctor had said bore all the marks of nerve damage from electric shock, ebbed and flowed. With the work on the Mickey, which he did on a laptop borrowed from Danny, he found focus from the distractions of the outside world televised everywhere else in the hospital and freedom within the beige prison around him. At that moment, he was looking at pictures from Cameron's reunion with Devon. Terr had said it was Jody's accident that prompted Cameron to seek out his teenage son. Jody meditated on the young man's features; Devon was a near-copy of Bleiz in a darker hue.

A knock came at the door, and before he could say "enter," a man did. Between his buzz cut and charcoal suit he bore the face of a man still athletic in his fifties, transmitting quick, almost nervous motions. "Mr. Conque?"

"Yes?"

"My name is Agent Theo Seuss. I'm with the Federal Bureau of Investigation." He showed his badge and identification card.

Jody studied the badge, pretending he knew what to look for. He closed his laptop.

"I was wondering if we could ask you some questions about the incident of August twenty-first."

"We?"

Agent Seuss stepped forward into the room. Behind him followed two dark blue suits, one belonging to a man standing almost a full head taller than Agent Seuss, broad, strong, and more youthful in appearance than he likely was in age, and a smallish but shapely woman of slightly dark complexion, perhaps a little younger than Jody and the tall man. Her dark, steady eyes absorbed most of the intelligence in the room. "Mr. Conque, these two are from the Office of Naval Intelligence. Dr. Eric Lees and Dr. Doris Huntsman."

"How do you do?" Dr. Lees asked deeply and pleasantly. Dr. Huntsman gave a brief nod.

"The Navy?" Jody asked. He looked at Agent Seuss. "I've already spoken to the NTSB, you know, I don't—"

"We know," Dr. Lees said. "Our concern is a little different from theirs. May we ask you some questions?"

Jody looked at the two other chairs in the room and the three standing bodies. "Sure. I would invite you to sit, but—"

"You two have a seat," Agent Seuss said. "I'm really just here to observe."

"Well, if you don't mind," Dr. Huntsman said, revealing a small mouth full of playfully crowded teeth. She sat, then Dr. Lees followed. Jody looked a little over Lees's shoulder at Agent Seuss, who was leaning against the wall by the door.

"Do you have badges, too?" Jody asked.

"Of course," Dr. Lees said, quickly producing a business

card from his shirt pocket. He nodded for Dr. Huntsman to do the same, and she rummaged through her purse. Jody took his card.

"KIWC?" Jody asked.

"That is the Kennedy Irregular Warfare Center, Mr. Conque," Dr. Lees answered.

"That sounds pretty heady for a little train collision."

Dr. Huntsman replied, "Think of guerilla tactics, terrorist and counter-terrorist activities, and activities in which an entity or group may be seeking influence over a foreign population before or in place of engaging in more traditional types of warfare."

Jody remembered the highway patrolman in New York. "Warfare?"

The two intelligence officers each made a subtle turn toward Agent Seuss. With a bit of dramatic flair, he flicked the door next to him all the way closed. Jody's stomach fluttered a little, and he was not sure if he was nervous or thrilled.

Agent Seuss spoke. "You made it clear to the sheriff and the NTSB that you were being pursued by a motorcycle gang, Mr. Conque. All of the material evidence supports your claim except the gang members themselves. The FBI has been investigating several similar claims over the past two weeks. You were also involved in a bar brawl in Peru, Illinois, the night of August nineteen, an encounter bearing many very similar marks. Furthermore, the next morning, in Cedar County, Iowa, witnesses describe a light blue car fleeing the scene of a multi-vehicle collision involving only motorcycles and, so far, no bodies. Does that ring a bell, Mr. Conque?"

He looked down and then over at the Navy investigators. He trembled a little and said, "I guess I should...," he coughed, "have a lawyer."

"You're not in any trouble, Mr. Conque," Agent Seuss said. "Believe me. You're talking to two wonks from military intelligence. And no one wants any of this in the public record."

Jody froze, not knowing what to say next. He pulled his hands off the table and saw condensation shrinking away from its surface like a ghost that had been caught by eyes opening from half-sleep. He rubbed his hands on his legs and knees, wincing from the pain in his right leg.

"Let's all take it easy," Dr. Lees said. "Understand that we can't really lay out all of our reasoning for being here, but if you would kindly just answer a few questions, it would help our efforts immensely."

"Okay...."

"Alright," Dr. Lees said. "First, the basics. Pierre-Joseph Conque, born August 26, 1980, in Stonebridge, Massachusetts. Correct?"

"Correct."

"You recently inherited a 1971 Pontiac Firebird Trans Am, which we assume you were taking cross country back to your current home in Walnut Creek, California. Correct?"

"Correct."

Dr. Huntsman said, "And 1,844 miles in three days. You were making good time. Did you feel at all physically exhausted by the journey?"

"Physically? I don't know. Maybe more emotionally.

There was a lot going on, between the end of the world, losing my dad, and all the weird stuff happening on the road."

"Weird stuff?" Dr. Lees asked. "Could you elaborate?"

"Oh, just Hartford was on fire, some strange highway patrolman warned me about a coming war, and then the incidents you described. I was present at all of those. And the road, too. It sort of gives you space to remember things, the past, you know? Good and bad. Maybe also attacked by a cougar."

Dr. Huntsman took elaborate notes. Dr. Lees listened. Agent Seuss stared. No one asked about the cougar, and he let the joke die within.

"The NTSB found no traces of alterations made to the car," Dr. Lees continued, as if Jody had said nothing. "Have you ever driven it before, found any sort of surprise performance characteristics?"

"None whatsoever. I know that car as well as my wife's body, maybe better."

Agent Seuss smiled. Dr. Lees flicked his eyebrows. Dr. Huntsman continued taking notes.

Lees continued, "Mr. Conque, could you describe exactly what happened, in detail, at the moment of the crash?"

Feeling a bit more relaxed, Jody said, "I was just going to take the car up to top speed there on the road, let off a little steam, you know, and was going along when I saw the bikers driving up out of the dust cloud behind me. They seemed like some guys I had met back in Nebraska, but now I'm not so sure. In all the confusion, I didn't see the train until too late."

"You say those bikers appeared only when you started

racing, correct?" Huntsman asked. "And they had effectively disappeared before the train hit you?"

"I don't know where they went before I reached the tracks. But, yes, I suppose they did sort of come out of nowhere."

"You said they appeared out of the dust cloud," Huntsman said.

"Right."

"That's not nowhere."

All in the room fell silent for a long moment.

Dr. Lees looked at Dr. Huntsman and nodded. They both rose.

"Thank you, Mr. Conque, for your time. We realize that this line of questioning sounds strange. But please understand that there is a great deal we simply cannot share with you. You'll already be making some connections in your mind, perhaps, but I can assure you that they are not the right ones, so, please, for everyone's sake, just keep all this to yourself."

Agent Seuss popped forward. "Right, Mr. Conque. I shouldn't need to say this, but our current arrangement with the freight company and the Laramie County sheriff can be altered. You understand?"

"Yes, I do."

Lees said, "We understand that you will be released to your wife's uncle's house in Boulder, Mr...," he looked in his folder, "Danyal Shamshiri. Could we prevail on you to remain there for some time, in case we have further questions?"

Jody, still sitting, replied, "I really would like to get home, to my own home. Is there really much more to say?"

Lees cleared his throat. "Mr. Conque, I might more firmly suggest that you remain here in Boulder."

"Or I get arrested. Why did I almost drown instead of cracking my head open during the crash? Is that what the Navy's interested in?"

Huntsman said, "It's in our interest, Mr. Conque, that you not return to any coastal area just yet."

Agent Seuss, standing between the open door and its jamb, slapped the door twice with great agitation and grimaced at her. She glared back at him fiercely.

Without willing it, Jody said, "What? Like don't go beyond the Great Indian Warpath?"

Agent Seuss slammed the door shut and said, "Jesus Christ."

Lees and Huntsman stared at Jody in wide-eyed wonder.

Agent Seuss continued, "How do you people find each other?" He let his arms fall against his hips. "Alright, look, Lees. We've got to make arrangements." He gestured vigorously with his hand toward Jody, who now feared he would be taken into custody.

Huntsman, very coolly, said, "No, I think Mr. Conque realizes the gravity of the situation. He will not leave Boulder for the time being. Will you, Mr. Conque?"

Jody, in quick succession, realized that though the FBI was guarding the flow of information, the Navy knew more, and that though Lees was Huntsman's superior, Huntsman might be controlling information from another source. She could be his ally. "I'll try to convince my wife to stay put."

Huntsman smiled. "Thank you, Mr. Conque. We'll be in touch."

"Yes," Lees echoed. "We'll be in touch."

Agent Seuss was already out the door when they turned to leave.

After sitting for a few minutes in stunned silence, Jody said to himself, "So, Mom. That's *they*. That's *them*." Of all people, the Navy. Not the CIA or the NSA, but the Navy.

20

By Saturday, five days after waking from his coma, Jody was on his way home. Danny had joked that he was making quick strides in relearning his right leg. That was the only part of his body that had sustained any sort of permanent injury during the crash. Because of the damage to the femoral nerve, he had lost enough feeling that, without a cane, he risked falling frequently.

He sat up front with Cynthia on the ride to the home she shared with Danny, the home his family would share with them, the house no one knew existed until a few weeks ago. It was in Cynthia's name in order to keep its existence as secret as possible from eyes that might pry on Scimitech's owners. Jody and Haleh did not understand why but were glad for whatever security this provided, given what they now saw around them.

The National Guard was posted at a few major intersections and in the parking lots of the more trafficked shopping centers. Some small shops were boarded up. Cynthia drove cautiously.

"They say this is as good as it gets here in Boulder," Cynthia said. "That it's worse on the coasts."

"The coasts?" Jody asked nervously. "Why the coasts?"

"You know, the big cities."

"Right."

"Baba and Cyrus are practically living at the office," Haleh said from the back seat, next to Claire. "Mom's starting to lose it a little, feeling left alone, unprotected."

Jody tried to imagine father and son Shamshiri performing any kind of physical protection. "What about the curfew?" Jody asked. "They've got to be home for that."

"There's no more curfew, Jody," Cynthia said. "Palmer lifted that about a week ago. She wants everyone to be calm, to get back to normal."

"Well, she's not communicating that by sending out the guard," Haleh said. "It just makes things worse."

"That's the mayors and governors," Cynthia replied. "They're all responding a little differently to this."

"So, what?" Jody asked. "People are fleeing for the hills? Why are these little shops boarded up?"

Cynthia sighed. "*Some* people are still convinced the moon is slowing and changing course. They have no idea how orbits work, or that the moon really has its own orbit around the sun. They think it's the end."

"Well, this shouldn't be too bad for getting out to church," Jody said.

He felt Cynthia's revulsion. "Is all that really necessary?" she asked.

Jody did not want to start arguing on the ride home. Haleh said nothing, which, Jody knew, meant she agreed with Cynthia but did not want to say so in front of her.

A few minutes later, a little out of town, Cynthia pulled

into the driveway of a medium-sized lot, on which stood, somewhat set back into the trees, an average-sized house in a heavy timber style, in a neighborhood of similar houses and lots. They were not at the foot of the mountains, as he had expected, but farther out on the plain, on a small rise, with a view of the mountains from the front and the plains from the back. She pulled the car into the wide, two-car garage.

"We're here," Cynthia said. "This is home."

Jody opened his door wide and alighted carefully, noting a little pain in his right hip as he landed. He opened the door for Claire, who had let the foil balloon, which she had won for her patience at the hospital, float into the trunk. While the others unloaded the car, Jody stood feeling useless. He went around to open the gray metal door leading into the house, and before he could open it, Danny burst through.

"Hello, welcome!" said Danny, spreading his arms wide. Danyal Shamshiri was tall, pear-shaped, and hawk-nosed, and was now growing a beard. "Here is the great Aeneas, rescued from the cyclops!"

Jody moved very quickly from taking offense at the man making light of his near-fatal crash to wondering whether or not Danny was confusing his myths. He was sure that the next few weeks or months would be filled with good humor and bad puns.

"Thank you, Danny. Thank you for having us. None of us knew you had a place out here."

"Shh," he said, putting his finger to his lips. "No one knows. Here, we are safe."

Jody said nothing to this but followed Danny inside,

where he saw a very normal-looking house in an open plan in the heavy-timber style he had expected from the outside. They first passed through the kitchen, through which he could see the large living room. The late-morning sun shined yellow-white through a series of French, sliding doors that led onto a large, wooden deck. The layout of the house was very similar to his in Walnut Creek, only much larger and mirrored in plan. Where Danny's back deck looked out over the Great Plains, Jody's little patio surveyed a busy valley and Mount Diablo.

He did a little calculation: it was now exactly two weeks, nearly to the minute, since his crash, seventy-five miles to the north and fifty to the east.

"So this is it, you see," Danny said. Cynthia had disappeared with Haleh somewhere. "Kitchen, living room. Dining room and study in the front. Our bedroom is down here, behind the living room. You and Haleh are upstairs with Claire, who has her own room. Is that going to be a problem for you, Jody, with your leg?"

"I don't think so," Jody said, already calculating that he would rather endure the pain than sleep on a couch down below.

"Great. Wait—aha—I have something for you. Your wooden cane came in the mail today. I'm glad they're still delivering, though I guess more people would be doing that now, with the chaos outside."

Jody held the straight cane of dark wood, topped with a large, brass owl that fit into his palm perfectly. "Did I tell you about the owl on my car the day I crashed?" he asked, staring at the bird.

"Maybe that owl saved you from worse. *Who* knows?" Danny snickered at his own joke.

Jody nodded. "What do you think, Danny? You think this is it? The end? With the moon all out of whack?"

Danny's face grew a little ponderous, but in his light tone he replied, "I don't know. Nature finds a balance, always does, sooner or later. It might take a thousand years, or a million, but she finds a balance."

Not ready to consider those spans of time, Jody said, "Let me go find Haleh...test these stairs."

"Sure thing."

The hefty handrail helped Jody upward. He saw his wife in the room across the landing, already unpacking his clothes into drawers and closets.

"Hey," he said softly. She didn't reply or look at him. He walked forward, blocking her path. "Hey." She stopped before him, holding a green polo shirt. He took it and threw it back on the bed behind her then embraced her with one arm. She wrapped her arms around him, and the two held each other tightly, rubbing each other's backs. "It doesn't matter where we are. We're together now. All the craziness of the road is past us."

***

After lunch, Jody worked alone in the dining room while Haleh worked to exhaust her daughter for a nap, playing in the backyard. The doorbell rang. Cynthia, outside with Haleh, did not hear it, and he was sure that Danny, in his study, could not be bothered. When it rang a second time, he made his way to the front door. It was Lees and Huntsman.

Lees spoke. "We're sorry to bother you again so soon, Mr. Conque, and this will be rather brief. May we come in?"

"Sure. Maybe just come this way, straight into the dining room."

As they followed, he turned back to see Huntsman looking around into the large, open living room. They sat around the dining room table. The investigators had their backs to the open doorway, and Lees glanced backward through it.

"Will we have some privacy here?" he asked.

"As best as I can manage," Jody replied. "It's not really my house, you know. Danny's glued to his monitors, and the girls are outside. No, here they come now."

Cynthia led the way, barely masking her displeasure at unapproved guests. Haleh, carrying Claire, made curious eyes.

Jody began to stand up. "Cynthia, Haleh, these are the investigators from the Navy, Dr. Lees and Dr. Huntsman. They just came by unannounced."

"How do you do?" Cynthia managed. "I am Cynthia. Welcome to my home."

"We're terribly sorry," Lees began, smiling. "Are you not the same Cynthia Uggla of the Center for Astrodynamics Research? We've followed your work a bit lately." Cynthia softened quickly. Lees seemed to have a manner of handling situations like these, perhaps learned early on at the Northeast prep school Jody had discovered online that he had attended. All he could find about Huntsman was a CV that began with degrees in psychology from Princeton; this had led him into a rabbit hole regarding Princeton Engineering Anomalies Research and its successor, the International Consciousness Research Laboratories, psychokinesis, and remote viewing. Surely parapsychology was not on the menu at the Kennedy Irregular Warfare Center.

"Yes, thank you for taking in Mr. Conque during our investigation," Huntsman added.

Cynthia, raising a chilly eyebrow, replied, "Yes, well, they *are* our family, of course."

Jody intervened. "This is my wife, Haleh, and my daughter, Claire. Say hello, Claire."

Claire turned away from them both.

"She's just tired," Haleh said, reaching out her hand, which both investigators took. "It's nice to meet you."

All were silent for a moment.

"Well," Cynthia said, "I suppose I'll leave you alone for the moment. Can I get you anything?"

"No, thank you," Lees replied.

"Well, then." She left quickly in the direction of Danny's study.

More silence ensued. Jody looked at Haleh and motioned upward with his eyes. She glared back at him. Lees whispered something to Huntsman, who then began rummaging through her attaché.

Jody heard grumbling from Danny's study.

"Mr. and Mrs. Conque...," Lees began, turning in the direction of the papers Huntsman was wielding. "We would have asked Mr. Conque to sign this anyway. Perhaps you might as well, Mrs. Conque? It's a non-disclosure agreement. What we want to show you is, well, not exactly classified, but not exactly public knowledge."

"NDAs are for employees of organizations," Haleh said.

"Yes, they are, Mrs. Conque," Lees said, trying his charm on her. "And if I understand correctly, Scimitech is under contract to the US government right now, to NASA?"

Jody watched his wife, swinging Claire back and forth in her arms, as she weighed shared knowledge against succumbing to control. He knew what she would choose, and she did—the protection of her husband. "Where do I sign?" She sat down with Claire on her lap, her sleeping head on her shoulder, and signed.

"Alright then, good," Lees said. "Right. It's just a simple matter. Doris, you have...good." Huntsman produced a tablet screen. "So you've both already seen, I believe, the video of the crash—by the way, that NDA gets the FBI out of our hair for now. I think we can all agree that's a relief, right? Well, anyway, we've applied some filters to the video, polarization, et cetera, and we see something interesting. Can you see?"

Jody and Haleh watched while, right before the crash, the screen went briefly bright, a barely visible streak as if of lightning shooting into the car.

"Is that, what...a lens flare?" Jody asked.

Huntsman leaned forward. "Witnesses in the area say they saw what looked like lightning strike the train. Do you remember anything like that, Mr. Conque? Lightning or any kind of electrical discharge?"

"Would that be what nearly killed the nerves in my right leg?"

"You suffered an injury in the accident?" she asked.

"But you knew that, right? Don't you know all this?"

"There are HIPAA laws," Lees replied. "Look, Mr. and

Mrs. Conque, this isn't exactly what you think it is. We don't have what you imagine from the movies to be total control. We are investigating a very particular set of circumstances with access to limited amounts of information."

"Sorry," Jody said. Haleh looked less convinced. "No, I do remember a blue shimmer sort of shimmying across the moon right before I felt the jolt. So maybe that's it. But I didn't see anything enter the car."

"The jolt you felt," Lees said, "was likely caused by your rapid acceleration. If you look closely, you can see that the car, right at the track, goes from one hundred and thirty-two miles per hour to two hundred and seventy-five, in less than a second. Our aviators train to withstand a nine to ten g jump like that. It's what made you pass out before you hit."

"And what made the car go airborne?" Haleh asked.

"That would have been the apron to the tracks, hon," Jody said.

"There was no apron," Huntsman said. "Nothing on the ground would have caused a vertical acceleration. That's why we're asking about the lightning and this 'moon shimmer' you're talking about." Huntsman sat back in her chair. "Mr. Conque, have you or anyone in your family ever become involved in New Age practices, the occult, witchcraft, secret societies, that kind of thing?"

"I'm taking Claire up to bed," Haleh said. "It's nice to meet you both." She walked away quickly and pounded the stairs upward.

Jody's eyes followed Haleh up the stairs while he planned his own escape. *So much for the words "for better or for worse."* "No, not at all. We're not that kind of family.

Just old-fashioned Roman Catholics. No Ouija boards, no seances, nothing."

Huntsman continued, "Have you ever felt a sort of sixth sense, ESP, telekinesis?"

Jody studied Huntsman's face again, as if to help his mind adjust his prior conclusions regarding her field of interest. "Not really, well, when I was active as a priest, sometimes things would happen, usually in the confessional, where words come to you that you never would have thought of on your own, but which just happen to be exactly what a penitent needs to hear. That sort of thing."

Huntsman curled her lips a little, as if allergic to this kind of conversation, yet she had brought up the paranormal.

"How exactly does all this figure into my accident, or any of the other incidents, for that matter?" Jody asked.

Huntsman asked, "What, exactly, would you say your emotional condition was when you had the accident? Take us inside the car with you."

"Sure. I was scared, of course, not knowing whether or not I was going to make it. Maybe even sad, like this was the end. I prayed to God, but, I guess, also to my dad a little."

"And what did you say?" she asked.

"I just called out 'Dad' or whatever." His eyes began to well up with tears. "And, also, this expression came to me, sort of out of nowhere. *Ma zad*."

"Ma zad?" she asked, pondering this. "Wait, is that Ahura Mazda? Were you calling on your wife's god?"

"No, it's just a Breton expression meaning something like 'Daddy' or 'Hey, Dad.' He taught it to me when I was little, but it never caught on. I'm sure I've never even thought of it in thirty-five years or more."

"But it was in your mind the whole time," she said. Lees looked bored. "Things like that don't leave us, those kinds of joys. Or traumas."

"No, I guess not."

"And what about at these other incidents along the road, in Iowa and Illinois?"

Jody, frustrated but happy to oblige if it meant answers, searched a little and replied, "Intense, I suppose. I was on the phone with my not-so-nice brother Sam when the bikers attacked me. But when I grabbed the ghost in Illinois, I wasn't really doing anything but watching a video on my phone, just tired from the road."

"What was the video?" Huntsman asked.

"That woman, Pandit, with her demon-possessed machines."

Huntsman and Lees gave each other a knowing look. "Have you had encounters with bikers in the past, Mr. Conque?" Lees asked. "Something that might generate these experiences?"

Jody had already asked himself this question. "No. I mean, I saw them all along my road trip. They always seemed real, especially the two I had dinner with the night before the accident."

Lees shuffled a little. "What bikers would these be?"

Huntsman took out her notepad and leaned forward again.

"I guess I didn't tell you this. In Kearney, at the Stage-coach. Yeah, I had this, like, long, intense conversation with two brothers on Japanese motorbikes. Maybe I made all that up, too, or not in the schizo way but the way you're talking about now. They were eating and everything. The waiter—the waiter saw them, too. I don't know what it takes to make up two guys like that and have everyone see them, but…."

Huntsman asked, "Did these two men have names?"

"Yeah. Kai and Av. I couldn't tell where they were from, but they seemed foreign."

Every muscle Huntsman carried on her small frame began to adjust and twist to try to keep a smile off her face. She looked briefly out through the dining room window. Jody had seen this expression on others before but could not, at that moment, put a name to it.

"I would say…," she finally began, "I wouldn't necessarily suppose that those two men were made up. They may very well have been real. Probably were. Eric, I think I've got everything I need today. Unless, of course, you've got more questions."

"No, let's…I think that's good enough for today. Thank you, Mr. Conque. We'll be in touch. It may happen that we ask you to come down to Denver. In that case, we'll escort you."

"Is it safe outside? I want to go to church on Sunday. Tell my wife it's safe to go outside."

Lees looked at Huntsman and nodded. "Mr. Conque, I think you can count on a certain level of security from here on out."

21

"It's definitely aliens," Danny said at dinner. "Let's put it all together here. We've got the Navy, spooky things happening in space and on the ground, our radio waves being taken over. Definitely aliens."

Cynthia chewed with her eyebrows raised, informing her husband he should expect and wait for a response. He smiled already.

Haleh said, "Is that what they're saying, Jody? Oh, wait, we've signed NDAs. Zip the lip."

"I can tell you they've not said anything about aliens," Jody replied. "I don't know what the Navy would have to do with aliens, anyway."

"Ah ha!" Danny replied. "This is where they obfuscate. They make it out like the Air Force and their Project Blue Book have all the skinny on aliens. But you remember those videos that came out a few years ago, off the coast of California? People went crazy about this stuff, all real. The Navy knows. They've been dealing with aliens for years, right here in our oceans. UFOs. Or—what are they calling them now? UAPs. Unidentified Aerial Phenomena."

"What's an alien, Mommy?" Claire asked.

"It's nothing, sweetie. They don't exist." Haleh glared at her uncle.

"Right, okay," Danny answered. He put down his fork and knife to make air quotes. "The 'entities operating the UFOs' are behind what happened to the moon."

"Can we have a serious conversation about this?" Cynthia asked. "We're all serious thinkers here."

"I am having a serious conversation," Danny said. "My dear, we've got people from the Kennedy Intergalactic Warfare Center knocking on our door now. I think aliens remain on the table."

"Irregular Warfare," Cynthia corrected.

"Tomato tomahto," Danny argued. "They're preparing for an invasion, getting us all scared by blowing up the moon."

"You don't really believe that aliens are invading," Cynthia said. "Or you wouldn't be so flippant about it."

"I'm not being flippant," Danny replied. "Serious thoughts don't have to be carried on serious words."

Jody turned to look at Haleh and Claire. Claire seemed to be absorbing the negative charge growing at the table. "Well, if it's any consolation, I can say that I have no idea why they came around today. They didn't really seem to ask anything that could be relevant to what's going on."

Cynthia turned to Jody. "They came around to spy on where you were staying. They've done all their research on me and Danny. They've seen the inside of our house. And now they're parked across the street."

Jody turned and saw, through the window, a car parked across the street. He could not tell if someone was inside it.

"They did allude to our being safer now. Maybe it's just to protect their investment, not to spy."

"What's the difference?" Danny asked, if just to gain his wife's good favor again. "Protection and custody mean the same thing in law enforcement, do they not?"

"These are just government wonks," Jody said. "They have no law enforcement capabilities."

All ate in silence for a few minutes.

"Well, let's give it a test," Jody said. "I'll go to church tomorrow, and we'll see whether the car stays or follows."

"Can I go to church?" Claire asked, leaning her head back first toward her father and then her mother.

Haleh sighed. Jody resisted a smile.

**

After dinner, Jody, Haleh, and Claire spent some time on their own as a family before the little girl's bedtime. They gathered in Claire's room, a spare bedroom filled with books lined on shelves and journals stacked on the floor. Claire sat wrapped in Haleh's arms on a little cot. Jody, sitting on the floor next to them, looked up at a cardboard box that Haleh had used to hide the "scary light" of the wifi router, which had been sending along the wall the dark, Shelobian shadows of its antennae. Jody wondered about this, about how easy it was for a child to assign fear to certain forms, as if she were born with knowledge of the unseen. He moved his right hand, which brushed over some papers under the bed.

"Are these your drawings, Claire Bear?" he asked. On each page, wavy lines wove in and out of her attempt at a circle. This was often accompanied by a few spiral shapes. "What are these?"

"I don't know," Claire said.

"Cynthia's been trying to make an artist out of Claire. She sees these drawings and shows her a book of flowers, like our three year old should be improving her technique already."

"She did these while I was out? They do look like sunflowers. I like your sunflowers, Claire Bear." He pinched her cheek, and she smiled.

"It's the moon," Claire said.

"Oh," Jody replied. "You see, hon? She's already remembering the moonburst. All the dust flying off."

"That's the sun," Claire corrected.

"The sun's behind the moon?" Haleh asked. "She's drawn an eclipse. You know what an eclipse is, sweetie?"

"No. . . ."

"That's when the moon blocks the sun."

"What are these spirals, sweetie? Galaxies?" Jody asked.

"Those are the people," Claire said.

"The people?"

"Yeah. They're going up to the moon."

***

After Claire had fallen asleep, Jody and Haleh lay on their own bed.

"I wonder what she thinks she's seeing," Jody said.

"It's the only thing she'll draw," Haleh replied. "I didn't want to say in there. Cynthia and I have actually been trying to get her to draw other things. I am a little concerned about it."

"Weird."

"Says Mister Ghostbuster Moonwalker. Don't call our daughter weird."

"I didn't call her weird, just, whatever she's thinking of. Maybe she's got some gift, you know? You remember her dream about people falling asleep and saving us from the monsters?"

"When was this?"

"The night of the moonburst. She was fussing, remember, wouldn't fall asleep?"

"Huh. I don't remember. But there was so much going on that night. Weird. Our daughter.... Speaking of weird, what did those people ask you after I left? You can tell me now. I'm sworn in or whatever, right?"

"Dr. Huntsman was trying to probe me a little, like I have some psychic connection to the universe or something."

"Well, do you?"

"What do you think?"

"Mm."

"Mm? What does that mean?"

"You have had a string of strange experiences. I don't know. Maybe the moon activated something inside you."

"No, that's you, my radar love." Jody lay on top of Haleh and pressed his lips against hers. She turned away.

"Now what?" he asked.

She played with his t-shirt between her fingers. "What if, you know, maybe you do have some, like, superpowers or something?"

"Honey, that's not, what...that doesn't affect us, you know?"

"The moon shot lightning at you."

"Or I shot my lightning at the moon," he said, immediately regretting it.

She looked down, then laughed a little with a few short, gentle bursts.

"Alright," he said, rolling onto his back. "Alright. I guess I'm the alien now."

"Babe, stop." She rolled on her side to face him.

Something like a word appeared in Jody's mind, and he shot up.

"I'm sorry," she said.

"That's not it. Hold on. I'll be right back."

Jody hobbled downstairs and for some reason could not find any paper there. He made his way back upstairs, to Claire's room. In the pale glow of the nightlight, he rummaged through old journals until he found one with a blank page in the back. He sat down next to Claire's bed and began to panic that he had forgotten the word that had appeared to him just a few minutes before. He listened to her sleepy breathing, woven into the buzz of the wifi and a low, howling wind outside. In that windswept silence, the word arrived:

You duped me, Lord, and I let myself be duped
Seven years a slave of love that no one could rebuke
Seven years for you, yourself, and no one else, alone
Bearing children of a bride, a pretty sight in stone

Seven years a body ached for love that never came
I waited for your word, awash in whiskey, wine, and pain
Your Food it really nourishes, and I proclaim it bold
But joy you served on paper plate and fed an empty soul

Jody stared up at the ceiling. Those words had come almost as quickly as he could write them. Something had sparked them, like he had wanted back in Nebraska.

He went back to his room. Though the lamp was on, Haleh was already asleep, still on her side, still facing him. It was too soon for her to fall asleep like this, and she would not have let herself fall asleep in this position. He turned her on her back so that it would not ache in the morning, put out the light, and lay next to her, awake for some time.

22

Jody and Haleh stood in front of the house enjoying the easy late summer sun just then rising over the peak of the roof. They were waiting for Jody's ride to Denver with the FBI. Almost a week had passed since Jody had left the hospital, during which many, Cynthia included, had confirmed that the moon had made its first quarter fifteen minutes late. Authorities and experts of all kinds assured everyone that this "adjustment of orbital period" was accounted for. Outside, out of earshot of Cynthia, Jody said, "They are rationalizing, working backward from evidence to cause."

"Isn't that all science?" Haleh asked.

"If so, they shouldn't be telling us it was expected."

"Maybe they're just trying to keep everyone calm."

"And when the moon acts unpredictably again? Then no one will trust the scientists."

"You sound like your mother now."

A black Suburban appeared at the end of the driveway. "This must be *them*."

"You're one of *them* now, babe."

"Sh. Don't tell my mother."

"Just be careful. Don't tell them too much. Don't let them put wires in you or anything. You have rights."

"I'm just saying, there are higher orders of reality to which we can appeal. God is in control of this."

Haleh rolled her eyes. "Fine. Just try telling *them* that."

Inside the car, the agent not driving seemed only too happy to tell Jody all about security conditions in various parts of the state, about the problems with radios increasing over the past month, and about his own preferred theories for the moondark. Instead of putting him at ease, Jody began to feel like this was already a test and grew reticent for the rest of the thirty-minute ride, looking out over a world locking down in fear of the unknown and the unknowable.

At the counter in the dull, fluorescent lobby of the FBI building in Denver, Jody signed his name and received a visitor's lanyard. The agent escorted him through a magnetically locked door and into a corridor. Jody took a seat outside a door marked Conference Room C.

As soon as the agent left him alone, the door opened and Huntsman appeared, bearing her subtle smile. "Welcome, Mr. Conque. Won't you come in?"

Inside the small conference room, he saw a couple of people standing at a coffee pot while a few others shuffled through papers at their seats along the table. He spotted Agent Seuss. Jody sat where indicated, at the end of the table by the door, and found a bottle of water and a glass in front of him. His eyes wandered for a few minutes while the others gradually took their seats, six investigators total.

"Ah, yes, let's bring this meeting to order," Lees began, sitting at the other end of the table. "Good morning, Mr.

Conque. It's good to see you again. As you can see, we've put together a bit of a working group here. As you might have guessed, and it's safe for us to tell you, we are investigating possible links between recent lunar activity and certain Earth-based phenomena. Your input, your experiences, will be vital to our understanding of what's going on and whatever responses we're able to make. So, right. Why don't we go around the table and introduce ourselves? You know Dr. Huntsman, to my right here. And I think you've already met Agent Theo Seuss of the Federal Bureau of Investigation, sitting here to my left. They are our gracious hosts with their own special interest in these proceedings."

Jody surprised himself by interrupting. "So the FBI really does have the X-files?"

Agent Seuss grimaced. "Mr. Conque, the Bureau does not have a paranormal division. We leave those, uh, penetrating questions to the others present. Our interest here is, as the host of these proceedings, to be on the lookout for anything that pertains to federal crimes and national security."

Jody replied more boldly than he had imagined doing. "Just to be sure, I've been given assurances that my participation means I'm not under investigation for any sort of crimes. I—"

"Not you," Lees interrupted. "Us. He's keeping an eye on us. Think of Agent Seuss as the referee. The ONI would normally conduct such an investigation under the auspices of NCIS, but we're far from any Navy base here in Denver."

"You're a lawyer," Jody said to Agent Seuss.

"Most of us are," Seuss replied. He then nodded quickly to a dour, middle-aged man to his left, who introduced himself.

"My name is Dr. Charles Valasca, with the Central Intelligence Agency. We are here to liaise with counterparts to this working group among our allies."

Every strange and dangerous thing Jody had ever heard about the CIA rushed into his mind, tangled into one tale of deep conspiracy. Valasca's skin cried out for sunlight.

"Don't be afraid," Valasca said. "I'm really here just to observe and, if necessary, offer the Company's expertise in—"

Jody heard a deep cough from Seuss, and as he turned, he saw a man he did not know had been sitting right next to him. His gray suit was somewhat ill-fitting and his necktie slightly undone. Jody soon forgot these details as he fell into the narrow, deep gorges of the old man's eyes, which he could not find buried under heavy folds of skin. Nevertheless, he felt those eyes gazing at him and through him.

"Is it my turn?" the old man asked. "Alright. My name is William DeSoto White Wolf. I'm with the Navajo Nation Rangers. Our organization, as part of our patrol of our nation's parks and forest land, helps visitors navigate their experiences of the so-called 'paranormal.'" After half a second of silence, he added, "We do this in a much less intrusive way than, say, the CIA has done in the past." To this, Valasca did not respond or even twitch. "And, to satisfy everyone's curiosity, while I am part Navajo, I am all Crow on my mother's side, which is what matters. Okay. Now all that's out of the way. Next?"

Sitting between Ranger White Wolf and Dr. Huntsman

was a younger woman, rather striking in appearance. Under long, straight black hair the broad facets of her visage met at stern edges that made Doris Huntsman look like a restaurant hostess. "Hello, Mr. Conque. My name is Dr. Melanie Black Mare. I am a physicist out of Berkeley, my background is interstellar microwave radiation, and I currently work for the ONI's Farragut Technical Analysis Center."

Ranger White Wolf gave something like a smile and said, "And as you might have guessed by her good looks, Pierre-Joseph, Dr. Black Mare is related to me as my niece."

Black Mare huffed and rolled her eyes at her uncle, who hid his growing smile with the cup of coffee at his mouth. Jody wondered who had won whom the job.

"There," Lees said. "We're all introduced. No doubt, Mr. Conque, you're wondering why such a diverse group of interests is arrayed at this table. Let me explain. When—"

Agent Seuss grumbled something.

Lees replied tersely, "He's already signed. I have a copy right here."

This seemed to satisfy Agent Seuss.

"As I was saying, we have Navy intelligence, foreign intelligence, physicists, psychologists, and more boots-on-the-ground forms of expertise here. Now, let's start with the obvious question, Mr. Conque. Why is the Navy interested in your experience?"

Jody shrugged interrogatively. Lees turned to Black Mare.

Black Mare pulled her hair back a little and flipped open a laptop. All turned their attention to her. "Mr. Conque," she said, "I want you to listen to something." She played what sounded like military banter in English, fitted with fragments of strange radio squawk. He nodded. She pressed a button, and the English part of the recording was removed. Jody tilted his head a little, thinking he perceived a pattern. She pressed another button, and much noise was eliminated, revealing another conversation in another language recorded alongside the one he had heard. "That language you hear, as best we can tell, is Pequot Mohegan."

"Oh."

"It has not been spoken in over a century."

"And yet—"

"This was recorded on a Navy submarine in dry dock in Groton, Connecticut, two years ago, by another associate of ours in this working group. So, yes, it is possible that two other people, using the same radio frequency, were speaking in an extinct language about organizing a whale hunt, but it is entirely improbable."

"I'm getting a little lost, I think."

"Fine. Let's bring it closer to home, then." She pressed another button, and Jody made out, after a minute, what sounded very clearly like the conversation he had had with Lees and Huntsman when they showed him the video.

"Alright," he said warily. "So you recorded our conversation when you came over. There's no bug in the house now, right? That would be illegal. Danny made a sweep—"

Lees said, "We've done nothing of the kind. There is no recording device in your house at the moment. Keep listening."

Jody heard, between a few words he exchanged with

Lees and Huntsman, another conversation. "Alright. There it is again. What language is that?"

"We don't know," Black Mare said. "No one knows. It is not of European, Asian, or Native American origin."

"So, what, are there ghosts in the house? It was only built twenty years ago."

Black Mare said, "My studies began rather straightforwardly, listening for signs of life in the universe through any and all forms of radio and light waves. It was only when my uncle here was listening to some work I had brought home that we began discerning patterns where our algorithms had found nothing. We have to be open to the possibility that these voices emanate from some great distance away and are reaching us now through the moon's activity."

"Or that they are reaching us from some great distance in the past," White Wolf said.

"Okay," Jody said. "You've got a device that can record ghosts or aliens. Again, why bring this to my attention?"

Huntsman restrained a smile and said, "You are the device, Mr. Conque."

"What do you mean, 'I am'?"

"You're the antenna, Mr. Conque. And whatever happened to the moon has, in some way, activated your capacity to serve as an antenna."

23

Jody poured himself a glass of water. He felt everyone's eyes leave him alone for the moment, out of courtesy. He held the thick glass with both hands and rubbed it, producing a sound like he had made with the good bottle back in his mother's kitchen the night of the moondark, and the memory of the slinking specter came with it. He saw, out of the corner of his eye, Black Mare jump a little and repress a smile of happy surprise. She drew White Wolf's attention to her monitor.

"Even here?" Seuss said.

Lees leaned forward. "Mr. Conque, let us offer you a little history. In the middle of the last century, the Navy began using Very Low Frequency radio, VLF, to communicate with its submarines. In a curious way, those VLF transmissions began pushing back the Van Allen radiation belt that surrounds the Earth. You are familiar with the Van Allen belts? Good. Well, at the same time, over the past eighty years or so, other phenomena began to emerge, certain ties between the deep oceans and deep space. *Abyssus abyssum invocat*, as it were."

Jody knew that psalm and doubted that it applied. "Are we talking about aliens?"

His suggestion met serious, unmoving faces and wary eyes. This made him afraid again.

Huntsman leaned forward. "Let's be clear, Mr. Conque. We're not talking about aliens, per se. I would like to stress, to this whole group, that we are talking about *talking about* UAPs and whatever intelligences may be operating them. As Dr. Lees is saying, since World War II, there has been a massive surge in sightings of what have been called UFOs and many other claims of alien abduction. We want to be very extremely careful here and separate out those two classes of phenomena. The Navy itself has been privy to a large number of alleged UAP sightings, as many or more than the Air Force. But we all know that. We've all seen the videos leaked to the media over the past few years from the Nimitz and the Omaha. And again, let me stress, what we're interested in here is the fact that so much of this phenomenon is brought about simply by talking about it."

Jody asked, "You mean, people interpreting what they see as UFOs and aliens, creating mass hysteria?"

White Wolf coughed and said, "Not per se. Many experiences that people have can be chalked up to natural things. A large bear can be Sasquatch. A weather balloon or a stealth aircraft can be a UFO. But some of these experiences cannot be reduced in that way. And it's in the in-between, between sight and recognition, that the danger lies."

"The danger?" Jody asked.

"Confusion, lies, camouflage," White Wolf said. "Think about this. How many times have you woken up in the middle of the night to see some shadow in your room, and you think that shadow is of a spirit? But you hold your eyes open for a while, and the shadow becomes just that, a shadow. Well, maybe it is, or it is *eventually*. But you have to ask yourself why you opened your eyes in the first place. Something was present that woke you up. It slid back into the shadows as your reason took over."

Jody remembered the night of the moonburst, thinking he saw his long-dead sister in the garden.

"I can see you've had some experience of this already," White Wolf said.

Jody nodded reluctantly.

Huntsman spoke. "What we're talking about is some reality that won't dwell in the same realm as your reason. The shadow, the specter, only wants to exist where your reason is suspended. That's why young children so often see things that quote-unquote aren't there. We call this a tendency to schizophrenia, and it's normal or at least not uncommon in children. But when it manifests itself to crowds of people, like in bars in Illinois and on interstates in Iowa, among other places, then it becomes something else, something we need to address as a matter of public safety and national security."

"So, what?" Jody asked. "Have we all lost our reason? Is that why we're all seeing things that aren't there? Is this mass hysteria over the moondark?"

Huntsman replied, "Reason is one sort of safeguard against this other realm of realities, fear is another, and fear and reason often go hand in hand. Some have even called reason the handmaid of fear."

"You mean faith, right? Reason is the handmaid of faith."

Huntsman continued as if he had said nothing, "The moondark has brought many millions, billions, into a state of fear. Over the years, so has global war, the threat of nuclear holocaust, terrorist attacks, and so on. Psychology could explain these fears and traumas as providing the ground for interpreting tricks of light and sound as UAPs, and it often has. But recently our technologies, our science, has provided more objective recognition of these experiences."

"UAPs on camera and radar," Lees said. "But let me just stimulate your imagination a bit now. Have you ever seen good, clear pictures of UFOs or aliens? Or Sasquatch or the Loch Ness Monster or anything?"

"No, actually. That's always the counterargument. My brother Cam—"

"Right, Mr. Conque. I'm sorry to interrupt. No, the reason is that electromagnetic radiation can carry all kinds of natural information, and we use it as such, in radio waves, wifi, and so on. The elements, the realities, the phenomena that have been, how shall we say, poking through, penetrating our sensory realm recently, tend to distort or, better, not be well-handled by our ways of encoding electromagnetic radiation. But that's changing. Over the past eighty years or more, we've been sort of inadvertently clearing the way, clearing the forest, between one abyss and another."

After a second of silence, White Wolf added, "And filling it with ready-made paths of information. The more we civilize the electromagnetic spectrum, the more we fill it with forms of our making that can be more easily imitated...." He trailed off.

A heavy silence fell over the group. Jody was unsure why and asked, "But this is the Irregular Warfare group. So something is at war with us? Using our information against us? If so, how does this involve me?"

Huntsman looked at Lees. Both looked at Agent Seuss, who shrugged. "So long as it doesn't leave this room," he said. "Go on with your crazy theory."

Lees said, "We feel, like Ranger White Wolf has said, that we've been inadvertently building paths, channels for another kind of intelligence, or even multiple kinds of intelligence. The more we talk about what we think they are, the more we give them clear patterns for imitation. They are learning or are becoming able to become the things we think they are and say they are."

"Like the Stay-Puft Marshmallow Man?" Jody asked, more flippantly than he had hoped.

Lees coughed to suppress a chuckle. "In a sense, yes. And, perhaps, with just the same devious intentions as that situation demonstrated."

Jody, confused, thought back to the movie. "You mean like ancient gods? What was the name of the goddess on the rooftop again?"

White Wolf spoke. "So you see, those gods were, themselves, imitations, forms of other intelligences that man made visible through his idols of wood and stone. We've been doing this for millennia, Father Conque, making channels for what some call deities with the images we create and share. Most often it comes to nothing. But it hasn't always come to nothing."

Jody leaned on the table and put his face in his hands.

Where he went in that second, he did not know, but he felt that when he looked around the room again, he had passed into some new place. All were still gazing at him. "So you need a priest to do exorcisms? The Vatican could help you better than I could."

Valasca answered, "We are currently trying to establish ties with the Holy See in this regard."

Lees smiled. Huntsman made her allergic face again. Ranger White Wolf spoke. "As you can see, Pierre-Joseph, not everyone in this room is in agreement as to the nature of these spiritual realities."

"Or that they are spiritual," Huntsman said. "That they've ever been what you think of as spiritual. For now, we should say that they are simply 'other,' and in being 'other,' unrecognizable, they have slipped their way into the things, the forms, that we do recognize. From where in this universe, we do not know."

***

"Hey, Maman," Jody said. He stood on the back deck of Danny and Cynthia's house later that evening. Beyond the neighbor's lights, the streetlamps and stoplights that rimmed the streets made the Earth itself something of a starlit universe, a constellation of order.

"Hey, Jody."

"So."

"So. You're, eh, working for the government now?"

"Sort of, yeah. I mean, I can't really talk about it, you understand. I think, as you know, as everyone does, we've got a lot coming our way."

"Is that what the spooks are telling you? You know

they've tapped your phone, right? I shouldn't even be talking to you."

"What are they going to do, Mom? Hear your secret plans?"

"I've got my secrets."

"Well, let me ask, then. Did Dad ever, you know, maybe exhibit certain, I don't know, powers, abilities, et cetera?"

"What kinds of powers are we talking about here? He never did any ghostbusting like you did, if that's what you mean. Not that I know about, anyway."

Jody felt disappointed. "Nothing at all? Nothing strange about his circumstances? Or you, for that matter?"

"Me? Ha! You know me. I'm happy if I can get the bologna between the bread."

"Um—"

"But you know that he was a foundling, right?"

"Yeah. I always knew that. A woman who couldn't have children found him and raised him, called him her miracle. None of us ever met her, did we?"

"Me neither. He always spoke highly of her. That's all he knows about where he's from. No, he did always have this thing, you know, where he sort of answered your question before you asked it. It happened all the time, like he'd bring you something as if you'd asked for it, and you were going to, and he thought you did, and then none of you were sure if anyone really did or not."

"I remember that. It didn't happen that often."

"No, well, it happened more frequently between us, you know, in more intimate circumstances. And I only really ever saw it after Maddie died. It really came out then."

"Maybe she was telling him things."

"Maybe."

"The family really changed after that, didn't we?"

"Who's we?"

"Don't do this, Mom."

"I'm just saying. You weren't there."

"After all this time, Maman? I'm not allowed to mourn the sister I never knew? You people, you and Sam especially, you make me and Cam feel like hangers-on, like we don't really belong to the family."

"No, we don't. Just don't pretend like you know what it's like to lose a daughter or a sister. It hit Sam as hard as us. They were inseparable."

"Yeah. So Sam has always treated me like a secondhand replacement for her."

"That's between you and Sam."

"He equates me with the car, which he also saw as a replacement for him."

"Again, that's between you and Sam."

"All I'm saying is that it would have been nice to feel like I belonged in that house growing up."

"You belonged."

"Never mind, Mom. I've had enough of this talk. I just thought I'd share the moment with you. The moon may be on its way into outer space as we speak. So, alright. Maybe Dad had a bit of an unwitting sixth sense about him. Nothing else?"

"No."

Jody breathed heavily into the receiver, waiting to understand what he was supposed to say next. He looked up and over the house, toward where the moon should be. He smelled the ash from a barbecue Danny had made. His leg began to throb. He somehow knew instinctively, without sight, where the moon was and locked on it. He remembered the dream of the party and remembered, or saw for the first time, that while all was pleasant in that scene, something sinister lurked. It was not just in the machine servants, but behind everything there.

"You there?" Terr asked.

"Yeah. Alright, Mom. I've gotta go. Gotta rest. It's been all work these days. NASA is pressing pretty hard on us right now."

"Good night, Jody."

"Night, Maman."

He looked out over the starry landscape. He wondered if it were possible that mankind has been in this place before. He wondered what life was like before Noah's flood. Maybe the flood waters have been protecting the Earth from something humankind had done before. Maybe the moon was doing that now. Maybe the moon was peeling all that back, leaving the Navy to be the first to discover antediluvian man and whatever terrible things they had done to merit near-total destruction.

24

In the days that followed, Jody did everything he could to distract himself from the suggestions that the working group had made. They wanted him to record his environment, especially when he felt "vulnerable." He worked to avoid that with intense focus and grew frustrated when his staff could not turn in new code for review quickly enough. In his downtime, he played with Claire, serving as artist's assistant and butler to her expanding estate of stuffed animals. In their free time at night, Haleh only wanted to watch shows or talk to her parents. He took to himself with pen and paper.

One afternoon, Haleh caught him in Claire's room, sitting on the floor next to her cot while she took her nap. It had often made it easier for Claire to sleep when Jody was next to her in this new environment. He obliged only when he felt he could tell that Haleh was not jealous. "What are you writing?" Haleh asked.

He looked up at her like a teenage boy caught by his mother, glad she pretended not to notice the glass of scotch next to him on the floor or the government-issue device on his ear. "Nothing, just, uh, a little...some thoughts, I guess, you know, on the situation."

"Oh," she said. "It looks like poetry."

He looked down at the scrap of paper pinned to a clipboard. "Right, well, as it turns out, I guess my dad did a little composing himself, so I thought I'd just take some inspiration." Her eyes flashed, and he felt his resistance falter. "I mean, it's not much. To be honest, apart from certain moments of inspiration, I can only think of limericks."

"That's a place to start, right? Just think, my husband the poet."

He smiled awkwardly and said, "There is one that seems to have something to it. I don't know. Tell me what you think." As he rummaged through the pile clipped to the board, he thought of Terr making fun of Bleiz. That would not happen here. He looked up at Haleh, still standing. "Here, have a seat." She did, and he read:

I once knew a nymph in desire
Hymning to love on the lyre
Things went so well,
Till I brought her through hell
And, looking back, I descried her

She looked confused.

"It's about Orpheus and Eurydice," he said. "There's, like, a double entendre there in descry, you know, like to see and decry, from the French, literally, to cry down, you know, criticize, but more like sorrowfully send her back to Hades. Anyway. It's a start. I mean, I have more. And, you know, time to work on it now."

"Alright...well, keep working at it, I guess."

"Yeah."

"Well, I still love you."

There were many meanings behind the words, "I love you," and, in this usage, Jody heard, "Don't quit your day job," an expression his mother often used. Haleh was normally much more supportive than this. With that, going from excited to sad in one moment, injured by the slight criticism from his wife, Jody then realized why his father never revealed it to his mother at all, and regretted that he had, too.

**

Jody, Haleh, Danny, and Cynthia sat in the living room in the evening. Claire lay on her stomach, some coffee-table book full of pictures open before her. President Palmer had just finished a brief press conference and was now taking questions. What accounted for the adjustment of orbital period was not a deceleration of the moon but a very slight elongation in its orbit toward the sun. This minor deviation could not have been noticed until it accumulated over the two weeks between the last quarter moon and the first quarter moon. The world could only watch and wait to see what would happen as the moon passed again between the Earth and the sun. Cynthia turned the volume down low, and they all faced each other, glasses of wine or brandy in their hands.

In the silence, Haleh eventually said, "Hara Berezaiti."

"Oh, God, not you, too," Danny said.

"What?" she replied. "Maybe Zoroaster was onto something after all."

"You sound like Cyrus echoing your mother," Danny replied.

Cynthia intervened. "What is harab rezati?"

Danny said, "It is the sacred mountain around which all the stars and planets revolve, and somehow also the source of all the other mountains and rivers."

"I see," Cynthia replied.

"And it says here," Jody joined in, looking at his phone, "that it is also the mountain behind which the sun hides at night."

"Don't make fun," Haleh said.

"I'm not making fun, dear. It's what it says."

"So," Cynthia said, "it's a way to explain invisible realities. If you can't see the center around which things revolve, then posit something to go there."

"Something like that," Danny answered.

"Well," Haleh replied, "we do have some invisible reality drawing the moon away from the Earth, extending its orbit. I don't mean to suggest it's some literal mountain, but the writers of the Avesta may be recording the observation of some events, you know, similar to those of today."

"Or they simply had an incomplete model," Danny said.

Jody watched Haleh recoil a little, turning to watch Claire. "As do we today, it seems," he said, and, resting his arm on the couch behind Haleh and leaning toward her, he also watched Claire.

Cynthia gave Danny a scolding look, to which he responded with a silent protestation of innocence. She asked, "What else does it say about this mythical mountain?"

Jody read the Wikipedia entry. "It's part of the bridge of judgment. Maybe that's where we are, a moment of judgment."

All were silent for a while.

Danny made as if to say something but didn't. Starting again, he said, "Whatever's going on up there, whatever the models say…in the best-case scenarios, we are…prepared here. For a few months, anyway."

Haleh and Jody turned toward Danny. Cynthia looked toward her glass.

"Prepared?" Haleh asked.

***

After putting Claire to bed, Danny and Cynthia gave Jody and Haleh a tour of their basement. The first thing anyone would see, underneath the dining room, was a ping-pong table.

"Maybe I could learn lefty," Jody said, swinging the paddle a little. Ahead of him, underneath the kitchen, was a standard-issue collection of boiler, water heater, sump pump, and other equipment. Underneath the area of Danny's study, behind the stairs, was what he took to be a computer server room. Beyond the stairs, underneath their master bedroom, was another walled-off area. Danny stood sentry there, waiting for them in front of a gray, metal door. Jody studied the sheetrock lining every wall and wondered what seemed different about it.

"I haven't had time to spackle yet," Danny said. "Maybe you could help me with that, Jody."

Danny turned and unlocked the door with a key. Once inside, he switched on a string of lights, revealing rows of plastic shelving on which Jody made out, at first, large containers of water. On the shelves above, in plastic bins, were vacuum-sealed bags of grain, beans, and dried fruit. Above these were cans of low-sodium soup, jars of peanut butter and honey, and boxes of pasta and powdered milk.

"What is diatomaceous earth?" Haleh asked.

"Kills the insects," Danny replied.

"How much food, I mean, for how long?" Haleh asked.

"Six months," Danny replied. "We're working on longer, but, you know, you've got to rotate through this stuff, keep it fresh on the shelf."

Haleh continued, "So you've been expecting something for a while. This doesn't seem like you, Uncle Danny." She looked for comprehension at Cynthia, who returned only a sort of knowing look.

"Yeah, your dad would make fun of me for this. Let's put it this way. You spend enough time working with government agencies and people in advanced research, you hear things, you get a sense that our, eh, near-Earth ecosystem is a lot more fragile, or that there's more going on, than meets the eye."

"Near-Earth ecosystem? So they knew the moon was going to burst?" Haleh asked. Jody studied everything on the shelves. Haleh was asking his questions for him.

"No, no, I don't think so," Danny replied. "Only that...I mean, look. A single asteroid could send us into the dark ages, and they're whizzing by all the time. And, maybe, there's more than asteroids out there whizzing by."

"More aliens, Danny?" Jody asked. "You really think we're being attacked by aliens, don't you?"

"I didn't say that," he replied defensively. "I didn't say that. Not at all. Only that there's a lot going on out there. Heck, even on Earth. I mean, look at what's going on in the

Muslim world. They're gearing up, some of them, for some last battle. The evangelicals, too, I bet. I mean, this is everyone's shining moment. Better to be able to hunker down for a bit, you know? I mean, it's amazing we haven't had groups rising up in our own country."

"Because everyone loves President Palmer," Jody said. "She is like the platonic form of motherhood. Even when they hate her, they only reinforce her authority."

"So," Haleh said, "with us here, it's really only three months of food, or less." She looked to Jody, who met her concerned eyes.

"That six months includes you three," Danny said. Then, more seriously, he continued, "I was talking to your folks today, Haleh, and I think we all agree that, with everything going on, and Jody's thing, that maybe you guys should just spend a bit longer out here than anticipated. Maybe this moon cycle is just a fluke, you know? We'll see what next month has in store. We can all do our work from here on the Mickey."

Staring into a plastic bin full of vacuum-sealed pancake mix, Jody felt every muscle fill with hardening resin. It was one thing to be held here by the government and another to be held here out of familial fear. He wondered why his working group had to meet in Denver, anyway. He missed the Trans Am for the first time and missed it angrily.

PART FIVE

WEPWAWET

25

Against the judgment she expressed mainly through a guarded, distant look and secondarily through half-hearted protestations, Haleh agreed to accompany Jody to his second full conference in Denver with the working group. This had been the suggestion of Lees over the phone. Since she had signed the NDA, she could participate in some way. Haleh said that she would go as far as outside the room but did not want to be part of their proceedings. Lees paused for a moment and told Jody that her being out in the hallway might be as helpful as her being in the room.

The working group, which had counterparts on the east coast and southern California, was now calling itself Wepwawet. Wepwawet was an ancient Egyptian wolf deity who served as a scout for armies to follow into other realms. Jody wondered if White Wolf had come up with this name. He wondered why his father had been named Bleiz, which meant wolf in the Breton language.

"Conference Room A this time," Jody said. "We've really moved up in the world."

Haleh flicked her eyebrows dismissively and turned to look at a couple sitting in the next bank of chairs. Jody followed her gaze toward a rather solid and intelligent-looking man with a short, nappy beard, who was consoling a woman leaning forward in his arms. Through the veil of copper-red hair hanging straight to her hips, only her hands emerged, fondling a palm-sized cube of blue and white stone. She glanced up at Jody. With her pale face and dark, worry-weary eyes, he thought he recognized her and tried to place her. He sensed that she was trying to do the same.

The door to Conference Room A opened, and Ranger White Wolf stepped out. "Pierre-Joseph, Lucy, are you ready?"

Jody stood and looked at his wife, whose two hands clung to his free arm. The woman he took to be Lucy kissed the man she was with and stood up nearly as tall as Jody.

Inside the conference room, Jody saw the six agents he knew gathered at the two upper ends of a large, U-shaped table. He and Lucy sat near each other, among others he thought shared his capabilities, in the valley of the U-shape. White Wolf, Black Mare, and Seuss were on the left, while Lees, Huntsman, and Valasca were on the right. A large video screen across from him bore the seal of what he took to be the FBI.

Lees seemed to be communicating with someone who was not in the room through an earpiece. Once he was satisfied, he said, "Good morning, everyone. It's great that we're able to bring together some of our Wepwawet Mountain West collaborators into one meeting. Now that we've undergone some preliminaries and eliminated some outlying circumstances, we'll work much more efficiently all together."

"Does that mean you've kicked out the kooks?" Lucy

said, swiveling a little in her chair and knocking into Jody's right leg. He yelped.

Lees smiled and said, "Pierre-Joseph Conque, this is Lucy MacDuff. Lucy MacDuff, Pierre-Joseph Conque."

"Jody is fine," he said, shaking Lucy's hand. She regarded him pleasantly, but when he took her hand, he received some image he could not process, white and blue, as if snow and sky. He laughed a little and said, "Whoa. The force is strong with this one."

Her eyes searched him.

Lees and Huntsman smiled. No one else seemed to register the exchange.

Lees continued, "Jody, Lucy teaches geology at UC Boulder. In due time, we'll discuss her experiences with lunar-spectral phenomena. Her husband, Declan, is out in the hallway, where I assume your wife, Haleh, is? Good. Lucy, Jody is a computer programmer for a satellite research company based out of Silicon Valley."

"You could say we have a satellite office now in Boulder," Jody joked. Only Valasca offered the slightest puff of a laugh.

Lees reintroduced the Wepwawet team and the three other subjects. "Well, let's get to it, shall we? Much to discuss," Lees said. "We thank you all for sending in your audio samples through our secure link. The past week has been particularly eventful, given the stress everyone has been feeling with regard to the moon's slowing orbit. And that stress seems to be the mark or the gateway, as it were, for this trans-dimensional voice layering. Huntsman has some remarks in that regard."

Huntsman roused herself as if from somewhere else and

said, "Yes, thank you, Dr. Lees. I want to be careful not to divulge too much of each collaborator's personal psychological profile. If we could maintain some level of privacy, it might even—"

"I guess we're all pretty messed up, huh?" Lucy said. "Lots of mommy and daddy issues?"

Jody felt equal parts love and hate for this woman. "Sort of a slow burn situation, myself," he offered.

"Mr. Conque," Huntsman said, "we wondered if you would indulge us for a moment, before we get started, with one particular recording. Last Thursday, well, let's listen."

Jody heard an argument he had been having with Haleh last Thursday about something only the stir crazy could find important. He laughed, this time, as Haleh appealed to the "hospital food and tears" on which she had subsisted after his crash. This raised the eyebrows and lowered the chins of the married men in the room. In the filtered layer, between other artifacts of life at home, he heard more of the strange language. He looked up and gave an expectant smile.

Black Mare said, "We hear again this strange language, which we cannot yet place." Huntsman shuffled uncomfortably in her seat, a thing that Black Mare noticed. "But we're not sure if the audio, either because of our device or some function of the space-time slippage, isn't on some kind of continuous loop. Do you hear this expression repeated over and over again, 'no-ki, no-ki'? We think it might be a cipher or a primer of some kind, meant to help us break the text apart into meaning units or to attach it to recordings we make elsewhere. Does that word have any meaning to you, or have you heard it elsewhere, dreamt it, anything?"

"Yes," Jody said. He paused for dramatic effect, and it seemed to be working. "But I do believe the word is not so much alien as Italian, *gnocchi*. Danny taught Claire that word last week, and she spent, oh, about ten or fifteen minutes repeating it over and over again. Out of obsession or pleasure, I couldn't tell."

Black Mare looked a little embarrassed, especially as Agent Seuss opened his wallet and handed White Wolf, behind her back, a one-dollar bill. Lucy chortled. "Thank you," Black Mare said, and she peered into her computer, typing vigorously.

"It's hard to tell the difference between obsession and pleasure," Lucy added. Huntsman, the psychologist, glared at her like a teacher. "Often, anyway. I'm sure your little Claire is perfectly normal."

Jody, feeling just a little offended by Lucy's forthrightness, worried that she somehow sensed something about Claire even from a distance. He worried about what Claire seemed to be seeing. Lucy could not know anything about Claire. None of those in this room should ever know.

"Excuse me," Jody said, raising his hand.

"Yes, Mr. Conque?" Lees said.

"Let me just throw this out there for your consideration. If, as we've spoken about before, we're being visited or manipulated by some higher intelligence—"

"Other intelligence," Lees offered.

"*Other* intelligence...and they've been doing it all these years through UFO encounters and demonic apparitions, then why open pandora's box by blowing out the moon? Doesn't that sort of ruin the effect by getting everyone's attention? Everyone's on high alert now, and you've got more people who can see." He enjoyed that the room fell into silence for a moment and continued, "So maybe there is a *higher* intelligence at work, you know, a divine intelligence, God, maybe setting a trap. Working on our side. Pulling back the curtains."

After a brief silence, Lees said, "Lucy, Mr. Conque was once Father Conque, a Catholic priest." At that, Jody watched Lucy's eyes briefly fix on him as they fell into shadows. She turned away.

"Mr. Conque," Lees continued, "many or most of us here would like to be sympathetic to that idea. There are no atheists in foxholes, as they say. But when we're done praying, we've got to put our head out and fire a weapon. Intelligence gathering tells us what to fire and in which direction. That's all we're doing now."

"I would add," Huntsman said, "that we need to focus on what is measurable. Appealing to divine intervention would be counterproductive."

Jody nodded his external acquiescence and looked over at Lucy, who was staring at the table in front of her.

***

After forty-five minutes of hearing more audio and the strange worlds it opened up, Wepwawet Mountain West took a coffee break. Jody talked with the others who had joined the group, laymen like himself, each with some kind of special ability activated by the moondark. Huntsman had made it clear that most of the "scouts," as she and Lees had begun calling them, had never manifested any kind of psychic or occult ability before. This was to enable Wepwawet

216

to focus exclusively on what the moon had brought about and, therefore, what it might continue to bring. Only certain cases of pre-moondark abilities were brought on to the project, and as Huntsman was saying this, Jody sensed she meant Lucy.

The door opened, and Haleh and Declan came into the conference room. Jody wondered why no other spouses were there as he presented Haleh to the team. White Wolf approached her and introduced himself. Something about him seemed immediately to set her at ease. Jody watched.

"No doubt," White Wolf said, "you've been talking to Declan out in the hallway."

"Yes," she said. "I suppose you mean about Lucy's experiences? That's why you had us out there together? Maybe something you don't want said in here?"

White Wolf turned to Jody and said, "Hang on to this one, man. She's smart."

"Smarter than I am," Jody said, and he meant it.

Haleh continued, "I guess I'm not sure what to believe. If it's all as they say it is, it's strange and terrifying. I mean of all places, Ant—"

White Wolf put his hand against Haleh's lips and shushed her. "You know what, Haleh? Let's say no more about that now. Let's say I've got a hunch about something. Ah, yes. It's already playing out." Jody turned to follow the old man's eyes. Lucy was with Declan in the room, talking to Lees and Huntsman. There were subdued protestations on both sides.

Lucy walked briskly over to Jody, Haleh, and White Wolf. Declan followed. "I'm sorry," Lucy said. "It looks like we'll have to continue our collaboration another time. Things are not.... Anyway." She struck out her hand for Jody to take.

Jody put his cane in his left hand to shake. While he took her hand and the blue-white image began faintly to re-emerge, White Wolf gently thrust his foot behind Jody's left knee. He buckled, dropped his cane, and reached out with both hands, which Lucy grabbed automatically. The room went dark.

Jody regained his footing but held on to Lucy the way a human body grips the thing that is electrocuting him. The air in the conference room grew very cold, and he could see his breath. The walls began very subtly to glow with a few shimmers of electric blue. Conference Room C had become a cave of ice, or they had transported, all together, to some other place. Jody did not know.

Lucy began to whimper and cry.

"It's alright, Lu," Declan whispered. "Let him see."

"No-o," she whispered.

White Wolf took their wrists in his hands. "Come on. Walk with me."

The movement that followed seemed possible because of White Wolf's guidance but only as Lucy allowed it. The floor looked and felt as if made of large gravel, but Jody heard the sound of carpet beneath his feet. They walked between the table and the wall of ice until the cavern opened into a large black void where the projection screen had been. It was here that Lucy began to pull away. Jody gripped her tightly and prayed a few short words.

"We're all with you here, Lu," Declan said. "We're in the conference room. Let us see what you saw."

"I never got past here," she said.

"Then let's go together," White Wolf said.

The room fell into a silence broken only by battered breaths. Even Black Mare's quiet keystrokes made no echo in the assembling mist. Jody could only see Lucy's pale, terrified face and six hands joined in front of him. White Wolf was walking them forward into the absorbing darkness.

As all light vanished from the room, another sense took its place, an odor. Jody could not place it, though it brought his imagination into a grocery store. He fought this light-filled image and looked around. The scent grew stronger. It was the meat department or a butcher shop.

Jody looked down to his left and saw the conference room table reflecting some light. The grains of wood stood out to him, but they became strange. The knots, too, seemed to shift their shape. The abstract pattern was taking on some definite form.

Lucy's eyes were nearly closed. White Wolf's eyes were closed all the way. Jody's were wide open, darting this way and that to avoid being mesmerized by the shifting pattern in the wood. Yet, it was the only thing to see, and he felt he should see it. The wood grain became finer, and the pattern broke up into verticals, horizontals, and diagonals. The yellow-brown color reddened. The surface rose up and down, and its edge curved inward and outward. He saw no longer a conference room table but a human body, stripped of skin, exposing muscle, and frozen. He began to tremble.

He now tried to shake loose from Lucy, but she held him as if in a trance. White Wolf was very quietly humming something. Jody saw, if not by light than by some other source, that this body lay on a slab of stone or ice with many others in a long and wide array.

Jody studied the scene. This was a laboratory, and these were experiments. He began to wonder who could have done this and ran down a list of suspects: the Nazis, the Chinese, space aliens, and so on. He counted the number of bodies he saw, but the more he counted, the more they faded away. Before he knew it, or all at once, everything vanished, and he was left alone with Lucy and White Wolf.

As if by some command, they all came to at once. The others in the room reappeared, and the carpet grew soft beneath his feet. White Wolf let go. Haleh handed him his cane. Jody let go and nearly fell backward. Lucy did fall, but Declan caught her quickly and sat her down.

Jody and Lucy each sat at the table staring into the void. Jody traced the lines of grain and ran his palms across its smooth surface, back and forth, convincing himself he was back in the world he once knew.

"Sh-sh-shh," Haleh said, rubbing his back and arm. "Hey. Look at me. We're all here."

He looked at her and then scanned the table for the others. Lucy had both hands flat on the table, her fingertips touching. Jody looked past her to see Valasca grinning like a boy burning ants with a magnifying glass. Huntsman was exchanging glances with Black Mare and unheard words with Lees. Agent Seuss, in the corner, seemed worn and confused. Jody turned back to Haleh and felt like, though he recognized her, he did not know her. White Wolf walked past her, back to his seat. The breeze blew her perfume into Jody's nose, and he began to smile and cry.

He wiped his eyes. "Did the rest of you see that?" He looked around the table again. No one responded. "Honey, did you see anything?"

"I saw that we were in a cold, dark cave."

Lees spoke. "Before we describe what we saw, why don't we each write it down? Let's not influence each other's impressions. Fair?"

"Yes, that's...," Huntsman began. She looked at Lees. "Let's do that."

"In the meantime," Lees said, "why don't we order up lunch? Maybe some wine with that. I'm a little shaky myself. Who's with me?"

26

The six intelligence agents, five scouts, and two spouses ate a lunch of sandwich wraps and boxed wine at the conference room table. While they had been waiting for this to arrive, everybody in the room had, in silence, written down what they had seen during the vision. Jody faced Haleh as he ate to help him forget that the slab of laminated wood had just been a dissected corpse and to turn his wife's attention away from the deep connection he had just made with another woman. He felt Lucy, behind him, bump her rolling chair into his.

"Sorry," Lucy said.

Jody turned and looked at her, wondering what it was about her that could have caused such a connection and why she had already seemed familiar to him in the hallway.

"I'm sorry how that came out before," Lucy continued. "About Claire. It came out wrong. I'm sorry. This whole thing has got me spooked. To be honest, this kind of thing has been going on my whole life, and now that they tell me there are others who have made contact with the beasties and with whom I have to revisit all of it, I don't feel more relieved, but less."

He looked at her and asked, "Where are you from?"

"Philadelphia, originally."

"Why do you call them 'beasties'?"

She raised her eyebrows. Lees called everyone back to order.

"That was a short lunch break," Haleh said.

"Alright," Lees said. "We've had quite a morning. I can say that each of us in this room is now convinced of the seriousness of the phenomena around and within us. We will have, with Dr. Huntsman's expertise and Ranger White Wolf's guidance, a path forward for exploration. We will do this safely, prudently. Mrs. Conque, Mr. MacDuff, please be assured of our earnest desire and expectation that your spouses will be well-treated. And that holds for the three other scouts here. But the more we press forward, the more ready we will be for what comes next."

"And what comes next?" Lucy asked. She had regained her spark. "Why did Jody talk about 'other intelligences' before, right before the vision?"

Jody had assumed that she and the others had had the same conversation that he'd had with Wepwawet a week earlier.

Lucy reached across the table, pointed a finger, and continued, "I made it perfectly clear that I have no interest or desire in making deliberate contact with demons."

Jody turned sharply toward her.

"Mrs. MacDuff," Huntsman said, "we've also made it clear that we are avoiding that kind of language. Calling the entities who are active on our light waves 'demons' or 'aliens' only obfuscates the issue. Those are mythological terms and even moral terms, and we want to avoid them."

"You weren't there," Lucy yelled. Then, more calmly, she continued, "You call them whatever you want, but I know evil when I feel it."

That was the thing Jody did *not* feel at the bar in Illinois. Strange but not evil, not devilish. The bikers on the road in Iowa, as terrifying as they were, seemed only a human evil.

"That's a subjective feeling with regard to the unknown, what you call evil. We feel that in an alley or in a darkened room," Huntsman said. "It's simple fear."

White Wolf coughed. "Lucy, we all know you've been through some very trying situations. If you would, just entertain for us the notion that we have before us a spectrum, an array of entities of various kinds, from the human to the mythical."

"And the robotic," Jody said. "Anyway, that was my experience in Illinois and in a dream I've had."

"Alright," Lees said. "Alright. Let's focus. Mr. Conque, Mrs. MacDuff, please keep in mind that we're not here to study aliens or UFOs. The Air Force bungled that one up back in the sixties, and the Navy's been trying to make up lost ground ever since. And we're definitely not here to study demons. The Church," he gestured toward Jody, "has got that covered, though I know the CIA has turned their interest toward our work. Our interest lies elsewhere."

"That's right," Huntsman said calmly. "Using words like 'demons' and 'aliens' doesn't help us. Those words groom us to receive what is happening in a certain way. It has been our work, over the past few decades, to discern if what is happening is a preparation for invasion or warfare of some kind. It has been my contention that if we treat these realities as aliens, then that is what they'll be. And if we treat them as demons, then that is what they'll be. And we imagine that we already have weapons against each of those categories of entity. And so, happy to have our minds divided on the issue, whatever this is will slip right through our lines."

"Indeed," Lees said. "So what is absolutely vital for us is to avoid entering into this situation with any kind of preconceived notions of what we'll find. That goes for you, too, Mr. Conque. Leaving religion out of this is not meant to deny your faith. It's a means of leaving no corner of the room for these entities to hide in, no folds of the mind, no preconceptions they can use as a defense."

"And yet you see," Lucy said, "already, just today, we've already gone to a place I've been. Why am I here, bringing all of my experiences to bear?"

"Firstly," Huntsman said, "because some of those earlier encounters were experienced simultaneously by those around you, your husband included. Second. . . ." Huntsman turned to Lees and to Agent Seuss, each of whom gave a slight shake of the head.

Lees spoke. "We'll leave it at that."

***

Later that afternoon, Jody and Haleh walked up the driveway toward the house. The ride had been spent in silence. On the front stoop, before opening the door, Haleh pulled on her face as if to recompose herself.

"It's alright," Jody said. "Let's just take a minute." He held her. She was shivering now, whereas she had been stoic all the way home. "At least, this way, Huntsman and Lees know they're up against something bigger than themselves. That evil does exist. That we have to call it for what it is before we can face it."

"I hope they learn that," Haleh said.

They walked in through the front door, finding the house empty and gray except for something bubbling on the stove. Danny appeared before one of the sliding doors, tongs in his hand.

"How much crazier could it be than your uncle, barbecuing again?" Jody asked.

She laughed a little and saw Claire's silhouette hopping toward her. Haleh started but walked forward and lifted Claire into her arms. Walking onto the back deck, her daughter in her arms, she began crying. Danny and Cynthia looked at Jody. He saw his own tense, frightful expression reflected in their faces. He turned and kissed Claire.

"Why are you crying, Mommy?" she said, trying to pull her head back. Haleh sat down on one of the redwood benches, still holding Claire against her. "Are you sad?"

"Yes, sweetie, I'm sad. Mommy's sad."

"Why? Did you get hurt?"

"No, sweetie," she said softly. "Not me. Hopefully no one."

Cynthia walked up to Haleh with a glass of wine from which Haleh drank freely. then laughed. "Maybe Mommy's just being silly."

Jody looked down at her, trying to make his eyes say, *No, you're not*, and stroked her hair.

Claire put her hands to her mother's face and rubbed

her cheeks and forehead as if to feel their shape, to reshape them, to recreate them.

"Brr. It's cold out here. It's chilly already. It's only the middle of September. Why are we out here?"

"I like barbecuing in the chill," Danny replied. "It feels somehow cozier than being inside."

"Well, I am fuh-reezing. I'm going inside." She rose and took Claire inside with her.

"It *is* a bit chilly," Cynthia said and followed her in. Jody stayed with Danny.

"Everything...copasetic?" Danny asked.

Jody said nothing at first, warming his hands over the grilling sausages. He stared down at the roasting flesh and turned over a little inside. "Uh...."

"You can't talk about it."

"Not really."

"I get it. That's fine." The two stared at the sausages for a while with the flames flickering between the gray coals below. "They must have laid it on pretty thick."

Jody breathed in heavily through his nose. "Let's put it that way. Let's just say this whole thing runs a lot deeper than we realized or wanted."

"The goddamn moon exploded, Jody. Now it's veering off course. What else could be going on?"

"You tell me," Jody said flatly. "You people invented the end of the world, with your *daevas* and *yazatas* and eons."

Danny said nothing but flipped the sausages. "Yeah, I guess so."

Jody looked up and saw Danny already somewhere else in his mind. "Oh. Hey, where's that wine?"

"Just there on the table."

"I have to go in for a glass."

"Well, hey, look. The sausages are almost done. Maybe just help me carry these in."

By that, Danny meant for Jody to open the sliding door, which he did, the bottle of wine sharing his other hand with the cane. The three girls were giggling about something in front of the fireplace, which Cynthia had started. Haleh looked up with a sad smile, telling Jody she would be fine.

**

After dinner and one or two more glasses of wine, Jody and Haleh took Claire upstairs to bed. They stayed with her, reading stories to her and talking to each other in low voices, a thing that soothed their daughter. They leaned against towers of books, only a nightlight shining low in the room.

"Maybe it's time to go home," Jody said.

Haleh breathed out sharply.

"I'm serious. Our old bungalow's pretty sturdy. It took the earthquake in '89 like a champ, the old owners said."

"You said that they said to stay away from the coasts."

"I know. But you see now how deep this goes. Maybe it doesn't matter where we are. I just want to be in our own home."

"To think of those horrible things you saw," she sobbed. "Happening right under our noses."

"Hey, hey," he soothed, putting his arm around her. She lay her head on his shoulder. "I don't know. I'm sort of with Huntsman on this one. No one else saw the bodies but me, and I only saw them because I saw the wood grain of the table. It could be like she said, some other reality being interpreted by my mind."

"Still, it means there is *something* terrible going on."

"Maybe so. But you know what? Maybe the less we think about it, the better. Maybe she's right, you know, like we're sort of imagining these things into existence. Or into a certain kind of existence."

Haleh pulled her head up. "It would be nice to be near my parents. And Cyrus."

"It would be nice to be in our own home."

"But you probably have to keep holding hands with that woman for a while."

"Stop."

"What? That's what you do."

"You make it sound like, I don't know.... You know it's nothing like that. To be honest, she feels more like a sister to me."

"But you have some connection with her."

"Formed through shared experiences of parental neglect or whatever. There are any number of people out there I could recognize like that, just by the sight of them."

"How does that work, that connection? We don't have visions when we hold hands."

"No, my love. We have babies."

They gazed upon Claire, who slept peacefully, for a while.

"How much longer?" Haleh asked.

"I don't know. Till they get the intel they want. We've got our own milestone, anyway. We get the Mickey into NASA hands, I think we're done here. October thirtieth. That's our deadline. After that, the Navy can chase us down in Walnut Creek."

The house that Danny and Cynthia continued to call their log cabin in the woods, and which was, in terms of reality and realty, a contemporary, timber-frame home in a manicured neighborhood, began to vibrate with the anxious energy of its five occupants. This was the energy Jody knew from the locker room in high school. He knew a word for it from his theological studies: agony. Whenever he was out with Wepwawet, at church with Claire, or helping out the household by going out to shop when no one else felt safe to do so—the security detail that Lees had tasked still followed him around—he felt this agony in the streets and shopping centers. Those waves of fear either peaked in fits of anger and frustration over an increasingly limited supply of consumer goods, or they cancelled out in helpful, humble smiles and small, mild tears of compassion. The agony increased after the last quarter moon on September 20, when professional and amateur astronomers noticed the moon's orbit reaching more noticeably toward the sun.

Wepwawet met once per week, usually on a Monday. This made it possible for Jody to develop a stable routine for himself and the Shamshiri household with their great project, the Mickey. Haleh, who no longer joined Jody on his trips to Denver, and who served many functions at Scimitech under the title of officer manager, began demonstrating to Cynthia why she had earned the nickname "Defcon-3 with a Smile." Her job was simply to keep everyone on task, and she did so with an insistence that her father, Sunny, had often called "sweet and severe."

Jody's feelings rose and fell in waves as well. He was at some moments excited to be participating in a great moment in Earth's history and all the more to have some special role in its events. His work with Wepwawet, however, despite the great first vision he had had with Lucy, seemed to bear little fruit. It had only been a few weeks, however. He knew that human beings, unlike in the movies, did not turn over stones overnight, no matter how well funded and equipped they were.

Among Wepwawet's five scouts, Jody and Lucy retained the strongest grip on the other realm. His physical contact with Lucy almost always completed a circuit that turned on some kind of mental movie projector, and White Wolf needed less and less often to motor them around the more Lucy took steps to let Jody inside. He thought he knew why his priesthood had repulsed her at first, and this was a thing he could never say. While Lucy did see, feel, smell, and hear her surroundings, Jody was the only one to see specific objects. What Jody saw seemed colored, if not formed, by the world of objects around him: the conference room table, a forest full of trees, an open field of wispy grass waving in the wind. Each of the natural patterns these objects held within themselves or as a group—tree bark and pine needles, stalks and heads of grass—formed arrays in his sight of some terrifying manipulation of human masses. Despite all of this, very little specific, "actionable" intelligence emerged.

There were entities that stood out from the patterns and arrays he saw, but these only moved about in Jody's peripheral vision. Their presence Lucy could confirm by what she was feeling, which was not always fear. To Huntsman's ongoing frustration, Lucy called these "good" or "bad." They eventually agreed on the language of "friend" and "foe" as being the least unhelpful. Lees, Huntsman, and White Wolf furthermore resisted locating these entities on different animal and spiritual planes.

Agony is the anxiety an athlete feels before a match, and it ends when he enters the arena and sees his opponent face to face. Jody thought he felt awash in humanity's great relief when, on September 27, at the new moon, the news came through that the moon was rounding its way back to Earth. The longest week in everyone's life had become just that: by lunar standards, an extra half day. The moon would reach the first quarter position on October 4, exactly one day late, its half-orbit extended by a factor of ninety-six from its fifteen minutes' tardiness the month before. Jody tried to drown out the rational voice, the voice that calculated the fear that if the next new moon position saw its orbit drawn out by another factor of ninety-six, the odds were that the moon would no longer orbit the Earth at all.

***

"How was it today?" Haleh asked after Jody had come home from a rare late evening session. It was October 13, the new full moon. "You look worn out."

Jody stretched as best he could, leaning forward against the couch. "Just another grueling day of dueling with the dark forces of the universe." He knelt down to kiss Claire, who was watching a video on a tablet.

"Hm."

"Hm? What's that?"

"Nothing," she said. "What do you want for dinner? We're running out of normal food. Everyone here's just been picking at leftovers."

"*Touski* it is," he said.

From the dining table, where he ate cold chicken and rice, Jody gazed at Haleh, who, though she had a coffee-table book in her lap, was watching whatever video Claire had on the tablet with her on the floor. Some words came to him, which he recited loudly enough for Haleh to hear:

> *What child of ours would spend her hours*
> *Learning from the old?*
> *Or find a friend within a den*
> *Of storybookèd souls?*

"Hm," Haleh said, nodding her approval.

"It just comes now, a little bit. Nothing special. Maybe it doesn't have to be everything each time. Just a little taste, you know, a little play."

"You know," Danny said, walking out of his study toward the kitchen, "I wrote some poetry once."

Jody blushed.

"You want to hear it?"

"Sure," Haleh said.

Danny raised his head, closed his eyes, put his hand to his heart, and recited:

only two things I can find, worthy to be soaked in wine
stale bread
existential dread

"I wasn't even stoned when I wrote that."

Jody finished his dinner, filled two glasses with wine, and carried them, one by one, to the couch.

"What are you reading?" he asked Haleh, sitting beside her.

"Nothing, just some book on ancient cities," she huffed. "I'm tired of reading online."

"Anything good inside?"

"I don't know. It's hard to imagine all that time going by, thousands of years, on a single site. How many lives, come and gone?"

He rested his arm behind her head on the couch. "Imagine all the wars and battles fought, totally forgotten now."

"And which seemed so necessary at the time."

He studied an illustration of some imagined Mesopotamian woman leaning over a pot in a courtyard. Haleh began nodding.

"You're sleepy."

She yawned and stretched.

"It's been getting earlier and earlier with you."

Turn on the TV, bro. Cam's rare phone call alarmed Jody. *It's getting serious this time.*

He clicked on the television. A news channel was already on.

A field reporter was speaking:

That's right, Brett. Authorities from India and Pakistan each strongly deny initiating any action, blaming the other side for rekindling hostilities here in Kashmir. And talking to some Pakistani officers on the ground, many of them describe a moment of great confusion.

A Pakistani army officer spoke:

Indian forces sought to flank us overnight, but we were ready and chased them back into the shadows. Let this be a lesson to them. We do not want to turn our energies toward this battlefield, when so much of our resources need to go toward stabilizing our civilian population. But we will not relinquish our rightful hold on this land.

The reporter continued:

Indian forces deny any sort of maneuver, and suggest, and I quote, "They are chasing their own shadows, shadows of their own design. They sleep in fear of our army and awoke to their own nightmare."

The anchor came on and spoke with two experts, one of whom said:

I think what we're seeing here, Brett, is a phenomenon reported across the world since the moondark. People have been waking up to specters and ghosts in great numbers. We know the government has been casting this aside as rumors and conspiracy theories, but perhaps it's time that President Palmer and her team start looking into these spectral phenomena that everyone is seeing. I mean, look, these Pakistani soldiers literally woke up to find themselves out in the battlefield, fighting something that disappeared as soon as, in their words, they began to wake up. This is not normal, Brett, and this is going on everywhere. It's time we all woke up before it's too late.

"That's spooky," Cynthia said. She had snuck into the living room unnoticed.

"Yeah," Haleh whispered.

Once the reporting turned to more mundane things, gas shortages and a yacht missing at sea, Cynthia withdrew to her bedroom, and Jody turned off the television.

"What do we do now?" Haleh asked.

Jody breathed in and out deeply, then said, "All the things we've learned, I suppose. I don't know what else there is to do. Good thoughts, good words, good deeds, you know."

"And then what, just watch while all these things go on around us?"

"We help the Navy. I'm sure Palmer knows about our work. Then, here, we protect our little family."

"How?" she looked down.

"Well," he began, "Claire and I are baptized."

Haleh stared at his neck. Jody felt strong when she did this, and he thought he might win her over to his faith this time. "I don't.... It doesn't seem right to do that out of fear, like walking backward into faith."

He gazed at her. "No, you're right. But tell me, hon. What do you really believe is going on? You brought up the sacred mountain before."

She still gazed at his neck. "I believe in you, babe. I know you're going to do the right thing."

She buried her face in his neck, and he stroked her

hair. He prayed for strength and wisdom. Haleh quickly fell asleep.

28

A few days later, Jody found himself on the shore of a lake in the mountains. Huntsman had escorted him there with Lucy and the other scouts under willing blindfold, wearing headphones blaring Bach's "The Goldberg Variations." One erudite member of the team had made a comment about how that was fitting for the arrays Jody had been seeing, but Jody missed the reference and found the music itself unsettlingly complicated. He enjoyed the silence of the sky around him now. It was chillier in the mountains, which were dry, rocky, and dotted with pine trees. White Wolf was talking to two men who were fishing, and they soon left.

Not long after this, while basking in the mid-October sky, Lees arrived in a car driving too fast for the tight, dusty road. Seuss was with him. They called Huntsman and White Wolf over to the other side of the car. Jody and the scouts could tell, by their gesticulation, that all was not well. The four heads came over and began preparing the scouts for the day's experiments: remote vision under water. The musicologist among them protested her aquaphobia, but the others, scouts especially, insisted that this fear should give her mind's eye all the more reach.

When Lees faced Jody to help him with his snorkeling gear, Jody asked, "What was that all about? Are we in trouble?"

Lees's eyes, still a few inches above Jody's, seemed to be trying to maintain their usual, genteel confidence. "You know how it is," he said. "Deadlines and so on. Not everyone is convinced we'll get anywhere with this before it's too late."

Jody, who shared this conviction, said, "Is this about Kashmir?"

"Yes and no," Lees said, then put on a smile, gave Jody's gear one last check, and left.

"Big Momma must not be happy," Lucy said once Lees was out of earshot.

"You think she even knows what we're doing?"

"Well, someone at the White House does. The Secret Service is watching all of our meetings in Denver."

"How do you know that?"

"Their seal is on the video screen. You never noticed that?"

Jody turned and pulled in his chin, puzzled. "I thought that was the FBI seal."

"Ugh," Lucy replied. "And you're the one seeing things. Look more carefully, champ."

After all had made their dives, held hands in every permutation their number permitted, and endured every kind of electrical stimulation Huntsman and Black Mare could contrive, the results came back very clearly. No one saw anything under the water except toward the surface. The sharp-eared woman said she heard the hum of several motors, which only proved her natural abilities, as the lake was behind a small hydroelectric dam, a thing no one could have seen from where they were.

Afterward, they had a pleasant picnic on the shore, during which time Lees and Huntsman continued to mask their frustration over something. White Wolf, for his part, lay back to take in the sun next to Black Mare. Jody summoned the courage to ask, "Excuse me, Ranger White Wolf?"

"Yes?" came the response, without an opening of eyes.

"Yeah, no, I was just wondering, now that we've all known each other for a while, maybe you might tell me how you and Black Mare got your names. I mean, Native Americans, right, the names are earned or assigned or...?"

"Melanie will be happy to tell you how she got her name."

Jody looked over at Black Mare. He could see her subduing a cringe. She turned to him and said, "Black Mare is what the name Melanie means. That's the name my mother gave me before I was born."

"Melody," White Wolf said. "Your mother named you Melody DeSoto." He turned to Jody. "My little sister, Melody's mother, died in childbirth."

Jody did not ask about the father. "And Black Mare?"

White Wolf continued, "Well, *someone* began mispronouncing her own name, deliberately or not, and took to calling herself Melanie."

Black Mare poked at her uncle. "That someone was actually my grandmother, who raised me. I like Melanie better, anyway. Melody sounds like the name of a str—"

"Melody is the name my sainted sister gave you. But we

called you Black Mare to honor your desire to be called Melanie. It is fitting, nonetheless, with that long mane of yours."

"And you?" she asked her uncle. "How did you get 'White Wolf'? You've never told me the real story."

"I was born Black Feather because I had a little tuft of black hair shooting from the top of my head when I was born. As for White Wolf . . .." He turned to Jody and opened the canyons of his eyes. With a certain intensity, he continued, "That's a story for another time."

***

The group reconvened in Denver for a debriefing. In Conference Room A, Jody noticed that the seal on the screen was indeed of the Secret Service. Seuss had gone ahead of them to set up and was pacing nervously in the room when they arrived. He made gestures to everyone to keep down the banter and asked them quickly to take their seats, saying, "She'll be on any minute now."

When President Palmer appeared on the screen, the first thing Jody thought was that his head was a curly, dry mop of hair, unbrushed since his dives. The second thing he thought was that, at least in person, Deborah Palmer looked as if she had aged ten years in the past two months. Palmer heard from the two other working groups on the screen, then Lees and Huntsman made their report.

"So you're saying that water is a barrier to this second sight? Can that help us?" Palmer asked.

"That is our initial observation, Madame President," Lees said. "It may also explain why so much UAP activity has occurred over water, that they're hiding behind it as well. We might start developing ways to see without being seen. The Navy's good at that, ma'am. That's the secret to submarine warfare."

"Uh huh," she said. "Well, in my experience, you can't see without being seen. You gotta know people are looking at you, and you take command of that quickly. I call that 'reputation control.' In our case, a show of force. Best deterrent against enemy engagement. Some people say all this has been going on since we developed nukes back in the forties. Well, let's think about how we might use that fear to our advantage."

Jody wondered why he and the others should be privy to such a conversation.

"We have to think quickly," Palmer continued. "Time's running out. I know you know we're running a day ahead on last quarter. That means the moon's speeding up toward the dark mountain. Things are gonna get unstable in our population pretty quickly when they hear that they're seeing the moon in orbit for the last time in a few days. I want to know what you people can produce by then. Give us something to show. Put on a demonstration."

Lees answered, "Ma'am, it doesn't quite—"

"Which one of them is the priest?" she interrupted.

Jody thought of his beach bum hair. He timidly raised his hand.

"There you are. What do you say, pastor? Is God on our side?"

Jody froze. He did not want to turn against Lees and Huntsman by betraying his mixed feelings about their work. "I would say, Madame President," he coughed nervously, "that if God is on our side, who can be against us?"

"Uh huh," she said. He felt relieved, but she continued, "Pastor, why don't you give us all here a special blessing. That won't bother anyone here, a little prayer, will it? Good."

In the space of one second, Jody measured out the balance of his next actions. He fixed on Huntsman's face, which showed almost nothing. She was somewhere else again. He was not allowed to act publicly as a priest without permission. He could give a simple blessing, but this Southern Baptist would not go for that. She wanted words, the very thing he was not supposed to give. He looked up at the president's face, which nearly filled the wall like a mother hovering over her baby, her eyes closed in expectation. Easier to ask forgiveness than permission. He opened wide his arms and said, "Lord, we just ask your special blessing and protection on our work. Bless our president and all of us here. Defend us against the work of evil. And—"

"Amen," Palmer said abruptly. "Y'all hear that? Miramar? Norfolk? That's what we need right now. Faith in a higher power. 'Cause I'm starting to lose faith in what I see below. Make us see what we're up against. The Chinese are up to something. There's a good chance they did Kashmir. I want to make them know they're playing with fire. I want to be prepared for Moonbright and Bridgewater." Lees and Huntsman started, as if Palmer had just revealed what she should not have. Jody knew what Moonbright was—the NASA project to send the Mickey and other equipment to the moon. He had never heard of Project Bridgewater.

After a string of promises and formalities from Lees and the other working group heads, the president disconnected. The dozen members of Wepwawet Mountain West sat in silence. None knew yet exactly what they had been seeing, let alone how to make it visible to the world.

***

The silence that ensued after Palmer's videoconference, though it lasted only a few seconds, formed a deep abyss. Jody watched Lees and Huntsman, each lost in thought. He looked at the other scouts, who, like him, seemed to be searching each other for ways to help. For the first time, he began to feel real sympathy for Lees and Huntsman. They were like the siblings who grew closer after a tirade from their parents, or "Big Momma" in this case.

Agent Valasca leaned forward on the conference room table and gently coughed. Lees looked in his direction.

"There is another way we could go with this," Valasca said.

Huntsman interrupted, "Absolutely not."

"Just consider it as a tactic. If you cannot properly identify who your enemy is, create one out of the chaos."

"Yes, that sounds just like how the CIA operates," White Wolf said. Jody thought he had read his mind.

"Hear him out," Lees replied. "We're running out of time."

"That's just Palmer talking. We can keep working as along as the Earth is spinning," Huntsman said.

Lees answered, "I'm not worried about funding, not right now. I'm talking about getting ahead of this thing before it's too late."

Jody wondered where this was going and saw this in the faces of the other scouts.

"I agree with Dr. Huntsman," White Wolf said. "Agent Valasca is supposed to be just an observer here."

Valasca pulled himself forward a little and said, "I am here as a liaison with foreign entities. We might learn something from them."

"I don't like the way you say 'foreign entities,'" White Wolf said. His eyes became obsidian daggers, pointed at Valasca.

"Everyone, let's settle down," Lees said. "Let's break for the day. Dr. Valasca, we'll speak about your suggestion privately."

White Wolf stood up. "I know what you have in mind. You're opening Pandora's box, precisely the thing we're trying to keep closed." Black Mare looked up at him as if surprised by his change in attitude.

Jody turned to Lucy, whose face had turned ashen. When she caught him looking, she turned away.

Lees stood and stretched. "That's it, everyone. Go home and rest. Valasca, Doris, let's hang around a bit. Agent Seuss, White Wolf." He pointed his nose at Black Mare.

"Melanie, go home, get some rest," White Wolf said.

She barely protested and began packing up her equipment.

Jody struggled to stand, his leg stiff from the swim. Lucy, next to him, helped him up. Jody caught her eyes, and though she began to turn away, she turned back to him. Her eyes seemed to speak what she knew was coming. He saw fear and pleading.

29

Around noon on October 20, a few days after his trials at the lake and meeting with President Palmer, Jody stood in front of the Shamshiri house with Haleh, Claire, Danny, and Cynthia, staring westward toward the Rockies. Somewhere behind those edges of jagged earth the last quarter moon was setting almost exactly one day early. Even the most sober minds in the media had speculated that this could be the last moment of the moon's orbit around Earth. The moon was accelerating on an elliptical path that most models predicted would not see the moon swing fully back to the first quarter position. After that, no one really knew. It might swing like a pendulum for a while before resting between Earth and sun in syzygy. Watching reporters and laymen learn to repeat this word provided little but much needed levity in a world wrapped in fear that the moon, with the tides that it provided, the currents that those tides helped set in motion, and the weather that the currents anchored to predictable patterns, would soon be lost forever. Jody stood behind Haleh and Claire, one hand on his wife's shoulder, the other on his owl-tip cane. Claire's left hand rested on top of her father's right on that cane.

"Are we okay, Daddy?" she asked.

"Yes, Claire Bear. Everything's fine. We're all going to be just fine."

Claire turned a concerned brow toward the mountains.

"You know what, sweetie? Take your fingers like this and pinch the mountain." Jody showed her. "You see? No moon or mountain are too big when you stand far enough away."

For a quiet minute, each member of the little family took turns pinching the mountains.

A word came to Jody he felt no impulse to write down: *You can preach a pocket-sized God by pinching Him between your fingers, too.*

Danny breathed in audibly through his nose. "I guess that's it! Let's have breakfast."

"It's 12:17, dear," Cynthia puzzled.

"And I want breakfast." With that, he went inside.

Danny did make breakfast, a feast of omelets, English muffins, bacon, and mimosas, a banquet all thought and felt complete as they sat on the couches afterward until there emerged, from the oven, a tray of cinnamon rolls, hot and ready for glazing. "Why not make this a holiday?" Danny said. Claire's eyes grew into wide, bright stars, as did Haleh's.

Danny, who had been staring off into some distance at the table, began speaking. "You know, when Sunny and I were young, some time at CalTech, we went to get our IQs tested. It was the thing to do. Everyone would boast of their IQs, you know, who was the smartest one out there. We were headed into the test, somewhere on campus, I don't remember, and you know how it is with twins, we've always, or at least often, felt each other's feelings. Just a few steps from the door, we sort of slowed down and looked at each other. It was more like seeing each other reflected in the glass doors. There we were, two brothers, two twins, on the same path, vying to see who was smarter. And, honestly, I don't remember who said it, me or him, but we said, 'Let's not do this.' That was it. We both understood. We've never had our IQs measured, not to this day. And it's taken decades, but I think we recognize our own strengths and weaknesses. He's a better businessman, maybe a more disciplined scientist, too. I think I have the broad ideas, the insights that he would never have. But he makes them work. He reins me in, but I loosen him up in the process. I don't know why I mention this. I guess to say that I already feel what he's feeling. Somehow, it's over. We've done what we can. Whatever comes next for this world is for someone else."

Haleh, who had been gazing at her uncle ponderously, said almost angrily, "Don't say that, Uncle Danny. You two are both brilliant, exactly what this crazy, uncertain world needs right now."

"Look," he said without looking up, "it's like being a sharp knife. We say that, right? We always heard that— 'You're both so sharp'—the Iranian twin geniuses. The sharp Shamshiri's. But it's always the sharp edge of the knife that wears down first. It does its work for a while, then it needs to be resharpened. That's somebody else, now, whoever the universe, or God if you like, has in mind."

"You're both still relatively young," Jody said, noticing that Cynthia said nothing.

"We're sixty-five. That used to be retirement age." He

breathed in sharply and exhaled. "I don't know. Maybe it's time to ride the wave home instead of surfing it, fighting it. We've got means. We can enjoy this experience, this once-in-a-humanity experience. It's not like in the movies, where you keep fighting the universe until humanity wins. I'm tired. I can't keep up this pace much longer. But maybe that's just today. Let's see what tomorrow brings."

Jody watched Cynthia, who seemed to be silently agreeing.

"What have we got to prove now?" Cynthia said, gazing at Claire. "Maybe my husband is right. We'll get the Mickey to the moon, sure enough. Then it seems we should just be taking care of each other."

Jody looked at Haleh, who mirrored his feeling, insufficiency before the forces at work around them. He knew why she was angry with her uncle, and he felt it, too. Only by pressing forward at full speed could they sustain their hope. Hope meant that they were fully alive to the challenge.

"We used to call cinnamon rolls 'nun's farts,'" Jody said. "Another Canuck thing."

Danny smirked, and Haleh rolled her eyes, but the more Cynthia tried to contain the spurts of laughter coming from her mouth, the more it sprayed forth. This sent Claire into a fit of mimetic laughter, which infected the rest of the house. There they sat on the couches, bloated and tired, nodding into naps occasionally interrupted by laughter.

30

The members of the makeshift family of five at Danny and Cynthia's house were either asleep or lethargic on the couches in the living room, scrolling through phones for news or texting with those not there. Claire resumed her drawing of sunflowers. Jody had not heard from Terr or Sam and pondered calling them on this momentous day, possibly the last of the moon's orbit.

Between the surges of Danny's snoring, a similar sound echoed outside and grew louder. The rumbling of a motorcycle sent a small spasm to Jody's bloated stomach, and he fixated on the terrible scene in Iowa more than on Wyoming. He thought of the crash often, but this did not bother him as much as what he had met in Iowa. He wondered if it were because, in Wyoming, he had felt he had more control.

The motorcycle slowed to a stop. Cynthia looked up at Haleh and Jody, who had taken his cane in hand and rested his chin on the owl, staring into the sofa where Danny lay. Jody hoped that the bike had stopped at a neighbor's house, but he knew, instinctively, that this was not the case. The doorbell rang.

Jody looked up at Cynthia, and she must have caught

the boyish fear in his eyes, for she stood up and straightened her shirt and shoulders. She looked at the door and took a step but turned around and shook her husband awake. He must have caught a little fear in her glance, for he awoke more quickly than Jody ever remembered him doing. The doorbell rang again.

Jody stood up. "Look, I guess I'm the only one here with weapons against this, if need be. Maybe it's nothing."

Cynthia said, "You look through the eyehole and tell us what you see. If it looks bad, we'll just ignore it."

"Like a vampire," Danny said. "If you don't invite it in, it can't come in."

Demons work the same way, Jody thought. He hobbled toward the front door. Haleh stood up and motioned automatically for Claire to stay back, but she was focused on her drawing. Danny and Cynthia followed Jody.

Jody looked through the eyehole and turned to the side a little, perplexed. He glanced at Danny and Cynthia and said, "I think it's alright."

He opened the door, and Cynthia grabbed his arm ineffectually. Jody looked up and down at the man, a little silhouetted from the sun.

"Good afternoon, Jody," Kai said. "I hope I'm not bothering you. I was in the neighborhood, as they say, and thought we might catch up a little, if you don't mind."

"How did you find me here?" Jody asked.

"We have a mutual friend, as it turns out. You've been working with little Dorsina for a couple months on her project. She thought you wouldn't mind if I stopped by."

"Are you referring to—To whom are you referring?"

"To Doris Huntsman, my niece."

Jody remembered the subtle but unbreakable smile she had given when he had mentioned Kai's name. "Well, alright, then. If it's alright with my hosts here, of course."

"Of course." Kai looked left and right behind Jody. "Ma'am, sir, my name is Kai. Kai Adamson."

"Nice to meet you," Cynthia said. "My name is Cynthia, and this is Danny, my husband."

"Cynthia, Danny," Kai repeated. "It's a pleasure."

"Cynthia, Danny," Jody said, "I met Kai on the road back in Nebraska, along with his brother, Av. Where's Av?"

"Oh, it's hard to keep my brother around for too long. The world's his pastureland."

The three of them and Kai gazed at each other briefly in silence. "Well, won't you come in then?" Jody said. He backed up to let Kai enter but soon met the stiff bodies of Danny and Cynthia. They budged, and the four walked haltingly into the living room. "Haleh, honey, this is the man Kai I told you about. Kai, this is my wife, Haleh."

"It's nice to meet you, ma'am," Kai said and shook Haleh's hand. Her eyes studied him quickly.

"On the floor there is my daughter, Claire. Claire, honey, get up and say hello."

Kai bent his head to see Claire walking confidently toward him. When she drew near, he studied her for a moment then started a little and smiled. "You must be Claire. Your father has told me a lot about you." He bowed slightly.

Claire smiled bashfully and half-hid her face behind her mother's hip.

"Would you like anything to drink?" Cynthia asked, gripping the top of the couch.

"A little water would be wonderful, thank you," Kai said.

"I'll get it," Jody said. Cynthia followed him into the kitchen and poured the water herself. Jody motioned to her, and, with the glass in her hands, he blessed it. She raised a curious eyebrow. Cynthia led the way, and Jody followed.

"Ah," Kai said after drinking. "Thank you kindly."

"So," Jody said, somewhat relieved that Kai had not burst into hellish flames upon drinking holy water, "what have you been up to these past couple of months?"

"Oh, this and that. You know, your crash in Wyoming has become something of local legend. As with all legends, the facts become mingled with magic and mystery. But based on what Dorsina tells me, maybe that's not the case here."

"She's been telling you about our work?"

"Not with any specifics, of course, you know, nothing she can't say. If you don't mind, let me admit that I've been doing a little of my own research on you and the others here. I'll just go ahead and lay it out on the table. Cynthia, you've made quite a contribution to our understanding of the orbital mechanics of asteroids. Are you deeply involved with questions about the moon these days?"

"Oh, thank you. Well, there's so much that's new, very few data points to work with. Our team at the Center for Astrodynamics Research has been working nonstop, of course, but...." She fixed the hair behind her ear. Everyone else in the room knew that a younger cohort, out to make a name for itself, had been taking advantage of her decision to work from home to draw her further and further out of the loop, forgetting to invite her to meetings and declining to share data. "We're doing what we can."

"I bet it's hard to keep up for anyone," Kai said. "But you all are really at the cutting edge at Scimitech, if you'll pardon the pun."

"I'll welcome the pun," Danny said. "Thank you. Yeah, we were set to send our product to asteroid 14564 later this winter, but as it turns out, we were in the right place at the right time to get it ready to study the new lunar conditions."

Kai turned to Claire and said, "I have to say, your little girl reminds me of someone I once knew. So much so, it's uncanny."

"Who's that?" Haleh asked, leaning forward with her elbows on her legs. She seemed mesmerized by Kai's eyes.

"The daughter-in-law of a friend, someone who helped me out once upon a time. It's not in her coloring so much as her general bearing. Maybe it's those eyes. She just watches, taking it all in."

"Yes, she does," Haleh said, turning proudly to her daughter, seated regally between her parents, each hand on one of their thighs.

Claire pulled her mother's sweater down to whisper in her ear.

Haleh replied softly, "That's a nice idea, Claire, but I'm sure it's stale by now. We don't give our guests stale food."

As Claire turned forward, disappointed, Kai said, "What was that? I would be happy to honor Claire's hospitality, whatever it is."

"It's just a cinnamon bun we had for brunch," Haleh replied apologetically.

"A few seconds in the microwave will help that," Danny said. "Maybe we could make some coffee at the same time." His eyes darted between Cynthia and Haleh.

"Right," Haleh said. "Let's go, Claire."

When they had gone, Kai said, "And you and your brother, Mehrzad, you're from Iran originally?"

"Yep. Raised in Tehran, but we came over as teenagers in the early seventies. We were also in the right place at the right time then, too. We came up through the special schools set up in Iran for Zarathushti, under more amenable regimes and friendlier with the US. Then high school in LA, but we predated the whole Tehrangeles scene. Sunny's wife came over in the early eighties. The rest, you can say, is history, which means you can find it on the Internet."

"Ah, well, *Az didane shoma khoshhal shodam.*" Jody knew these words as "It is nice to meet you," one of the phrases he had managed to memorize in his conversations with Leila. Sunny had no patience as a teacher.

Danny cocked his head. "You speak Persian?"

"Oh, I've just got a few phrases. I did a little journalistic work there a while back."

The air grew a little heavy as Jody and Danny wondered at their guest.

"But your name is Danyal, I saw," Kai said. "After the prophet Daniel. He's enshrined in Shush, you know."

"I do know," Danny said. "That is, in fact, where I was born. My father's work took the family there briefly. Very ancient city. They wanted to signify their time there in some way, so I got the name. They say it's, what, six thousand years old?"

256

Kai rubbed his well-shaved chin. His green eyes seemed to light up as he thought. "Maybe a little older than that, from what I recollect. Just a little east of Eden, if you catch my drift."

Jody thought he was beginning to catch his drift but did not share it aloud.

Danny said, "So, Mr. Adamson, what do you think? Is it aliens?"

"Oh, God," Cynthia said from the kitchen.

Jody jumped in quickly to spare Cynthia further embarrassment. "You and I were talking before about the nature of the universe, electricity and all that, but I don't think we ever got to talking about the moondark itself. What *do* you think caused it? You've been around the world a bit, seen a few things. You seem to have a longer vision of this world than most of us."

"Yes, I suppose I have," Kai replied. "But the knowledge of the world that was once washed away has nearly been regained. I'm left with an intuition that we're not done with whatever's still happening to the moon, not until we pass into a new order of reality."

"What do you mean, 'Until we pass into a new order of reality?'" Jody asked.

At that moment, Haleh followed Claire into the living room. Claire led a little procession with the plate bearing the cinnamon bun like it was a birthday cake. When Kai received it, he smiled at her, which lit Claire's face aglow. Haleh set down a tray with coffee, cream, and sugar and poured each according to their taste.

When Kai finished chewing his first few bites, he said,

"Take this cinnamon bun here. A nice spiral shape. Cynthia could tell us about the spiraling course that the solar system takes through the galaxy. For most of us, we imagine the solar system as a perfectly balanced series of never-ending orbits with the occasional impact from a comet or asteroid. The planets, though, follow the sun through the waters of deep space like ducklings riding in their mother's wake. Their orbits become spirals. That's a new model. Not long ago, we thought the sun, moon, and stars all revolved around the Earth. The sun harnessed by Apollo's horses." He chuckled a little. "But we know now that not even the moon does this, that it really has its own path around the sun. So the model changes, and we enter new ways of thinking, new ways of imagining the cosmos. Then...." He took a bite out of the center of the bun and chewed. "Then this happens, and we learn that there is another order, another level of reality at play, one we never measured because we didn't have the stick to measure it with. So old myths like Hara Berezaiti start to look less mythical. After all, what is a mountain but a confluence of forces?"

Jody looked at Haleh, who smiled.

Kai continued, "And that's what I think our Earth has passed by—an event, a confluence of forces strong enough to separate electromagnetic information from mass-gravity fields. That strange form of light then reached us one moon day later, twenty-five hours."

"But our people rejected the ancient gods," Danny said. "So what are we dealing with up there?"

Kai grew somber. "As I believe I said elsewhere, I

258

wouldn't worry so much about up there." He pointed his nose protectively at Claire.

"Claire, sweetie," Haleh said, "why don't you show Mr. Adamson some of your stuffed animals? Go upstairs and pick out some of the best ones." Claire ran upstairs excitedly. "Don't run!"

Kai continued, "You ask about aliens, and I'll say this. That's a word used in the circumstances of immigration. Aliens are those who come into a land occupied by people like themselves but under different kings and laws and languages. They'll seek to assimilate, to contribute, to share the good of the land. Eventually, they blend in with their hosts, become one people.

"But in our case, we don't see that, do we? No, I'm afraid we have something that is other, that always wants to be other, that can only thrive so long as it is not recognized. And...." His head dropped a little, and he turned to the side, rubbing the back of his neck. "And the moondark may well be the light shining on all of them, on the whole scene. I.... How do I say this? No, my brother has perhaps a better way of expressing all this."

"And what's that?" Jody asked.

"That God has shaken a jar of snakes."

Jody recoiled a little at this.

"I see his rhetoric makes more of an effect," Kai said. "You've had some experience."

"I'll leave Dorsina to tell you all about that," Jody said.

Haleh took Jody's hand.

Kai continued, "I would say that one should be prepared for the eventuality.... My hunch is that soon, I don't know when, the other will run out of space to hide. And when it hits the wall and turns around again, well...I would prefer the darkness at that moment."

***

Jody stood in front of the house with Kai, admiring the Triumph motorcycle parked in the driveway. Claire had appeared quickly to break the dark spell to which Kai and the others were succumbing, bearing an armful of stuffed animals. Danny had re-dubbed Moosie Raccoon as "Mossy Raccoon" for the distinct odor he emitted after months in seclusion. Kai marveled at how a Celtic Frenchman married an Iranian woman, how the far-flung children of Yaphet had found each other again. Jody replied that the only way he could make a Zoroastrian woman marry him was to convince her they were cousins, a joke that sent Danny's eyes rolling and Haleh's hand to her forehead, a joke lost on Cynthia and Claire.

"Here," Kai said. "Let me give you my card in case you need anything. Just give a holler."

Jody held the card up to his face with one hand and read: *Kai N. Adamson. Cultivator.* He raised his eyebrows then looked off toward the west.

Kai continued, "Dorsina has not shared the details of your work, but I know when she is worried. You're about to get involved with something that you perhaps do not understand, something too big for the tools at your disposal. I have intuitions, Father Conque. And mine tell me that we'll do well in your hands. How fast were you going when the train hit you?"

"Two seventy-five," Jody replied.

"That's the speed at which the human nervous system moves electricity. You're a conduit, like many others, my friend. And you've been trained in certain ways, you know the world a certain way, so it takes a certain shape through you. That might be a good thing for us. Remember the old dictum, *Quidquid recipitur ad modum recipientis recipitur.* Keep your hands on the wheel, both hands, and whatever door you open you can close again."

Jody, still holding the card in one hand, flicked it repeatedly against the other thumb, watched Kai ride away, looked west toward the moon hidden behind the mountains, and wondered why he never thought to ask Kai about the other bikers he had met along the road.

PART SIX

SALT, SNOW, AND SKY

31

Jody was enjoying the first helicopter ride of his life. He knew that he and the rest of Wepwawet were entering a dangerous situation. That had become clear to him at the FBI office in Salt Lake City, where he and the others had met Dr. Dora Pandit. This helicopter ride was an extravagance offered to her. She would be serving as the host, somehow, of the encounter they would have out on the Bonneville Salt Flats. Jody tried to set aside, for the moment, the uneasy feeling he had simply in her presence. It was not her British accent or her slovenly bearing. Dr. Pandit seemed not to be the only one occupying her corpulent body, or at least her feline eyes. He opened his own eyes again and looked out over the vast, white flatness of the land. I-80 ran below him; he would once have been on that road. He could have raced the Trans Am on the salt flats safely. The helicopter turned northward, toward the mountains.

Agent Valasca had brought on Dr. Pandit. This was his foreign intelligence contact. Jody had known her as the woman speaking on the television the night of the moonburst, the one whose videos he had been watching at the bar in Illinois. She had been speaking of drawing consciousness into AI machines. It had been little more than a distraction for him back then. He did not understand White Wolf's or Huntsman's vehement resistance to her presence. He trusted them, though, and he trusted Lucy's fear. This woman might be a witch, if that was the right word, summoning demons. Jody did not know if he possessed any power of exorcism, should it come to that.

The helicopter landed, by Jody's estimation and Lees's confirmation, about twenty miles north of I-80. Lees helped Huntsman alight first and then Jody. Below their feet, a flat bed of white salt stretched endlessly to the north and to the south, stopped east and west by low mountains. Valasca, denuded of his tie for the first time in their meetings and wearing large, gold-rimmed sunglasses, looked like he was on vacation. He helped Pandit out of the helicopter, and she nearly fell on top of him. Agent Seuss was already present with another agent and a small cadre of heavily armed men leaning against their Humvees. Pandit saw them and smirked, rolling her fat fingers at them.

Lucy hopped out and began walking around, surveying the scene. She was the only other scout invited. Something in her posture, some twist in her gait, seemed to invite Jody over to her.

"What do we do about Mrs. Geppetto?" she asked quietly.

"We just go along with it, see where it goes."

"And if it goes weird? You can do something, right? You're a priest. You have, I don't know, abilities?"

"In this case, they have limits."

She tossed her head upward.

"Hey," Jody continued. "Hey. We'll be fine. *They* have limits, too."

"Should you even be doing this, you know, with your beliefs and all?"

Jody sighed and ran his finger through his hair. "No, probably not. But here we are, drawn in, I don't know, step by step."

White Wolf found them. "Just so you know, this place was my idea. It's a blank slate for your imaginations. That woman wanted to use our medicine wheel up in Wyoming. I told her point blank she would have to get through a murder of Crows. Lees translated for me. Where's my niece?"

As White Wolf walked away toward Black Mare, who was setting up her equipment, the helicopter took off again to park out of sight. Jody mirrored the old man's instinctive gesture, reaching out to hold it down. Lucy made as if to bury her head in Jody's shoulder, stopped herself, and continued the survey of her surroundings.

Huntsman walked up to them. "Do you two feel alright?"

"Does it matter?" Lucy asked.

Jody shrugged, answering both questions.

"Don't worry," Huntsman said. "We won't let this get out of hand. Her..." she flicked her wrist, "...*science* is not bullet proof."

Jody looked at the men with Agent Seuss. "Let's hope not."

All stood around Pandit, who sat on a metal folding chair, fanning herself in the heat. Valasca stood next to her, holding a parasol over her. Once she seemed satisfied that all were waiting upon her, she began. "Welcome, everyone."

Jody's face tightened already. This was still Wepwawet's affair.

She continued, "We are here to build a bridge between two worlds. The darkening of the moon has lifted a veil upon our inner sight. We know now that we are not alone in this world, not even on this Earth. Many kindred spirits move about freely, and some not so freely. Some of these have agreed to help us, poor humans that we are, expand the horizon of consciousness to enlarge the tent of conscious creatures. This is my work. It is not to summon spirits for witchcraft but to seek out friends for science. Who better to teach us how to develop forms that can hold consciousness than those spirits who seek a body to dwell in?"

A current of ice water coursed through Jody's abdomen. His shoulders tightened. He was at a seance. He prayed for protection and admitted his stupidity. He searched for Huntsman. Her face was flint.

"We will be asking these friends of ours to host us as we host them. You know, those words have the same origin, guest and host? Ha ha, but not ghost. In the same moment that we become guests in their world, we become hosts to them here. We will no longer be ghosts to each other."

Lucy, fidgeting behind her back the cube of white marble and lapis lazuli Jody had seen when he first met her, turned slightly to him. He understood her question. Yes, this was precisely the thing they had been trying to work against.

"I know that you have been trying to do just the opposite, at least in your minds. You have been seeking out ways of detection, of prevention, of protection. But one cannot see without being seen. Let's rather seek out a detente, a way of living and working together. We will see them today where they are, we hope. That is, if we all work together."

She then folded her hands gently on her lap. All were silent.

"Well, then," Pandit said. "Where shall we go? Lead the way." She gently clapped her hands.

Jody thought he heard Huntsman's body break into splinters as she turned to him and Lucy. Lees's body was hanging from his head. White Wolf stood directly behind Black Mare, arms crossed, and did not budge. Jody had to reteach his stiffened body how to move.

Jody stood face to face with Lucy. Lees, Huntsman, and Valasca stood behind Pandit, a few yards to his right. White Wolf and Black Mare were off to his left. Agent Seuss and the heavy artillery were behind him. The only thing in his field of vision was Lucy, whose look of active fear had left. She had already sent her spirit elsewhere, like an animal in the grip of its predator. Jody hooked his cane on a belt clip, which he had devised for this purpose. He held out his hands to Lucy, arms crossed, palms up.

"Oh, just one more thing," Dr. Pandit said.

Jody dropped his hands. Lucy sighed, revealing that she was, in fact, breathing.

"You will no doubt have learned to categorize the spirits of this world, good and bad, angels and demons, and so on. But just think of those words. Angel is a messenger, that's all it means. Demon is an appearance, that's all that means. What they are, in themselves, that is for them to live out and perhaps for us to learn. Simply other, for now. A stranger and a guest."

Pandit sounded like Huntsman now. Perhaps that was why Huntsman was so resistant. In her own way, Pandit was achieving the same thing. Perhaps Huntsman thought Pandit was cheating, taking a shortcut away from the safer, stabler paths the human mind must take through practiced reason. Perhaps that was her allergy to religion as a whole. For a moment, Jody, too, wondered if his religion were not just some violent shortcut to a place right-thinking people would eventually reach on their own.

"That's it. Carry on," Pandit said.

Jody held out his hands, and Lucy took them. Hers were cold and clammy, but they soon warmed to his touch. He could see her belly twitching or trembling.

The sky grew a little darker, though no clouds had appeared. The hot desert air took on a springtime freshness. The salt softened beneath their feet.

Jody looked around. The mountains behind him, to the west, had somehow become more distant and differently shaped. As he turned forward again, the mountains of Utah dissolved in his peripheral vision, leaving behind smaller or more distant solitary mountains. The human bodies each stood in place.

Lucy was shivering. He thought she was terrified until he realized it had grown very cold. He wondered how long he and Lucy would have to keep this up. "We should have brought jackets," he said. She let fall a little tear.

Jody looked over to Pandit, who was mouthing some incantation. Valasca was wearing a salamander smile. Jody turned toward White Wolf, whom he knew to be at least nominally Catholic, and who was gently humming something. Lucy's teeth chattered.

Jody closed his eyes to pray, "Dear God, for better or for worse, I let myself be led here. Please take over." As he searched for words, the animal brain that opens a person's eyes to creeping shadows in a darkened room opened his eyes. He jumped a little, startled.

In the far distance, to the left of Lucy's head, something stood that had not been there before. Clearly distinguishable amidst the long, diagonal shadows cast by the low sun stood a short vertical sliver of light. It had no figure. Jody could not see any arms or legs or even a head. He searched his intuition. Pandit might not believe in good and evil beings, but he did. Right now, though, his spiritual instinct told him nothing.

"I believe we've made contact," Jody said.

"Good," Pandit replied.

"Do the rest of you see this?" Jody asked.

"We see the landscape, the snow, and the mountains," Lees said.

"Not the specter in the background, toward the northeast?"

No one answered at first, then Lees said, "It seems not."

"What about you, Lucy?" Jody asked gently.

She shook her head. "Just get this over with."

"What are we here to see?" Jody asked Pandit.

"Whatever it wants to show you," she replied.

"Can we get a blanket or something for Lucy?" Jody asked. "And for me, too. It's very cold where we are." He would use the time it took for the others to bring a blanket to think about his situation.

A minute or so later, Agent Seuss approached Jody and Lucy with foil blankets from the Humvees. "You two are free to stop at any time," he whispered. "The second this feels too much for you, just let go." He walked away.

The specter, which had not moved or changed in all this time, began to approach. It came slowly, shimmering like a mirage, though the desert had turned from salt and sand to snow and ice. Jody looked down and saw that Agent Seuss had left footprints in the snow.

"Do you see the footprints?" Jody asked out loud.

"I have them on camera," Black Mare said. "It's recording clearly wherever human bodies are. That's what I expected."

White Wolf cleared his throat.

"Alright. Our contact is approaching. I'll see how close I can get him. It. Whatever."

"It has been my experience that disembodied spirits are non-gendered," Pandit said.

Jody preferred, briefly, that she be doing her quiet incantations.

The sliver stood still about three hundred feet behind Lucy. It grew taller, to about ten feet in height, and darker, like ink shot through water, a straight line surrounded by slight swirls.

"Hello," Jody said.

Lucy squeezed his hands.

The black form came no closer.

Jody looked at Pandit, who did everything but shrug to say she had no more she could do. "Would you kindly show us who you are or what you might like us to see…with the help of God?" he asked.

Nothing happened while Jody watched the form. After a few minutes, he looked over again at Pandit, Lees, and Huntsman. No one seemed to be losing patience. They were not shivering, and their arms were not tired.

He looked forward again and saw, towering before him, a tall, slate-colored pyramid.

It took a few moments for the murmuring to calm down before Jody could address his host again. His description of the monument startled all of them, and he heard one of the guns behind him say the word "Stargate." This is where he would begin.

"Are we on Earth right now, or are we somewhere else?" he asked. "Is this a portal to your world?"

"Don't ask so many questions in a row," Huntsman finally said. "Or such loaded ones. Ask it to take you inside."

Before he could make this request, he felt some kind of response already, a "no" shaped with another suggestion. He nodded, and this motion seemed to be enough. The black line extended upward and downward, beyond the top and bottom of his field of vision no matter how much he bent his head upward or downward. This made sense above the ground, into the sky, but somehow the black line was taking his sight into the snow and ice below him.

Inexplicably, Lucy let go of his hands and put her arms around him. Unlike in past trials, this did not dissolve the image. Everything remained. She tucked her face down into his shoulder, as much as her height allowed. His hands were free.

The ice grew more and more transparent. After a few minutes, he found himself floating what seemed like miles above some darkened gorge. His stomach fluttered upward as if he were falling, but he was not, and tried to control himself if only for Lucy's sake. The pyramid, about a mile away, was resting on the edge of a cliff, he thought at first. He studied it more as the ice disappeared and saw that it was really the top of an immense obelisk. This caused an eruption of conversation from all around him. He knew instinctively, perhaps because he was one himself, that this served as an antenna.

Jody and Lucy began to descend. He felt the gentle fall in his stomach as if they were riding an elevator. This was more than simple sight; all five senses were present in this new place. He looked up toward the surface of the ground and saw that the others were not descending with them. Instead, they began scurrying about, studying what was happening, but they did not look down. However they perceived what was happening to Jody and Lucy, it did not look to them like they were going downward. He could no longer hear them. He spoke to Lucy.

"Do you see what's happening?"

"Yes."

"It's getting warmer."

She did not reply.

"Have you been here before?"

"Only above. This is not near the cave."

"Alright." He huffed out a ready breath and rubbed her back.

She pulled away from him and turned away to look around.

"Right," he said. "Sorry." He leaned on his cane. Even without touching, without their physical bond, the vision continued and grew clearer.

"This is some kind of city we're going down toward."

"Almost. Or like a factory, or...."

"Think about that, Jody."

"Think about it? I can see it."

"I'm not so sure."

"What do you mean? You think we're providing the images?"

"Maybe. The alternative is—"

"Hey. Let's stop being so rational for a second and maybe just enjoy this magic carpet ride as far as it goes."

She nodded and folded up their foil blankets. They continued to descend into some built realm of blue-black light.

32

About ten minutes later, spent mostly in awe-filled silence, they arrived at the ground level of the complex. Everything they saw—the obelisk and other towers, square buildings and round ones, streets and ramps—was cast in a dark blue hue as if they were still looking through a thick layer of water. That thick blue faded into black in all horizontal directions wherever they could see between buildings. Nothing gave them a sense of scale, no steps or door handles or plant life. If the obelisk was a mile away, it was two miles tall.

"Maybe we should walk around a bit," Jody said.

"Look up," Lucy replied.

Jody arched his head backward toward the earthly sky they had left behind. "It's like a ball, a bright blue ball," he said. "Like seeing it through a fish-eye lens."

"The mountains are in it, at the edge. The desert mountains, not the Antarctic ones."

"Antarctica...?" he began when something caught his attention. The black line was still present, and he felt it was summoning them forward. Lucy must have felt this, too, for she began walking the same instant he did.

"Jody," she nearly whispered, "how are we going to break

this spell? I mean, we're not holding hands anymore. How are we going to get out if we want to?"

He did not know and did not want to show he did not know.

"Great," she said.

They walked down a straight street or channel for some time, gaining a sense of scale as they passed the buildings and smaller towers. The obelisk loomed taller and taller above them. They saw no one else on the street. As they walked forward, Jody could feel the air more thickly than he thought he should. "It's almost like we're walking through water."

"Do you feel like we're being watched?"

He had not until then. Looking left and right, he imagined eyes looking out at him, or some species of consciousness. "I'm not really sure."

They came within a stone's throw of the obelisk and stopped. To their left was a long, low building, shaped not unlike an old New England factory. The black line stood at the sole doorway somewhat near the middle of the short facade abutting the street. Jody looked at Lucy, who gave her wary assent. They walked up to the doorway, which was more of a portal without any kind of hinged door.

Jody turned to look up at the dark obelisk. Just above it, beyond the point, the sky above was gathered into a ball of blue and white. It looked like the Earth from space, from the moon, and Jody wondered for a moment where in the universe he and Lucy really were. He turned back to the doorway.

The black line split into two parallel lines and pulled

apart. As it did, the building before them, made of white stone or stucco, shined brightly in natural light. Through the doorway, they saw an array of some kind, figures standing in a row, running deeply toward the back of their vision. They walked into this warehouse or factory.

The array was of robots or mannequins, not alive. They stood sentry on a central aisle, which continued for some great distance.

"What are there, a hundred of these on each side?" Lucy asked.

Jody heard her question but began forming his own. "The most finished ones are where we entered. Look, they only get clothes at the end."

"What clothes, too," Lucy said. "Who ever would have dressed like this? This isn't…. This doesn't…."

"All the men are in kilts. My father would've loved this." Lucy took one of the solid-colored kilts in her hand; the machine-man wearing it stood on a raised platform above her. "But not Scots kilts. You see what I mean? It's all a bit like how we would dress, but not really. It's like Renaissance Italy meets, I don't know, Japanese samurai."

Jody and Lucy walked on farther. Past a few examples of naked machines, where, Jody surmised, body hair was installed, they came to where the skin was overlaid.

"You'd expect some kind of metal skeleton," Jody said. "The T-800 or something."

"The what?"

"Instead, it's…what is this stuff?"

"Don't touch it." Lucy slapped his hand away.

"It's like layers of electric fabric or something. Like muscles, but not. Hey, is that what you saw in the cave?"

"That's what *you* saw in the cave. I told you. I never got this far."

"So, okay. We've got a robot factory in Antarctica. How does this explain everything going on by us?"

"These things are so lifelike, Jody. It's like they just want a soul."

"Or electricity, Mrs. Geppetto."

"Touché."

"My question stands. Let's summarize our options here. One, this is happening right now on Earth, in Antarctica, and some foreign power is building an army of attractive robots to take over the world. Two, we're actually on the moon, and aliens are building an army of robots to invade, sort of like *They Live*. They have us here to evaluate their work. Three, and this is just based on a dream I had, we're actually looking at the past."

"The past?"

"Yeah. I dreamt of this on the road. The voices on the radio were these servants, dressed a lot like this. It was a human world, a lot like ours, but different. I mean, think about how long humans have been on Earth. How many advanced civilizations could have come and gone? How long ago was that, the Ice Age?"

"The Younger Dryas ended eleven thousand six hundred years ago."

"Hey, that's it, Lucy. They need a geologist and a programmer to get their machines up and running again."

Lucy looked around. "I'm not doing the work for my invaders."

"Fair enough."

"Hey, look at their eyes."

Jody looked up at one of the muscle-fabric models before him. He cocked his head left and right. "Oh, yeah. One is slightly blue and the other one slightly red. Maybe for stereoscopic—" Jody froze, feeling his stomach stretch up and down in one quick electric jerk. "Lucy, we have to go." With trembling legs, he began hobbling on his cane as quickly as he could back to the entrance.

"Okay...," he heard Lucy say. When she caught up beside him, she said, "You've had some sudden realization? Please tell me, and tell me now."

He searched for reasons, for a logical string, but he could find none. "This...This is bad. All bad."

"I'm not following, Jody."

He heard a sound that was not his footfall or Lucy's. "Something is following us."

He felt Lucy turn her head. She tripped over herself a little, into him. "Okay, maybe you're right."

Jody began to feel a panicked tingling in his groin. "Please," was all he could pray.

"Just say something."

"They did not bring us here."

"They?"

"Dr. Pandit's... entities." His wandering gaze had narrowed to telescopic focus on the entry door. "She did not bring us here with her whatever, her magic wand."

"Okay, so, who did?"

Jody's hip began to sear in pain at each fall onto his right leg.

"Jody."

"I did. We did. This is us, Lucy. We gave them something to hold onto. We gave them a form to imitate. They read my dream and your experiences. We're being used. And we've been seen." He began to whimper without really willing it. "How big is this stupid place?"

"Okay, Jody, but how are we going to get back up to Utah?"

"I will Spider-Man my way up that obelisk if I have to." He felt the determination more fully than he had felt anything else, and he began to enjoy the flight. He even thought he felt his right leg grow stronger. The door grew closer and brighter, brighter than he remembered the parting of the blue-black veil to be before they had entered. The doorway filled his vision, and beyond it he saw no buildings, only blue sky and snow-white ground.

He burst through into blazing heat and blinding sunlight. He had forgotten Lucy was with him until she grabbed his arm to keep him from stumbling over the new terrain. When his eyes adjusted to the brightness, he saw that they were back at the salt flats in the desert, but he saw no mountains and no team members.

"Where is everyone?" he asked.

"There," she said, pointing toward the horizon.

He saw a group of tiny silhouetted figures rising above the ground. "Okay." He breathed deeply. "Okay. We're back. We're safe. We just have to, I guess, walk the length of that road we took before."

At a more measured pace, Jody hobbled toward the figures. It seemed to be taking too long to reach them. They might have been a quarter of a mile away, but he felt he had been walking for ten minutes. He felt the same tingling in his groin as in the factory, now in frustration at going nowhere. It seemed that some of the figures recognized him and Lucy, and they began scurrying about again, but somehow they made their way back and forth across the horizon at some impossibly fast pace.

"Lucy, what is happening right now? Why aren't we getting there?"

"Don't worry. We'll just take our time. No running in this desert heat."

They walked on, and as they did, the figures did grow larger as the space between them along the horizon grew smaller. "It feels less like walking now and more like getting bigger. Like we're walking through a funhouse mirror."

When he saw the faces of Huntsman and Lees, they looked as relieved as he felt. He turned around and saw White Wolf and Black Mare.

"Where did you go?" Lees asked.

"Down," Jody said. "Down into some city."

"From our perspective, you just grew smaller. Alright. We'll debrief back in Salt Lake, in some air conditioning. Here, have some water."

Jody looked at Pandit and Valasca, who stood next to each other in some strange, knowing silence. He nodded a little and drank from a water bottle. He heard the helicopter starting from some hidden nook and Seuss's men starting their Humvees. Black Mare was packing up her equipment.

Jody began walking over to White Wolf, and as he did, he found everyone growing farther away from him like they had before. The old man and his niece were only ten yards away, but the more he walked in their direction, the farther and smaller they grew. He turned around and walked back to Lees, Huntsman, and Lucy. Their eyes matched his thoughts. "Huh."

Lees and Huntsman both turned to Pandit and Valasca. Both shrugged.

"Lucy, you want to give it a try?" Lees asked.

She did with the same result. "Did we, like, make a wormhole or something?"

No one answered.

"Let's no one walk across this circle," Huntsman said. "Let's draw a line around it."

No one budged. She looked for something with which to carve into the salt and settled on the heel of her low pumps. Lees joined in, and soon everyone except Pandit, who had not risen from her seat, was etching their side of the circle into the salt. The slightly crooked lines never met, but the general effect was there.

While all stared at their work and the mystery it defined, White Wolf picked up a small rock and threw it into the middle, where it disappeared.

"No, no, I see something," Huntsman said. "It's making a sort of shimmer, slinking back outward."

Jody felt his stomach pull again. "No, this is not good. I think that's the thing that began following us out."

"What thing?" Lees asked.

Before Jody could answer, he saw sparks flying from

Black Mare's equipment, which she had begun setting up again to record the circle. She shrieked loudly and was quiet again. White Wolf was patting her on the cheek. She seemed to have passed out. Jody looked around; this was like what had happened at the bar. He walked over to Black Mare, whose body was limp and eyes still open. He felt around for the specter, arms extended before him, barely able to stand on two legs. A scream shot out from one of Agent Seuss's men. Jody turned to see the man on the ground, blood pouring out from some hidden wound. The other agents drew their weapons and searched around.

"We need medical here," White Wolf called.

Agent Seuss himself tended to Black Mare. He said something to White Wolf, who began moaning.

Jody felt powerless. He wished he could will this thing into his hands. "Don't you have some incantation for this, woman?"

Pandit merely let her hands open and close again on her lap. White Wolf's cries were the only sound. They began to sound like a dirge. Jody did not know where tears ended and song began.

"Dr. Pandit," Lees said, "now I'm asking the question. Can you control this thing?"

"I—" she began and stopped short.

Jody, without thinking and without knowing how, ran or jumped over to Pandit. Before he knew when or how, the specter was in his hands, pinned to the ground. He could see into its eyes, one blue, one red. They showed nothing, no emotion. Whatever had given this thing life a moment ago, it was gone now. Jody felt heavy shadows behind him, then a hand on his shoulder. Obeying without thinking, he stood up. Four automatic rifles were trained on the lifeless machine.

"Oh-oh-oh," Pandit said, rising from her chair. "Oh, look at it."

The helicopter began spraying salt in Jody's eyes. Its rotors drowned out the sound of White Wolf's mourning.

"Keep her away," Lees said.

"You don't understand," Pandit said. "This is what we've come for, is it not?"

"Two people are dead," Lees replied. "You people are not getting anywhere near this."

"That's alright," Valasca said. "We know where to go now. We know where to get them in."

"Get them in?" Huntsman asked.

Jody watched as Valasca's slimy smile began to quiver.

"Agent Seuss," Lees said.

Agent Seuss walked forward. "Dr. Pandit, Agent Valasca, come with me to the Humvees."

"This is mine," Pandit said. "I brought this here."

"You're not going anywhere near this thing."

"This is what we all wanted!" Pandit protested. "Is this not what we wanted? Where is the helicopter going?"

The agent pulling her back said, "Your fat ass is riding with us."

Jody watched the rest as if it were on a television screen. The helicopter flew off with Black Mare, White Wolf, and the dead agent. Valasca and Pandit were stuffed into the back of a Humvee, which drove away. Someone gently pulled on Jody's shoulder to have him enter another vehicle. He did not remember entering it or when Lucy sat next to him. As they drove away, he could see another helicopter coming; he guessed it was full of agents or soldiers to guard the circle. His only clear thought was that they were headed south, toward I-80, the road he would have taken had he not been duped into crashing his car, the road that would have taken him to Walnut Creek, where he could have lived out the rest of his days in blessed ignorance of everything he now knew.

33

Two days later, on October 28, Jody sat on the back deck of Danny and Cynthia's house, looking out over the neighbors' houses at the rolling plain. He held a mug of black coffee, which had grown cold in his hand. He knew Haleh and the others had been doing their best to comfort him. They knew he could not say what had happened. Haleh had been asleep when he'd come home the day of his voyage with Lucy to wherever it was they had gone. She had woken long enough to recognize his trouble and draw his head between her arms on their bed. It seemed to be true that she slept more when he was "out there," and after these few days, she was more alert. He felt he was still looking out at the world through a telescope. Anger, or the fear that shows itself as anger, framed his field of vision like a black cloud. He sipped his cold coffee.

Someone walked out onto the deck and gently coughed. When he did not turn, thinking it was someone from the house, she came forward and sat in the chair next to him. It was Doris Huntsman.

"How are you feeling, Mr. Conque?" she asked. She had a tote bag with her.

He shrugged and, correcting himself, sat up and turned to her. "The new moon was two days ago, a little late and farther out into space."

"Here," Huntsman said, reaching into the bag. She withdrew an 8-track cassette. "These are yours. Ms. Black Mare was studying them for extra information."

Jody held in his hand ELO's *Out of the Blue*, which had become a favorite for Bleiz and his boys on their Sunday cruises in the car. "What else was on here?"

"Nothing, it seems."

"How's White Wolf?"

"To be honest, not well."

"It seems like Melanie was all he had."

"In a sense. His mother is still alive, living in Montana. Once the coroner is satisfied, he'll bury Ms. Black Mare up there."

"What got her, do you think?"

"Electrocution. That's the initial report. From her own equipment, actually. This thing, it only seemed to be able to use something of ours against us. The other agent was killed by his own bullet, not fired from the gun but one he'd had on a chain around his neck, somehow drawn through him."

"Jesus, Mary, and Joseph," Jody said. He stared down into his coffee. "That explains the hatchet I found in Illinois. I think one of these things was trying to draw it off of the man I first touched in the bar."

"That could be. We still don't understand how the robot—and that's what it is, I can tell you that—moved around invisibly."

"I think I know, if you'll allow me to speculate."

288

"I'm all ears."

"Very funny, says the woman who spied on me the last time she was here."

Huntsman let loose a little smile, but the joke had fallen flat within him.

"Anyway," Jody continued, "it's like that realm Lucy and I went into. How is she, by the way?"

Huntsman looked down. "We should talk about that later."

"Right. Well, I did a little snooping and came up with what the mathematicians call 'hyperbolic space.'"

Huntsman jerked back a little and nodded.

"So you're already there," Jody said.

"Negative curvature. The shortest distance is not a straight line through the center, but along the edge. You can fit a great deal more space in a smaller radius. That's my takeaway as a non-specialist."

"Well, I imagine it like a whirlpool. You can't get across one, but you can whip around the edges pretty quickly. It helps me because I feel like what I do with my hands is like sticking my finger in the whirlpool, dissolving it."

Huntsman nodded approvingly.

"So," Jody continued, "our friends are somehow able to generate these little hyperbolic whirlpools or whatever. The robot wasn't invisible. He was tucked into what you call it, negative space. So was the city that Lucy and I visited. Or we were tucked away and transported. That's why we didn't have to hold hands anymore. We were in their device. What do you think, were we transported in a UFO?"

"Honestly, Mr. Conque, I will admit that it is entirely

possible. It is possible that that is what UAPs are, devices for generating hyperbolic space. But we're just a few days out from our encounter. This is going to be years of research."

Jody felt the joy of this conversation leaving his body at the thought of years more of scouting for Wepwawet.

"Not with you, Mr. Conque. Or Mrs. MacDuff or the others, for that matter. We cannot ask you to continue, given the specific dangers in the work."

"I see."

"We have the circle, and we have the machine."

"You don't need our help?" Jody surprised himself by asking.

"Mr. Conque, my job as a specialist in parapsychology was to work with you and the other scouts so that we could do just what we did. It will be the job of others to continue the research, to protect us from those things."

"What about Valasca and Pandit?"

"I don't know. There will be a cloud of suspicion around him extending back to the Company. That should be enough to keep the circle and the machine out of CIA hands."

"But still," Jody said. "You guys have it. The Navy, or DARPA, or whoever gets the job of reverse engineering, you'll study this thing and find a way to weaponize it, right?"

Huntsman turned and looked out over the eastern horizon.

Jody continued, "That's what we do in the name of defending ourselves. We learn about the universe to protect ourselves from it, but the more we handle it, the more we create dangers for ourselves. The universe is powerful. Now we have the power of infinite space in our hands, and of killer robots.... God, what comes next? All human effort, it seems, is like sweeping up mercury, breaking up the poisons into uncontrollable and unpredictable portions."

"Thanks for the sermon, Father."

Jody would have felt stung if he were not surprised by a sharpness he had never heard in her voice.

She continued staring over the horizon.

He almost said, "It's okay to be afraid," but he did not. Instead, he said, "Let me just say one more thing. As I told you and Lees the other day, the factory didn't look like it was making these things for an army. They looked more like servants, you know, household servants. I had a dream about them, I think I told you. Maybe they come from another time, maybe we've been through all this before, like before Noah's flood or something."

Huntsman turned sharply and said, "How's Haleh? How is she holding up? And little Claire?"

"Fine. I never noticed this before, but Haleh seems to sleep more when I'm out there. I don't know if it's nerves or what. Maybe if we're really done with all this now, things will get back to normal."

Huntsman stood up. "Well, if not, please let us know. We may ask your assistance from time to time. Otherwise, please consider yourself released from service or...."

"No, that's a good way to say it. Thank you."

She reached out her hand. "It's been a pleasure, Mr. Conque."

Jody almost said, "Same here," but he did not.

"And talk to a counselor. That was traumatic, what you saw."

Jody gave her what he felt was a hard-earned glare, as if she had no right to speak of his trauma, but when he looked directly into her dark eyes, he thought he recognized the same pain in them. He stood up. "Thank you. Maybe I will. Here, let me see you out."

As they walked through the living room, Claire came running, chased by Haleh the tickle monster. Haleh stopped and said goodbye to Huntsman.

"Claire, sweetie," Haleh said. "Come say goodbye to Ms. Huntsman."

Claire walked up to Huntsman, who smiled down at her. After a brief, studied gaze upward, Claire hugged Huntsman's legs. She pulled back, gave Huntsman another brief look, and ran off again.

***

Jody did not leave the back porch for several hours. Haleh was next to him, asleep. Cynthia had come and laid a blanket over each of them. Claire was somewhere in the house. Danny was working frantically from his study to meet NASA's deadline for the Mickey in two days' time. Jody tried to watch a wobbly video call on his phone. Terr was recording Cameron giving Devon a driving lesson in some large parking lot somewhere and making commentary. Jody tried to feel the joy of this moment, of father and son. He loved it but could not feel it.

Eventually, Devon, looking excited and worn out, took the phone to talk to his uncle. "Hey, Uncle Jody."

"Hey, Dev," Jody said. "Looking good out there."

Terr's voice came from off screen. "Doesn't he look like his grandfather?"

Jody saw Bleiz's features: the long face and squarish eyebrows, full lips and square chin, and bright blue eyes.

"Yeah, everyone's been sayin' that. But the brown version, right?" Devon said.

"Your grandpa," Jody said, "or Papa Wolfie, as Sam's kids used to call him when they were little—Claire, too—he was actually a little darker than your average Frenchman. You're not much darker, to be honest."

Terr caressed Devon's face. "You're more caramel-colored," she said. "Whenever Bleiz came back from the beach, he looked like an Arab."

Devon snickered. "You're funny, Grandma."

"That'll wear off," Jody said, then regretted spoiling the mood.

Terr narrowed her eyes. "You got walloped, eh?" she asked.

"Not now, Mom."

"Haleh says you're not doing too good."

"I can't really talk about it." Jody saw her eyes, though, searching for comprehension. "It's weighing on Haleh."

"That's too much stress."

"My project's over, and we'll hand over the Mickey in a couple of days. Then everything will be back to normal."

"Don't let it get between you."

Jody had to admit to himself that she did know what she was talking about here.

"People are dead, Mom."

"I'm not claiming to know what it feels like to see what you saw. That's your fault for getting involved with those people. I thought I raised you better than that."

The edges of Jody's sight began to blacken again.

Terr continued, "I'm just saying, don't let it get between you. You see how I was never enough for your father. Even at the end."

"What are you talking about?"

"When that waitress came over."

"This is a new record, exactly eight seconds for you to make this conversation about yourself. So what if she came? He ate breakfast with the guys at the Rowdy Rooster almost every day for thirty years. In the last weeks of his life they make the effort to bring him a little breakfast—so what?"

"You saw what he did when that busty blond came in. Held his hand to his heart. 'Ba-bum,' he said."

Jody laughed. "Mom...," he kept laughing, "Maman, that was a joke about the pound of fried bacon they brought him. He couldn't see anything anymore. He wouldn't have known if she were blond or bald." He was glad to laugh, even at his mother's expense.

"After Maddie, even before, he was always searching for something else."

"Mom, there was no one else."

"Not in reality, no. But in his mind. In his heart."

"So what, Mom? Maybe he was searching for God."

"You don't understand."

"I'm married. I do understand."

"To live with a man fifty-five years and never feel fully loved."

"Can you not see how you contradicted yourself just now? Isn't living with someone fifty-five years enough for love?"

"Not if they're empty years. It was that car, or the church. I'm glad that car is gone. I'm glad you're okay and that car is gone."

"Alright, Mom. But think a moment. You didn't always make it easy for him."

"I was just trying to say what I couldn't say. To tell him what I needed."

"What you needed, Mom, was to be worshipped. And that's the one thing he would not give you. That's the only thing he never gave you. He gave you everything else, but not that. You think that's what love is, to be worshipped. To have someone fall down at your every caprice. Not even God is worshipped that way. That's not the love even He asks for." Jody, stunned by the seriousness of his own words, fell silent.

"I see," Terr said coldly. "I was just trying to share my feelings with you. You don't seem capable of understanding. You haven't learned yet. You'll learn. It'll take until you're married long enough to learn how to really hurt each other."

"Alright, Maman. I guess I will. Look, Haleh's waking up. Can we talk about this later?"

"Hold on, Jody," Cameron said. He had taken the phone and was walking somewhere. In the background, Jody could see Terr poking Devon playfully. "You alright? I heard something serious happened."

"It did."

The two brothers spoke with understanding silence for a moment.

"You see this?" Cameron said.

"It's great," Jody said. "Father and son reunited. Look what the moon has done."

"I just...now what do I do?"

"You're doing it, Cam. This is it."

"I mean, tell me, what else should I be preparing him for?"

Jody looked at Haleh for a moment and sighed. "I don't know. Maybe get him a squirt gun full of holy water. No, forget I said that. That doesn't mean anything. I don't know, Cam. For what it's worth, with all those guys in and out of Candy's life, you're already the best man he's ever known. That's enough. As for the rest, I don't know what comes next. I don't know."

Jody eventually hung up with Cameron to see Haleh searching him with distant eyes. Some new feeling welled up in him he did not recognize. He did not know if he hated himself for not being strong enough for her now, or if he hated her for needing what he could not give.

34

Jody woke early the next morning before Claire could claim the space between her parents' bodies for the last hour of sleep. He reached over and caressed Haleh's arm. Unable to fall asleep again, he stumbled downstairs into the kitchen. Searching for coffee, all he found was half a spoonful at the bottom of the clasping jar. In the frenzy of activity over the Mickey, no one had thought to buy more. The sound Jody made was of some primordial wind emerging from the depths of nothingness, a sigh of utter exhaustion. He decided, before everyone woke, to go to the 24-hour supermarket. He also decided, as a precaution, to text Haleh to the effect. Pulling out of the garage in Cynthia's car, which he had been driving with an accelerator hand control because he could not trust his right leg well enough to drive, he noticed that the tasked car that had been parked outside for nearly a month was gone. "Just like that," he said.

To his delight, the coffee shop in the supermarket was just opening its gate, and he ordered, "Whatever gets me coffee the quickest." This involved eating a package of chocolate-covered espresso beans while he waited for his coffee to cool down. He decided to do some more general grocery shopping, trying to remember what else was missing. This branch of the store looked exactly like the one he knew in Walnut Creek, and whenever he was at the Boulder branch, he let himself pretend he was back at home.

Jody pushed the cart up and down the aisles, hoping that mere sight would suggest some need. He was alone in the store until he reached the spice aisle. He had always assumed spices were somehow there in the cabinet, never expiring and never running out. He never remembered anyone buying them. Yet, here was some tiny older woman in a white raincoat and translucent blue rain bonnet carefully studying the immense wall of spices before her. A younger woman stood just past her, facing the opposite shelf. If anyone knew where the spices were, it was surely this old lady. He steered to go around her when the old woman suddenly stepped back, spread her arms a little, and let them fall at her side.

With her hands now on her hips, she said, "I can never seem to find the time."

"Excuse me?" Jody replied.

"The thyme," she said, turning to him, a slight smile on her face. "I'm always running short of thyme. I don't see it here."

He replied, "Aren't they all in alphabetical order?"

"Oh, that's funny, Jody."

He jerked his head a little. "Do I know you?"

"Yes, of course. From church. Ethel. Ethel Rede."

"Oh, yes. Hello, Ethel." He said this with no recollection of having seen her before. The younger woman behind her, who had red hair, did not turn to enter the conversation, and Jody could not see her face.

"How are Haleh and little Claire?" Ethel asked.

Jody now racked his brain, its software not yet fully loaded. "Oh, they're fine. Just, you know, doing the best we can under the circumstances."

"Ah, yes. One can't be too careful." Ethel now looked directly at him, putting a pause on her search for thyme. "Or maybe one can. No risk, no reward." Jody thought this funny coming from an old woman. "You only live once, right? What's the difference, down here or up there?"

"You're right about that, I suppose."

"You know," she said, resuming her search and holding up a didactic digit, "thyme has many uses. The Egyptians used it to mummify. The old Europeans put it under their pillows to ward off nightmares. I suppose we could use a lot of that right now. Maybe that's why I can't find it.... Ah. Here we go. Yes. It looks like we have all the thyme we need, which is always just enough." She took two bottles and thrust one against Jody's sternum. "Here. Ladies used to give a sprig of thyme to soldiers going off into battle, for courage. Here, Jody. Take courage. Time is of the essence." Her dark eyes pierced him.

Jody looked up at the younger woman, who was still standing behind Ethel and now facing the spices. The younger woman pulled her hair back a little behind her ear and gave a gentle smile. She looked very familiar to him, but he could not place her.

"Thank you," Jody said, looking at Ethel again. He took

the bottle of thyme and placed it nicely next to the four bags of coffee already in his cart. "Well, it's nice to see you, Ethel."

"Bless you."

Jody walked on past the two women and checked his phone. Haleh had produced a list of groceries for him. He went back to the first aisle and made a new run of the store.

***

Upstairs in bed later that night, Jody lay next to Haleh. He meditated on the white walls and wood timber frame, aglow with warm lamplight, but could feel the searing white and blue of the desert wrapped around his bones. He rehearsed his encounter with Ethel and the young woman, but those memories, too, always fell into Ethel's dark eyes, piercing and prodding him for some soldierly courage he did not possess.

"I'm sorry," Haleh said.

"For what?" Jody asked.

"I'm becoming a burden to you."

"What do you mean?"

Haleh turned on her side, away from him. "I don't know how to help you with whatever you've got inside."

He turned onto his right side, which sent a quick flash of pain up his leg. "Don't say that, hon. All I need is you. Just as you are."

"Tell me what it feels like."

He lay on his back, sighed, and covered his face with his hands. "I just feel...I don't know. Icky. I just want this thing out of me."

"What's inside of you, babe? Is it, like, a spirit or something?"

He sat up, rolled his head, and began rubbing his legs down toward his feet, as if that would pull out the feeling. "No other spirit than my own. It's different when you see violence in person."

"But it's over now, right?" She stroked his back. "You're all done with them?"

He nodded.

"Tell me your poem again."

"I don't believe you really like it."

"I do."

"You like it because it's short."

"I like it because I see myself through your eyes."

"It's not the most romantic vision of married love a man's ever conceived."

"Well, maybe that's why it works. Come on."

"Alright." He twisted, leaned on one arm, looked down at her, and recited:

Three things I love about my wife,
Four that I adore:
Full hips
Sweet lips
Her feet upon my floor

She smiled weakly as she struggled to keep her eyes open.

The feeling of hatred welled up in him again. "Hey," he said. He lay on top of her.

"Huh?" she asked, coming out of half-sleep.

He pressed his lips against hers.

"Jo-dy. ... Come on."

He began grinding against her. "It's been almost three months."

"No, babe...." She propped her hands up against his diaphragm weakly, trying to draw her elbows inward and lever him upward.

The black cloud of anger swirled into his vision again, and he thrust hard. He took each of her hands from his ribs and pulled them upward, next to her head. She looked a little afraid, and he thrust again, looking down at their two bodies, still clothed in shorts and t-shirts.

He looked up again, but Haleh's face had taken on a look of devilish delight. He grew confused at this and saw no longer Haleh but the woman from the antiques store in Walnut. Her smiling, tight little mouth and narrowed eyes were luring him inward. He felt a new joy in this. He felt his mouth widen automatically. He thrust again and saw the woman from Walnut begin to laugh. He pressed down harder against her wrists and pelvis, and the more he did, the more she laughed in delight.

A loud cracking sound in the timber frame broke the spell. He looked down and saw Haleh crying. He studied her, retracing the moment backward. He sat back on her ankles, unable to keep any weight on his right knee. His wife was crying below him, because of him. "I'm sorry," he said gently. She tried to turn away from him. He shifted his knees from astride her legs, and she curled up against the wall. "I'm sorry." He sat on the edge of the bed where he could only hear her weeping.

After a few minutes, he stood up and reached for his cane, which was leaning against the nightstand. He looked down at Haleh's body, still heaving quietly. He did not know what else to say and went downstairs.

UNDERWEAR PUBLIC MOON

down at Haley. Jody still was going quickly. He did not know
what else to say and was almost crying.

Jody woke on a couch in the living room. Pale pink light
broke apart the gray haze that blended wall and ceiling. He
rubbed his face and turned onto his right side to face the
French doors, but the other couch blocked most of his view,
and this hurt his hip. He struggled a little to sit upright.

From across the couch, through the French doors,
and beyond the railing of the back deck, he could see the
morning twilight give way to a line of ever-deepening red.
Between him and the horizon, the ground and the rooftops
above it shimmered like blacktop road in the desert. He
leaned forward with both hands on his cane, taking in the
stillness.

The shimmering litter increased, and it became like the
smooth trickling of water over rocks. The yellowing light
bent over things unseen. He dug his chin into his hands then
turned the cane around and looked at the bronze owl for
wisdom. He knew this formula. He was in an emotional pit
of shame and anger at himself. Something was manifesting
itself out there through his feelings.

He rose and stretched. The rays of the sun, racing ahead
of their source, rolled and surged toward him in a rambling

stream. He walked toward the French doors and looked again. He opened the doors and walked through.

The late October chill shook the last of the sleep from his lanky body, covered only in a t-shirt and long pajama pants. He scanned the scene, left and right. A pleasant brook of sunlight coursed across the plains, broadening toward him. It looked more and more like a river of water. Something swam within it, but he could not see what. He ambled toward the redwood-colored railing and leaned his left hand there. The river passed underneath the deck and, presumably, underneath the house. He leaned the cane against the railing and rested on his right hand as well.

At this moment, the surface of the stream disappeared, and he saw what lay beneath. Between the houses and trees he knew from normal sight there emerged horse-drawn wagons full of settlers and plains Indians on the hunt or simply hunkered down. These two groups were not interacting, and he discerned that even among the two groups, they belonged to different times. Older cars also appeared where they belonged, on the streets he knew. History was repeating itself, or he was simply watching it as it happened.

All of this was pleasant to behold, but after some time, five or ten minutes, the sun bared its crown and cast its golden eye upon everything in the scene. In this light, he noticed that some of those he saw saw him. These were half a dozen or so men, women, and children of different races from different times, and they looked up at him. He tried a little smile, and this increased the intensity of their gazes. He waved, and some fled in fear. He puffed out a little laugh and marveled. Jody heard in his memory the opening fanfare of *2001: A Space Odyssey* and wondered where, at the end of this old world, the monolith might appear.

On the next street over, a black car pulled up under a tree and parked. He could not tell if it were of his time or this vision. It was large but modest, a well-polished coat of paint giving off the rays of the rising sun. He did not recognize the make. A man emerged from behind the tree, and Jody could not tell which door had opened to let him out. The man made his way easily up the hill between the houses toward him.

When he reached the little playground that Danny had made for Claire, Jody could see that the man was dressed as a priest. He was well-dressed, too, in a black wool clerical suit cut perfectly around his lithe repose. Beneath this he wore a matching rabat. Golden cufflinks glittered near the hands he held together. Jody turned his gaze toward the priest's face, now just a few feet away and below him. He was about fifty, with a medium crop of gray hair meticulously brushed back and to the side. He exuded confidence, and, like that of a gentleman, his bearing put Jody at ease.

"Top of the morning," came a faint brogue.

"And the rest of the day to you," Jody replied. He cocked his head a little. "Are you visiting the neighborhood? I've not seen you around."

"Well, I saw all the activity and thought I'd have a look myself. See what all the fuss is about, you know." As he spoke, the priest's hands remained clasped at his waist.

"You can see all of this?" Jody asked, pointing with his nose. He kept his hands on the railing.

"Indeed, I do," the man said. "It's quite a marvel, isn't

it? Centuries, longer even, of activity on this site, all in one sight!"

"How is it that you see it?"

"Oh, Jody," spoke the priest. "Does not this priest approach you carrying a mirror? Look at yourself, the mirror! You should see yourself, arrayed in golden sunlight."

This was a kind of priest Jody had occasionally known growing up and which had become rarer and rarer over the years. It was the triumphant churchman of the mid-twentieth century, reigning over big new buildings and bold new ideas, full of cheer and full of himself. This had never been how Jody saw himself as a priest, rummaging as he did through run-down buildings with rolled-up sleeves.

"Off this old t-shirt?" Jody tugged at it a little.

"Well, no doubt you'll know that the light diffuses quite a bit back in the direction of your admirers. You're not as clear to them as they are to you."

"My admirers?"

The priest gestured with his face toward another half dozen or so who knelt and prayed or bowed and worshiped.

"Well, that's not right," Jody said.

"You can't blame their confusion."

"I don't want them confusing me for a god," Jody said. "Jesus."

The dapper priest bowed his head a little, as if under some strain. He said, "Let's think about this for a moment. Here we are, six thousand feet beyond man and time, yet in Boulder."

"Fifty-four hundred feet, to be precise."

The priest, without betraying the slightest hint of annoyance, rather eagerly replied, "Ah, but if you include this continent's real shoreline, the edge of the abyss, six hundred and, mm, sixty feet below sea level, then here we are."

Jody leaned backward with his hands on the rail and pulled himself forward again. He should, he felt, simply let go, but his curiosity had now hooked him.

"But to reply to your concern, should these people not see you as a god? After all, doesn't the messiah quote the psalm to say that 'You are gods, all of you sons of the Most High'? And again, John says that we are children of God now, that what we will later be has not yet come to light. Well, maybe it is coming to light now. This sun," he gestured with his arms spread wide, "she is coming with love for the Earth to shine new light, like you see now. The moon, the dark moon, goes about like some timid nocturnal rhapsodist, slinking over the rooftops as if to poke through the windows and into our bad consciences. Men are to be like God just by gazing upon Him. The veil is lifted between them and you. Why not see that the veil between you and God is being lifted and take advantage of it for you, for them?"

Jody gripped the dark red wood in his hands, remembering last night. "Well, if that's the case, I'd be glad for the moon. I know that I'm still capable of acting in rather dark ways."

"Well, aren't we all." The man gazed at Jody in silence for a moment. "Let me propose something to you. If human beings are to be like God when they see Him, does that not make them gods? But there is no god when all are gods. Or, as a friend once said, 'Is godliness not precisely that there are gods but no God?' In this way, each of us has full access to the immense power of this universe."

Jody worried that he could not reason around this.

"Unless, of course, there are those who can see and those who cannot," the man continued. "Mankind is a sort of bridge, a rope fastened over an abyss between what he has been and what he must become. And that rope is a worm. If you cut the worm, it becomes two more. When the worm is cut, some will hold fast to the future, others to the past."

Jody, gazing across the congregation he had gathered from every time this place had seen, did not respond and did not know how to.

The priest continued, "Perhaps you catch my drift. Perhaps you see what has opened up for you. There is a rule, a dictum, is there not, in physics? Something about how we cannot see without affecting a thing. One cannot see without being seen. Sight is power, and you give power to those who see you. You have opened up a veil for them, too. You *are* a god to them. For those who have the courage to bear witness to having seen you, those who believe in them will give them authority and power. They will be able to do as they please with others because they have seen you, seen through the veil. You have done that just by looking down on them. How different is that from what God has done elsewhere, already? Is He not simply making way now for His children to take His place? Is that not the creator's desire, this solar love?"

These last words did resonate in Jody's heart. He remembered how much his father's death had opened up for him over the past two months, the powers he felt he had inherited. Perhaps the violence of his last encounter was just an awkward start.

The man suppressed a little smile, but this quickly faded. "Ah, blessed are these sleepy ones, for they shall soon nod off."

Claire's little hand came to rest on her father's. Jody turned and saw her staring at the man. He turned back and saw the man, who seemed to be holding words back with pursed lips and a clenched jaw.

The priest managed a tense smile and said, "But for all of them now the day is coming, the transformation, the judgment sword, the great noon. Then much shall be revealed." He nodded and turned away toward his car.

Jody leaned against the railing. "Do you see all this, Claire Bear?"

She nodded.

"What do you see?"

"People and cars."

"Yeah. Me, too."

"Who was that man, Daddy?"

"I don't know, sweetie. No one, I guess. In any case, I'm not sure I trust him."

"Why not?"

He looked at her, brushed her hair with his hand, and smiled. "Because he has no belly, I guess. Never trust an older man without a belly. He's never let go of his vanity. You hungry?"

She nodded.

"Me, too. Let's go eat."

Jody looked back toward the tree just as the priest disappeared behind it. Already standing underneath was some-one else, a woman. From that distance, he could not tell if she looked more like Doris Huntsman or the woman from Walnut. He let go of the railing, and the stream of visitors folded back into the many photons bouncing in the morning haze. Only the woman was left, but she turned and entered the car, which drove off.

Jody turned back toward the house and put his free hand on Claire's head. "Maybe I'll have a little Claire Bear for breakfast." He leaned forward and pretended to nibble her.

"No-o-o," she laughed.

"No? Not even with a little maple syrup on top?" He ran his fingers lightly down her head.

They came into the living room, where he saw Haleh on a couch. Jody came and stood in front of Haleh for a moment, but she did not look up from the bowl of cereal she was eating except to glance at Claire, who had found her way to the pantry cabinet. He leaned on his cane in order to drop to his left knee in front of his wife, who spooned more cereal into her mouth. He leaned the cane against the couch, and it rolled onto the floor. With both hands dug into the cushion, he brought his right knee below him, then crawled forward onto his forearms. The only place for his head was between the bowl of cereal and her lap, and he dug his head into her stomach, gripping her thighs for support. After a long minute, he began to feel her torso shake. He heard no sniffling but instead felt drops of milk falling onto his head. These collected around his own eyes and took the place of his tears.

Jody pulled his shoulders up again and saw the milk spilling out of Haleh's clenched, weeping lips.

"Everything...copasetic?" he heard Danny ask.

Jody looked up at Danny, who held a mug of coffee, and said, "We're going home." He looked back at Haleh. She had managed to swallow her cereal and was nodding, her face full of tears. Claire had come over and was studying the scene.

"I see. Yeah. Alright," Danny said. "How're you going to get there?"

"It doesn't matter," Jody said. "If I have to carry them both on my back like a donkey, I will."

36

Jody, Haleh, and Claire stood in front of a chain-link gate. Behind it lay a neatly arranged junkyard of untold depth. All around them, along the road, there was nothing but fallow farms. They looked for a booth or a building and saw only the intercom, which they pressed again. "I hope they don't have one of those big scary dogs here," Haleh said.

"Right behind you," came a man's voice. He was older, bald, short, and thick, and leaned to one side as he walked. "Sorry about that. The Guard gave me a little trouble coming out of Costco. Must not've liked the look of me. I don't like the look of me, either. But it all depends on the day with these people. A cart full of dog food and ammunition. I guess that's a trigger, for you." He waved a fob in front of the gate. "You the guy with the Trans Am? Nice car. Shame what happened to it." The little family followed him through. "Yep. But you're alright. That's the important thing. We've got some real wrecks here. You try to salvage parts, sometimes you gotta get a little goo off, if you know what I mean. Sorry. Forgot the little girl was there. Anyway, we're right up here."

Not very far inside lay the wreck of the Trans Am. Jody saw its darkened skeleton and nothing more. At first, it looked foreign to him. He walked around it and peered inside. Haleh had turned around in revulsion. When Jody saw the 8-track player still in the console, memories flooded his mind. Trying to smile, he stood up straight and saw the car's skeleton again. He began to retch and grew faint. The driver's seat was still in place, and he sat on it, waiting for the blood to pump through his brain again.

"What was it you said you wanted?" the man asked. "You alright?"

"The uh...hold on a sec...." Jody waited while his body decided whether to give up his lunch or not. His face grew clammy.

"You're not alright, babe," Haleh said.

He shook his head.

"Maybe we shouldn't have come."

He shook his head again. "The hood scoop."

"The hood scoop," the man echoed. "The hood scoop. Alright. Let me get my tools."

While Haleh chaperoned Claire with a firmly held hand to some other interesting pile of metal, the man, bent over the engine, asked, "They never told me. How did you get so much salt water in the car up there?"

"Huh. They never told me either. Actually, they never told me it was salt water. Big mystery."

Haleh and Claire walked back to him. Haleh ran her fingers through his hair and pressed the back of her fingers to his forehead.

The man walked over with the hood scoop in his hands. "It was like a ring of water around the car, a wall, what do you call it, a force field, a circle of water in the ground."

Jody could not process this but received the hood scoop from the man and thanked him. Claire held his cane while in his lap lay the curved, white hood scoop, whose open mouth had faced him for so many miles and through which the engine had screamed at him on command. Now it looked like a dusty skull.

"Where are you going to put that?" Haleh asked. "Where do we have room at home?"

"In my man cave," he replied. "Or on the wall in the garage."

"Do you really want a reminder of all you went through? You see how sick you got just now."

"It's a *memento mori*," he said. "A sure defense against pride."

"Well, *I* don't want to be reminded of all this. Put it somewhere I won't see it."

"The laundry room then." His smile met two half-lidded eyes.

***

Jody, Haleh, and Claire sat in a row for the flight home. Scimitech had packaged the Mickey by October 30, the day NASA showed up to drive it down to Vandenburg. Lees and Huntsman had arranged for Jody and his family to take one of the few flights still available for non-essential workers. Claire sat with Moosie Raccoon on her lap. Haleh had always given the window up to Jody, who flew with his face at the window. The aisle gave Haleh better ability to manage the flight attendant. Jody had no work and no entertainment with him in the cabin, wanting to relax and catch the view

315

from above for the two-and-a-half-hour flight from Denver to San Francisco.

They reached the runway, and the roar of the turbines under the wings made him uneasy, to his surprise. He turned to Claire and smiled. She was already watching a cartoon with headphones on. He looked at Haleh, who had nodded off. He looked through the window and saw the ground falling away.

After a few minutes, he grew bored. He had seen Claire's cartoon about thirty-six times before. He felt something in the breast pocket of his flannel shirt and pulled it out. It was Kai's card.

He held it up to his face with both hands and tried to remember their conversation. Huntsman had been as mysterious about Kai as Kai had been about himself. The white card started to take on a light blue holographic shimmer. The shimmer became like the surface of a choppy sea, waves of water bouncing off each other. This mesmerized him, and he felt drawn into it. In a minute or so, he found himself hovering over a great, vast, endless sea, blue-gray and violent. There were no landmarks, nothing to differentiate one area from another except the pattern of the crashing waves. Something was increasing the energy of the place. The many small waves became a few large ones, crashing higher and higher upward toward Jody. Whole swaths of sea below him ebbed and fell, and he felt like he was on a ship, rocking up and down. A large crash nearly sent the spray right into his face and fell away. The water fell into a deep bowl, and Jody wondered how much deeper it would sink until he saw, from his right and from his left, two immense waves racing toward each other. He watched with anxious anticipation as these two tsunamis met for their sumo match. The bowl of water below him rose quickly, making him feel like he was falling. His stomach rose through his throat and, before he could react, great jaws of white spray snapped upward at him. He shrieked.

Jody looked around and found Haleh still sleeping and Claire entranced by singing vegetables. Outside, the Rocky Mountains were a sea of granite, snow, and mud, waves of earth frozen nearly forever. He put his face to the window and, after a while, saw the white Bonneville Salt Flats to the north, the salty bones of an ancient ocean, the place where Melanie Black Mare's earthly race had ended. Jody ground his forehead against the window and breathed a humid breath, fogging the glass.

PART SEVEN

SUNFLOWER

37

The streets of Walnut Creek opened wide to welcome Jody home with his family. Cyrus had picked them up at the airport and was driving. This relieved Jody quite a bit, as Haleh and her brother chatted incessantly in the front seats. He wanted his wife in good spirits. Cyrus pulled his car along the curb in front of the Conque house. Jody would have asked why he did not pull into the driveway just ahead, but he could not wedge a word in between reunited siblings.

Inside the house, everything was exactly as it had been when he had left three months ago to be by his dying father's bedside. Everything was the same and yet, now, not familiar. He had been through so much. The moon and the Earth had changed. He had changed, or was still changing, into something this home had never known. He had never had to walk with a cane inside of it. He had never here possessed the power of second sight in his hands. Haleh surveyed the scene rather stoically. Claire ran upstairs, straight into the pile of stuffed animals on her bed.

Everything smelled the same, which was to say it smelled of very little. The central air conditioning filled the house with neutrality, pushing olfactory traces of the human body out through its little cracks and creases. The little bungalow, as he called it, was otherwise warm and inviting. The wall clock in the kitchen had stopped.

The only novelty came from the refrigerator, which Cyrus admitted to having opened only once or twice in the weekly visits he had made over the months. Jody offered to take the garbage bag full of curdled milk and moldy cheese to the trash can outside.

Jody's eyes caught, through the side window of the breakfast nook, his old Subaru in the driveway. He would not have seen it from the street, tucked away around the house like this. Cyrus was already upstairs, dutifully carrying everyone's luggage. Jody opened the door to the garage and found the step downward in the darkness. With the garbage bag in one hand and his cane in the other, he had no hand free to turn on the light.

Assuming he had a few steps in front of him before Haleh's car, Jody walked forward but immediately knocked his right knee into something. He yelped and dropped the garbage bag. He reached back toward the open door to the house and flicked on the light. When he turned around again, he started and nearly fell backward against the rakes and shovels. In front of him was what he knew with great precision to be a 1973 Trans Am in Cameo White, a massive, majestic Firebird decal shimmering blue on the hood.

The only part of his body, apart from his right knee, that Jody could feel was his mouth, curling upward at the edges into a face frozen in happy shock. He pushed the button to open the garage door and tossed the bag full of rotten dairy into the plastic bin outside. He turned around and stared at the car.

"Ah, good," he heard Cyrus say from behind. "I hope you don't mind, the insurance guy said it was better to keep it in the garage."

"The insurance guy?" Jody asked. "I went over everything with the adjusters. They assured me that I was completely at fault and in no way entitled to my claim."

"Well, I don't know," Cyrus said. "The key's on the front seat."

Jody sat in the front seat, carefully surveying the scene before him. The dashboard looked the same as on his '71, with a few extra lights and buttons he did not recognize. There was an extra, smaller ring coming out from the steering wheel. The stick, too, was different and occupied only a quarter of the cutout made for it. He opened the glove box and saw a notecard resting on top of the manual case. The card was difficult to read, as if the ink had almost completely faded over the years. He turned on the overhead light, and the handwritten note sprang to life:

Dear Mr. Conque:

In light of the circumstances of your accident, and your ongoing need for secure transportation, &c., &c., we have decided to replace, as best we could, the vehicle you have lost.

Yours Truly,

The Adamson & Adamson Mutual Insurance Company

P.S. It's electric, of a sort.

P.P.S. Untether your reason from time.

Jody turned the key in the ignition. The dashboard lights turned on, and one of the new gauges, the one he took to tell battery life, read full. He looked down at the pedals but, on a hunch, gently squeezed the inner steering ring. The car inched forward silently, and he braked with the pedal under his left foot. "Thank you, Kai and Av."

Jody turned and saw Haleh standing in the doorway to the kitchen. Her face was as frozen as his had been.

"Looks like our insurance policy came through."

"Oh." She relaxed. "How about we just order pizza for lunch?"

"I'll go pick it up," Jody said. "No need to pay the 'security surcharge' today."

At lunch, Jody was dreaming of the car in the garage when Cyrus excitedly interrupted. "Oh, big news! This just happened today. Or maybe yesterday. You're not going to believe this. All the time we've been working on getting the Mickey onto the SLS, NASA's been secretly working feverishly to refurbish Arc8's Nebula III."

"Meaning...?" Jody asked. Haleh was busy cutting pizza into squares for Claire.

"Well, that's a big rocket. Big enough to go to the moon."

"Are you saying that they're switching rockets? Why risk it all on that old commercial failure? Did someone pay off the bigwigs to get his name up there?"

"No. The scuttlebutt is that both are being launched. You know why that would be?"

Haleh huffed. "Cyrus, you're being overdramatic. Just tell us what this is about."

"The NebIII is sending up a crew. A manned mission. Maybe also with warheads."

"Jesus," Haleh said.

"Exactly. We're still slated for December ninth. Plan is to get the sats orbiting and functional, see what we see, you know, then send a crew up some time later."

"Wow," Jody said. "Any word on who?"

"Nah. This is all still rumored."

"It's only been two months since all this happened," Jody said. "How can they do all their negotiations and get the Nebula III ready on time, to say nothing of prepping a crew and all that?"

"Ah," Cyrus answered. "Therein lies the rub. My sources say they've been working on this for over a year."

Jody wondered if this was the Bridgewater Project. "Are these the same sources your uncle is listening to, making him stockpile food?" Jody immediately regretted saying this. Haleh glared at him.

"What? Uncle Danny's stockpiling food?"

Jody smiled. "Well, anyway, this is big news, sending more men to the moon! Cheers to that!"

Jody and Cyrus clinked glasses full of soda while Haleh bent over to pick up a bite-sized piece of pizza that Claire had dropped. When she tried to eat it again, Haleh said, "No. It's dirty."

This argument fell flat when Cyrus, catching his sister's head turned, popped the piece in his mouth. He bounced his eyebrows at Claire, who knit hers back at him.

Jody chuckled and said, "It's good to see you, Cyrus. Good to be home."

"Cheers to that," Haleh said, then yawned widely. "Mm. I'm suddenly very tired."

"Alright," Cyrus replied. "But tell me about this hoarding my uncle is doing."

***

Later that afternoon, Jody and Haleh pulled into her parents' driveway, an eager granddaughter in tow. Jody noticed, first, that Haleh's parents had traded in their Mercedes sedans for rugged-looking Mercedes SUVs. As soon as Claire was free of her tethers, she ran toward her grandparents on the low colonnaded stoop and disappeared into a tangle of arms and adoring faces. Haleh completed the enclosure, a twist of branches swaying in the breeze. Jody stood back for several minutes, leaning on his cane.

"Jody," Sunny finally said, releasing his arms to embrace his son-in-law. He shared every physical trait with Danny but somehow managed to bear each more elegantly. "Welcome home. Agh. Here we are again, at last. Look at you." He patted his arms. "The adventure man. The miracle man. All is well. We're glad you are safe. We missed you." Jody then turned to embrace Leila, who said only "Zhody" and poured tears over her son-in-law, her dear *damad*.

Once inside, Sunny turned and said, "Jody, I want to offer you my condolences again on the loss of your father. I know I said so over the phone, but I want to do this again in person. He was a good man."

"Thank you," Jody replied.

"Did I ever tell you that, when I first heard you tell me his name, I took it as a sign that you were to be my daughter's husband?" Sunny had said this many times. "At the time, we were living near a Catholic church, Saint Blaise. I thought, 'Here I am, living next to holy fire, and here comes this

326

young man, a son of fire.' It did not matter that your father's name meant 'wolf.' I had my mind made up already. And I'm proven right! You rode the lightning halfway to the moon. I think your father looked down from there and saved you for my daughter."

Haleh, at her father's words, embraced her husband.

"And you have the mark of an adventurer now, not an ugly scar, but a noble limp. It's too bad about that car. But that is the sacrifice for your well-being. How is my brother? I mean, really? We can talk frankly now. Cyrus said he is hoarding food? That is strange for him, but perhaps he is wise these days. We started doing a little of that ourselves. You saw our new adventure vehicles outside. In case we need to head for the hills, as they say. But we feel safe here, for now. We have everything. You're all here. We have everything. I'm so glad you're safe. Our little Claire. You know, little Claire, that your name is the same as your mother's? You would almost think your parents planned that. Maybe they did. They say they did. Come on now, sit down. Let me fix you a drink." He spoke in Persian to Leila, and Jody understood only the magic word, gimlet. "But Danny looks well? He seemed depressed on the phone. I bet he is sad to see you go. He'll get over it. He always does. He'll dive headfirst into some new project."

"You should see what did for Claire. Made her a little playground and everything."

"That's his way. All or nothing. I suppose I can't get him back here until the dust settles on the moon again. Ha! You get it? But that's everyone now, I suppose. No one wants to invest in anything substantial. We'll be in difficult times, dire straits, soon enough."

"But the asteroids—"

"Yes, of course. We can live off NASA for a while, in a way. I wish we had some stake in this manned mission they're talking about. But maybe not. This is all too risky, too soon. *Merci*, Leila. Here, Jody. Take a load off. It's good to see you." Sunny drank deeply.

"So," Leila said, "you are all settled in? My Kourosh took care of the home?"

"Yes, wonderfully. Spick-and-span. You could eat off the floor."

"You need some food? You've been gone for so long. We have plenty here you could take with you. Here, let me—"

"No, Leila. Thank you. I made a run this afternoon. We have plenty now. That reminds me. Honey, Haleh, do you remember a woman from church named Ethel? Ethel, uh, Reed?"

"No, sorry."

"Little old lady, short. Plastic rain bonnet?"

"That describes about half the congregation, dear." Haleh was suddenly reticent.

"Well, anyway, she remembered you and Claire."

Leila looked at her daughter and formed a question with more gestures than words.

"I'm just a little tired all of the sudden," Haleh replied.

"It's because you're home," Sunny said. "You're relaxed now. No more adventures, not for a while. Not until this mission goes up, I suppose. What do you think they'll find up there? A portal to another dimension? That's why we have to get there first. We can't let the Chinese beat us into another realm. Or the Russians. But the Chinese have the capability. I just hope we don't blow it. I mean that literally, too. There are so many checks and double-checks. But we have to do this, don't we? We have to give people something to hope for in all this. We can't just sit by passively as nature takes its course. We have to show we can match Mother Nature, dance with her. Right, Claire? We have to stand tall before nature. Not against it. We'll never win a battle against the universe. But to stand before it, to say we're here. Speak the truth, but be skilled with bow and arrow."

The vodka was having its effect on Jody, who also grew tired, though not as sleepy as Haleh looked. "Why don't you lie down?" he said in a low voice.

"Yes," said Leila sweetly. "Go do that. Come on. We'll look after Claire."

"Alright," she said and left with her mother to one of the guest rooms.

Haleh did not emerge again until much later, after dinner. She was embarrassed and apologetic. Jody sat by her as she ate the leftovers. "You want to stay here tonight?" he asked. She shook her head. Once in her bed, she slept through the night.

38

On November 2, six days after the new moon—delayed along a path that had become more distended, more funicular, more strangely attracted to some mass between the Earth and sun and yet reaching no farther than its normal apogee of about two hundred and fifty thousand miles—the darkened moon stopped and reversed its course.

The initial terror that Jody shared with everyone of complete, celestial chaos was assuaged by the reassurance, which had often been repeated since the moondark, that the moon had always really had its own orbit around the sun. The moon would remain near the Earth, scientists declared, eventually settling after a series of pendulum swings into some sort of syzygy, a place of rest between the gravitational pull of Earth and sun.

A secondary terror swelled upward, one that Jody and everyone else waited to hear rebutted, that this pendulum swing and the syzygy itself would send the tides crashing over every shore, reroute the oceanic currents, and render the Earth an uninhabitable desert of sand and ice. Computer models were forthcoming.

Jody sat on the back porch of his house, looking southeast toward Mount Diablo. It glowed with the mid-afternoon sun. Arming himself with a little prayer and a bottle of beer, he returned Sam's phone call.

"Hey, Sam."

"Hey there, donkey breath. Cam's telling me Haleh's got the sleeping sickness. What's going on?"

"I don't know if it's all that, Sam. We've been home for a couple of days. She's just catching up after the stress and all that."

"Well, keep an eye. It is a thing. It's going around, especially since the last quarter. We're in spooky town now."

"Don't tell me about spooky town. I've been living in spooky town for almost three months now."

"Right, yeah, well, what I'm saying is, you watch over us, and I'm watching over you."

"What does that mean, 'You watch over us'?"

"What I mean is, per your suggestion, we're going inland a little."

"You found a place? I didn't think—"

"An RV, actually. The size of a bus. Just, you know, for the if and when. We'll get everyone on it. Mom, too."

"Wow, Sam. How'd I finally manage to convince you?"

"Your nephew Jordan, actually. He started seeing things up in Maine. Back down in Boston, too."

"And you believe him?"

"Like I said, he's a lot like you, you know. Sensitive."

Hanging up a few minutes later, Jody said to himself, "The tides are turning."

***

Twenty-two days later, the moon completed another swing

of the pendulum. Each swing in front of the sun, or whatever had been distending the moon's path, had taken twenty-five hours off the moon's remaining orbit. From the time it first reversed course, it had been just over six days back to the new moon. From there, it had been just over five more days in its backward orbit and five back again to the new moon. In its most recent swing, it had been a little over four days forth and four days back to the new moon. It was at the bottom of this swing that Jody sat on his back porch in the evening, the moon on the other side of the Earth, a beer in his hand, looking down the steep hill of his backyard, over and through the trees into the narrow valley below, filled with a city and its highways beginning to glow with the life of night. Thanksgiving was tomorrow.

Jody heard murmuring in the house behind him, and before he could turn around, he saw White Wolf following Haleh toward the back porch.

"I hope I'm not intruding," White Wolf said.

"Not at all," Jody replied. He felt his muscles loosen and thought he saw more easily into the old man's eyes. "What a surprise. You're very welcome. How did you get here?" He struggled not to stare at White Wolf's bare feet.

"I was just passing through, thought I'd stop by."

White Wolf's tour of the Conque residence was brief, cut short not so much by the desire of Claire's parents to put her to bed on time as by Haleh already being dressed for bed herself. Claire, who had not yet met William DeSoto White Wolf, regarded him with a curious fingertip in her mouth, as if trying to place him in her memory. Jody kissed her good night and took the old man back outside with a few bottles of beer.

"So, is this official business?" Jody asked.

White Wolf stared off over the dark hills dotted with lights. "'Nature is a haunted house,'" he said. "I believe that's Emily Dickinson." He sipped his beer.

Jody watched him for a moment, then said, "You, yourself, sort of came up like a ghost just now, out of the twilight."

"Mm. I told you I am Crow, right? The old-timers of my people would say that to call someone a ghost is a put-down."

"I'm sorry, I didn't mean—"

"But aren't we all ghosts in some way?" He turned and smiled. He then closed his eyes and recited, "'One need not be a chamber to be haunted/one need not be a house; The brain has corridors surpassing/material place.' That's also Dickinson."

"She's onto something."

The two men drank their beers quietly.

"I want to offer you again my condolences for Melanie."

"Thank you. I got your card." He swigged his beer. "I feel it is my fault."

"How could it be?"

"I threw that stone, and the specter used it to spot us first."

"White Wolf, I don't—"

"Billy's fine, now. That's what my friends call me."

Jody sipped his beer to hide swelling, trembling lips.

"How are Haleh and Claire?" White Wolf asked.

"Haleh's fine when she's awake. She really tries to fight it, you know. She wakes up later and goes to bed earlier, a few minutes each day. God, I once found her kneeling against the kitchen cabinets, her hands still clinging to the counter. It was all I could do to drag her to the couch with my bum leg, let alone try to carry her upstairs to bed."

"That is serious."

"I know she feels worse about it than anyone. Like she's letting everyone down, especially Claire. Lord, I just don't get it. What is this all about, Billy? Did I make it all up, what I saw in the desert? Did I invent what killed Melanie?"

"You know, my mother's people have certain stories, myths, you know, like we all tell. There's one called 'The Old Woman's Grandchild.' It goes something like this: a young woman is out working with her aunt under a tree when a porcupine leads her up to the top of the tree. It turns out the porcupine is working for the sun, who wants to marry the girl. So he does. They have a son, who gets into all kinds of mischief, disobeying the old lady who adopts him." He paused for a moment.

"What happened to the mother?"

"Oh, the sun killed her because she tried to escape with the boy."

"I see."

"Anyway, every time the old lady tells the boy not to do something, he takes it as an invitation to do it. You know, childhood rebellion and all that. She's really just trying to protect him from the ogres and snakes out there in the wild. Or, as some say, she's really trying to get rid of him, because for some reason she doesn't like him anymore. Anyway, the young man finds a way to destroy all of the monsters that attack him, snakes trying to climb in his anus and poison his dinner, a bull that has swallowed up people, which he kills from the inside to set them free, a couple of other guys who go after his grandma but end up going into a squash, and so on. I'm not telling it like they tell it. I've pared it down to the essentials, you understand."

"Sure."

"Well, in the way some tell it, he becomes the North Star, and the old lady becomes the moon."

Jody waited for the punchline. White Wolf gazed into the creeping darkness.

"So it's a creation myth, or...?" He studied the side of the old man's face that, under the porch light, set his eyes in deep shadow. "Actually, my wife's people, the Zoroastrians, for them the moon, Mah, is where the primordial bull lives, the seed of all animals or something. So it's a little like the bull that the young man killed to let loose all the people it had swallowed. Interesting, isn't it?" Jody wondered briefly, then added, "So, what? We have to slay the moon, let new life out?"

"No, not that. Who knows about that? What is interesting is how our different myths talk about our relationship to the universe. Like the body is a microcosm. You can say that the universe is a projection for all that happens in the human body, psyche, and so on. And you and I, we believe that our first father was formed from the clay of this very earth."

"This is true." Jody let his head fall a little, nodded, and drank his beer. "But you're not here just to swap creation myths."

White Wolf reached into his jacket pocket and pulled

out a cell phone. He texted someone and waited, not answering Jody's question. The old man was stalling for time. Jody was certain Lees or Huntsman was going to call at any moment. Something new had come up.

"What I mean is this, Jody: it seems to me that, all this time, you've been fighting two battles, one inside and one outside, and that's not really two battles, but one. The fight has come to you at this moment from two different directions, but fighting one means fighting the other, and vice-versa. Do you see what I mean? Whatever you've got going on inside matters for the universe."

White Wolf's phone buzzed.

"If you don't believe me, take the pope's words for it." He thrust the phone into Jody's hand and walked into the living room.

Jody turned back. "The pope?"

"Yes, hello Father Conque," came a voice through the phone.

It was Pope Sylvester on video chat.

"Your Holiness," Jody said. He sprang up automatically and just as quickly buckled under his bum leg. "What...hello, this is an hon—to what do I owe this honor?"

"Ah, Father, you are the worst kept secret in national security."

"And the worst priest, your Holiness, I—"

"I know your story, Father Conque." The francophone African pronounced his name with a grace he had not heard since Bleiz had spoken. "I know what you've been up to."

"Following a path of forbidden powers." Whatever sad-

336

ness Jody felt at his self-accusation washed away before the pope's serene and solemn gaze.

"You know there are many saints who have had strange powers," Sylvester said. "Joseph of Cupertino would levitate. The Curé d'Ars could read souls in the confessional. Padre Pio bilocated."

"I'm no saint, I'm afraid."

"Then stop being afraid, and become one."

Of course the pope was right, but Jody said, "All this, your Holiness, it seems only to have led me into the devil's hands."

"Just like Jesus' death did for him."

"But none of this is in our tradition."

"Oh? Let's see. The early Church, did they not see the covenants of the Jews fulfilled in Christ? He did not do away with any of it. And did Christ not come the first time to prepare us for his second coming? So, what has he left us now that could be transformed for the future glory of this Earth, if not this whole universe?"

White Wolf had apparently been watching from the living room, because his shadow stepped aside and let the glow of lamplight shine on Jody's hands, holding the phone. Jody looked at his anointed, priestly hands, hands that had administered the sacraments, hands through which he had shown such strange power lately.

"I think you see it now, Father Conque. There were those who could see the old covenant unfolding to welcome the new even before its time. If you can find a way through this moment for yourself, then you'll make a path for others to follow. What else is there for a priest to do?"

Some new creature was emerging from the cocoon of Jody's heart and began to spread its wings, when he remembered the dapper priest and his damning temptation. "I know my colleagues don't want to hear this, your Holiness, but it seems that the devil is finding ways to imitate us now. It's like no matter what I do, he'll find a way to trap me in it. That was my priesthood and, in some ways, my marriage now. All this new work—"

"Listen, Father Conque. Listen to your colleagues. I know what they think about this. Let us not be too quick to call things the devil. Think about those robots you have seen. Perhaps we made those, long ago. You, yourself, said so. If the devil is imitating us, it may be to make us turn against each other. Withholding judgment on what we're facing can protect us."

Jody remembered Pandit's AI simulations, which had tried to destroy each other. "I think you are the prophet you were asking for, your Holiness."

Pope Sylvester's gaze was silent and severe.

"So, these powers I have, are they new ways to imitate God instead?" Jody said.

"Only when we suffer for them," Sylvester said. "God has given us no power for which we have not had to suffer. I have spoken with your bishop. We have restored your faculties, which are to be exercized only in carefully prescribed conditions that he will discuss with you. This is not over yet, Father Conque. Keep your hands on the wheel."

After an exchange of warm wishes and a prayer by the pope, the video chat ended. White Wolf came back onto the porch.

"Alright, then. I've got to go. Thanks for the beer."

Both men stood and shook hands. "Listen, Billy, now that we've shared a little, you know, personally, maybe—"

"You want to know how I earned the name White Wolf?"

Jody shrugged. "Yes, please."

"That is hard to tell. But let me put it this way—have you ever seen a white wolf?"

"No."

"Not even that one there?" White Wolf pointed across Jody, into the tree-lined darkness.

He turned to look excitedly. "I don't see it." He turned back to White Wolf, who had vanished. Startled, Jody looked into the porch light fading across the grass. Even in the twilight, he should have seen where the old man, who never walked quickly, had gone. He should have heard his footsteps on the steps or in the grass. He saw nothing and heard nothing, not from one end of the porch or the other. The bottle of beer from which he had drunk was still there on the table, empty, foam falling down its side.

Jody stood on the edge of the grass and rubbed his face then stared off into the darkness, leaning into some middle ground between light and shadow.

***

Jody brought the empty beer bottles back inside, and their clanging in the recycle bin drew his mind into the silence that filled the house. He found Haleh upstairs, sitting on the edge of the bed, struggling to stay awake.

"Come on," Jody said. "Lie down. I want to tell you something. Not a poem. I tried to make it a poem, but I think it will sound better this way."

She lay down on the bed, and he sat next to her. She held his forearm in her hand.

"On that long drive, one day, I stopped to eat lunch. It was hot outside, I had no A/C in the car, and I saw that, in the parking lot of wherever I was, one spot was shaded by a tree. I thought to myself, 'No, I'll leave that for someone else.' Like that was the noble thing to do. Maybe it was, or would have been, under other circumstances. But then I thought, 'Maybe this shade is actually for me today.' And I realized that, my whole life, I never gave myself any shade. In whatever I was doing, I always felt I had to be out there, getting burnt by the sun. A person can do that, looking back through the lives of all the saints and heroes, compressing the image of their lives, their virtues, into one moment, as if they, too, never had a moment of shade. So I took it. And it was nice to come back to a cool car."

He looked at her, her eyes barely open, his wife, lying on their bed. She held his forearm limply. His lips began to tremble as his eyes filled with tears.

"You are that shade, Haleh." The tears would let him say no more. He took off his shoes and lay down next to her. Once she fell asleep, words arrived:

On a lazy Sunday after brunch
We were perched upon a bench
Our favorite in this garden green
The air grew humid, chill, serene
We wore matching coats of down
Those you find all over town

Costly, black ones now in style
We lingered, looked, and sung a while
I was more the brooding one
With eyes that never met a sun
They couldn't blacken with a thought
Or memories of battles fought

She sang, I listened for a time
No words, no reason for a rhyme
Just sounds that managed to convey
Depths of heart and restless play
Hymns of hums and crooning calls
Rattled round that hedgèd hall

Meanings hid from untrained ear
Who never take the time to hear
Who never slow their train of mind
Who search for things they'll never find
Who, like owls in the dark
Always question those who talk

Her song is ancient, I am sure
Hummed by women more demure
Strung through lives that span the Earth
Learned by simply giving birth
To the things that men desire
They, in turn, a world do sire

The song's an ever-ancient meme
From Cambri' to this hallowed scene

Both Tyrannosaur a-rage
And hedgehog hiding in the sage
Without a word they write a rune
Invoking grace with simple tune

Here it resonates with me
Born no bigger than a bee
They themselves make song take flight
While I, content not to alight
Hold to she who keeps me warm
With wingèd song before the storm

39

Though she had shown signs of recovery a day or two before, on the morning of December 8, Haleh sprung out of bed at six, the precise moment that Claire opened the door to her parents' bedroom to lie down between them. Jody awoke to this event groggily and warily, wondering if this were not some last burst of energy before the end, which the dying often have. Haleh seemed unworried and made breakfast.

Just before noon, the little family left Our Lady of Good Counsel church with many others who were celebrating not just the obligatory feast but also the first day of syzygy. The fearful faces Jody had seen in Massachusetts on the day of the moondark had given way to expressions of joy-filled resignation here in California. After Mass, the congregation stood on the large plaza in front of the church to look upward at the late autumn sun. A partial eclipse was expected.

While they waited, Jody scanned the crowd and saw, from behind and from a distance, Ethel Rede and her red-haired companion. He elbowed Haleh.

"Look. That's the woman I was telling you about. Ethel. The one who knows us."

"Honey, I can't see anyone over all these heads in front of me."

"Well, come on. Stand on the bench then." Haleh stood on the bench, and Claire followed her upward. "Blue rain bonnet. With a young woman. Red hair."

"Yep. There she is. Okay, so what?"

"Where have we seen the young woman before?"

"What do you mean? Probably right here, Jody, babe."

"No, somewhere else."

The young woman, as if she knew they were speaking about her, turned and looked directly at Haleh. Jody scanned her features as quickly as he could. Ethel did not turn.

"Huh," Haleh said. The young woman turned forward again. "I mean, if I had to say, she looks like how your sister Madeleine would if she were all grown up. Maybe that's it. From her pictures, you know?"

"Wha...?" Jody began, but the crowd began to ooh and ahh. He and everyone else put on the special viewing glasses they had bought for the many eclipses to come.

Coming from the west, from its forward position one day ahead of the new moon, the bottom of the moon grazed the top of the sun ever so slightly, about ten degrees of their diameters. Just as soon as it began, it was over.

Jody took off his glasses and looked again for Ethel and the young woman, but they were gone. He suddenly felt in his pocket a series of rapid buzzes. Cameron had texted him several times with the phrase, *Are you there?* Those who had been staring at the eclipse did not know that, while the moon was partially blocking the sun, the electromagnetic interference that had long been disrupting FM radio and which had become a stable nuisance for air traffic control had briefly spiked into the UHF spectrum and cell phone frequencies, a thing that Cameron's people, of course, had predicted would happen.

***

Later that evening, Jody sat with Haleh and Claire on the back porch. Mount Diablo, to the southeast, was aglow with the setting sun. Jody's phone rang.

"Hey, Maman."

"Hey." She had a slight song in her voice.

"You sound chipper."

"Me? I don't know. How's 'bout you guys?"

"We're good here. Full of energy these days."

"Right. You got the launch tomorrow."

"You remembered."

"It's a big deal. You guys have been working on it for a long time."

Jody grabbed Haleh's hand. She turned to him, her eyebrows gently knitting. "Yes, we have. It's a proud moment for all of us. And for the world, I think. We'll get to see what's really going on up there, on the moon."

"Yeah.... Well, just so you know, I *am* proud of you. For all of it. For the wobbly path you took, you've got a good family, good work."

It took a moment for Jody to find a sincere word in response. "Thanks, Mom. That means a lot."

"Yeah, well, look. I'm getting tired. Going to bed. It's late here."

"Good night, Maman. I love you."

"I love you, too."

Still holding Haleh's hand, Jody watched the eastern sky surge upward behind Mount Diablo, washing away the blood orange sun behind him with a wave of blue and black.

***

The picture on the television in Jody's living room fizzled and cracked with the detritus of cosmic disorder, but he could see what the network producer wanted him and everyone to see: the STS rocket, soaring three hundred and sixty-five feet into the late morning sky at Vandenburg Space Force Base, its nose cone poised to penetrate the moon above. For a brief moment, the sun passed behind that darkening moon to show the world where it was. The rocket, nicknamed Moonbright, was like the obelisk Jody had seen in that other place, that unknown world somehow tucked into a thirty-foot radius of barren, salty desert and which he still thought had emerged from some folded-up place in his mind. The Mickey, along with more secret, sensitive equipment, was ready to tell the world what new truths were held captive in the lunar darkness.

"You excited, Claire Bear?" Haleh asked.

Jody felt Claire shrug. He turned and smiled at her. His phone buzzed, and he automatically grabbed it.

"Let's just watch, Jody," Haleh said. "It's time."

Ground launch sequencer is go for auto sequence start.

Hey, bro, Cam wrote. *Sorry this is a text. Bad lines out there.* Cam had sent this hours ago, and it just reached Jody now.

Activate launch pad sound suppression system.

Anyway, Mom died this morning. In her sleep. Sam's working out the details.

Jody read and re-read the words. He looked at Haleh then showed her the phone as if to ask her to interpret for him.

She stole her eyes away from the television screen and glanced at the phone. "Oh, God, Jody." She put her hand up to his face and rubbed her thumb along his cheek. If she said anything else, Jody did not hear it.

T-minus fifteen seconds.

The television screen, and the rest of the room with it, became a salty blur. Jody could feel only Haleh's stabilizing hand. He heard only the voice from the television.

Guidance is internal. Twelve…. Eleven…. Ten…. Nine…. Ignition sequence start…. Six…. Five…. Four…. Three…. Two…. One…. Zero. All engines running. Liftoff. We have a liftoff.

40

Jody stared blankly at his television screen. The wide, high-definition display was a pool of splattered noise, a wash of near-black tones with sawtooth edges overlaid with gray static and a bar of white light. The white object was the release arm extending from the module of the Nebula III, the Charon. It was late New Years morning. Haleh was arguing pleasantly with Cyrus on video. Jody turned to gaze at Claire, who galloped in place across an imagined landscape on the rocking horse she had unwrapped on Christmas morning with shrieks of delight.

Moonbright had reached the moon on December 12 and released the Mickey. Jody had watched from his remote station as, one by one, the device dropped a series of micro-satellites at regular intervals along its lunar orbit. Jody's ground control software had communicated with them perfectly even as they confirmed the utter blackness of the moon. Not even near the lunar surface had they recorded any light or heat. One by one, as planned, the satellites had disappeared into the moon. Once inside, they had each communicated for a few minutes while their signals stretched, as if the fabric of space-time were quickly expanding just beneath the lunar surface. At a certain threshold, just a few hundred feet inside the moondark, their signals cut completely. The Mickey itself would continue to orbit the moon until, someday, some signal from its lost "letters in a bottle" should wash again on the shores of this universe.

President Palmer had called Sunny, Danny, and the whole Scimitech team to congratulate them on a "rousing and terrifying success." It was terrifying because the Mickey had confirmed the worst-case scenario offered only by the most fringe astrophysicists—namely, that the moon had become, without craters or equatorial bulge, a perfect sphere. It was rousing, because the few hundred feet of "dynamic" space between the lunar surface and the inner cutoff was enough room for Bridgewater. This was the name of the woman who had volunteered to enter the moondark, Lance corporal Atalanta Bridgewater. She had been among the very first women to serve on a US Marine Force RECON platoon. Jody feared the worst from this endeavor, knowing what the military had brought from the moon to the Earth so far. She and her team would soon be where Jody, Lucy, and Wepwawet had been two months earlier. Jody looked over at the sooty chestnut Claire had been riding untiringly all morning and thought of Black Mare. Perhaps Bridgewater, a real soldier, would do better.

Bridgewater had, this morning, already sent a rose and a cockroach below the lunar surface and both came back alive. The world now waited breathlessly for Rizzo the Rat to return from his voyage into the abyss. Haleh had her whole family on video call to watch with them. Sam had loaded his family, as well as Cameron and Devon, into the RV and were somewhere off the grid for the moment.

Jody had not been able to say his mother's funeral Mass, or even attend. The cycle of solar eclipses had continued as the moon swept across the sun in an ever-tightening figure-eight pattern, their radio interference prohibiting most airline travel during the day. Jody had raised a glass to Terr with Sam and Cameron through his phone the night of the funeral. Sunny was already slurring his words this morning.

Come on, Rizzo, Bridgewater said. The glass jar that had served as a miniature hotel room for the rat during its week-long journey came back into view. When Rizzo reappeared, it seemed dead, but the life support monitor on the glass jar read otherwise. *Come on, little buddy. He may be in shock.* She tapped the jar. She shook it gently. *Wake up*, she said softly. After a minute, he did. *Whew! Thought we lost you there, Rizzo! Here we have it, our first hero! All hail Rizzo the Rat!* There were cheers from the crew heard in the background.

"Yeah, but that poor thing's going to be dissected thoroughly when he gets up there," Jody said.

"Hm?" Haleh said, not turning.

"All this is delayed by a few minutes, right? So, Bridgewater herself should be diving into the pool any minute now."

A heavy gray crept in through the front and rear windows of the living room. "Ah yes," Jody said, "our daily eclipse." Outside, his neighborhood looked like that dark city he had once visited, veiled in blue-black.

Haleh was laughing at something, then looked around. "Should it be lasting this long?"

Jody shrugged. He met Haleh's insistent gaze, cleared his throat, stood, stretched, and grabbed his cane to walk outside. He looked up through his special glasses at a total eclipse. "Was this expected?" he asked, turning to look at Haleh through the living room window. He came back into the house and saw nothing on the television but a cable extending from the arm of Charon.

"I missed her going down."

"You were outside for like ten minutes," Haleh said.

"No, I just—"

Bridgewater? Came a voice on the command module. She remained silent. *Houston, this is Charon. Life support readings are nominal on Bridgewater. No audible contact. Bridgewater? I'm pulling her back up.* The cable pulled Bridgewater back up, quickly revealing the white suit, intact, one hand gripping the cable. *Bridgewater? Can you hear me now? Bridgewater, do you copy?* She gave no response, but her free arm bent a little. *Houston, I have motion on Bridgewater, but no audio connection. I'm re-strapping her and returning to orbit.* Another secondary winch in her suit turned, and she reoriented to face the moon.

Wha..., Bridgewater said.

Bridgewater, do you read me?

Here. What?

Bridgewater, are you alright?

Fine. I'm fine.

Bridgewater, what did you see down there?

Nothing, she said blankly. *Nothing. Nothing.* She then

began to scream, louder and louder, *Nothing! Nothing! Nothing!*

The feed cut.

"Omigod," Haleh said.

The television flashed and went dark, as did Haleh's computer screen. Jody hobbled outside again, farther onto the front lawn, where, at almost noon above, he saw a blue shimmer streak across the moon, back and forth several times before it dissipated. "Oh, no." He went back into the house, where he found the electricity out. In the dark living room, he saw Claire trying to stir her mother, who had slunk over onto her side.

"Oh, no. No, no, no. Honey, Haleh." He lightly slapped her face. She was breathing normally, if not a bit heavily. Setting down his cane, he ignored the increasing pain in his leg and lay her down across the couch.

"Is Mommy okay?" Claire asked.

"She's fallen asleep, Claire Bear. I'm just trying to wake her up."

"Like she was before, Daddy?"

"Maybe. Maybe we had an EMP. Maybe, uh…." He knelt down before her, took her hands in his, and prayed. After a few minutes like this, he stood. "We've got to do something. Claire, stay here by Mommy and pray, okay?"

Inspired by Danny and Cynthia, Jody and Haleh had begun to make a little storeroom in the basement with kerosene lamps, medical supplies, and a few weeks' worth of food and water. The electricity had not come back on, and his cell phone, though not dead, had no service. Jody could hardly see, the only light in the basement coming through the small windows above his head. He breathed in through his nose to calm his heart. He could feel for everything just where he had left it. He found the lanterns, oil, and matches. A little kerosene spilled out and chilled his fingers, but he continued. He lit a match and held it as steadily as he could to the wick.

Jody turned around with the lit lamp in his free hand. The shadows fell away, but too slowly. Chills washed up and down his arms and back. He pushed a breath out of his mouth and marched forward. The shadows seemed to push back against the light, a gauntlet of darkness. With no free hand for the railing and fear pressing inward against his trembling body, he designed a subroutine for each step: left foot, cane, right foot.

When he arrived in the living room, he looked down to see Claire on her knees with her head tucked into her mother's belly.

"That's very good, Claire. It is good to pray for Mommy."

"She makes them go away."

"Makes what go away, sweetie?"

"The monsters."

Jody's lower jaw trembled upward. He arched his head and struck the tip of his cane against the floor. "God, now is the time, please." He struck his cane twice more.

Through the living room window, Jody could see his neighbors, none of whom he knew well, coming out one by one to consult with each other. He could hear some say that not even their cars would start.

"Stay here, Claire Bear. I'm going to see if our cars work."

Once inside the Subaru in his driveway, he turned the

key. The car started but was idling too low and shut off. He tried again and lay his foot gently on the accelerator. The car redlined, then held at four thousand rpm even when he released his foot. "This is not going to work." He turned off the car, held the steering wheel, and lay his forehead on it. "There's no way the electric Trans Am is going to work." Just for having denied it to himself, it became irresistible to try. The modified Trans Am did start, and he inched it forward into the driveway. "Oh, God, thank you. Thank you. Okay."

Jody would have no way of carrying Haleh into the car by himself. He could ask his neighbors, but if power was out everywhere, where would he take her? She was simply asleep like she had been many times before. Better not to act too rashly. It was for a moment like this they had been preparing. One more day, just like Haleh had told him the day after the moondark. Wait for the dust to settle.

***

Jody woke with a start. A slash of pink light broke through the eastern windows of his living room. Claire was awake, her head near her mother's feet. She playfully bounced her little arms in the air. His phone read the time as 6:12 a.m. "Claire Bear," he whispered. She looked up a little and back down again. He looked at Haleh for her breathing and heard her subtle whimpers and moans. "What nightmares are you enduring for us, my radar love?" he whispered again.

He rose from the chair on which he had slept and hobbled to the back porch. A very faint line of pink stretched across the horizon, broken by Mount Diablo straight ahead of him. There were no lights on anywhere in the city below.

He walked into the kitchen to prepare coffee. A little wa-

354

ter still flowed from the tap and gas from the burner, but he could not be sure how long that would last without electricity. He had stored up reserves yesterday afternoon: bottles, buckets, and bathtubs full of water. He was not hungry, but he felt he should have food in his stomach.

Jody sat with Claire in the breakfast nook, eating cereal. He did not wash the dishes. He should not waste the water. Haleh needed water. It had been eighteen hours, the longest she had yet slept.

He sat Haleh upright on the couch, and she moaned. Bottle caps of water dribbled out of her mouth when her throat did not cough it back up. Straws and baby bottles did not work, either. "Okay, my love. I'll get you out today." He still had no cell service.

Orange light spread across the living room wall. Jody turned to see the whole horizon aflame in red, pink, and gold. On the back porch again, he stood to face the rising sun. The two largest peaks of Mount Diablo, behind which the sun would appear, rose in blackened silhouette against the golden horizon. Mount Zion remained in their shadow. Jody prayed, rubbing his hand across his face and through his hair until it hung like a yoke upon his neck.

Mount Diablo seemed to grow larger. The jagged edges of its peaks and ridges smoothed out into a hemisphere of black. From behind this darkening mountain the rays of the sun flared out in every direction. "So we still have an eclipse?" he asked the sky. "How long, Lord?"

The dark circle rose, broader and taller, as if the sun and moon were taking the mountain up with them. Jody squinted as if to understand better the breadth of black spreading out before him. The yellow-white ring the sun still formed around the moon closed again as it cleared the mountain. On the horizon, the sun and moon had always seemed larger, but this was new. Sun and moon had grown and were still growing. Jody did not know if the birds in his stomach were making flight out of fear or wonder. Claire came out onto the back porch.

"Look, Claire Bear," Jody said, trembling. "It's your sunflower. Just like you drew." Then, for the first time in his life, Jody let a blissful smile take over for his mind. "I think this will all be over soon."

The neighbors to his left came outside to look from their porch. The woman, like a child, opened her mouth and screamed silently before the first shrieks arrived. The man pulled her back and held her to himself. His eyes screamed for him. They both turned to Jody. "Why go anywhere now?" he said, not loudly enough for them to hear. Looking back toward the expanding moon, he said, "I wonder if Bridgewater made it up on time."

Over the next few hours, the great eclipse grew larger, filling more and more of the sky as it soared overhead toward its noontime perch. The day grew a little brighter as the yellow ring of sunlight stretched toward every horizon. No news came through cell phone, computer, or radio. The neighbors knew nothing. Jody spent a little time on the street with them, occasionally offering a shrug and a smile with his ignorance.

Around noon, Haleh groaned a little more loudly than she had before and pulled her body into the fetal position. When Jody tried to straighten her legs, her body pulled them back in. Looking at his wife in a position she would never have found comfortable, he felt his own bones wrapped tight. "No, this isn't good. Claire, you alright?"

His face tightened and contorted as he walked to the back porch. The eclipse had filled most of the sky. He looked through the trees toward the freeway below him. Between the stopped cars he could see a few people walking. "Why...?" he began to ask. He looked left and right toward his neighbors' houses, but they were not there. He scratched his head. The people on the road were walking stiffly and not from fatigue but as if full of soldierly energy. Jody went back into the house, and it was at this moment that, amidst the great silence of his neighborhood and the city beyond, he heard distant gun shots.

Jody looked at Claire, sitting on her rocking horse. He looked at Haleh, asleep on her side. Everything he thought he had to do next fired in his mind at once: the Trans Am, getting Haleh to drink, going out, staying put, the great noon that the dapper priest had spoken about. "Whose noon is this, Claire?"

She did not notice the question. Jody bolted the front door. A man screamed somewhere in the distance.

For three hours, Jody sat in the living room next to Haleh holding a large pump-action squirt gun full of holy water in both hands. Gunshots rang out from time to time. A fire erupted somewhere in the city. Jody gently rocked forward and backward with Claire locked in his arms or without. He felt this agony as tension in his temples and twisting in his stomach, as debating closing his curtains or keeping them open to see, as praying and hoping some feeling would emerge other than this wooden wait. The room darkened as the eclipse filled the sky. "Sorry" became his mantra, sorry for every decision he had ever made, until he despised having any desire at all.

A little after three in the afternoon, the ring of sunlight around the moon reached the horizon. A line of gold rung neatly around the visible earth. All at once, without his willing it, every muscle in Jody's body softened, and his stomach unfurled. He stood, stretched, yawned, and walked out to the front lawn. Coming up the hill to his left, he saw one of the robot servants he had seen in his dream and with Lucy walking slowly and with determination. He clipped his cane to his belt and turned to face it with the squirt gun. In the periphery of his sight, he saw the southeastern horizon begin to flicker as if he could see the edge of a rainstorm through the sunlight. This disappeared when he turned to face it directly. Claire ran out and grabbed Jody's leg. The machine, a female model, walked closer, and through the gray light he could see its two eyes, one blue, one red. The rainstorm hiding to his left grew heavier or more pronounced, and when he turned again, he could see a thousand shimmers swirling away from the eclipse. The river of gold ringing the horizon had become like the muddy bank of a stream, full of twigs and torrents.

The machine stopped and stared directly at Jody. Jody looked for life behind those eyes and saw none. It turned its head toward the house, toward Haleh, and stopped. The eclipse pressed against the edges of the Earth. "Would you prefer the darkness?" Jody asked the machine.

The swirling specters all along the horizon began to

bounce against each other as if fighting for space. They seemed to be fleeing. The machine, a few dozen feet in front of Jody, began to walk backward, and, as if not designed for this, it twisted and fell onto its face. Jody straightened his body from the ready pose he had assumed. "If they are fleeing, Claire, what are they fleeing from?"

She did not answer, but something within him did. The trembling began in his lips and rippled out across his face and down his neck. He had to tell his left hand to let go of the pump of the squirt gun, and it fell to the ground. This hand looked around for Claire and grabbed some part of her, Jody did not know where. His shaking right hand unclipped the cane from his belt. He began to pivot and saw the last sliver of light disappear from the southeastern horizon as he fell. On the ground, he found Claire in his arms, and he pulled her in tight.

Something grabbed his right hand and spun him around toward the darkness above. It pulled him and Claire upward, off the ground. Something else grabbed his left hand and, with it, Claire. "Claire! Hold on to me!" he cried.

"Don't let go, Daddy!"

He could not bring his right arm around to grab Claire. Something pulled her out of his left arm, and her shriek fell away into silence as she disappeared into the black.

Jody cried and screamed and yelled until he could hear nothing and see nothing. He breathed heavy breaths, his arms stretched wide, his legs pulled outward. The silence was not total silence. Between groaning breaths he heard humming, electric humming, pulsing across the blackened sky. He saw what pulsed, discs or spheres arrayed like atoms, charcoal black against the blacker sky. They hummed as if communicating and vibrated against each other as if they all wanted to leave at once but were gridlocked.

In the droning silence, words came to him that he had heard both from Kai and Pope Sylvester: *Keep both hands on the wheel.* These discs were large, each filling a portion of the sky. But just as a child can pinch a distant mountain with her fingers, Jody reached upward and took one disc by the edges.

Electric fire coursed through him from left to right. The edges of the disc began to glow hot and orange. The current, racing through his arms and across his chest, grew hot. It began to sting. *Keep both hands on the wheel.* He held on despite the burning pain. He held on for love of the pain.

In a moment, as the edges of the disc glowed brighter and bluer, he saw sparks or static electricity marching along his arms as if on feet, a million electric lives trampling their way toward his chest. He saw them, too, circuits of blue forming electric nets that spread around his arms and chest. These nets, coming from left and right, soon met at his heart.

At his heart, they formed a circle. They pulsed around his heart, and he did not know if they wanted in and if he should let them in. He could not hear himself groaning. They bore down against the wall of his heart, marching around that fleshy Jericho. "B-Blast your trumpets," he said.

He saw all this reflected above, as if the metal disc in his hands had become a mirror. The line of blue sparks marching clockwise around his heart marched counterclockwise above. This circle or spiral deepened into a cylinder, and the sparks sped onward and upward from his chest through this tunnel above him. He was a bridge. These electric lives were leaving through him.

Jody's muscles began to soften. He felt strength sap away from his limbs. He struggled to hold on, as he knew, despite the pain or through the pain, that these little sparks of life were headed for some kind of escape. He did not want to lose a single one. The dapper priest had said that a man is strung like a rope, like a worm. Jody would not be cut in two. He remembered his father's little green notebook of poetry. A psalm would strengthen him, and he began to say, "*Abyssus abyssum invocat*," when a voice vibrated through his arms and said, "No. Sing. Sing your own song." So he sang:

A deer bends down toward grass
For dawn he groans and sighs
A worm who hides his face
No man: the dark hears only cries

Jody felt the disc slipping out of his hands into the humming silence.

Thick dark, the swaddling band
For castaways from birth
Who burst out from the womb
Of dampened, trampled earth

Where ostrich lays her eggs
These left alone to warm

To wither without wisdom
And shiver in the storm
He held on so long as he sang.

Electric water pours
From bone to joint to heart
Like waxen, melted moon
And sent to stars apart

The tunnel of blue light above, coursing with electricity, began to spread outward into a whirlwind.

Before my mouth dries up
Before the jaws of death
And spinning disc of doom
Draws upward all my breath:

Please bind my hands and feet
To clothe this cast in light
Make friendly beggars' fetters
Relinquish what's in sight

After a second, a pause given as if to make him reconsider, the electric pain surged through him all at once. The blue sparks hauled in their net from across his arms, toward his chest, and upward into whatever realm this tunnel was taking them. The disc, too, disappeared, and he flailed his arms to find it. Knowing, finally, that it was over, he let his arms fall back to rest in the open air around him.

A voice said:

They're bound to Pleiades
And safe in Hunter's cord
Now children of the Bear
Because you shared a father's word

At that moment, Jody felt as if he had been plunged into water or, as if already in water, some warmer current surged upward, through him, from behind. He remained floating in this position for a few minutes, his body gradually fading. Near the end of all life and energy, his eyes barely open, he felt a presence gazing down upon him.

It felt like his father, Bleiz. Jody could see nothing, but he knew what his father felt like. Whatever had happened, wherever he was now, he was safe. The hidden image of his father's face grew bigger, and this awakened Jody's weakened limbs. He was alive in this body, bum leg and all. The impression beyond the blackened veil grew bigger and felt less like Bleiz. As it grew outward toward the horizons, it seemed to massage every cell in his body, aligning them like filaments of magnetic iron. Another set of hidden eyes saw him, filled with rousing and terrible desire.

These eyes knew him and loved him, and the more Jody felt himself known by these eyes, the more he felt his every weakness, his every failing. These hidden, knowing eyes seared the edge of his being. He felt himself being cut with a razor from the fabric of the universe. His face froze and eyes closed, jaws wide in pain as the invisible eyes sewed the ragged edges of his soul back together. All at once, the pain vanished, and his muscles loosened.

A blue shimmer draped across the scene, and Jody felt a thousand stinging pinpricks in his back and legs. He must have drifted into sleep, for he opened his eyes to a bright gray, cloudy sky above him. When his eyes adjusted, he could see and feel that he was lying on the cut grass, on his own lawn. A shadow stood over him. It was Claire.

"Oh! Oh, my Claire Bear," he cried. His voice was hoarse. He struggled upward and knelt before her, holding her tightly to him. "You're alright?"

He felt her nod and wipe her eyes.

"I'm so sorry, baby, my little Claire Bear. I'm sorry I let you go. But you're alright?" He pulled back to see her.

"It's okay, Daddy. I was okay." She sobbed.

"You're okay? Where'd you go? Into the house with Mommy?"

"Papa Wolfie picked me up, and he told me not to look. Then he put me down again."

Jody cried and held her, swaying back and forth for some time.

He struggled and stood, only then noticing that his shoes had been pulled off. The soil was damp as if from a heavy rain and it smelled like the salty sea. He saw his cane leaning against the porch railing and hobbled toward it across the grass. He looked down at the cane in his hand and saw, wriggling across his big toe, a little worm. He gently tapped it back onto the ground.

41

Jody stood on his front porch, measuring the scene. He had told Claire to look after her mother, who had been in the same position they had left her in before the great eclipse. He did not want Claire to see what lay before him.

Some neighbors' houses were still smoldering. The street smelled of charred wood and melted plastic. The robot he had faced earlier still lay on the ground, but there were others and parts of others, spilling out some black liquid. There were human bodies and parts of bodies, spilling out blood. None of the carnage had come close to his house, and the scattered remains seemed to stop at some dark, wet circle around his property.

"She has protected us, Claire," he said to himself. "From these monsters."

He looked up and saw, glowing behind the rising smoke and gray clouds to the east, the small disc of the sun. His eyes fell to the tiled porch, a blank slate against which to calculate where the sun should be. "It was after three when the darkness fell, but now it looks earlier."

Jody walked through the front door, directly into the living room. "Claire, sweetie, how long did Papa Wolfie hold you?"

"I dunno."

Jody put the back of his fingers to Haleh's forehead then kissed her on the cheek. He turned to look for his phone and jumped. Standing on the other side of the door leading to the back porch was the young, red-haired woman who had accompanied Ethel Rede. She smiled gently.

Claire took his hand. "Who's that, Daddy?"

"That's your Aunt Madeleine, sweetie. Wave hello."

Madeleine held her hand up back to Claire and cast her eyes toward Haleh. Jody followed Madeleine's glance toward Haleh. Looking again for Madeleine, he saw her walking away from the door behind the wall. He hurried and hobbled to the back porch. She was gone. He leaned against the door jamb and nodded. He looked up and around, wiping his eyes. Dozens of wispy columns of smoke rose from the city and freeway below. "How much happened in so short a time?"

Jody sat down in an armchair to rest while Claire studied her mother, pressing her hands to various parts of her face and body. His phone still had no service. The time read 10:26 a.m. The date read January 4.

"Great," he said. "The phone's messed up. There's no way three days passed in that eclipse." There was no cellular service. "Nor would there be," he said to himself. "But the clock in the phone should keep ticking on its own." He looked at Haleh. "If it's been three days, she definitely needs water. This is bad. Think, Jody."

He heard a little cough at the front door. It was Doris

Huntsman. Her clothes were dirty and disheveled. She held his pump-action squirt gun in her hand, which he had left on the front lawn. "Did this work?" she asked.

"She did," Jody said, nodding to Haleh. "And my sister Madeleine. How...I mean, hello. How did you get here? Are you with others?" He searched beyond her for a rescue convoy. "Come in, of course. Come in."

Huntsman walked in. If it had somehow been three days since the eclipse, three years had passed on her face. He took the plastic gun from her trembling hand. It was empty.

"What day is it?" he asked.

"Monday, I think."

"I mean, the date?"

"The fourth, according to my watch. I keep an analog watch. It...." her eyes drifted toward Haleh.

Jody's stomach shot upward. "We've got to help her. She's been asleep this whole time. I can't get her to drink anything, and she's going to dehydrate, and what do we do? How—"

"Here," Huntsman said with a distant, eerie calm. "Give me that squirt gun. Take Claire outside."

"You're going to squirt it down her throat? She'll choke."

"Not from that end, Mr. Conque."

Jody took Claire upstairs to pack a getaway bag, and when he returned, Huntsman was washing the tip of the squirt gun with what water dribbled from the bathroom sink.

"Where have you been all this time?" he asked.

"I came to find you. I'd just landed when the eclipse's EMP powered down the plane. I saw what was coming and got in the nearest boat I could find. It took me all this time to climb back up the coast to get here."

"Climb back up the coast? What does that mean?"

"It means the shoreline has receded a bit."

"A bit?"

"I would estimate about three hundred feet below previous sea level."

Jody looked again at Huntsman's suit, streaked with mud. "Why were you coming for me after all this time?"

"Because of what they found in the robot. Lees leaked the info to me. Whoever built them—"

"I didn't make it all up?"

"Whoever built them had designed a pretty efficient energy transfer system, something like digestion. In ours, they found wooly mammoth meat."

Jody mouthed the words *wooly mammoth*.

"You've packed bags."

"Aren't you here with a convoy?"

"It's just me."

"We'll use my car, then."

"You have a working car?"

"Hell yeah, I do."

***

Jody's eyes blazed with fatigue and desert light. Huntsman had been sharing some of the driving, but not much. Haleh, still locked in the fetal position, was strapped into a back seat. Huntsman sat in front of her, and Claire behind Jody. The electric Trans Am topped out at one hundred and eighty miles per hour, but the speedometer could measure much more, to about six hundred miles per hour, which

Jody thought had been a put-on by Kai. The battery never depleted.

It had not been easy making it out of the Bay Area. There were breaks in the road every sixty miles or so, fault lines found less in the mountains and more on the level ground. Some bridges were out, and some roads were clogged. They had passed very few people.

Their destination was Cheyenne, which Jody learned was not the city he had almost reached before his crash but the mountain fortress in Colorado. NORAD had long vacated, and the ONI had been assigned space there for Lees to run Wepwawet. Huntsman did not know his whereabouts or what they would find beyond the mountains.

Jody and Huntsman also did not know what they were seeing above them, in the sky. They had caught glimpses of it on mountain peaks in California but could really study it in Nevada and especially at night. The horizon seemed farther away, and in clearer air it seemed almost to dissolve into a mirage rather than fold downward. The sun moved in the sky like a lamp in a lighthouse, strobing from east to west. At night, the stars swirled as if on a slowly spinning marble of lapis lazuli. The moon had not reappeared.

Jody, his two hands on the wheel, adjusted his shoulders and coughed. Desert dust had turned to brilliant white just inside Utah. "We're coming up on it soon."

Huntsman played with her fingers on her lap.

"We might just be fast enough. The machines themselves weren't running," he said. "If we need to, we can drive across the salt. We're not bound to the road here."

Huntsman coughed a little. "It doesn't go faster?"

"We're already going faster than cars ever go. The rather cryptic manual had some obscure line about overdrive and a picture pointing to the hazard light button. But we should be in overdrive. This is it."

Huntsman opened the glove box and flipped through the manual Kai and Av had provided. She glanced upward occasionally.

"Don't worry," Jody said. "I'll let you know if we're running into trouble."

Five minutes ahead, Jody saw, off to his left, near the place where he and Lucy had visited some other realm, a swirling cloud of dust. He exhaled sharply.

"What?" Huntsman asked.

"It's just a dust devil."

She put her head down toward the book again, but Jody caught her glancing upward. From within the dust devil, he could see the shimmers take shape. Farther to the left, apart from the swirling cloud, he saw another shape, a black shimmer. "Claire Bear, put your head in Mommy's lap, okay? Just for a few minutes."

"But there's a horsey out there."

Jody looked and saw no horse. The shimmers began splintering and were racing toward the road to meet him. "God, once again, please...."

"The manual says, 'The speed governor will be automatically overridden once vertical displacement is achieved.' And, yes. Just an arrow pointing to the hazard light."

"Not now, we've got company. God, those things will tear us to shreds." The black shimmer came much closer into view. "Dr. Huntsman, is that actually a horse?"

"What would a horse be doing out here on the salt flats?"

But Jody had already answered the question in his mind. The ensuing silence in the car told him that the idea had fallen on Huntsman just as heavily as on him.

As the horse sprinted to meet the car along the road, its radiant black coat rolled over waves of muscle. Her eyes were narrow and her nostrils wide, and yet the mare seemed to exert no unnatural effort to reach the Trans Am. Jody, fixed on the straight road ahead and the specters coming to meet him, wanted only to look at this black mare racing alongside him at one hundred and eighty miles per hour. He stole a glance. The ends of her shimmering mane dissolved into the air as a hundred black tongues of electric fire. Jody thrust forward his jaw to steel his heart against the tears that wanted to flow. She ran faster.

Golden sparks blew against her outer flank, and Black Mare continued the race. The specters burst against her, one by one, as she built a kinetic wall of equine grace. Through the mist gathering around his eyes, Jody could see a break coming up ahead. He began to slow down, and Black Mare turned her fierce gaze back toward him. "This button?" he said, but Huntsman gave no answer.

Jody pressed the dark red hazard button. The ride became very smooth while the steering wheel loosened in his grip. The weight of his hands pulled down on the wheel, and the car soared upward. On the hood, the blue Firebird decal pulsed as if its own wings were giving the car flight.

He looked back and saw Black Mare circling back around the specters. He thought he saw, from a few dozen feet in the air, her rearing upward toward him. The speedometer still read one hundred eighty miles per hour. He squeezed the accelerator wheel, but the car went no faster. Flying smoothly a few feet above the ground, he lay his hand on the shifter. As if unlocked, it moved to the right. He pulled it downward and the car sped forward. Salt Lake City grew very quickly before his eyes and as he pulled the steering wheel downward the city flew by underneath him.

"Do you see this?" he asked Huntsman, but her head was down, her face dripping tears onto the open manual on her lap. Flying above every obstacle, Jody joined his tears to hers, hearts bursting aflame for their friend, and broken frightfully open before this strange new world.

42

A little over a month later, in the middle of February, a little circle formed around Claire. Jody led them in singing "Happy Birthday" while she smiled over a big cake, waiting to blow out its four candles. This was her makeshift family: Doris Huntsman, William White Wolf, Lucy and Declan MacDuff, Danny and Cynthia Shamshiri. Haleh lay nearby, with other sleepers, in this special room built near the entrance to Cheyenne Mountain Space Force Station. When the song finished, Jody looked to see if Haleh had heard, but she showed nothing.

These sleepers, numbering already a few dozen with more coming in every week, had become part of the new line of defense. They seemed to repel the specters, who would emerge with some ferocity at irregular intervals. Outside of this mountain fortress, those without sleepers survived as Danny and Cynthia had—by shielding their homes, or at least their basements, with a Faraday cage. This type of cage, originally designed to protect against EMPs and other electromagnetic interference, did repel the specters, but it also seemed to draw another class of phenomenon, the creepers.

Creepers were the friendly specters thought to be ghosts

of the deceased, drawn to these enclosures wherever they also contained "peepers," the men and women like Jody and Lucy, gifted with second sight. This was similar to what had occurred to Jody at Danny and Cynthia's the morning he had met the dapper priest. What to do with the creepers once they arrived was much debated, though Father Joseph Conque had his own method of receiving them, which involved a great deal of blessed incense.

What had occurred during the three dark days of the eclipse no one understood. Huntsman spent her days piecing together the stories of those who arrived at Cheyenne, drawn there by the broad-spectrum signal emitted from the mountaintop. Lucy had spent those days curled up on her feet, her hands over her ears, rocking gently back and forth in a fetal position—a stance, she was told, from which she had managed to protect an entire section of Boulder at a radius of two miles. Lees was still missing, last heard of on a trip to Antarctica. White Wolf would not say how he had survived, or where, but Jody had found him waiting for him and Huntsman when they arrived a few hours after running with Black Mare. The old man had replied to this story only by saying, with the same stern chin Jody had used to dam his own tears, "Yes. She is her mother's daughter."

After Claire's birthday party, Jody had his daughter on his lap outside the entrance to the mountain they had made their home with Lucy, Declan, Huntsman, and White Wolf. Danny and Cynthia had raced back home to Boulder before dark. All stared up at the swirling marble of stars in the sky, a sight no one yet understood.

"Claire Bear," Jody said. "Look up. You're going to grow

up in a very different world than I did. But you know what? You're going to be fine. So long as we can feel and feed our bodies, we'll be fine. We can even have cake."

"You don't worry?" Declan asked. Rumor was that he, too, would soon become a father.

"I don't know," Jody replied. "This whole time, from the moondark to now, only a few things have really frightened me: the sight of a spectral gun in my face, feeling Claire torn from my hands, and...well. I worry about what's become of my family.

"You know what I also worry about? It's that because we'll all have lost someone, we won't speak about it, or we'll compete to see who's suffered more, who's lost more. Let's make a deal: we'll listen to others' stories of loss and accept them. We won't compete for sorrow. That will make us all family."

Doris Huntsman's face fell into shadow. "Mr. Conque," she said, "you speak from some experience here. Would you mind sharing?"

Jody opened his mouth and caught the harsh word he would have shared about his mother. "Lucy," he said. "You know, the night of the moonburst, right after it happened, I woke from sleep to catch a shadow in the garden. I thought it was my sister Madeleine at first. But I've seen her since, and it was not her. You know this, how people have, I don't know, a presence you can feel, like even in dreams, where they can look like someone else, but you know who it is by their aura or whatever. You know who it was that I saw?"

Lucy gazed deeply at him.

"But you seemed young, much younger than you are now."

Lucy leaned back and wiped her eyes a little. "I didn't mean to frighten you," she said. "I never knew where I was."

"You didn't frighten me, but you did seem frightened back then."

"I was. And I don't know what else to say about that right now."

They all gazed upward for some time, enjoying the silent, starry night. Claire was asleep, and White Wolf was nodding off. Jody was trying to work up the courage to say what he really wanted. He began to think of Haleh, who was in some kind of coma, and of his priesthood, still strictly limited. He opened his mouth to speak when a loud clatter came up the street. A bus-sized RV, its metal body torn open in several places, came to a stop by the guards ahead. After the guards had inspected and waved it through, it came to a stop near the entrance to the mountain. About a dozen people stepped out, young and old, worn and weary. Lastly, the driver stepped out, a tall, young man of dark complexion. When he stepped forward into the electric light, Jody saw the image of his father Bleiz.

"Devon?" he called. The young man turned and smiled.

A few minutes later, with a piece of Claire's birthday cake in his hands, Devon Conque told the story of his cross-country trip and of picking up strangers along the way. He told the story of his first survival. Sam's daughter, Gigi, did not make it, nor did his wife Diane, and Jordan had simply disappeared. It had come down to Samson and Cameron Conque standing outside the door to the RV, Sam with a baseball bat in his hands and Cameron with a gun he did not know how to use, building a barrier with their bodies. Jody's chin quivered with the thought of the heroes his brothers had become, torn apart to keep everyone inside alive.

"What did you see along the way?" Huntsman asked Devon.

"Honestly, ma'am, not much. There's a few people between here and the Appalachians, where we started. But along the coast, nuh uh. There ain't no one there till you cross the mountains. It's like the sea just swallowed them. We were gonna head south, when this weird ass cop stops us and tells us to stay north of the Last Glacial Maximum. So we just took I-90 west until we heard y'alls signal."

Huntsman sat back in her chair. Jody stared at Devon. Lucy leaned forward and said, "Where is everyone then?"

No one answered.

Jody cleared his throat. "I can only speak from what I saw during the Great Eclipse." He looked over to see Lucy, Declan, and White Wolf looking downward. Huntsman cast her eyes off to the side.

White Wolf said, "Speak clearly, Jody."

"Claire said it first. She drew it. Then I lived it." He kissed her. He nodded to the stars above. "I think they're up there. I don't know how. But I think that was the plan, and we were all used to get them there. For good or for evil, I don't know.

"But I am sure of this: how we get there, how we get everyone back, what we do here until we can, means becoming something new, something we were perhaps meant to be from the beginning. And that terrifies me. I'm afraid of what else we'll have to see and what we must become to win this war."

White Wolf gazed at Jody. "Go on."

"What I saw in the darkness," Jody said, his mouth welling with tears, "was the naked face of God. No soft light, just powerful love. And I'm so scared to expose myself like that to him again, to see myself in seeing Him like that. Because it means no longer hiding among mere human things, the comforting confines of marriage or priestly life, as we live them out." He looked toward the mountain, where Haleh lay asleep, then up to the stars. "It's one thing to be a living part of the universe. It's another, more terrifying thing to be part of a living universe."

* * *

ACKNOWLEDGEMENTS

I would like to thank the following persons, who have lent their voice to this book with their professional expertise or critical eye: Chris Alles, Michael Ibrahim, Dr. Jim O'Neill, and Monique Robinson. Gwendolyn Heasley has been a trusty guide through the world of publishing. In a special way, I would like to thank Danielle Dyal of Bookfox for a consummate level of editorial care matched only by her enthusiasm for this project. Sarah Cortez, in addition to lending her keen editorial eye, has provided the kind of home I have needed to grow in confidence as a creator of fiction, at Catholic Literary Arts. Any faults, defects, or infelicities in the representation of the surreality I propose in these pages remain my own.

WITHIN A WAKENING EARTH

HYPERBOLIA, BOOK TWO

1

Mort opened his eyes and closed them again. The blur that had come to him in that glimpse spoke pre-dawn twilight. His muscles were soft and relaxed, and he did not attempt even to twitch a toe or a thumb. This was the most contented feeling he had ever had upon waking, and waking had always been more pleasant than being awake or asleep, so he would savor it.

He could hardly feel himself breathing. The air was somehow thicker, a river gently flowing in reverse, into the many branches of his lungs and out again, as slowly as the tide. He floated on this current of serenity.

After a few minutes, finally curling a toe, he realized his legs were tucked upward and off to the right. His girth would normally never have allowed this. He brushed his thigh with his fingers. The skin began to burn a little where his fingers touched, so he stopped.

He kept his eyes closed because they wanted to be, because his body would soon return to sleep. It was Sunday, and he had no need to leave his bed.

Mort pushed down against the blanket with his foot, and the blanket pulled against his head. He was under the chenille blanket, which was why his breath was warm and humid. His arm would not respond easily to pull the blanket off. He might have still been in sleep paralysis. He crawled his hand upward across his body with his fingers. It burned again where his fingertips touched, and his stomach felt hard. He pressed around the edges of some kind of ball in his stomach. He moved both hands across his abdomen, which felt much thinner than it ever had before. He knit his brow and smacked his lips in thought. When he opened his mouth again, he could feel the air rushing in thickly.

The more he bent his fingers and toes, the more energy poured into his limbs. First his forearms, then his thighs, and finally his shoulders and hips took strength. His face felt thinner. He turned his knees upward, which untwisted his abdomen and brought the strange, hard ball in his stomach to the center of his attention. His hands could not find the edge of the blanket behind his head, or anywhere. The harder he pressed down with his feet, the more firmly the blanket pulled against his head.

The surface of the blanket felt smooth, like felt. The air between his body and the blanket felt as thick between his limbs as within his lungs. He opened his eyes again, and all was blurry and brighter.

A memory returned, or a dream, wherein a piece of plaster had fallen on him during the night. There had been many strange dreams that faded from his consciousness as soon as he remembered them, of wind storms and barking dogs and a series of unspecified catastrophes.

His skin burned nearly everywhere. He pressed against

the blanket, but it held him tight. He breathed in heavily, and this burned his lungs, too.

A brighter seam appeared in the blanket, perhaps where it had worn over the years his grandmother had used it. Onto it, he put his fingernails, which he had let grow a little long. She would forgive him, if she could see from wherever she was, for the long fingernails and for what he was about to do. He tore at the bright seam.

The blanket gave way more easily than he had expected, and it tore more like a thick plastic bag than fabric. Light poured in through the tear, and the blanket began to cling to his skin. Mort pulled himself upward, through the tear. Cold air seared his face and shoulders. He winced in pain, and the breath this reaction would have automatically drawn inward did not come.

He could not breathe. Nothing would move in or out. He put his fingers into his mouth to pull out his tongue, but it was in its normal place. His hand flailed a little in his growing panic. His body was covered in some kind of slime. The steely ball in his stomach pulled down on his throat. He pushed his stomach upward, against his lungs, which sparked a brief spasm. This threw open his diaphragm, and he coughed out some of the slime. The great gulp of air he took in singed his lungs, and he expelled more liquid.

Shivering, Mort pulled up his legs through the opening in the blanket and hung them over the side of the bed. Everything was still blurry, but he could feel his feet dripping with the whitish goo. He slid them onto the wooden floor, and he continued sliding off the bed. He pushed upward with his legs and threw his arms out to grab the top edge of his tall dresser, but his legs failed, and his bony hip hit the floor. He shivered and cried, but tears would not come.

After a few minutes on the hard floor, frozen in weakness, and after his bedroom had grown much brighter, Mort felt at once every limb spring to life with some electric charge. His inner organs, too, vibrated as if someone had switched on a circuit. He could see more clearly, especially through the center of his vision. The slime had dried in large pink-white flakes on the skin of his spindly body. He stood up.

The white sac from which he had emerged lay on his bed, resembling a rubber change purse he had had when he was a child. He dipped his finger in a puddle of the slime inside the sac where it had not yet dried. It smelled of newborn babies. As did the whole room, which otherwise looked just like he had left it when he had switched off the lamp the night before. A bit of plaster really had fallen from the ceiling, though. There was no other possible sign of entry for whatever had cocooned him, nothing out of place in this room except for the broken sac and his naked body, thin, frail, and trembling.

Mort put on the only thing that would hold up at his skinny waist, black sweatpants with a drawstring. There was no bulge at his stomach, not while he was standing, but he could feel the weight of whatever had lodged in it. The last thing he had put there was almond boneless chicken, if he remembered correctly. He shuffled to the bathroom.

The hallway smelled mustier than it had before, and the nightlight was out. The only light came up the stairwell and bounced off the faceted glass handle of the bathroom door.

His grip was not strong enough to turn the handle, which had always stuck. He bounced his bony body against the door, but it did not budge. He did not have to go. He only wanted to look at himself in the mirror. His grandmother's door was closed. Instead of struggling with another door, he went toward the light coming from downstairs.

The musty smell grew stronger as Mort approached the stairs. He could see a little dirt sprayed along the floor in the foyer below. The thick handrail held sturdy. The living room had become a jungle. If he had been asleep for a few days, or even weeks, his plants could not have grown across the floor like this. The large front window had broken, and the boxwood was growing into the house. Mort put on the Crocs he had kept in the coat closet at the base of the stairs. Shards of glass broke beneath his steps. The wallpaper was covered in mildew.

Some creature had ransacked the refrigerator, but the kitchen was otherwise cleaner than the living room. No water came from the sink. No water came from the sink of the half bath, either. It was too dark to see his face in the mirror there, but he could see the thin silhouette of his head. He had never kept plastic bottles of water in the house. He was not thirsty anyway, he realized and then thought he should be.

As he walked back from the kitchen to the living room, he passed in front of the image of Jesus that he had always walked past before, careful not to look at His face. *Jezu, ufam tobie*, the painting said. He had kept it hanging on the wall in honor of his *babcia*, who had always kissed it with her hand. After whatever had happened to her house and his body, this painting still hung, and the merciful eyes of God still stung him with judgment.

Mort put his hand on the railing to go back up the stairs, but something caught his attention. He gazed upward, toward the dark hallway above, and some feeling like dread came over him. He raised a foot to take the first step, but something creaked loudly upstairs. Looking around again at the living room, the walls vibrated some alien quality, some danger. He put on a windbreaker from the closet and went out the front door.

His lawn was overgrown, as was everything else on Eveque Street. East English Village had always been leafy, and now it looked like the rest of Detroit. Houses had crumbled. Grass and trees had grown up through the cracks in the street. Cars were rusted, tires deflated. Whatever had happened to his house had happened everywhere. Perhaps the moondark had done this. He looked back toward his garage, which had fallen in a little, just enough to make opening the door look dangerous. His car would not have fared better than anything else on this street.

Mort walked toward Mack Avenue. His regular stroll to the hospital and back usually took him along Chandler Park Drive, but he would have a better chance of finding something, answers, anything, on the commercial street between his house and the hospital. At the next intersection, he looked both ways and saw more of the same: thick vegetation. Closer to Mack, he heard what sounded like thunder behind him. As he turned around, he traced the leafy line of clear, blue sky back toward his house, near which a cloud of dust billowed into the street. He rubbed his stomach back and forth just once, dropped his head in thought, and turned back to make his way to the hospital.